# DRAWING DANGER

L.E. Luttrell

A CIP catalogue record for this book is available from the British Library.


ISBN 978-1-9999334-1-8

ISBN 978-1-9999334-0-1 e-book version

Typeset in Great Britain by Set-to-Print Ltd, Burnley, Lancashire

Published by Woolloomooloo

Printed in Great Britain

For Megan – a talented creative writer

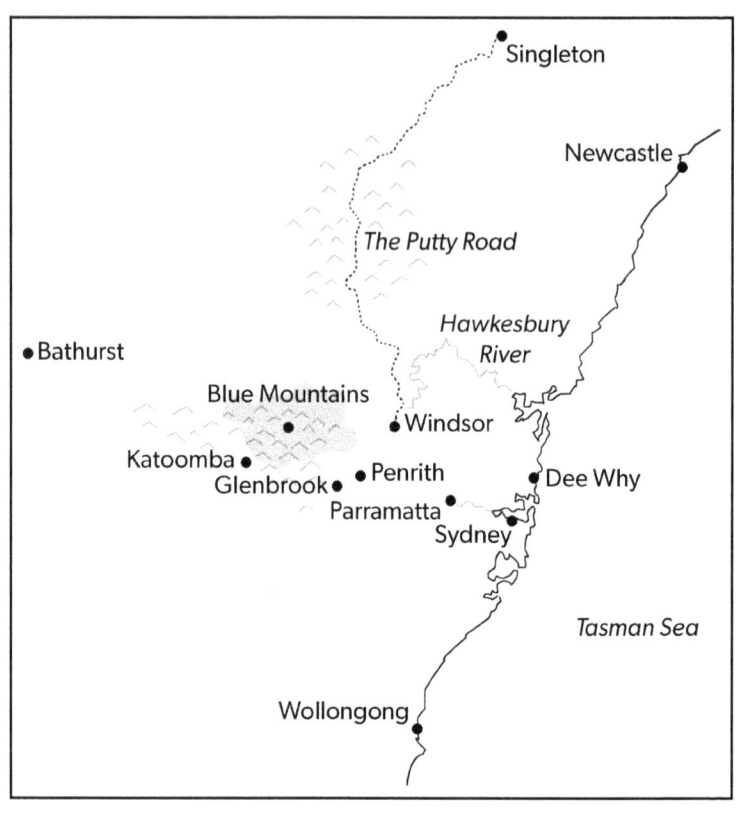

Map showing a small part of New South Wales referencing some of the places where the story is set.

# 1

**Melbourne, Australia. December 1980.**

Everyone who knew her said that Mia Adjudovic had a big mouth – in more ways than one. Women were envious of her thick sensual lips and wide smile, as well as her beautiful face and curvaceous body. Men found her irresistible, and lusted after her. The problem was that the illusion was shattered as soon as she spoke. Instead of the expected deep, husky, sexy voice, she emitted irritatingly high and whiney squeaks. Mia's more mature colleagues agreed amongst themselves that she reminded them of the silent movie character Lina Lamont from 'Singin' in the Rain' whose voice was so atrocious when 'talkies' were being introduced in the story line of the film, they used young Debbie Reynolds's voice to dub over her as part of the plot. But instead of an American accent, Mia, of course, has an Australian accent, being the first generation born of European immigrants.

As well as being subjected to a barrage of grating sounds, people found Mia's habit of gossiping and honesty disconcerting. Honesty that wasn't appreciated – speaking without forethought or invitation. Trivial throw away comments that could deflate a person's confidence in seconds ('I don't like your hair like that, it doesn't suit you … you should …'). She seemed to have no awareness of how inappropriate, unkind or even dangerous her outspoken thoughts could be. Like now.

Mia hadn't gabbled about her latest romantic liaison as she normally did. If she had, it would have undoubtedly been helpful to detectives leading the subsequent investigation. But Mia had not told a soul about the man she was currently seeing. He was a work colleague who was married. Her friends, and most certainly her family, would have frowned upon an affair with a married man. She is just about to make the biggest blunder of her 26 years and speak out without thinking it through clearly. Again.

Mia has just admitted her lover to her flat where she has been ensconced all morning taking a 'sickie' from work. She really had been feeling sick last night after her lover had left, recollecting what she had seen. Despite drinking several glasses of water, Mia can still taste the residual bitterness of the food she lost last night after he left. His feral odour lingered in her bedroom long after his hasty departure so that she hadn't been able return to her own bed. Instead she'd camped out on the couch with a sheet where she returns to after he enters her flat.

She burrows under the sheet to hide the slight trembling in her hands. Last night her whole body had been shaking. It has eased, but she can't seem to still the trembling. This morning she'd switched from one TV channel to another to discover whether the violent attack she witnessed had made the news. There was nothing though and she has decided she needs to do the right thing by reporting the incident. Her father had never been punished for the years of violence he inflicted in his family. She can't allow this man to think he can do what he likes to others like her father. Mia can sense him approaching the couch but she just can't look at him.

'What's wrong Mia?' he asks knocking the sheet out of the way, grabbing her arms, and pulling her up from the couch. He wraps his arms around her, holds her tightly kissing her cheeks saying 'Why are you off work? You look fine to me. I've got time for a quick one if you're up for it.'

Underneath the deodorant and aftershave he must have put on this morning, she can still detect the pungent odour she smelt last night. It revolts her. Why has she never noticed it before? Mia shudders as he removes her silk dressing gown revealing her naked body underneath and runs his hands down her smooth back. The last thing she wants is a repeat of last night's bedroom antics.

'I saw what you did last night,' she squeaks, squirming free of his embrace and taking a step back. She feels vulnerable in her nakedness and folds her arms across her body.

'What do you mean you saw what I did?'

'I saw what you did to that club owner, Dougie, or whatever his name is just before we left the club. I came looking for you. You said you would only be a minute and you were gone for *ages*, leaving me alone with all those pervs at the bar. So I went looking for you. I heard you arguing with him. When I reached his office I saw what you did to that man. It was horrible. You might have killed him. He might even be dead.'

After witnessing this scene the previous night Mia had rushed back out into the main room of the club. Within minutes her lover had re-appeared and aggressively grabbing her arm, began walking her out of the club murmuring, 'Come on, we're leaving'. He'd moved so fast she'd almost had to run to keep pace with him, stumbling in her high heels. Not that he had cared.

It was only a five minute drive back to her place from

the club, which was completed in silence, but Mia could sense the hyped up violence still coursing through him and even in the dimness of the car interior could see the way he gripped the steering wheel, his adrenalin exaggerating every movement. His behaviour reminded her of her father, who seemed almost euphoric at times after attacking her brothers for some minor misdemeanour. Her father had been a man who took pleasure in violence. She is beginning to believe her lover may be similar, something she'd not been aware of before last night. On the return journey, Mia had sat in the car frozen with fear, just as she had done as a child, expecting to be the next victim.

Once they had entered her flat last night she'd been too terrified to say anything to him and his aggressive sexual behaviour left her feeling violated and sick.

Since making her decision this morning about what she needed to do she had begun to feel more confident and determined. And if she was honest with herself, stubborn. Her mother constantly tells her she has a stubborn streak, which is not becoming.

'You didn't see anything Mia,' he says, drawing her back from her thoughts. 'I know Dougie well and I found him like that. He said some clowns had just done him over. Said he didn't want the cops or an ambulance called and he'd get one of his boys to see him right.'

'No, that's not what happened and you know it.'

'So what are you saying Mia?'

'I'm sorry, but I'm going to have to report it. What you did was wrong. I don't care what he might have done, or if he's a crim, which he probably is, running a place like that. I wish you hadn't taken me there. Now everything is going to come out about us as well. I didn't want people at work or my family knowing about us.'

'There's no need for *anyone* to know about us Mia. And I wish I hadn't taken you there either. You can't say anything. It'd be the end of my career and marriage.'

'Well you should've thought of that. I've already left a message for someone to call me back.'

'So you haven't actually spoken to anyone yet or told anyone anything?'

'No, but I expect someone will be calling me any time now,' she says turning away from him to the window as though expecting someone to arrive at her door imminently.

The man looks at Mia and cocks his head to one side considering his situation. She has made no mention of the large wad of money he pocketed after bashing the club owner, Dougie. Clearly she had returned to the bar area before that happened. At least he was safe in that regard. He knows Dougie will not be reporting either the assault or anything about the money. After all, Dougie had agreed to pay him anyway. He'd just helped himself to a larger wad because the drongo had broken his word and tried to hold out on him. The bashing and the money were to make Dougie understand that he couldn't do that. Not to him.

'You shouldn't have made that call Mia,' he says quietly.

Too late Mia realises she should have kept her mouth shut. As she turns she sees that he is pulling a pair of gloves from his pocket and has removed the tie of her silk gown.

She freezes for a moment as he moves toward her, then ducks to the side and attempts to get around him, but he is too quick for her. Before she can let out a scream the tie is pulled tight around her throat and she is dragged back across the room. All she can manage is stifled rasps as her life ebbs away.

He is thorough – or so he believes. He dresses himself in taped bin liners, including one around his thick hair and sets about cleaning and clearing the flat. He strips the sheets and the thick flannelette sheet that is acting as a mattress cover, from the bed, packing them, the silk gown, and the tie, into a bin liner to take with him. He vacuums and washes all the floors and then removes the dust bag from the vacuum cleaner throwing it into the liner in the rubbish bin to take with him as well. He wipes down all surfaces and starts the dishwasher. He's satisfied he has done enough.

Armed with his bulky load the man looks down at the woman who has been his lover for the past few months and says, 'You never were very bright Mia – nor could you ever keep your mouth shut. Now look what I've had to do.'

He's never liked grasses, and he couldn't let her report him. Even if she had he probably would've got away with denying her accusations and sticking to the story he'd fed her. He knows Dougie would be likely to back anything he said, especially with what he has on him. But then it would have been a nightmare situation. Suspension pending an enquiry. His family finding out. Probably the break-up of his marriage. His bosses keeping closer tabs on him. No he couldn't have that, so she had to be silenced.

Checking through the window that no one is around in the street or the park opposite, he awkwardly opens the door and leaves.

# 2

**Sydney, January 1987**

Catelin Brant is bent over her drawing, concentrating on getting the right shape. She keeps doing it wrong and has to keep rubbing it out and re-doing bits of it. Her drawing skills are improving, but she is still not skilled enough to capture the image that is in her head. She hasn't heard her stepmother come into the room and is startled when she hears her speak.

'Didn't you hear me call you Catelin? Lunch is ready and we are all waiting for you. What's that you're drawing? Who is that supposed to be?' asks Janet leaning over for a closer look at what Catelin has drawn.

'It's the man who killed my mother,' Catelin says, 'only I can't get it quite right.'

'Don't be ridiculous Catelin. You were only six years old when that happened. As if you could possibly remember. Now stop this nonsense and come downstairs for lunch.'

Catelin sighs and abandons her drawing. Janet, whom she is supposed to call Mum, would never understand. Whisked off to her father's house in Beecroft, Sydney, following her mother's death in Melbourne, Catelin now lives with Janet and her half-sister Rosie who is three years and seven months her junior. She loves Dad and Rosie, but she struggles to feel any strong love for Janet. She finds it very difficult to call her mum as her father insists she should. She would never call Janet 'Mummy'. That was reserved for her true mother. She avoids addressing Janet directly as much as possible, but when she is left with little alternative, the word 'mum' comes out half strangled from her throat. She believes she is being disloyal to her own mother by calling Janet 'mum'. It's not that she doesn't care for Janet who is a loving mother to Rosie and treats Catelin well enough. She does care for her, but it is not the same as it was with her own mother and never would be.

After putting away her drawing, Catelin picks up a picture of her mother which she keeps on her bedside table, 'I promise you mum, no-one is going to stop me doing this. I will keep doing the drawings until I get it right. And I will make the police take notice of them. One day we'll get him.' She puts the picture back down and follows Janet downstairs and enters the dining-room where she hears Janet mumbling something to her father before going into the kitchen. Her father and Rosie are sitting ready at the table. They are about to eat their traditional roast on a scorching hot Sunday. The air-conditioning has been turned on to cool the room. Her father is in the process of carving the meat joint. Looks like lamb today, Catelin thinks.

'Mum tells me that you have been doing one of those silly drawings again,' Dad says, avoiding mention of exactly what he is referring to in front of Rosie.

'What silly drawings?' asks Rosie? 'Do you mean the ones Catelin does of the man who murdered her mother?'

'See what you've started now,' Janet says as she brings some dishes in to the table.

'I'm not the one who brought it up,' Catelin says moving into the kitchen to collect more vegetable serving dishes. *Why can't they just leave me alone!*

The sisters had first discussed Catelin's drawings when Rosie came into her room one day after school last year. 'Some of the boys have been teasing me about the colour of my hair,' Rosie had sobbed. 'Calling me horrible names. All of us kids with red hair get teased. I don't know why. My hair isn't ginger and frizzy like some of the others and I don't have their freckles either, but I still get teased.'

'Children will always find something to pick on in others,' Catelin had told her. 'Just so they don't feel so bad about themselves. Your dark red wavy hair is the most beautiful colour and don't let anyone tell you otherwise. It always looks lovely. With your green eyes and smooth creamy skin, you look like a beautiful princess.'

'Do you really think so?' Rosie had said cheering up. 'I've always wished my hair was the same colour as yours.'

'My hair?' Catelin had asked surprised. 'My hair is a boring brown. And almost straight. Why would you want to have hair like mine?'

'It's not just brown. It's golden as well. Sometimes when you have been in the sun and you're all brown it also looks blonde in places. Your hair is a lovely colour – it matches your blue eyes and tanned skin perfectly. Not like my lily white skin. You don't have to cover up when you're out in the sun like me.'

'Your skin is silky and smooth. It's just perfect Rosie.' Rosie had sat looking at her, unconvinced. It was then she had noticed Catelin's drawings.

'Anyway, who's that you are drawing? Is it daddy?' Rosie had asked.

'No. Don't tell dad or your mum. I'm trying to draw the man who killed my mother, only I'm not that good at drawing faces yet. I have to keep practising.' Catelin had previously explained to Rosie that a bad man had killed her mother and that's why she had come to live with them.

'I won't tell them. But why are you drawing him?'

'One day I want the man to be caught. I need to keep drawing him until I get it right so that I can give a copy to the police when I'm older. And so I don't forget what he looks like.'

Since then Rosie had asked Catelin to show her any of her new drawings. Rosie had told her that were getting better and encouraged her to keep doing them.

'I told her she couldn't possibly remember what the man looked like, seeing as she was only six years old,' Janet comments, placing the last of the dishes on the table.

'Mum's right Catelin,' her father says. 'Just give it up. Otherwise it's just going to bring back the nightmares.'

'I don't have them anymore,' Catelin lies, avoiding a look in Rosie's direction. *Please don't say anything!* Rosie had come into Catelin's bedroom a few nights before, after experiencing a disturbing dream, asking if she could sleep with her for the remainder of the night. She'd given Rosie a comforting cuddle and they'd settled down, only for Catelin to wake some time later experiencing her own repetitive nightmare of the killer. This time the roles reversed and Rosie had cuddled her. The nightmares had been a regular feature in Catelin's life in the first few years following her mother's death, but now only crept into her dreams on rare occasions.

It was just a few weeks after she moved to Sydney to live with her father that Catelin began experiencing the nightmares. She was convinced, after waking from the horror of them that the murderer was in her room, hunched over near the door, waiting for her. If her father came in to comfort her she would plead with him to stay with her insisting that, as soon as he left the room, the man would come back. No amount of reassurance from him could convince her otherwise – after all she'd seen him time and time again with her own eyes. Sometimes her father would remain with her until she fell asleep again. But on those nights when he didn't come into her room, or if he returned to his own bedroom impatient with her fears, she would huddle down under her bedding terrified that the killer was going to come for her. It was only some years later that Catelin realised that the large looming shape 'waiting' for her near her bedroom door was in fact her bulky winter dressing gown (that Janet dutifully renewed - every two years) hanging on a hook on the back of her bedroom door. As Catelin always slept with the venetian blinds open (as really dark rooms frightened her) the shape would be accentuated when there was strong moonlight shining into the room or a light was on in one of the neighbours side windows. Although the neighbour's house was at least fifteen feet away, whoever used the room opposite hers never closed the curtains or blinds and so a small amount of light would filter into Catelin's room, casting shadows.

Her discovery that the dressing gown was 'the killer' occurred when Janet had removed it one day for washing and after waking from one of her nightmares Catelin was relieved to see the killer was not there. In the morning when she woke and noticed the empty hook, realisation dawned on her what the culprit was. Thereafter she hung the dressing gown in her wardrobe at night after she'd been wearing it and 'the killer' never reappeared in her bedroom.

Catelin believes she has almost banished the nightmares with her drawings. Through the sketches she visualises him in custody, paying for his crimes. No longer a danger to anyone else. She has even drawn him in shackles a few times, sitting in a prison cell or looking out of a cell window through bars. It is as though the drawings have given her increased powers and reduced his ability to instil fear in her.

'I still remember exactly what my friend Cheryl looks like and I was only six when she left our school,' Rosie pipes up in Catelin's defence.

'It's not the same at all,' Janet says. 'You and Cheryl were best friends and saw each other every day at school before the family moved away. Catelin only saw the man she is trying to draw a couple of times, very briefly.'

'It was enough,' Catelin says, 'to have his features seared into my brain forever. Anyway the drawings help me.'

'Enough!' her father exclaims thumping his hand on the table. 'Let's eat. Don't know about you, but I'm very hungry.'

When they have cleared the final dishes from the table Catelin's father asks the girls to return to the table. Once they are seated he announces, 'Now I have some exciting news to tell you. We're moving to London.'

'London?' Rosie and Catelin chorus.

'Yes my firm has offered me a senior management position in London. Your mother and I have discussed it and decided I should accept the post.'

'How long for?' asks Catelin.

'I don't know, could be permanent, or if we don't like it there I can look at transferring back to another position here in Sydney.'

'What about our house? What about my friends?' wails Rosie.

'We will ship some of our things to the UK. The rest

we'll put in storage. The house will be let out. It will still be our house and we can always come back here if we want.'

'When are we going and for how long?' asks Catelin, concerned about her drawings. What if they were still living in London when she is older and perfected her drawings? Can she take them to the police over there?

'We'll be moving in three months,' her father tells her. 'Just in time to arrive for spring in the UK.'

# 3

**London, April 1987**

The Brants find London very cold. Expecting warm spring weather in April, they are instead greeted with cold howling winds and rain. Luckily the new house they are renting has central heating, a new experience for the family, so they are nice and warm inside. When venturing out they have to don thick woolly scarves and warm rain coats with hoods. Umbrellas are useless in the winds.

They are in a suburb called Winchmore Hill, which is a fair way out of Central London. Howard Brant's firm had organised the partly-furnished rental for them following Janet's demand for 'a respectable suburb with good schools' before they left Sydney. Some of their prized furniture and other possessions have been shipped over together with some of the personal belongings they weren't able to pack in their suitcases. The house is a huge five bedroomed property and Janet Brant has enjoyed spending money to buy the additional furnishings they require.

The girls are enrolled in local schools and are due to start shortly after the Easter holiday break. Catelin is horrified to discover that she will essentially be in a lower year than she was in Australia. She thinks the system in England is strange. With her birthday in December, she was one of the youngest in her year at home where the academic year runs from January to December. In England it runs from

September to the end of August, with schools breaking up for summer holidays in July. Now she will be amongst the oldest in the year – but in essence a year behind where she would be back at home. Rosie, whose birthday is in July will be amongst the youngest in her year – instead of almost in the middle – and will be one year *ahead* of where she was in Sydney. Catelin hopes that she is not going to have to repeat all the things she has already learnt when she starts the new school.

Her new school is all girls, just like the one in Sydney. Catelin would have preferred to try a mixed school here in London. The new school she is attending is called a 'secondary' school, whereas in Sydney they called it 'high' school. Rosie tells her that her school is split into 'infants and juniors'.

Catelin had noticed that the girls in her Sydney primary school started to become nasty towards each other in the last two years there, as though they had suddenly undergone a personality change. In the few months she had spent in high school, it seemed to be even worse there, she'd thought, with it being all girls. She was somewhat relieved to be escaping it.

She had found it difficult to avoid becoming embroiled in the spiteful and bullying comments that were bandied about. Mostly Catelin kept quiet when her friends started making unpleasant remarks towards others, but sometimes found herself laughing along with them, afraid of becoming a target herself. Sometimes she couldn't stand it though and would tell her friends to stop picking on someone, asking how they would like it if someone did it to them, knowing how it had upset Rosie. It shut them up for a short time, but it wasn't long before they were at it again. Catelin wondered why kids did this to each other. She'd seen boys bullying other boys, from the all-boys school on her way home some days and wondered if the same thing would happen if they were all in a mixed high school. She doubts she will have the opportunity to find out.

Catelin's first day at her new school is difficult. She is starting at the school two terms into the academic year and friendships have clearly been established Catelin notices as the girls in her form group trickle into the classroom in clusters. Many stare at her in unfriendly silence after being introduced (as a new student from Australia) by the form teacher, who eventually pairs her up with a girl called Adhita Acharya.

Adhita later tells her that her name means 'scholar' in Hindi. It soon becomes apparent that Adhita doesn't have any friends in her classes, which is probably why the tutor has chosen her to pair up with Catelin. The other girls largely ignore both of them wherever they go, apart from the odd snide comment Catelin hears as they pass groups of girls. Either mimicking Catelin's Australian accent, making derisory remarks about aspects of life in Australia, or referencing Adhita's mixed heritage. Adhita ignores them, tells Catelin to do the same and makes no attempt to speak to any of them. Adhita tells her that both the English and other Hindu girls, as she refers to them, (rather than Indian, she tells Catelin because many of them were born in England so it is not correct to call them Indian) are rather racist towards her. The English girls because she is not considered English (although she was born in England) and the Hindu girls because she is of Anglo-Indian heritage. Adhita has much fairer skin colouring than the majority of the Hindu girls and she has hazel eyes (that appear predominantly green), whereas they all have brown eyes. She does have very dark brown hair though. Adhita says the other girls are only ever friendly towards her when they have to work in pairs and complete difficult science tasks as they know she can provide all the answers.

Adhita explains that she is considered to be Anglo-Indian because both her parents have one English parent and one Indian parent. In her mother's case it had been her father who was English and mother Indian, with the reverse for her father, which is why Adhita has a Hindu surname. She said her father wanted his children to have Hindu names (whereas her parents are Isabelle and Adam). She explains that both sets of her grandparents left India a few years after independence from British rule as their young children were not accepted in society there. Her two grandfather's had both been doctors. One Indian, one British. Her parents had largely grown up in the UK, met whilst studying at university and married. They are both doctors and Adhita is the baby of the family. She has two older brothers – one just qualified as a doctor and the other has just started university – also training to be a doctor.

'I suppose you're going to be a doctor as well to carry on the family tradition?' asks Catelin.

'No, I'm going to be a mathematician.' Adhita says with finality.

The snubbing Adhita receives does not seem to bother her at all. She seems very confident and self-contained, Catelin thinks. She wonders if Adhita finds the task of 'buddying' with her and showing her around the school tiresome, but she seems friendly enough towards her. She finds Adhita's directness refreshing. She also likes the fact that Adhita doesn't become involved in name calling or react to any bullying she receives. She tells Cate that it doesn't remotely interest her.

The girl's friendship grows over the following weeks and Catelin asks Janet if she can invite Adhita back to their house one afternoon for tea. She has discovered that Adhita is partial to chocolate cake and asks Janet if she can bake a cake if Adhita wants to come.

'Adhita? What kind of name is that? Where is she from?'

'She's English. Born in London. Her family live between Southgate and Winchmore Hill in a large house. Her parents and one of her brothers are doctors,' Catelin says, hoping that this will appeal to Janet's snobbish attitude.

'Well I suppose that's alright then. You'll have to give me warning though so I can make sure I have all the ingredients you need.'

Arrangements were made for Adhita to come the following week, on a Thursday afternoon. Wednesday afternoon after returning from school and completing her homework, Janet allows Catelin to make her special chocolate cake. One that she used to do with her mother when she was little. She has never forgotten the recipe as the ingredients are just simple maths, as long as she weighs everything carefully (apart from the eggs).

Catelin can tell that Janet is surprised when she meets Adhita. She gives Catelin a scowl and Catelin suspects there will be a little 'chat' later. She ignores Janet's attitude and the girls quickly demolish the cake and drinks Catelin serves. They then remove themselves to Catelin's bedroom.

Adhita walks about Catelin's room nosing into the built-in wardrobe and looking at everything she has lying about the room, all the time asking Catelin questions about

Australia. Spotting what looks like a drawing pad almost hidden under a pile of books Adhita turns to Catelin and asks, 'Is it okay if I have a look at this?'

Catelin shrugs, and taking that to mean assent, Adhita pulls the pad out and starts looking at the drawings. After the first few pages, which feature an outdoor garden scene, every page contains a similar image of a man.

'Who's this you keep drawing?' Adhita asked. 'Is it your father?'

'No. And you need to talk quietly. I will get into trouble if she hears,' Catelin says pointing to the door.

'You mean your mother?'

'No, I told you she's not my mother, well not my real mother. She's my stepmother.'

'What happened to your real mother?'

'She was murdered by that man in the drawing when I was only six years old. I have been drawing him over and over and will keep doing it until I get it right. I'm almost there. Only, my father and stepmother don't want me to do it. They think I couldn't possibly remember what he looked like. They wouldn't take any notice of me when I was six, and they won't take any notice of me now. Cos I'm just a kid.'

'So you saw this man then? You saw him murder your mother? When you were only six years old?'

'Yes.'

'God Cate, that must have been terrifying for you. How did it happen?'

# 4

**Melbourne, December 1980**

'I'm sure it was just something she ate at lunch, but as she vomited several times, you understand I had to call you and ask you to collect her. Just in case she has a tummy bug. We don't want it being passed on to the other children do we Mrs. Brant?'

'No, you're right Mrs. Walsh. I'll put her to bed as soon we get home. If she is not better by tomorrow I will keep her off school. But if she is fine, I'll be bringing her in. I've got a lot on at school this week as we're approaching the end of year and breaking up for the holidays soon.'

'Yes, I'm sure you have. It's the same at our school and is the busiest time of the year. Thank you for being so understanding Mrs. Brant.'

Julie Brant is livid really. She is convinced there had been no need for her to collect Catelin after a bit of vomiting. God, in her school, if they sent home every kid who'd vomited, there'd be dozens of them disappearing every day. Particularly the younger girls when they have their period, their bodies making difficult adjustments to the changes each month.

Julie bundles Catelin into the car and suggests she lies down on the rug which she has spread out over the back seats. 'We'll be home in a few minutes darling, but if you feel as if you're going to be sick again, use these tissues,' she says handing a box over to Catelin. 'Or it's okay if you're sick on the rug as well. Just try to avoid getting it on the seats or the carpet on the floor.'

'Yes, Mummy. It was those sandwiches I had today that made me ill.'

'What was in them again, I've forgotten?'

'Peck's Paste. I told you I didn't want Peck's, that it makes me feel sick.'

'Yes, you did. I'm sorry.' *And perhaps you made sure you were sick.* A trip to the supermarket is definitely required. She knows Catelin doesn't particularly like Peck's, but the cupboard had been rather bare this morning. If she goes into school tomorrow I'll let her get something from the tuck shop, she thinks. There won't be any supermarket trips today though, unless Catelin has a miraculous recovery in the next few hours.

Julie pulls out and slowly turns into the road running alongside the park. At the next intersection a man steps in front of the car forcing her brake sharply. She hears a thud in the back and Catelin letting out a howl.

'Are you alright darling?' she asks looking in the rear view mirror where there is no sign of Catelin.

'Yes Mummy, but I fell on to the floor. It hurt a bit.'

The man is carrying some bulky rubbish bags which he's dropped. Some of the contents have spilt out from the bags and Julie can see that there are more bin liners and general rubbish inside them and what looks like bedding. *Funny thing to be throwing away with general rubbish.* She can see the man, who is looking hot and sweaty, is mouthing obscenities at her from the twisted face he is pulling but she can't hear him with the windows shut and the air conditioning blasting.

'Stay down there for a minute Catelin.'

Julie waits for the man to gather everything up and move across to a car parked on the other side of the road, outside the park. She notices the thick gloves on his hands – another strange thing to be wearing in this heat. She looks around and observes that the park is deserted and there is no one on the street. The intense heat must be keeping everyone indoors, she thinks.

'Why did you tell me to stay down Mummy?' asks Catelin popping her head up between the two front seats and looking at the man across the road.

'Just instinct Catelin, get back down quickly.'

Julie drives off, knowing the man's eyes are following her car, and a few minutes later when she arrives home, bundles Catelin hurriedly out of the car and into their house.

'What's wrong Mummy? And what's inst….instint?' she asks not sure if she has said the word right.

'In-stin-kt,' Julie says placing an emphasis on the 'kt' sound. 'It's when you automatically or intuitively react to something.'

'What's intu….?'

'You ask too many questions,' Julie cuts her off impatiently. 'Go and lie down on the couch. How are you feeling now?'

'A bit better. Why was that man wearing thick gloves on such a hot day?'

'You saw him?'

'Just a quick peep.'

'I don't know Catelin,' Julie sighs.

'Was he a bad man Mummy? Is that why you asked me to hide?'

'I don't know Catelin. Maybe. Now do you want a drink? And the TV on, or one of your books to read?'

Catelin is immediately distracted and quickly forgets about the man.

The following day Catelin seems fine and Julie sends her to school. When she collects Catelin from the after school club she discovers that she is unable to proceed along her normal route. The road is cordoned off with police tape. There are several police vehicles outside a small block of flats on the corner where she nearly hit the man yesterday and there are a lot of people coming in and out of the block. A crowd of onlookers have gathered across the road in the park. Julie pauses, deciding the best alternative route to take. Catelin, sitting in the back, leans between the seats and points at a man talking to some other people.

'Look Mummy, there's that man we saw yesterday.'

Julie looks across to where Catelin is pointing just as the man turns and looks directly at them. There is something about the look on his face that sends a shiver of fear up her spine. She backs the car up a little and does a quick left turn, finding that her hand is shaking.

'What was happening there Mummy?'

'I don't know Catelin. Looks like something bad has happened,' Julie replies, not really wanting to talk about it. She thinks there is something about the whole scene at the block of flats that isn't right. What had the man been doing there yesterday?

'Was it the bad man who did it?'

'Did what? What are you talking about?'

'I said …well I meant … was it something the bad man did?'

'I don't know Catelin, and I don't know if he is a bad man. He might have just been helping the police.'

'I don't like him anyway, he was pulling rude faces at

you yesterday,' Catelin says with finality.

Catelin knows she should be in bed. Mummy told her to get into her bed and said she will come in soon to read her a story from the one of the new books she got for her birthday the other week. Mummy let her sleep with her last night and, with pleading, has agreed to her sleeping in her bed again tonight. She likes to sleep in Mummy's big bed and feel her close to her. But Mummy is busy on the phone talking to her friend Betty so Catelin is sitting at Mummy's dressing table trying on some of her beads. Mummy has been acting strangely since they arrived home. Not really listening to her, making Catelin be quiet while she watched the news. She asked her what was wrong a couple of times, but her mother said, 'Nothing.' Catelin knows this is not true as she can hear what Mummy is saying to Aunt Betty as she sits in the hallway of their single storey house just a few feet from Catelin.

'Do you think I should call the police, Betty? He is definitely the man I almost hit yesterday. Even Catelin recognised him and she didn't see what I did. He was behaving very suspiciously I thought yesterday. It is a *murder* enquiry according to what I've seen on the news. And you know, I am sure I saw a car similar to the one he got into outside the park, parked opposite our house yesterday afternoon, shortly after we arrived home. There was someone sitting in the car, but I couldn't see if it was him. Do you think he might have followed us?'

Catelin is aware that her mother has stopped talking. Betty is telling her what to do, she thinks. She knows Mummy is talking about the 'bad' man they saw both yesterday and again today.

'Yes, he might have been helping the police,' her mother

says, 'but there was only him there yesterday. No police. And then there were all those bin liners he was carrying and what spilled out of them. I'm sure that wasn't normal.'

The sound of the doorbell prevents Catelin from hearing the next thing Mummy says. The doorbell rings again and Mummy finally says, 'Okay, I will. Look, I'd better go, there's someone at the door. I'll ring you back after I've called them.'

Catelin removes the several sets of beads she has around her neck, closes the bedroom door over a little and stands behind it waiting to find out who is at the front door. Probably Mrs. Ostopolou from next door who is always calling in with strange, wonderful treats she has cooked. Catelin hears her mother call out 'Oh,' before her voice is cut off. She can hear scuffling in the hall, the door slamming and something crashing to the floor. Her mother is making weird choking sounds. Catelin's heart starts beating very fast and she is afraid. She opens the door and peeps out into the hall. No one is there and the umbrella stand has been knocked over. The sounds are coming from the front living room. Catelin creeps along to the living room door and she can see a man with his back to her holding her mother tight around the neck. Her mother is struggling and she can see the man is hurting her. She wants to run up and hit the man and tell him to let her mother go, but she knows she is too little to stop him. Instead she turns and runs back to her mother's room. She knows she has to hide.

Catelin pulls open her mother's built-in wardrobe doors and steps inside pulling the doors closed behind her. She climbs across the mountain of mess on the floor of the cupboard pushing aside clothes hanging on the rail. She squeezes in behind them flattening herself against the wall and pulls the clothes she has moved back in place. There is just a small gap between Mummy's dresses that lets her see through the louvre doors. Mummy had had the louvre doors fitted to their built-in wardrobes earlier this year. She had complained that the fitter had put them on the wrong way around. She had wanted them with the louvres sloping down. Instead, fitting them while they were out for the day, they'd returned home to find the man gone and the louvres were sloping upwards. Mummy complains that they are difficult to clean like that. But Catelin knows they are great for looking through when she plays 'hide and seek'. She waits.

It is quiet in the living room now, but she hears heavy footsteps treading across the floor boards. Catelin knows the man is coming to look for her. She hears him moving around the house and then coming into her mother's room. Catelin can see him looking around the room and then looking across at the wardrobe. It's the man they saw yesterday and again this afternoon! He walks up to the wardrobe and she can see him peering in. His face looks strange with just bits of it showing now. His eyes are very scary. Although she knows he is looking into darkness and can't see her, she closes her peep hole and shrinks back in case her eyes start shining like a cat in the dark. The doors of the wardrobe suddenly jerk open. Catelin holds her breath and can feel a trickle of pee running down her leg inside her pyjama pants.

Just as she thinks she is about to faint from not breathing she hears the wardrobe doors closing, his footsteps fading and the front door slamming. She doesn't move, terrified he is just pretending and is still waiting for her. Silent tears slide down her face. She knows the man has hurt Mummy and she doesn't know what to do. She lowers herself on to some boxes beside her.

She must have fallen asleep because she wakes later to the sound of the telephone ringing. It stops and everything is silent. Is it safe to come out now? She is uncomfortable with her wet pyjamas and she can smell her stinking pee. She hopes Mummy won't be too cross with her. She pulls the clothes aside, climbs across the piles and steps out of the wardrobe. There is just the faint sound of the television coming from the living room. Catelin can't remember the television being on earlier. She is sure Mummy switched it off after the news. Perhaps Mummy is okay and is in there watching something. She creeps out into the hall. The light is off there but she can see from the street light filtering in that the umbrella stand is still lying on the floor. There is no light on in the living room either. Just some light being thrown out from the television. She finds her mother lying face down on the floor and runs to her. She isn't moving and doesn't answer when Catelin shakes her. What should she do? Run next door for help or phone her Daddy? She knows he is home. She spoke to him earlier just before Mummy told her to go to bed. The lock on the front door is still too high for her to reach without dragging the telephone chair over to it. She decides to call her father.

Catelin is good with numbers and remembers her father's phone number. Mummy lets her dial him each time she calls him. She goes into the hall and picks up the phone. She can just make out the numbers and carefully dials. Daddy answers after just a few rings.

'Hello Daddy, the bad man has hurt Mummy. Can you come and help us?'

# 5

**London, May 1987**

'I doubt the British police could do anything to help you with your mother's murder from here,' Adhita says when Catelin finishes her story and has told Adhita of her plans for the drawings.

'Well if we're still living here when I'm much older, I'll just have to get a job and save enough money to go back to Australia.'

'I'm really sorry about what happened to your mother Cate,' Adhita says sitting next to Catelin and rubbing her arm. 'It's really annoying when adults don't take any notice of what we say. I've had it most of my life with two older brothers - being just a silly little girl in their eyes.'

'You keep calling me Cate. I like that. Perhaps I'll tell my family that's what I want to be called from now on. Cate sounds more mature.'

'Good luck with that. I've realised parents make all their decisions taking no notice of what we actually want.'

Catelin remains silent throughout the family meal that evening, reflecting on the aftermath of events on the day her mother was killed. Talking about it with Adhita has stirred up unwelcome memories. Her father had told her to hang up the phone after she had called him and he had called Betty, Catelin's godmother, her mother's best friend, and also a friend of her father's when he had lived in Melbourne with them and was married to her mother. Her mother had once told her that she had become very upset following the deaths of her parents and sister in a plane crash. Catelin was only a very little baby at the time and of course doesn't remember any of it. Her mother told her she was so sad and depressed that she could barely look after Catelin and had little time for her father. So they had split up. Catelin thinks now, as a slightly older child, that her father should have been more understanding and remained with them. But apparently he was offered a very good job in Sydney where he was originally from - with the firm he is still with now - and Catelin's mother had not wanted to move there.

Aunty Betty had come around to the house immediately after Catelin had spoken to her father on the night of her mother's murder, using the spare key Catelin's mother had given her. Confronted by the evidence of what Catelin had told her father, Betty had quickly called the emergency services asking for an ambulance and the police. Then Betty had called Catelin's father to confirm the worst. Her father had flown down the next day to talk to the police and be with Catelin. They had stayed at Aunt Betty's until he took her back to Sydney.

Catelin had told the police, when they came to the house, that she had seen the man and could tell them what he looked like. Aunt Betty also confirmed that her friend Julie had said that Catelin recognised the man they had seen earlier that day when all the police were at the woman's house opposite the park. The murder that had been mentioned on the television news that night. The police dismissed Catelin's claims, saying there was a large crowd around the scene and never even took a description from Catelin. They believed she was incapable of accurately describing her mother's attacker because she had been hiding in the wardrobe. But it was mainly because she was only six years old.

'So Mum tells me your new friend is from India, Catelin,' her father mentions when they have finished eating. Cate was relieved that Janet had not brought up the subject with her earlier. But it seems she has with her father.

'No she's from England. Adhita was born here. In London. Her parents, who are both doctors, and from professional backgrounds where their fathers were also doctors, were born in India to one English and one Indian parent - *they* are both Anglo-Indians.'

'Then she's half Indian,' Janet states firmly. Cate thinks that Janet looks like she is about to say something else, no doubt derogatory, but she heads Janet off.

'You consider your father Australian don't you?'

'Yes, of course,' Janet replies.

'Well isn't it true that *his* father, who was a miner, came to Australia from Wales after the First World War with his family, but that your father, the youngest in the family, was born in Australia?'

Cate had deliberately mentioned that Janet's grandfather was a miner - work he continued after settling in Australia, because she thinks Janet is so snobbish. She was forever looking down on people who worked outside what is considered to be a 'professional' career, when that is exactly what her background is – on both her father and mother's side. Personally Cate doesn't understand Janet's snobbery, or the attitude of the girls at her new school. Either a person is a decent human being – or not. Whatever their background.

'Yes.'

Cate can see Janet flinch slightly and she knows Janet doesn't like to be reminded of her family's background.

'*You* don't call your father half-Welsh – or even Welsh. You call him Australian. Just as Adhita is English – or British. Her *cultural* background and ethnicity might be partly Indian, but her nationality is British.'

'It is an entirely different situation with my father.'

'No, it's not.'

'Girls!' her father interrupts and he and Janet spend the next few minutes debating the issue.

Cate watches and listens to the exchange between her father and stepmother with interest. She had been worried that Janet might attempt to prevent her from associating with Adhita, and clearly Janet has tried to get Cate's father on her side, but it seems as though her father doesn't have any problem with her being friends with Adhita. Cate's relieved, seeing as how Adhita is her only friend at the school. When they finish talking she announces that she wants to be called Cate from now on. Her father looks at her in astonishment and Janet scowls.

You'd think I just made some shocking announcement, Cate thinks. She suspects it is going to be an uphill battle with Janet.

Cate finds the work at school easy, just as she feared. Particularly in Maths. They are put into ability groups for the core subjects of English, Maths and Science. Following an assessment, she is placed into the top maths set with Adhita. Adhita however sits on her own doing specially assigned work. Her level is apparently far above everyone else. They are talking about putting her in for the new GCSE exams in maths and science next year. Cate doesn't believe she is anywhere near Adhita's level, but the maths work is still far too easy for her. Today the teacher has set the class a test. Cate finishes it in about five minutes and so turns to the middle of her History exercise book and begins one of her endless drawings of the murderer. She tends to do it in the middle of her books if she is in class, so then she can pull the pages out easily - and throw them away if she isn't satisfied with the drawing, as is the case most days.

The seating is arranged in long aisles, with each student having their own individual desk. Cate finds this idea of individual desks old fashioned. In her Sydney school they sat at tables grouped together – as they do in some of the classrooms in this school. The teacher, Mr. Pearson, remains seated at his desk at the front of the room once they are set any tasks, just occasionally standing and strutting up and down the aisles with his nose in the air and hands behind his back. Cate has witnessed him doing this at some point in almost every lesson and wonders what he finds so fascinating about a ceiling that is just covered in white flaking paint.

She is so absorbed in her work that she hasn't noticed the teacher, Mr. Pearson, approaching and stopping beside her.

'Drawing Miss Brant? You are supposed to be completing your maths test.'

'I've finished it sir,' Cate says passing him her completed paper.

'Hmph,' he grunts. 'We'll see just how well you've done then, and I'll take this thank you,' he says reaching down and yanking her book (with hostility), from underneath her elbows, where she has been attempting to hide it from him.

Cate sits quietly throughout the rest of the lesson, waiting for him to unleash his wrath. She is sure she will be kept behind at break for a dressing down. He has marked her paper and appears to be angry. Hopefully not about the test, she is sure she has answered the questions correctly. He can't accuse her of cheating as she hadn't been using her maths book. Probably about the drawing, she thinks.

As the end of the lesson approaches, Mr. Pearson makes the rest of the class stop and has the papers brought to him by two pupils who collect them for him.

He announces in a very loud voice that he wants Cate to remain, but dismisses everyone else when the buzzer sounds. When most of the girls leave he calls Cate out to his desk.

'So tell me young lady who is this supposed to be in the drawing? Some film star or something I suppose? Hmm?'

Cate remains silent. She is not about to tell him anything.

'Not going to tell me? Hmm? Well in that case you can remain in here through the whole break. And if you don't tell me by the time break ends, you can have a detention this afternoon after school. Perhaps then you will tell me.'

'That's not fair sir,' says Adhita who is standing nearby. 'Cate had finished her test and it's not as if she was disturbing anyone else.'

'This doesn't concern you,' Mr. Pearson says turning to Adhita. 'You can go now, as with the rest of you. Out now.' Mr. Pearson waves his arms at them all shooing them out of the room. Some girls have been lingering behind, Cate suspects so that they can hear her being told off and then have a dig at her later.

'But sir,' Adhita persists, 'these drawings are really important to her. She's trying to capture the image correctly of the man who murdered her mother.'

There are gasps from the other girls in the room. Adhita turns the colour of beetroot, realising that she shouldn't have said anything.

'I'm sorry,' she whispers to Cate and runs out of the room.

After a few moments Mr. Pearson repeats his instructions to leave to the girls who are still lingering. 'And you young lady will come with me,' he says to Cate.

She follows him through the school to the Head's office where he asks her to take a seat outside. He knocks and enters the room. Cate can hear muffled talking and a few minutes later she is asked to enter the office. Mr. Pearson is about to walk off, but turns and tells her that she achieved a 100% in her maths test. Cate thinks he does not appear to be too happy about it.

Cate has only met the Headteacher once, briefly, when she came with her parents to look at the school. Mrs. Summers, although quite short, is a rather formidable character, seeming impressively large and intimidating. She calls Cate into her office and doesn't invite Cate to sit down. Cate's hands are all sweaty with fear.

'What's all this nonsense about this drawing being the man who murdered your mother?' she asks Cate pointing to the drawing lying in front of her on the desk.

'It's true,' Cate answers in a quiet voice.

'I will not have such wicked lies told in this school, madam. I shall be asking your parents to come in to see me this afternoon about this. In the meantime you are not to go to any lessons. You are to sit in the sick room annexe and some work will be brought to you. You will sit outside my office for the rest of break and then a member of staff will escort you to the annexe. You will have your lunch in the same room. Do I make myself understood?'

Cate nods. 'Right, that will be all. Out you go.'

The rest of the day Cate spends in a room with a few desks which, she is informed, are for students who are not well or have a leg or foot injury and cannot get up the stairs. It is attached to the sick room and every now and then she can hear what sounds like someone vomiting. *Lovely!* She is brought some English and History assignments to complete. She was supposed to have PE this afternoon and no work is sent to cover this lesson so the woman in charge of the sick bay allows her to read her library book. She doesn't dare do any of her drawings. The afternoon seems to drag slowly.

'I'm afraid your daughter has been telling some dreadful lies,' Mrs. Summers begins with Mr. and Mrs. Brant. She explains how Catelin was caught in a Maths lesson drawing the image of a man whom her friend claimed was the man who murdered Catelin's mother and that, when she confronted Catelin with the picture, she claimed it was true.

'Of course I can't have girls telling such outrageous lies in this school. I hope you understand that Mr. & Mrs. Brant.'

Janet Brant nods as though in complete understanding.

'My daughter doesn't tell lies Mrs. Summers, at least not about important matters,' Howard Brant says. 'Her mother *was* murdered when Catelin was only six years old. Janet here is her stepmother.'

Mrs. Summers is silent for a minute then with pouting lips says, 'I wish you had told me this when we first met.'

'What, so you could refuse my daughter entry to your school? Catelin's mother was not some disreputable character. She was a High School teacher. We don't fully understand what happened, and nobody has ever been charged, but from what she had told a friend, she nearly ran over a man leaving the apartment block where a young woman was killed. We think my ex-wife was murdered because she could identify this person. Catelin was at home at the time, saw her mother being murdered and then ran and hid in a wardrobe. She became a little obsessed with trying to capture the likeness of this man for some years, although I wasn't aware she was still drawing him.'

Mrs. Summers is silent for a moment before finally clearing her throat. 'I see. Well I can't have this kind of thing going on in my school. She was doing this drawing in the middle of a lesson. Apparently she had completed a maths test and decided to spend the remainder of the lesson doing this drawing.'

'We understand and we're very sorry. We will be talking to her about it, I can assure you,' says Janet.

'How did she do in the math's test?' asks Howard.

'According to her teacher she achieved 100%. But that's not ......'

'That's my girl,' Howard says, looking smugly at Mrs. Summer. 'She always did particularly well in her maths lessons in Australia. From what Catelin has told us though, all the work this top class has been given so far she has already learnt in Australia. A shame your teacher didn't give her some more advanced work, then this incident would never have happened.'

Mrs. Summers sighs. 'You may well be right, I can see that she achieved top grades in the assessments carried out by her teachers. Nevertheless, I am not sure that this is the right school for Catelin.'

'So are you saying that because her mother was murdered she is not good enough for your school? Is that really what you are saying?' asks an angry Howard Brant.

'I'm saying that if she is so caught up with this ….. this problem from the past, it will no doubt cause difficulties with the parents of other students. I've already received a few phone calls from horrified parents of students who go home for lunch. There were other girls present in the room when Catelin's friend Adhita Acharya blurted out what I now know to be the truth about the drawing. Things like that spread very quickly around a school. It's half term next week. I suggest you keep Catelin off school tomorrow and over half term consider other options. I realise of course that it would be very difficult to find another school at this time of year. We will provide work for Catelin to complete at home to carry her through to the end of term. And we will of course provide her with a glowing reference with regard to her grades. But I suggest that you begin looking for a new school for her from September.'

'So am I right in thinking that you are expelling my daughter?'

'No, certainly not Mr. Brant, we have never expelled or permanently excluded any of our girls. I am merely stressing that you should be looking for another school for Catelin, one that will suit her better.'

'Suit her better? What do you mean by that?'

'One where it won't be such an issue or cause great controversy if she were to repeat the incident we have had today.'

'You've got to be kidding me!' Howard Brant says standing. 'You want me to *remove* my daughter because you never *expel* your pupils – my daughter who has done nothing that warrants expulsion anyway and was merely filling in time because your teacher didn't provide her with suitable work to match her ability. My daughter, who through no fault of her own happens to have a 'murdered' mother – and you are worried that this has upset a few parents. The murder did not even happen in this country. To be quite frank, I find your attitude deplorable.'

'We are a fee paying school Mr. Brant. If parents are concerned about their daughters associating with someone who they might consider an undesirable person, and I'm sure some of them would still think like that even if they knew the full circumstances, then I have to take this into consideration. Otherwise we might well be seeing a number of our pupils withdrawn and moved to other schools.'

'I thought that this school would provide the best education to suit my daughter's abilities. Clearly I was wrong. You aren't capable of it. Right, come on Janet, I've heard enough of this. We're leaving. Where is my daughter?'

'I think you'll find she should be waiting outside for you now.'

Visibly shaken by the meeting with the Brants, Edith Summers drops some Rescue Remedy onto her tongue. It calms her somewhat but, feeling she requires greater relief, she also swallows a nip of brandy from the small bottle in her drawer which she keeps for such emergencies. She hates this aspect of her job, being under strict instructions from her superiors on how to deal with awkward situations such as these. Making mountains out of molehills. The Chair of Governors had called her earlier this afternoon and demanded that she "remove that unsuitable antipodean child." She was tempted to tell her it was her business, and her business alone to deal with the matter, but the Chair, an unpleasant woman in Edith Summer's opinion, had claimed that she had the unanimous vote of the rest of the board on the matter and said "the child is not to return to the school under any circumstances - any circumstances whatsoever!" Edith herself had, of course, thought the child was lying – just like everyone else. But she didn't think it warranted removal from the school – just a severe reprimand and some form of punishment - including standing in front of her class and admitting she had lied to her friend. But to discover the shocking truth just made the whole thing worse. The girl had not lied.

She will draft a letter to the Board outlining the details of Catelin Brant's background and hope that the Governors will feel some guilt about their decision. She doubts it though.

Pearson is to blame for this incident she thinks. He should have given the girl more advanced work. Any fool could see that she required extending. She will have to have a quiet word with him to ensure that this type of thing does not crop up again.

'What were you thinking Catelin,' Janet spits angrily at her when they arrive home. 'Doing those stupid drawings in the middle of a test. We told you to stop doing them. Now look at what has happened. They want you to leave the school, the best private school in the area.'

'Private school?' Cate asks surprised. 'I thought you said it was a public school?'

'Well … it is. Sort of.'

'Now I am completely confused. If it is a public school, how can it be private?'

'In England, the term public school is applied to fee paying private schools. The other schools are either Church schools or Local Authority Schools – meaning the Council

- whereas we say 'State Public School' in Australia. We don't have the local councils running education, each state runs their own education. Here it is more local.'

'But how can it be 'public' if it is private? That's just stupid. Public means for everyone.'

'I know, I had trouble understanding it all. Apparently the term is usually applied to the bigger schools like Eton, Harrow or Rugby, but it is also used by some people to describe any smaller private school like yours. Anyway you are dodging the issue madam. When your father returns with Rosie we will have to sit down and discuss options. You won't be going into school tomorrow.'

'Yes, okay,' Cate sighs.

When Rosie and her father return they all sit down at the dining table. At first Rosie is asked to go to her room and not take part in the discussions, but both Cate and Rosie object and demand that she remain. Rosie reminds everyone that she is a member of the family as well and should have her say.

'So you know that the school don't want you back Cate,' her father starts. Since the recent request to call her Cate, her father and Rosie have willingly complied. Only Janet persists in calling her Catelin.

'Yes. I don't think I am going to lose any sleep over that. They're a bunch of bloody snobs anyway. Adhita is the only decent person I've met at the school.'

'Catelin, no swearing! What have I said about using that word?'

'Dad says 'bloody' all the time,' Rosie reminds her mother.

'Yes, well he's a grown up. You two are *not* to use it. I've …'

'I'd like to go to a mixed school,' Cate interrupts. 'I didn't realise that my school was a private one – not understanding that public means private here,' Cate says. 'And I'm fed up with the spitefulness of some of the girls.'

'What do you mean Cate?' asks Rosie.

'Never mind that now Rosie,' her father says. 'So you'd be happy going to a local authority secondary school? Are you sure? I've heard some of them are a bit rough. And I suspect the girls would be just as spiteful in a mixed school.'

'And the better schools may not have a place either,' Janet joins in.

'I like my school with mixed classes,' Rosie says. 'Apart from some of the boys who behave badly sometimes, I think it's really good. Of course the girls are always better at everything than the boys, apart from some of the sports, and so lots of the boys work hard to try and beat us at things.'

'Girls do statistically better at girl's schools,' Janet reminds her husband. 'We've talked about this, which is why we chose girl's High schools for Catelin in both Sydney and here.'

'Well I certainly don't want to go to another private school, and I really want to try a mixed school,' Cate says with finality.

'Okay,' her father says. 'We'll look around and see what is available. I will take tomorrow off and see what we can organise. I'll make calls, and arrange visits until we find a suitable school for you.'

After visits to several schools, Cate obtains a place in the school of her preferred choice. She thinks she will like the new school she is due to start in September. Her father and

Janet seem happy about it as well. Janet has been asking around the neighbourhood and it would appear that many of the local children, who seem to come from respectable families in her view, attend this school.

As a punishment for her part in the drawing incident, Adhita is asked to drop and collect work each day for Cate through the final half term. Cate lives very close to where Adhita walks to after school each day to wait for her mother, who works in a doctor's practice nearby. The girls don't mind and their friendship blossoms, much to Janet's disgust, Cate thinks. When they first met up over half term Adhita was very apologetic, saying how sorry she was for revealing what the drawing concerned.

'It's alright Adhita,' Cate had assured her. 'You don't need to keep saying you are sorry. I know you said it to try and help matters with old Pearson. I'm glad to be out of that school anyway. Apart from you I didn't like anyone there.'

Adhita had also invited Cate to visit her house over half term where she met Adhita's grandmother on her mother's side. This was the woman who'd married an Englishman. Adhita's grandmother, now a widow, came to live with them a few years ago Adhita explained and that it was common in Indian families for several generations to live together. Cate told her that it was like that with one of her friends from Sydney who came from an Italian background.

'I couldn't imagine Janet's mother living with us though,' she had told Adhita. 'They don't get on very well and there'd be non-stop arguments. My mother's parents are both dead and my father's mother died when he was young, so I only have one grandfather alive. My father doesn't get along with him so I don't ever see him.'

Naniji, as Adhita called her, had made them some butter chapattis and daal for lunch. They'd also had some left over vegetable dishes. All exciting new tastes for Cate who loved the food and made Adhita promise to teach her how to cook some of these delicious dishes one day.

'Only if you give me the recipe for your chocolate cake,' Adhita had replied.

# 6

**London, June 1991**

Whilst Cate made friends with both boys and girls in the school she transferred to in September 1987, it was Adhita whom she continued to consider her best friend. They regularly saw each other outside school over the following four years.

Cate has recently completed her 'GCSEs', whereas Adhita has sat her 'A' levels, apart from maths and science, which she took two years earlier. At 16 Adhita is preparing to enter university in September two years ahead of her peer group.

The Brant family had moved to a house just around the corner from their old rental. Janet had persuaded her father to buy a house, when it looked like they would be in London for some years. The Company had paid the first six month's rental of their original London house in a relocation package, but when they had to start paying the rent themselves Janet declared the cost prohibitive and didn't see the point of throwing so much money down the drain. The new house is only four bedrooms, but is plenty big enough to fit the family and accommodate visitors. Janet set about having a new kitchen fitted and decorating it to her preferred tastes.

Secretly Cate continued sketching her mother's killer and is now confident that she has the likeness exactly right.

She'd never again attempted to do one of her drawings in school, but carried on doing them in secret at home or when she was at Adhita's. She'd acquired a part time job in a local supermarket at weekends when she turned sixteen last December and is saving as much as she can for a return trip to Australia when she is 18. Now, broken up from school, both Adhita and Cate are about to start working full time at the supermarket over the summer. Adhita has been urging Cate to wait until she's twenty one and finished university to travel together to Australia. Her friend has declared that she will have finished her PHD by then and Cate will have completed a degree course. Cate is considering her options when her father throws a spanner in the works.

Over dinner one evening Howard Brant announces that he'd applied for and obtained a promotion with the Company back in Sydney.

'I will be leaving London in another seven weeks and returning to a Company rental in Sydney until the tenants move out of our old house and I can sort matters there. I've talked about it with your mother and we've agreed that you three will remain in London until the house is sold and can be packed up.'

'But we haven't even been up to Yorkshire yet Dad. You promised we'd go there,' Cate groans.

Instead of visiting places in the UK during holidays, the family had flown to Europe for holidays in France, Italy, Spain and Greece to bask in the sun. The girls had loved these countries, but apart from two short holidays in England, to Bath, Somerset and Devon, plus one trip to Edinburgh they had seen very little of the UK.

'We'll go as soon as Rosie breaks up from school. How does that sound?'

'I'll have to book some time off from my job,' Cate says.

'I'm sure that won't be a problem.'

'I don't want to go back to Australia Dad. I don't want to leave all my friends - *again*,' Rosie complains emphasising 'again.' Cate thinks if Rosie believes it will make him feel guilty she'll be disappointed. She knows once her father has made a decision he doesn't budge from it. He and Janet make these type of decisions without any consultation or discussion with her or Rosie.

'I'm sorry Rosie, it can't be helped. You'll be able to pick up with your old friends when we're back in Sydney.

'It won't be the same though.'

'I don't want to go at this point either,' Cate says quietly. 'I'd rather finish my 'A' levels first.'

'Look girls, there's always going to be something that you'd like to do or finish first. But as the person who brings the money into this household, I have to grab opportunities when they arise. Be very clear, we are returning to Australia.'

Janet seems quietly indifferent about the whole thing even though she has made many friends in London and has an active social life. Cate wonders whether Janet is really unhappy about the move but is just feigning indifference in front of them to support her husband.

Cate has her mother's original birth certificate and it shows that she was born in the small town of Hawes in the Yorkshire Dales National Park. Rooms have been booked at a bed and breakfast and Cate and Rosie are looking forward to exploring the area.

The day of departure finally arrives and they head off up the M1 then onto the M6. The journey takes them a laborious six and a half hours with stops and delays before they finally turn off the motorway and head to Kendal, where they are to spend the first night. They spend a short time exploring the town until Cate's father declares he is too tired after the long drive and they head back to their hotel to rest and freshen up before their evening meal.

In the morning they visit various sites around the area and then head off on the final leg of their journey to Hawes, which boasts to being the highest town in England, standing 850 feet above sea level. Their B & B is on the outskirts of the town surrounded by beautiful countryside. The family all express delight with the eighteenth century building providing twentieth century mod cons.

Cate approaches the manageress and asks her whether it is possible to find out more about her mother's family. She tells the woman her grandfather was called Scrope and her grandmother's maiden name was Metcalfe. She unfolds her mother's birth certificate showing the woman, who laughs.

'Scrope is the name of the old Barons and Earls from Bolton Castle. It's pronounced 'Scroop' like in 'loop', not with a long vowel. Your grandfather was probably descended from one of their illegitimate lines. They apparently had plenty of them and there are a few Scropes still around the district I believe. Your grandmother's name, Metcalfe, is very common in this area of Yorkshire. I was a Metcalfe before I married, but I've never heard of a Catherine Metcalfe in my family. There's hundreds of us around here though – all originally descended from the Metcalfe's of Nappa Hall. You'd have to look into Parish records to find out more about who you might be directly related to.'

Disappointed that she won't be able to immediately find some great aunts or uncles or cousins, Cate mentions looking in the Parish records over breakfast.

'We didn't come all the way up here to look at Parish records Catelin, we're here to enjoy the scenery.' *Trust Janet to prevent her from doing any research!*

With trips to Hardrow Force and Aysgarth Falls on the River Ure where they also had a glimpse at Nappa Hall, the family manage to see much of the surrounding countryside. They take walks along the river and also visit Bolton Castle and various tea rooms where they demolish delicious cream teas and cakes.

All too soon the trip comes to an end and they set off home. Cate is pleased to know her mother came from such a beautiful place and wonders why on earth the family left there to go to Australia. She asks her father if he knows.

'Opportunities is what your grandfather told me. They viewed Australia as a place of opportunities. Your grandfather was a joiner and there was a lot of new building going on in Australia. There was not much work back there in Hawes.'

It was on one of the final legs of a trip returning from England after visiting family that her grandparents and aunt, her mother's only sister, died in an aeroplane crash somewhere over Asia. Her mother had been unable to go as by then she was married and had Cate. With Cate's mother dying when she was so young, Cate knows very little about her mother's family. She had inherited some documents and old family photo albums. But many of the photographs have no names written on the back so Cate has no idea who they are.

One day maybe …. Cate thinks.

There are tearful farewells at the airport when Cate's father finally flies out in early August. Even Janet cries, which surprises Cate as it is rare that she openly displays any form of distress. Anger, irritation, yes, but never distress. It is the first time Cate has ever seen Janet cry.

Their house is under offer and they hope to exchange contracts in the next fortnight. Cate's father signed all the necessary documents before his departure. Until the exchange of contracts occurs Janet has been advised not to officially withdraw the girls from their school, as the whole deal could fall through and they would have to start from scratch. If that happened the girls would need to return to school for the new term. The offer had been accepted back in June, one week after it went on the market. Janet complains to Cate that she does not understand why it takes so long.

'It seems all back to front to me,' she tells Cate (who has noticed that Janet is beginning to communicate with her more like an adult than a child). 'Contracts should come first, not last. That's how we do it in Australia. We have *contracts* subject to satisfactory inspections. Not *offers* subject to the same. Offers that are meaningless really until the contracts are exchanged. I've a good mind to tell the agent to put it back on the market.'

'Shouldn't you wait until we see if they do exchange contracts?' cautions Cate. 'I'm sure that they do really want to buy the house. Their daughter is going to attend my old private school, isn't she, so they'll want to be in the area.'

'That's the reason, I've been informed by the solicitor, why they are exchanging so quickly. Otherwise it could apparently take four or five months. Quickly - it's absolutely ridiculous! When we bought Beecroft, we completed the sale in less than four weeks.'

Cate leaves Janet to her moaning and escapes upstairs to do some more packing. She has all her mother's family's documents to pack in her suitcase along with her precious drawings. She didn't want them to be shipped back to Australia just in case the ship sank en route. At least she will be back in Australia when she turns eighteen, so going to the police with her drawings will be much easier.

Contracts are finally exchanged and Cate is relieved to learn the house sale is due to complete on Friday 29th August. This daily hanging on has been driving Janet crazy and Janet in turn has been driving Cate and Rosie crazy with her whingeing and whining. Cate at least has been out at work most days, so Rosie has suffered the worst of Janet's rantings. She is finally able to hand in her notice at work and Janet notifies the school of their departure. Fortunately they don't have to alter the airline tickets that had been booked. Janet has already had to change their departure date once.

The day before completion Cate had a tearful parting with Adhita and her family, especially Naniji who she is particularly fond of. The girls have promised to write to each other and Adhita swears she will come out to Australia when she finishes university and has some money behind her.

When the phone rings at 2.30pm Janet, a bundle of nerves, pounces on it. Her conversation is brief and as soon as she is off the phone she shouts, 'Thank goodness! That was the solicitor. We've completed. Girls, run around and do a final check that you've left nothing in the rooms.'

'Again! Mum we've already done that *twice*,' moans Rosie.

Cate can't help smiling. Janet was exactly like this the last time they moved. Janet also checks the fridge, dishwasher and oven (although she had already done them earlier). The 'white' goods (which are actually stainless steel) are remaining as part of the sale and most of the furniture has been either sold or collected by various charities this morning with other miscellaneous boxes of items. One or two pieces the family had brought to England with them are on their way back to Australia by ship, together with other belongings. They had been shipped out some weeks prior and they'd all been surviving on reduced clothing and linen supplies. Janet's car was sold over a week ago and so she has had to make use of public transport.

'Dirty, smelly and inconvenient,' she'd moaned to the girls the day after her car departed and she was forced to catch a bus to the supermarket. The girls shrugged. They were used to it. Seemed fine to them.

They are to spend tonight in a hotel at Heathrow and then they will fly out in the morning. Cate is pleased to hear they are flying business class, not economy like they had to on their flight to England. Janet refused to suffer the discomfort of such a long journey like that again.

'It's alright for a short flight to Europe that only takes a few hours, but I am not doing a long-haul in economy ever again,' she'd told her husband before he left. So he'd left enough money for them to book their tickets in business class before he'd flown back to Sydney.

Janet says she has to go to the bank before leaving for the hotel to organise their money to be transferred to Australia. The girls sit in the back of the taxi and notice that the meter is ticking away. Cate had closed her bank account the previous day and has all her money with her in cash that she will have to change into dollars in Sydney. She hopes no will mug her before they arrive home.

'This is going to cost a bomb,' whispers Rosie. 'We

should have got out here with our bags and then hired another taxi later.'

'Mum didn't want to,' Cate whispers back. She realises she had just used the word 'Mum' for Janet. In the past she'd always said 'your mother' to Rosie. She thinks Rosie has noticed it as well as she is looking at Cate with a silly grin plastered across her face.

# 7

**Sydney, September 1991**

'Hello house!' Rosie shouts as they finally walk through the door of their old house in Sydney. She charges around the ground floor for a few minutes and Cate hears shrieks from the kitchen area.

'Come and look in here, Mum and Cate! Dad's even had a new kitchen fitted and taken the dining room wall out. It doesn't look much like our old house anymore.'

'It's called modernising Rosie. The house was looking a bit tired after the tenants moved out. Don't you like it?' her father asks. 'If not, don't blame me, blame your mother, she chose the kitchen cabinets and said she wanted to open it up. I was just following orders.'

'I think it's great. But how did Mum choose the cabinets while we were in England?' Rosie asks.

'Your mother chose the general design from a kitchen magazine in England before I left and so I had them made to her specifications.'

Cate can tell by the joyful smile on Janet's face that she loves the changes. She will be able to talk to them while she cooks dinner; the same way as she did in London.

'There's new mattresses in your bedrooms girls,' their father tells them. 'Why don't you go and sort your rooms out. Your old wooden bed bases are back in there and your personal boxes.'

The girls head upstairs to become reacquainted with their old belongings. After about an hour, Rosie walks into Cate's room and declares that she will probably give most of the things from her stored boxes to charity.

'I don't know why I kept all that old stuff. The only thing I want to keep are my books and a few of my cuddly toys. All those dolls. Ugh! You never played with dolls did you Cate?'

'No. They gave me the creeps. The only dolls I ever liked were rag dolls. Look I kept Lulu,' Cate says holding up a doll she'd just unpacked from a box. Her mother had given her Lulu for her fifth birthday.

'You haven't unpacked your suitcase yet Cate and I can see your drawing pads poking out from under your coat right on the top of everything. Are they the ones with *him* in?'

'Of course.'

'Are you still planning to go to see the police about him?'

'Yes, and Rosie you must promise not to say anything to Mum or Dad. Otherwise you know they will try to stop me.'

'I won't say anything, but you'd better hide them away before Mum spots them. You know how she feels about you drawing him.'

Over dinner that evening, a takeaway Chinese meal, as the house is still in chaos, the girls learn that they are due to start at Cate's old school in another few days. Rosie is annoyed to discover she will be going into the *lst* year (after just completing her second year in England) and still has another term to complete, whilst Cate will be jumping ahead and will have a lot of catching up to do.

'But you will be with all your old friends again Rosie,' Janet assures her when Rosie complains.

'Not all of them will be going to this stupid girl's school though. Why do we have to go there? I want to go to a mixed school,' Rosie whines miserably.

'So do I,' Cate adds.

'Don't argue,' their father says. 'It's all settled. Your mother will be taking you shopping for new uniforms tomorrow.'

'In a few weeks you'll be breaking up for the traditional September holidays. It will give you time to settle in and meet up with your old friends,' Janet points out.

Cate hopes that by now her peers will have grown out of their childish taunts towards others but worries that Rosie will have to endure some ribbing. Rosie has acquired a slight London accent that may give her trouble. Cate doesn't think *she* sounds any different to how she spoke before she left Sydney but she soon learns otherwise.

'Listen to you and your posh English accent,' some of her old friends say on her first day back at school, but all that is quickly forgotten as they are bursting to know what London is like. Cate tells them about everything she has seen including their European holidays. She tells them that they only saw a fraction of London, the UK and Europe and that one day she'd like to go back to explore some more.

'I'm green with envy,' Emma, one of her friends, says. 'Being in Europe for their summer – during *our* winter.'

'We didn't leave England this summer,' Cate tells her. 'So there were no long holidays in the sun this year. Actually *you* all look quite brown to me. You must have had hot days already this spring, have you?'

'Out of a bottle. Mine is anyway. But you're looking quite brown yourself,' Emma giggles in reply. 'So they actually have some sun in London do they?' And so Cate's friendships resume without too much difficulty.

Rosie also seems to settle back amongst her old friends with ease. Cate notices that her London accent quickly disappears.

The work load Cate has had to complete to achieve her Higher School Certificate thoroughly exhausts her. She'd had little time for socialising or taking relaxing holidays in any of the school breaks since she'd been back in school. Her parents had insisted she came away with them to the Sunshine Coast for two weeks over the summer holidays in January but Cate spent much of the time there completing assignments and studying. In essence she completed two year's work in 14 months rather than 24 months, and eight months ahead of when she would have finished her 'A' levels in England. Her exams are over by the beginning of November and she plans to take a few weeks off relaxing and doing very little. She won't have her results until January.

Cate has received confirmation of a provisional place at the University of Sydney, subject to her final grades, to complete a three year Batchelor of Design in Architecture Course. She is looking forward to going to University, but hopes the level of work won't be as intense as it has been since she's been back in Sydney.

After a short break to recover, Cate acquires a part time job in Coles, a supermarket group, working Wednesday through to Saturday to keep her going until the University course starts – if she makes the grades.

Cate has never forgotten her promise to her mother she made all those years ago and has ascertained that the Sydney Police Headquarters are located in Parramatta. She can catch two buses from home to get her there or take a train into the city and then back out to Parramatta. As soon as she turns eighteen on 6th December she plans to make a trip down there.

# 8

On Monday 7th December 1992 Cate Brant takes two buses down to Parramatta to the Police Headquarters armed with her folder of drawings. At reception she asks if she can see a detective. A Detective Sergeant Joe Paramo meets her and takes her into an interview room.

'How can I help you young lady?' he asks.

'My name is Cate Brant. Catelin is my full name, but everyone calls me Cate. I am eighteen years old. I have drawings of my mother's murderer here and wondered if you could tell me whether you can do anything from New South Wales or whether I have to go down to Melbourne in Victoria where it happened? The case remains unsolved as far as I am aware. I have asked my father about it several times over the years and he has confirmed that no one has ever been charged.'

Detective Paramo is shocked. It is the last thing he was expecting to hear. 'Perhaps you could start at the beginning,' he says, 'then I might be able to answer your questions.'

He listens as the young woman explains in detail the events that took place twelve years earlier, from when she and her mother first saw the man in question in the road outside a flat, then with the police at the flat the following day and her mother's murder that night. She assures him she had a very good look at the man on each occasion and at close quarters through the wardrobe door the night her mother died. She explains how she has been practising her drawings of the man ever since. She tells him about the family moving to England and how she was even asked to leave her first school because of drawing in a lesson and how she had finally achieved greater accuracy when she was about fifteen. She produces the first pencil drawing and places it on the table.

'This is what he looked like then. This is what I think he might look like now,' she says placing a second drawing down beside the first. 'I've aged him a bit seeing as it is twelve years since it happened.'

Detective Paramo examines the drawings. 'You've certainly got a talent here Miss Brant. These are very good. How sure are you that they truly resemble the man? I mean you were six years old when it happened and it was twelve years ago.'

'I've never forgotten his face. Never allowed myself to forget his face. I know it is him. Is there anything you can do from New South Wales?'

'Yes, but I will need all the details of your mother's name and date of birth first.'

The young woman provides him with her full name and date of birth and similarly her mother's details, where they were living at the time and what school she had attended. She shows him her birth certificate and some old school reports 'just to confirm the details I am giving you,' she tells him.

After noting everything down he looks up at her and says, 'This is what I will do. I'll send a copy of the drawings down to Melbourne Headquarters with the details and see if anyone recognises the face. Can I have these drawings to make copies from?'

'Yes. You can keep them. I have plenty more. How soon could you do that?' she asks him.

'We are quite busy at the moment, but I will get to it as soon as I can. Can you give me your contact details?'

She hesitates and pulls a face shaking her head. 'I don't want anyone at home to know about this. As you can imagine, it has caused quite a bit of trouble at home over the years with my father and stepmother. I've had to wait until my eighteenth birthday before coming here to see you, otherwise they wouldn't have let me come. They don't believe I could possibly remember what he looked like. Can I come and see you again instead?'

'Miss Brant, I must have your details if you want me to pursue this. I assure you I won't come around or telephone you at home unless we have some specific information to pass on to you.'

'Okay.' Reluctantly she gives him her home address and phone number. 'I'm working in Coles part time at the moment, but hope to be starting at Sydney University full time when the term starts in the New Year,' she tells him. 'How long before I should come and see you again?'

'Leave it until the New Year,' he says standing to convey that their meeting is over. 'This time of year Melbourne won't be quick to respond. It's probably better if you phone me.' Detective Paramo produces his card and hands it to her.

Joe Paramo thinks Cate Brant is a remarkable young girl. To have held the image of her mother's killer in her mind all these years and her determination to follow it up is impressive. He will certainly help her as much as he can. He faxes a request to Melbourne Headquarters for information on the murder together with the two drawings. He thinks it might be some time before he hears anything back from them. He places the drawings in a file and shoves it in his bottom desk drawer. The boss isn't in at the moment but he will mention it when he returns.

The woman who receives the fax at Melbourne Police Headquarters examines the copy of the drawings. There is something vaguely familiar about the face. Probably someone on their records she thinks. She spends many hours on and off over the next two weeks trawling through their records of known criminals, but can't find a match anywhere. When she looks into the records of the case she discovers that the murder of Julie Brant remains unsolved and is possibly linked to another murder of someone who used to work for them in admin. Not someone she ever worked with though. She sends a fax back to the detective in New South Wales who requested the information, informing him that the two cases remain unsolved and that she can find no likeness of the drawings amongst identified criminals, but has added the drawings to the case file. She gives him the name and details of the first victim.

Detective Inspector Ross Pullman is handed the fax sent to DS Paramo by one of the admin staff. He looks at it and approaches Paramo.

'What's this about Paramo? When did you get involved in this?' he asks placing the fax down in front of Detective Paramo.

'Oh sorry boss, it was a young woman who came in several weeks ago. Her mother was one of the murder victims. I sent off the request the same day to Victoria. I meant to tell you about it, except we were called out to the shooting of Cemel whatshisname. I completely forgot.'

'Tell me about it.'

Detective Paramo fills him in on Catelin Brant's visit and tells him about the drawings she has made. 'I have a copy of them here sir, if you'd like to see them.'

'Waste of bloody time. Don't spend any more time on it. As if a six year old would remember what someone looked like twelve years later!'

'I really think she has remembered what he looked like, sir. It was a quite a traumatic event for her. And she saw the man three times, not just on the night of the murder.'

'Forget it. We have more important things to be dealing with. It's not our case anyway. It didn't even happen in our state. It's Victoria's problem, not ours. I don't want you spending any more time on it. Understood?'

'Yes sir, only I should pass on the negative response we've had from Melbourne, just to close things down.'

'Fine, do that. And nothing more.'

# 9

**Parramatta Police Headquarters, April 1999**

'I'd like you all to give a warm welcome to our new Assistant Commissioner, the *real* James Bond,' the Deputy Commissioner says grinning to the assembled police staff in the auditorium. 'He has joined us after a distinguished career up in the Gold Coast.' The new Assistant Commissioner steps forward and gives a slight bow in response to the applause and laughter.

He's kidding isn't he? Detective Inspector Joe Paramo thinks. That'd be right - another Anglo of course rising through the ranks. Never anyone from other origins. James Bond – no wonder he's risen through the ranks with a name like that, he thinks. Judging by how old he looks though, Paramo thinks he was born before the Ian Fleming character was created.

Paramo wonders if he's related to the Alan Bond clan with his Bond Corporation, or the Bonds from the Bond clothing firm. Although, if his memory serves him correctly the founder of the Bond brand name, George Bond had no children and died with little money, after losing his company despite creating a multi-million pound industry back in the early twentieth century. It was even said that the current railway line running west from Parramatta was built to move goods and people to the factory he built at Wentworthville/Pendle Hill. And the suburb Pendle

Hill was named after a place he came from in Britain or something. Mind you, most place names in Australia were named after either British places or British officials from the days when Britain ruled the country he reminds himself.

George Bond might have had descendants through siblings though, he thinks. The Bond name is synonymous with Australians, famous for its underwear. He is, in fact, wearing one of their famous 'Chesty Bond' singlets today, as the autumn weather seems to have really set in.

Alan Bond, on the other hand, is one of Australia's richest men, and is considered a national hero and corporate criminal at the same time. Bond became a national hero after his team won the America's Cup back in 1983. He had previously been named 'Australian of the Year'. That's a bit of a joke now, Paramo thinks, as Bond is currently serving a jail sentence for corporate crimes. He was first jailed in '92 but was handed a 'get out of jail free' card on those charges. We got him again though Paramo thinks, for fraud (over a Manet painting of all things – Bond was an ardent collector of art) and syphoning off corporate funds. Bond was your typical millionaire, who believed he was above the law, basically diverting money from the company to fund his luxurious lifestyle.

If this new bloke is related to Alan Bond and his Bond Corporation lot, he might have plenty of dough, Paramo thinks. And power. Another reason why he might have risen rapidly through the ranks. The Bonds have some connections up in the Gold Coast he's sure. Isn't there that new Bond University up that way?

Disinterested in giving a personal welcome to the new Assistant Commissioner, Joe Paramo returns to his office. Best to leave all that nonsense to his DCI. It's about all Pritchard is good for he thinks. The networking and liaising. Attending meetings, going to lunches. Their old DCI did little of that. He liked to remain in touch with real police work. Besides Joe's taken an instant dislike to this new Bond bloke. He can't put his finger on why. Maybe it's just the name.

'What did you think of our new Assistant Commissioner then, sir,' DC India Hargreaves asks as he walks into the squad room. She is already back at her desk, so must have left the gathering long before him.

'I thought the Deputy Commissioner was joking at first about his name,' Joe says, cautiously evading the question. He avoids saying anything derogatory about senior ranking officers to anyone. All those thoughts remain in his head.

'So did I, but he's not. The information about his appointment is already on the system. Do you think he's part of *the* Bond family.'

'You mean Alan Bond's family?'

'Yes.'

'Could be, I couldn't really tell you. I know they have links with the Gold Coast so he may well be.'

'You didn't want to stay and meet him?'

'No, I thought I'd leave that to our illustrious leader. I gather you didn't wish to meet him either?'

'What and be accused of attempting to gain promotion by buttering up to senior male police officers! Not a chance.'

'Now who would think you capable of such a thing, India?' Joe says with an innocent face. He watches as India silently sweeps her arm around the room at the empty desks. As the only female detective, and much younger than many of her male colleagues, Joe knows there has been a great deal of resentment towards her as university graduate. But she is a grafter and has proved her worth time and time again. The boys are slowly coming around.

He smiles at her and retreats to his office. Once back at his desk, Joe thinks momentarily about this new assistant commissioner. There is something familiar about the man. He's never heard of him though and never had any contact with the police in the Gold Coast so it must be just that he reminds him of someone else. He can't remember who, but believes it will come to him eventually.

# 10

**Parramatta, October 1999**

As Cate is walking to her favourite café/bakery for lunch, she reflects on how her life has changed since she left school. University, marriage and now soon to have a baby! Just five weeks to go. Several of her old school friends have been married for a few years with more than one child.

But although she's turning twenty-five this coming December, Cate's not sure that she feels old enough for the responsibility of motherhood. 'What if I make a mess of it?' she'd asked her husband Marco. He reminds that her mother was only twenty-one when she'd had her.

'Everything will be fine. We will be doing it together,' he constantly re-assures her. Easy for him to say. It will be me going through the pain of giving birth. I will be the one sitting alone at home with a new baby, in a new house, in an area where I don't know anyone, Cate thinks.

Towards the end of her first year at university Cate had met Marco Rossi, who was completing his masters to qualify as an architect. When Marco became too serious after they had been together a year, proposing to her one evening, Cate decided that she was far too young at twenty years of age for engagements or marriage, so broke up with him to enjoy life as a single person with her friends in her new shared house.

At the time, Cate knew she was both inexperienced and

naive when it came to relationships, having gone no further than a few passionate embraces and kisses with boys at her school in England and she'd had no relationships whilst studying for her HSC. The idea of a quick grope and poke up against the brick wall near the bins at her school in London had held no appeal for her. Similarly, crawling into prickly bushes at the local park had not appealed either. She knew some of her peers at school had resorted to these measures with no other opportunities available at their homes. Cate yearned for more than that, and she thinks Marco set the scene for their first sexual intimacy just perfectly – a remote outdoor area where they'd had a picnic lunch one day along the Hawkesbury River.

Cate had partied hard during her 'single' days after breaking up with Marco and had one or two brief flings with other young men, but when Marco contacted her again after a ten month break, she jumped at the chance to see him again. Fifteen months ago they finally married, Cate by then sure that Marco was the man she wanted to be with, following their four and half years on/off relationship.

Cate had left university after her three year degree course in Design and Architecture. She'd had enough of studying at the time. For the past three years she has been working in the same firm as Marco, an architect's practice in Parramatta.

Initially Cate's parents weren't happy about her marrying into an Italian family – more Janet really, whose background was Methodist and expected to hear that Marco's family were strict practising Catholics and that Cate had to be married in a Catholic Church, but both Marco and Cate assured them that as a second generation Australian he had moved away from any church dominance in his life. Cate and Marco had decided to shun all church weddings and had been married by a celebrant outdoors in Parramatta Park.

Marco had wanted Cate to stop working six and a half months into the pregnancy, but Cate told him she was pregnant, not ill. Working at her desk is uncomfortable with her now huge bump but she uses her lunch break to exercise, walking several blocks before stopping at her favourite café/bakery for lunch. She treks back the same distance, using different blocks. It is seldom that Marco joins her for lunch as he often has meetings to attend or urgent work to finish.

Cate has asked for some time off the following afternoon so she can go shopping at the mall to purchase more items she will need for the baby. She finds the mall too hectic and busy at weekends. While lunching that day she starts to scribble a list of things she wants to buy and decides she will need to bring her car into work tomorrow for the shopping trip.

The following afternoon Cate drives up to the shopping mall and meticulously works her way through her list. She thinks this might be her last opportunity to buy some things for the baby. They are moving into their new house in just over a week up at Glenbrook in the Blue Mountains and Cate knows she will be so busy organising everything there that she won't have time to do much shopping before the baby arrives.

'Nesting' Janet had told her she would be doing in the new house and explained how women prepared a 'nest' for their babies. When Cate thinks about the woman she calls 'mum', she always thinks of her as Janet, but when she talks to anyone, or Janet directly, she always calls her mum now. Cate had been doing that since they returned to

Australia over eight years ago.

Marco and Cate currently live in a small one-bedroomed rental apartment in Northmead where there is little enough room for their bed in the bedroom.

'It will be impossible, once the baby is born, with so little space,' Cate had pointed out to Marco one the pregnancy was confirmed. 'We'll have to move.'

Cate would have preferred to stay in a location close to their work at Parramatta, but Marco had wanted to move to the Blue Mountains. He had grown up in the Blue Mountains, as his father was an engineer in the mining industry based there. His parents had since moved to Singleton, transferring to the mining region in the Upper Hunter Valley. Marco loved growing up in the mountains though and told her he wants their children (steady on Cate thought, I haven't even had the first one yet) to grow up there, so they have bought their first house in the costly suburb of Glenbrook.

They'd spent months looking across the region and settled on a quaint single storey house just a ten minute walk to the station in one direction and a ten minute walk to the school in the other direction. Although costlier than other areas they looked in, Marco argued that this suburb would suit them both better. 'It is the first main suburb of the mountains and therefore quick to exit onto the highway back to Parramatta for commuting. And there are regular trains to Parramatta and Sydney Centre. The area is safe and the local school has an excellent reputation. There's a number of shops for basic needs and we can always nip down to Penrith, now that it's a thriving metropolis, for bulk shopping,' he'd pointed out to Cate.

'You sound like an estate agent,' Cate had remarked at the time. 'What about bush fires?' With the mountains vulnerable to fire outbreaks, Cate had been worried about this.

'No, in Glenbrook it will be fine,' he'd reassured her.

The house has only two bedrooms at the moment, plus a room off the lounge they will use as a study/studio, but the plot is large and Marco plans to build an extension onto the back when they can afford it. One day he would like to build a large modern house on the block and has even drawn plans for the dream house to show Cate how magnificent it could be. The house purchase completed six weeks ago and Marco has been having work done there in preparation for the move.

On her way out of the Mall, Cate spots a picture in a shop that would be perfect for the baby's room, so adds that to her collection of purchases.

Heading home from her shopping at the Mall, Cate pulls off the main road to call into her lunch café/bakery. She'd meant to buy one of their fabulous family size pies at lunch time to take home for a quick meal tonight, but forgot. She drives around several blocks before eventually finding a parking spot near what she thinks might be part of a convent. Almost the whole block is taken up with a range of brick-built readily identifiable Catholic buildings, reminiscent of many that have been built across the state.

After returning to her car and stowing the pie carefully she is just about to turn the key in the ignition when she notices the front doors of the building close to where she is parked open, and a man in a smart suit steps out with another man in a priest's outfit. She watches inattentively, her mind on baby matters as the man turns and shakes the priest's hand and then begins to walk down the steps to the gates.

The man's features finally penetrate her consciousness and Cate's heart suddenly beats rapidly. She can't believe what she is seeing. It's HIM. Her mother's murderer! She is sure of it. A little older, a bit fatter, but she's sure it's definitely him. She instinctively ducks down and pretends she is looking for something on the floor of the car in case he comes her way. When she looks again she spots a large silver car driving off. It turns at the corner before she can note down the number plate.

He's in Sydney! He looks like he's a businessman by the way he's dressed, she thinks. She must go and find that detective and tell him. Cate pulls out and drives to the corner where she'd seen the vehicle turn. There is no sign of the car.

She heads to the Police Station and once again has difficulty finding a parking spot. After driving around for several minutes, she eventually finds a parking spot several blocks away. She arrives agitated and breathless at the Police Headquarters asking for Detective Sergeant Joe Paramo.

'You mean Detective Inspector Joe Paramo?' the constable behind the desk enquires.

'Yes, that's him.' Clearly he has been promoted. All the better, Cate thinks, seeing that it was Sergeant Paramo's boss (who was an Inspector if Cate remembers rightly) who blocked him from making any further enquiries before. If the sergeant is now the inspector here, Cate hopes there'll be no one to stop him making enquiries this time.

'I'm not sure if he is in at the moment. Who can I say is calling?'

'Cate Brant,' Cate says, knowing her married name would be meaningless to him.

Cate paces up and down the reception area still in an

agitated state. She desperately hopes Detective Paramo is here. To her relief he arrives a few minutes later.

'Miss Brant? It's been some years hasn't it? I can see things have moved on for you somewhat?' he says looking at her stomach.

'Yes, I'm married now and, as you can see, expecting my first baby.'

'I'm afraid I don't have any news for you, so if that's what you came for it was a wasted …'

'No, no,' Cate says cutting him off. 'I've got some news for you. I've just seen him. I've just seen the man who murdered my mother! Just a few streets from here,' she gasps.

'Okay, okay let's take you into a more comfortable space,' Joe Paramo says, looking around at the raised eyebrows of those within earshot. 'I'm worried you might give birth any moment in the state you're in.'

Detective Paramo takes Cate into a quiet room and asks her to take him through everything slowly. Cate explains about returning to her car when a man came out of what looked like one of the main Catholic buildings, shook the hand of a priest and left, driving off in a large silver car.

'It was definitely him,' she insists. 'A bit older, his hair is more greyish now rather than blonde and he was fatter, but it was him alright. He looks like a businessman.' Cate describes the smart suit he was wearing.

'You didn't manage to note down the number plate – or note what make and model the car was?'

'No I'm sorry, I didn't. I ducked down and hid in case he walked past me – it was just an instinctive reaction to seeing him and when I looked up his car was turning the corner. But if you went around to the building and asked the priest who he was I am sure you would find out his identity.'

'Yes. Right. I'll see what I can do, but can you do me a new sketch like the ones you did before? In the meantime, I'll make some discreet enquiries.'

'Yes sure, I'll do one at work tomorrow morning and drop it around, probably at lunch time. We have nothing at home I could use. Most of our things are packed away as we are moving soon.'

Cate forgets all about the drawing she agreed to do for Detective Paramo when other events take over. Labour pains start as soon as she arrives home. Then her water's break. In a panic she calls Janet. 'Mum what does this mean?' asks Cate. She's forgotten everything she has learnt at pre-natal classes.

'It means you need to get to hospital Cate. We'll come over as soon as we can. Ring Marco and make sure he comes home immediately and takes you in.'

Marco rushes home as soon as she calls him and drives Cate to the hospital. After a difficult labour Cate gives birth to their son, Milo, in the early hours of the following morning. It soon becomes apparent that all is not well. Milo is five weeks early and has to be placed in an incubator. He is so fragile the doctors aren't sure if he is going to live. Marco and Cate comfort each other as they watch Milo being attached to breathing apparatus and drips. Milo was one of the possible boy's names they had chosen and as soon as they laid eyes on him they knew it was the right name for him. Milo Howard (after her father) Rossi.

Cate'd had no time to tell Marco who she'd spotted the afternoon before. The murderer and the promised drawings slip to the back of her mind with her worry about Milo.

# 11

Detective Inspector Joe Paramo wanders home late the same evening he saw Cate Brant. He has been in his favourite watering hole consuming large quantities of beer followed by whisky chasers. There is never any rush for him to go home these days, he thinks bitterly. Not since his wife of twelve years left him and took their two sons with her. It has been six months now and he is still struggling to come to terms with their absence. Everything happened so fast. One minute he had a wife and two lovely boys, next they were gone. They had a comfortable home and, although the marriage was not perfect, he had no idea that she was seeing someone else. When did that happen? He knows he's always worked quite long hours – it was the nature of the job, but when Ro suddenly announced she was moving to Canberra with the boys to start life with her new partner he was gobsmacked. Never saw it coming. Now he only sees his boys on occasional weekends or school holidays when he has to drive down to Canberra and stay in a rented cabin so that he can fit the boys in with him. Gone is the spacious family home they had in Winston Hills; all he has now is a pokey little rental flat in Parramatta that you can barely swing a cat in.

He picks up a take away meal as he staggers home, a pattern that is becoming all too familiar as he seldom cooks a decent meal in what he has aptly named his 'closet kitchen'. He knows his weight has increased in the past six months due to his unhealthy diet and drinking. *Tomorrow, he promises himself once again. Tomorrow I will start eating better, cut back on the drinking and take some exercise.* A mantra he has recited many a time to himself over the past months.

Not bothering with a plate he sets his take away Chinese meal on the small table and finds the last clean fork to attack it with. There is insufficient space to fit all the little containers and so he sweeps a pile of folders on to the floor to create more room. Several burps and empty containers later he nods off where he sits, slumped back in his chair with his head resting against the wall.

It is still dark outside when he wakes. He checks his watch and sees it's only 3.25am. A few more hours sleep, he thinks. He looks at the mess on the table and the floor and assuring himself he will deal with it in the morning, he stumbles off to bed.

At 6.40am he wakes again, showers, dresses and decides he will clean up the kitchen and 'dining' area (a tiny alcove in the hallway outside the kitchen) before leaving for the station. At least that way he can return to a cleaner space this evening and have some clean utensils for eating tonight's take away. He removes all the smelly take-away containers, throws them in the bin and wipes the table clean of his messy spills. He bends down to pick up the files when he notices a drawing sticking out of one. A lightbulb goes on in his head. Copies of the drawings Cate Brant gave him all those years ago! He'd put them into a file and taken them home. His old DI had asked him to hand over the master file when he was finished dealing with it, but sure that the DI was planning to throw it in the bin, he'd made a copy and brought it home. Last week needing a storage box for things to pack in the car to take to Canberra, he'd emptied the one he had the files stored in and left the files on the table.

He picks up the relevant file and opens it. Another light bulb. He recognises the face. Even from these old drawings. Cate Brant, or whatever her name is now, was right. He is older and a little fatter. Christ almighty! This is a bit if a time bomb waiting to go off, he thinks. Better go to the Chief Inspector with this. He knows his Chief will handle it discreetly. But before speaking to the Detective Chief Inspector, he decides he should pay a little visit to the Catholic building Cate Brant described to him yesterday. Where she saw the man leaving. Then he will have definite confirmation on the name.


The large double wooden doors appear foreboding as Joe Paramo knocks at 7.45am. He feels a little guilty that he hasn't been to Church or confession since his youngest son's christening eight years ago. If he went to confession now he'd be in there for days with the many sins he has accumulated over eight years. The door is answered by a middle aged woman with a scarf tied around her head, a full apron tied over her clothes and holding a duster.

'Can I help you?' she asks.

'I'm looking for a priest who was here yesterday afternoon. He might well be the bishop. I'm not sure of his name, but he'd probably be late forties/early fifties with grey hair?' That was the description Cate Brant had given him. He shows the woman his badge.

'That would probably be the Most Reverend Jonathan Byrne. He *is* the Bishop of the Diocese. I'm afraid he's over at the Church right now.'

'Do you know what time he might be back?'

'I'm sorry I couldn't tell you. I know he'll be going

around to the Diocese office in Victoria Road later this morning.'

'What is this particular building?'

'It's Bishop Byrne's personal office and residence.'

'You wouldn't happen to know who the visitor was he had yesterday afternoon would you? He left just after 5pm.'

'Sorry, I only work in the mornings. Sister Mary Beth might know though. She often comes in about lunch time and stays in the afternoon to help the bishop with personal papers in his office.'

'Is she attached to the Convent here?'

'Yes, she is.'

'Okay, thanks. I'll call back this afternoon.'


Chief Inspector John Pritchard listens to what DI Joe Paramo is saying. At first he is confused as Joe appears to be telling him about two different murders in Melbourne in 1980. He asks Joe to repeat the story, just so that he is completely clear. He listens to Joe's theories about the murderer and examines the old drawings made by Cate Brant, and reads the brief outline DI Paramo has in his files on the deaths of Mia Adjudovic and Julie Brant in Melbourne in 1980.

'I'm sure there is a simple explanation for this Joe. You're saying this girl was only six years old at the time?'

'Yes, but she got a good look at the assailant. Apparently no one took any notice of her at the time, including her father. She never forgot what the man looked like and spent years sketching him until she got it right. I first saw her when she turned eighteen. That was almost seven years ago now. My DI at the time didn't want me to take it any further. I doubt it ever came to the DCI's attention.'

'Leave it with me Joe. I'll ask some discreet questions.

And don't go around to the bishop's residence again. I don't want to be receiving any complaints about you from the Diocese office. How are you doing though? I know life has been tough for you since Rowena left with the kids. Have you cut down on the drinking like I told you to? Word is you were in the bar until almost closing again last night.'

'What I do in my private life is no one else's business… sir,' he adds.

'It is when you come into work smelling like a brewery. Clean your act up Joe or I might have to take disciplinary measures against you.'

'Yes sir,' Joe says.

Joe Paramo slams the door as he leaves Pritchard's office. He knows it is a childish gesture, but it gives him great satisfaction to vent his anger. *Bloody stuck up righteous prick.* He realises he has been drinking heavily in recent months, but he has still done his job without any difficulties. And he has never drunk on the job, not like some of the bosses he'd worked for in the past. Always having a bottle or two in their drawers or cupboards and nipping at them throughout the day. He has never brought any booze into work with him. I just hope young Cate turns up with that new drawing, he thinks. Then we'll have the bastard! Lucky I made a copy of the Brant file before going to Pritchard otherwise it might be buried.

He is just looking through the Brant file again when DC India Hargreaves knocks and enters his office.

'Are you okay sir? Only you looked pretty upset when you came through the squad room.'

'Put it like this, I've had better days.'

'Anything I can help you with sir? I've finished all my

paper work.'

DI Paramo hesitates. He would like her help. She's a good sort, efficient at her work, but he doesn't think it would be wise for her career to involve her in the matters he has raised with the DCI. 'Thanks for the offer, but I've nothing for you that wouldn't get you into trouble,' he says shrugging.

'I can be discreet sir, you know that.'

'I know India, but there's a few things I need to do on my own.....on second thoughts though, there is one thing you could think about for me. I need to find out the name and hopefully contact details of a man who was visiting someone locally yesterday. I need to come up with a plausible excuse to approach this person or one of his staff to obtain the information. Say for example, that a witness saw the visitor, whose name I need to know, drop their wallet as they were leaving the first person's place and handed it in to us, only we don't have the person's identification in the wallet.'

'That's all a bit cryptic sir. And a wallet would be no good as it usually does have ID in it.'

'Yes I know. It needs to be something small and valuable that might easily drop out of a pocket. I need to know the identity of the person who was with this other party yesterday without giving them the real reason for it. It has to be a feasible item that a witness supposedly saw this person drop. Sorry to be so vague, but I can't fill you in on the details. Do you get what I mean?'

'Yes, I think I do sir.'

'Well if you can think about it this afternoon and maybe tonight. I'm sure you can come up with something creative. You can bring me your suggestions tomorrow. We'll talk about it then and decide the best course of action.'

'Okay sir. Will do.' With a puzzled grin on her face DC Hargreaves turns and leaves his office.

Be blowed if he was going to sit back and take no action on this despite what the DCI says. It was too important, for god's sake. Especially in view of who he has potentially identified as the killer. Also, he let the Brant girl down last time round. He has no intention of doing so again. She was in such a state when she came in the other day, it's clearly still really affecting her life. Despite what Pritchard thinks, Joe is absolutely sure that Cate Brant spotted her mother's killer the other day and, as he pointed out to Prichard, the killer is known to them. Cate's old drawings where she aged the man show a good likeness to how he would have looked seven years ago. It needs following up. He's convinced that Pritchard will do nothing about it though. Pritchard would be worried about upsetting his Catholic friends and causing a major scandal into the bargain. Personally Joe doesn't care if it does involve a bloody bishop. He only wants to talk to the man to confirm the name of his visitor. That would prove things once and for all. What the hell is wrong with that? This arrogant bastard needs to be stopped. There's two historical murders and god knows how many more there might be. After scribbling some notes, Joe makes another copy of the Brant file and places it in his drawer. The final copy, with his original notes, he packs in his bag to take home later.

By early evening Joe Paramo is wondering what's happened to Cate Brant. He's checked a few times with the front desk to see if anything has been left for him, but clearly she still hasn't been in yet. She told him she lived in Northmead now, but he didn't take down her address, nor her married name as he was expecting to see her today.

He's sure she will turn up again though and he plans to have something concrete to tell her by then.

'Afternoon sir, I wondered if I might have a quiet word,' Chief Inspector John Pritchard asks.

'Sure John, anytime, come in. How can I help you?'

'I wondered if you might be able to answer a small query I have?'

'What is it?'

'I know you started your career in Melbourne and wondered if you were involved in the 1980 Mia Adjudovic investigation? Do you recall that case?'

'Yes I do and I was on the investigating team. Why?'

'Oh just something that's come to light. It might explain things. What about the Julie Brant case? Were you involved in that as well?'

'Um, Yes I was. But not at the beginning. We were busy on the Adjudovic case. It was only later when it was thought that they might be connected that our teams worked together. Why are you asking?'

'Well the daughter of Julie Brant believes she saw the assailant who murdered her mother. She drew sketches of him. She claims she saw the man outside Mia Adjudovic's flat and again in her own house on the night of her mother's murder.'

'Julie Brant's kid? She was only a toddler wasn't she?'

'She was six years old. She did these drawings. Rather a good likeness I thought.' John places one of the older drawings completed by Catelin Brant on the table.

'So the kid did these drawings? What at six years old?'

'No, no, she did them about 12 years later. Which would probably explain the memory confusion. Mixing them up with what she'd seen at the Mia Adjudovic scene once the investigation had started. That and the fact that she was only six at the time.'

'Why are you bringing these to me?'

'It seems Catelin Brant saw the man she believed had murdered her mother yesterday afternoon and came to see Detective Inspector Joe Paramo in the afternoon. Joe is one of my DIs who this Brant woman first saw when she was eighteen.'

'Where was she supposed to have seen this person?'

'Coming out of the local bishop's residence yesterday afternoon.'

'Are you asking if that was me? Do you really think I have time to be socialising with bishops? You know I was at a meeting in the city for much of yesterday. Arrived back here about 4pm. Took the best part of an hour and a half to drive back. Some pile up on the M2.'

'Yes I heard about that. I'm sorry sir, I wasn't suggesting it was you. I'm just repeating what Joe Paramo was told by this young woman.'

'I didn't stay here long after I arrived back, just to leave some papers. Had to rush off for a late dental appointment, then drinks with friends.'

I didn't need all that information, DCI Pritchard thinks before saying, 'I knew there was a simple explanation. It's well documented that the mind plays tricks on witnesses after a trauma. And the child being so young at the time probably led her to being confused and then seeing similarities in people everywhere. Sorry to have bothered you with this. Are you still on for that spot of fishing we talked about the other week?'

'Yes for sure. Only not this weekend. I have to fly up to the Gold Coast to see the family. I'll be a little busy for the next couple of weeks. But after that would be fine.'

'Righto. You're on.'

DCI Pritchard leaves feeling fully satisfied that Joe Paramo is completely on the wrong track. He feels sorry for Joe, but he really needs to sort himself out.

Joe Paramo has not kept his promise to himself. He started out with good intentions, heading straight home after leaving the station at 7pm. He'd even called into his local convenience shop and bought himself a ready prepared meal to cook in the oven. It was a start. While the meal was cooking he'd washed all the dirty dishes and cleaned up the remaining files lying on the floor. By 9pm, appetite sated and several beers later he can't stand it any longer and decides to pop down to his local (where he hopes there'll no bloody spies to report back to Pritchard) for a couple of drinks.

It isn't so much the drink he needs as the company. He hates being alone in the shoe box that is his so-called home. He misses the kids. And Ro as well, if he is honest, even though they regularly argued in the last few years they were together.

He has a sense of someone following him as he walks to the pub and stops, scanning the street behind him only to see it's empty. He shrugs his shoulders and sets off again. It's just your paranoia about Pritchard and his spies, he tells himself.

While drinking at the bar he wonders why Cate Brant, or whatever her name is now, hadn't turned up today with the drawing. It seems out of character. He hopes she hasn't done anything stupid like attempt to start investigating matters herself. He'll give her a call in the morning, he thinks before realising he only has her old home phone number in his file. He'll wait and see if she turns up tomorrow. I'll decide what to do then if she doesn't, he reassures himself. And see what India Hargreaves has come up with for him.

At 11.20 pm he heads home again, not reeling drunk tonight, but pleasantly under the influence. He hopes the two double whiskies he'd had just before closing will ensure a good night's sleep. As he steps through the door of his flat he can sense that something is wrong. There is a reek of aftershave lotion that is not a brand he has ever used. Someone is either in his flat or has been in here while he's been out. He instinctively reaches for his gun, only to realise he doesn't have it on him. He'd left it in his bedroom after arriving home earlier. Before he can turn on the light, something hard hits him on the right side of his head and he topples into darkness.

# 12

'Anyone seen Joe Paramo this morning?' asks DCI Pritchard at the morning briefing, noting Paramo's dark and closed office. Heads turn and shake negatively. From what the other detectives have to say, Paramo wasn't seen last night at the detectives local bar hangout where he normally drinks. Perhaps he took on board what I told him, Pritchard thinks.

'He told me he was heading straight home last night sir,' Detective Constable India Hargreaves tells him. What was wrong with parents these days, Pritchard thinks – to name their daughter India? She wasn't from India and certainly didn't look Indian with her blonde hair and blue eyes! What is that all about?

'Can you go round to his flat after briefing Hargreaves? Take DC Khan with you. DI Paramo has probably slept in. I've tried phoning but there's no answer.'

'I don't know where he lives sir.'

'Well look it up for goodness sake. Personnel will have the details.'

'Yes sir.'

When DC Hargreaves and DC Khan arrive at DI Paramo's flat there is no answer to their knocking or calling. The letter box is in the lobby downstairs so there is no hole in the door they can look through. They leave and decide to return later if he hasn't surfaced.

By early evening DI Paramo has not appeared at the station and he has not phoned in with any excuse for his absence. Just as they are about to go off duty DCI Pritchard instructs Hargreaves and Khan to return to his flat. 'Knock the door down if you have to, but gain entry by whatever means. I want to know if he's alright. He hasn't been on the best form lately so I want to be sure nothing has happened to him.'

Khan and Hargreaves take an entry ram with them in case. Once again there is no answer to their knocks or calls. They notice that there is strong odour around the entrance door to the flat. Khan smashes the door in and they are immediately assailed by flies, the metallic smell of blood and the odour of a body in the early stages of decay. It has been an extremely hot day for October and the open kitchen window has attracted flies in what seems like their thousands.

'Oh my God!' DC Hargreaves calls out brushing away the flies as she enters the flat. Holding her nose and forcing herself to breathe through her mouth, Hargreaves follows Khan down the short hallway. They find DI Paramo in a windowless area outside the kitchen, slumped in one of his dining chairs, leaning against the wall. On the floor beside him is a gun. One of the standard weapons issued to members of the squad. There is a big hole in the right side of Paramo's head.

'Bloody hell! He's shot himself,' Khan declares. 'Better call it in.' Khan leaves the flat to report the death on their car radio. He asks for medical and forensic back up.

Covering her nose and mouth in an effort to avoid vomiting, Hargreaves leans over and takes a closer look at Paramo's body just as DC Khan walks through the door. 'Something about this doesn't look right to me,' she says choking back tears. She is trying to look at the scene dispassionately, but this was her boss. A man she admired greatly. 'Why didn't anyone report hearing gunshots?'

'Probably didn't hear anything, or if they did, thought nothing of it. There's a busy road outside. It all looks pretty straightforward to me,' Khan says. 'Poor bastard shot himself after a night on the booze.' He points to the empty beer cans and whisky bottle near Paramo on the table.

DI Paramo's death is considered a suicide. Everyone knew he was struggling after his wife Rowena had walked out on him taking their two sons. As a formality, Pritchard instigates minor investigations which reveal that Paramo'd had a few drinks in his local bar sometime shortly after 9pm, returning home about 11.30pm. The landlord confirmed he seemed quite drunk, but jolly when he left.

The post-mortem reveals large quantities of alcohol in his body and signs of a contusion to the same side of the skull as the gunshot entry wound. It is not considered important and it's assumed he knocked himself somehow in his drunken state.

A verdict of suicide is given and the case closed.

# 13

'Hurry up Rosie or visiting hours will be over. I'm waiting for you.' Howard Brant calls from the hallway.

Rosie comes through from the dining room and switches off the lights. 'I've been outside looking for Tabitha. She hasn't come in for her food this evening.'

'Never mind about the bloody cat. She'll come back when she's ready. We're off Janet,' he calls up the stairs to his wife.

'Give Cate and Marco my love,' Janet calls back to him. 'Tell them I will be down again tomorrow. I'm just going in for my shower.'

'Will do. Come on Madam,' he says ushering his younger daughter out the door.

The man observes Howard Brant and a younger woman, who he assumes is one of his daughters, leaving the house in Beecroft. He knows it is not the daughter he is seeking as this one has red hair. Unless it is dyed. The brief glimpse he caught of the kid in the car with her mother back in 1980 had light brown hair. Of course that could have darkened over time, but certainly not turned red.

A security light switches off in the front porch a few minutes after they drive away from the house. He'd cased the house a few evenings prior but could see, with all the lights on and both cars in the driveway, that there were too many people home. Tonight, with the father and daughter leaving, has provided him with a better opportunity. It is a quiet and hilly street with large houses sitting on wide blocks. Although it is only early evening, there is virtually no activity in the street and little noise penetrating the dense bushes and trees surrounding neighbouring houses. There are some lights still on in the Brant house, on both floors, so he hopes to find the woman at home. He crosses the road and checks down the side of the house. The front gates have been left open, no doubt for making access easier on the car's return. Another car is parked down the generous driveway that leads to a detached garage with access to the rear of the house. There is no sound of barking, so presumably there is no dog in residence, he thinks. He moves down the drive by the boundary fence, as far away from the security light as possible so that he doesn't trigger it, and then turns around to the back of the house. He walks towards a covered outdoor area until reaching a rear door close to the driveway. It's locked, but when he moves on and checks the next set of double sliding doors he finds them and the fly screen door unlocked.

He quickly slips into a large open plan living area that he can see leads into a dining area and kitchen. There are some lights on in the kitchen, but the other spaces are in darkness. He crosses through to the hallway where stairs lead up to another floor. He can hear the sound of water running. A shower, he thinks. Silently he ascends and checks out the bedrooms. There are two that are obviously the daughter's rooms judging by the décor and girly belongings and another that looks like a guest room as there are no personal belongings cluttering it. The family bathroom is empty so there is clearly another bathroom somewhere. He approaches the final room as the shower abruptly stops. He backs up to the guest room. He suspects it is not the daughter in the shower, probably Brant's wife. She'll do for information.

He steps out of the shadows as the woman, clad in a dressing gown, emerges from a doorway heading towards the stairs. She sees him and makes a startled little jump back.

Janet Brant emits a squeal as she jumps back in shock at seeing a stranger outside her bedroom. There is something familiar about him and she is confused for a moment. Is this someone they know? Someone they were expecting tonight? But how did he get into the house? Did Howard or Rosie leave the front door open?

'I'm sorry, but who are you and what are you doing in my house?' she asks nervously backing towards the bedroom door where she plans to rush in, lock the door and phone the police if necessary.

The man moves around her to prevent her from doing this.

'Where's Catelin?' he growls at her whilst forcing her to take steps back towards the stairs.

'Catelin?' Janet queries, not understanding why he would be asking this.

'Yes, Catelin, where is she?'

'She's ……. she's in hospital.' Realisation suddenly dawns on her. She knows now why the man is familiar. 'It's ….it's YOU!' she exclaims. Catelin *had* remembered what he looked like. She recalls the drawing she caught Catelin sketching all those years ago. Janet knew Catelin had continued sketching him as she had found drawings in Catelin's sketch pads whilst cleaning her room in the years that followed. Catelin didn't like Janet going into her bedroom, but, in Janet's view, she never cleaned the room properly. While Cate had not been around she'd often pulled everything out from under her bed and given it a good clean. This is where she'd seen the sketch pads. She'd said nothing further about them as it was clearly something Catelin was driven to do. She'd noticed the drawings change slightly over time and seen that Catelin had sketched what she assumed were older versions of the same man. She hadn't really believed that the drawings would actually resemble the man that Catelin claimed murdered her mother. But here he is. In *her* home. Many years later. Older looking, but she can still see the resemblance to the image of the man in Catelin's drawings. Why is he here now? She doesn't understand.

'Well I know who I am. Who do *you* think I am?' the man says.

'The man who Cate …Catelin draws. The man who ……,' she trails off. Janet looks around her. Should she make a dash for the stairs and run out of the house seeking help? She realises now the mere presence of this man in her home spells danger for her. And quite probably Catelin, or other members of their family. Janet decides that she will need to do anything she can to protect them.

The man can see the woman is afraid, but there is also a look of defiance on her face. 'What hospital is she in?' he demands. The woman doesn't reply. He steps forward and raises an arm suggesting he is going to strike her.

'Westmead Hospital,' she says cowering, as though expecting a blow that doesn't come.

'See that wasn't so difficult was it? Now what is she in hospital for?'

'She's…. she's just had a baby. He was premature and is not doing so well.'

'Is she married?' The woman nods. 'And her married name is?' The woman remains silent. He sighs and moves towards her again. This time it is clear she is not going to answer. Deciding she has served her usefulness he pulls her across to the top of the stairs and pushes her without a second's hesitation. The woman somersaults down the flight landing awkwardly at its base. He thinks the woman was strangely silent during her fall, which is convenient for him. With no loud screams there will be no nosey neighbours coming to investigate. He follows her down to where she is lying unconscious, her head on the floor and her body partly draped over the bottom steps. He snaps her neck just to be sure. An unfortunate casualty, but he cannot afford to leave her alive.

In the entrance hallway he finds a small alphabetised telephone and address book on a small table where the telephone sits. With gloved hands he looks up 'C' but there is no Catelin listed. He has to go through the whole alphabet until he finds what he is looking for. There is a phone number and address listed for a Catelin and Marco Rossi in Northmead. There is also a work number. He is sure this is the one, but to make doubly sure he flips through the remainder of the address book. He writes their names, address and phone numbers awkwardly on a piece of paper he takes from his pocket, replaces the book on the telephone table and exits the way he entered the house.

Howard Brant and his daughter Rosie return home with the car laden with presents that Marco and Cate have received from friends and colleagues for Milo. They'd offered to bring them back to the Beecroft house until the couple move, as there is no room in their flat. Taking an armful of goods Howard Brant asks Rosie to open the door so that he can carry the parcels using both arms. He is following Rosie through the door when he hears her scream and watches as she runs towards the stairs and drops down to her mother who is lying at the foot of the stairs with her neck twisted at an awkward angle.

'Mum, oh god no, Mum?' Rosie shouts.

Howard drops the presents and runs over to his distraught daughter. 'Janet?' He bends down and reaches out to touch his wife. There is little warmth in her body and he can see by her glazed staring eyes that she has gone. He witnessed the same look in his mother's eyes when she died.

'Don't move her Rosie,' he croaks barely able to hold himself together. 'I'll have to phone the police and ambulance services.' Rosie remains with her mother, calling out and speaking to her as if she might suddenly awaken, while he makes the emergency calls and explains, through tears, what they have discovered.

An ambulance arrives within ten minutes of the call, followed shortly after by the police. The paramedics inform the police that there is nothing anyone can do for her. They believe she has been dead for some hours.

Janet Brant is pronounced dead by the doctor who is called to sign the death certificate. Time of death is considered to be approximately three hours prior to the doctor's attendance. The police photograph the body and do a thorough search of the house. All agree that her death was a tragic accident after learning that Mr. Brant and his daughter have been to visit his other daughter in hospital and that Mrs. Brant was home alone. It is believed that, following her shower, she tripped on the stairs and tumbled to her death. One of her slippers was found near the top of the stairs while the second slipper is still attached to her left foot. The police note that the back doors to the garden are unlocked and Rosie admits she probably left them like that after calling for their cat just before leaving for the hospital. The cat has still not returned.

Howard Brant and his daughter Rosie remain frozen on a couch while a female police officer plies them with hot drinks, which they barely touch. It is several hours before Janet's body is removed and the police finally depart, leaving them alone in the now silent house.

'What are we going to tell Cate?' Rosie suddenly wails, breaking their numb silence. 'This will be too much for her on top of what's happening with little Milo.'

'We'll have to tell her Rosie. She is expecting your mother to visit them tomorrow. We should go down to the hospital first thing in the morning. I won't be going into work. Thank goodness your exams are all finished.'

'How Dad? How did this happen? I can't believe it. Mum was alive and well when we left. I can't believe she's gone just like that.' Rosie collapses into heart-wrenching sobs.

'I know darling. It's seems unbelievable.' He moves closer to Rosie and draws her into his arms while silent tears slide down his face. His heart and mind struggle to come to terms with what has happened.

# 14

'Dead? *Dead!*' Cate repeats in numb horror. 'No, no that can't be right. She was here just yesterday. How? What happened?'

Howard Brant explains the tragic accident that took the life of his beloved wife and mother to the girls. 'I know she wasn't your real mother Cate, and that you've had your ups and downs over the years, but she loved you like you were her own daughter and only ever wanted the best for you.'

'I know Dad,' Cate sobs. 'I didn't always love her, especially when I was younger, but I grew to love her over the years. Oh Dad, how are you and Rosie coping. I thought you and Rosie looked miserable when you both arrived.'

They'd left Rosie with Milo and Marco while her father asked Cate to take a walk with him to the hospital chapel, where they might have some privacy.

'We're both a bit numb today to be honest Cate. I don't think it has truly sunk in yet. I keep thinking I must tell your mother something or other and then I remember I can't do that anymore. Rosie spent hours crying last night. I could still hear her long after I went to bed. I think she cried herself to sleep eventually. I couldn't sleep and kept thinking if only I'd insisted she came back to the hospital with us last night, she'd still be here.'

'It's not your fault Dad, don't ever think that. Mum

spent a few hours with us yesterday afternoon. She loved coming in on her own during the day. Why would she want to come back again in the evening? And if you'd been home would it have made any difference? From what you've told me she broke her neck in the fall.'

'Yes,' he sobs, 'I wouldn't have been able to save her. They told me she died quickly. Her neck snapped. But Cate I hate to think of her being there all alone when it happened.'

'Oh Dad.' Cate reaches out for her father and they hold each other while the tears flow. After a while her father says, 'Look we'd better get you back to Milo. You need to speak to your sister as well.'

Cate embraces Rosie and they cry in each other's arms.

'Now I understand just a little bit of what you felt like when you lost your mother all those years ago,' Rosie sobs. 'I've got such a hollow feeling inside me. Does it ever go away?'

'It eases with time and life takes over. But you never truly forget.'

'You should have seen her Cate, she looked like a little girl lying there with her neck all twisted strangely and her eyes staring.'

Cate freezes and pulls away from Rosie.

'I'm sorry Cate, it must have brought back memories of what happened with your own mother.'

'Janet was my mother too,' Cate says. 'Not my birth mother but she was the one who mainly brought me up.'

'I know and I'm so sorry Cate, I've upset you,' Rosie sobs.

'No, it's nothing you've done Rosie, I've just remembered something. With Milo's birth I'd completely forgotten about it.'

'What's wrong? What's happened?'

'Don't worry about it. It's just something I have to do. Let's go and see Dad and Marco.'

The sisters re-join the men who have been discussing the planned move to the Blue Mountains over the weekend. Either Rosie or her father have clearly told Marco about Janet.

'I've told your father that I can ask around for other people to help out. He's got enough on his plate at the moment,' Marco tells Cate.

'And I've told Marco it's fine. It will help me take my mind off things. What about you Rosie?' Howard Brant says turning to his younger daughter.

'No, I'd still like to help. Mum would want us to.'

'If you're both sure …..' Marco says. Cate can see he feels uncomfortable about the whole matter.

'Yes we're sure. What time do you want us at the flat?'

'Eight am okay?'

'We'll be there. Come on Rosie we need to go. I have things to organise.'

The funeral Cate thinks, but doesn't say. She hugs and kisses both her father and Rosie before they leave. When they have gone she asks Marco to remain with Milo while she goes and makes some phone calls. She doesn't say who she is planning to call and fortunately he doesn't ask. Cate thinks he probably believes she is going to phone people to tell them of Janet's death.

Cate pulls DI Paramo's card out of her handbag and dials the number. When she asks to speak to him the phone goes quiet. 'Hello, is anyone still there?' she asks confused by the silence. Perhaps they're putting me through to him she thinks. Eventually a woman's voice comes on the line.

*'Hello DC Hargreaves here, how can I help you?'*

'I wanted to speak to Detective Inspector Paramo. We met last week and I was supposed to see him again the next day, but I forgot as I was rushed into hospital and gave birth prematurely to my son. He wasn't due for another five weeks.'

*'Oh. Is everything okay with the little one?'*

'He's making good progress and the doctors are optimistic. Is DI Paramo there? Can I speak to him?'

*'Can I take your name?'*

'Yes, it's Cate Brant. Well it was Cate Brant. I'm now married, but I didn't mention my married name to Detective Paramo. It's actually Cate Rossi now.'

*'What were you discussing with Detective Paramo, Mrs. Rossi?'*

'It was about my mother's murderer. Look is he there? Only I can't talk for too long, I have to get back to my son.'

*'No, I'm afraid he's no longer with us.'*

'What do you mean "he's no longer with us"? He didn't say that he was going anywhere when I saw him.'

*'I mean he'd dead. Sadly he died last week.'*

'Died?' Cate repeats in shock. 'How did he die? Was it in the line of duty or something? Only he didn't seem ill.'

*'No it wasn't in the line of duty and he wasn't ill. I'm afraid I am unable to tell you anything further. I could help you with anything that he was working on though.'*

'I just wanted to explain to Detective Paramo why I hadn't been in touch. He was expecting me to come in to see him with something. He wasn't murdered was he?' Cate asks with a sudden foreboding.

*'No, look I really can't say any more Mrs. Rossi. If you would like to see me sometime to discuss the matter you raised with Detective Paramo, I'd be happy to see you.'*

'I'm a little preoccupied at present with my baby son,

and my stepmother has just died as well. We're also moving house this coming weekend, so things are just crazy at the moment, but yes I might want to come and see you sometime.'

*'Can I ask how your stepmother died?'*

'She had a fatal fall down the stairs at home and broke her neck, just last night,' Cate tells her in a shaky voice, struggling not to cry.

*'I'm very sorry to hear that. As I said, you're welcome to get in touch with me when you have the time.'*

'Yes, thank you.'

Cate breaks the connection and stands for a time staring at the phone. Very strange, she thinks. First Detective Paramo and now Mum. She wonders how Detective Paramo died. The woman had said he hadn't been killed in the line of duty. He wasn't ill and he wasn't murdered. That just left an accident or suicide. He didn't seem the suicidal type to me, Cate thinks, but do we ever really know what's going on in someone's mind? And two accidents with people she knows in a short space of time. Is that too much of a coincidence? No, no, they can't be connected surely. Cate's thoughts are disturbed by a voice close behind her.

'Are you finished there love, only I need to make a phone call?'

She turns to see a man jigging about. 'Sorry,' she says and moves off, heading back to the baby unit.

DC India Hargreaves sits deep in thought following her phone call with Mrs. Rossi. She knew as soon as the woman said her name who Cate Rossi was. She had searched through DI Paramo's desk drawers when they returned from his flat, looking for any indication that he was suicidal, which she didn't remotely believe him to be. And she was looking for the case file she'd seen on his desk yesterday. She had found it in his bottom left drawer hidden under empty notepads. Secreting it into the rucksack, that she brought to work each day, she'd taken it home for quiet reading.

It seems that Catelin Brant had been present at her mother's murder in Melbourne almost nineteen years ago. The child was only six at the time. From what India could make out from DI Paramo's notes, Cate Brant (who he'd listed as Catelin) came to see him when she turned eighteen, in December '92 with the sketches she had made, allegedly of her mother's killer. There were photocopies of the sketches in the file. Not very good copies. India wonders where the originals are. Recent notes in his file refer to the fact that the same woman came to see him last week, claiming to have seen the killer leaving the local bishop's house that day. Joe Paramo had not noted down Catelin Brant's married name though.

Cate Rossi was to complete a new sketch of the man and drop it in to Joe Paramo the next day. The conversation India has just had explains why that didn't happen. She wonders if DI Paramo spoke to anyone about the matter. DCI Pritchard perhaps? Perhaps that's why the DI was in such a bad mood the night he died. She'd seen Joe Paramo returning from the direction of the DCI's office not long before she approached him. Maybe the DCI told him he couldn't go around to the bishop's house again or make any enquiries on the matter. But Cate Rossi's supposed sighting of her mother's killer - surely that should have been followed up? From what she could make out from Joe Paramo's notes, he had been around to the bishop's house early in the morning on his last day at work and spoken to a cleaner. He had jotted down the name of a Sister Mary

Beth to speak to, who he has noted only works there in the afternoon. Joe clearly wanted to know the name of the bishop's visitor, a man whom Cate Rossi identified as her mother's alleged killer. Joe had written down *'Find a reason to return to the bishop's house,'* which he'd underlined. This must have been why he had asked her come up with that excuse - and it was for approaching the bishop or Sister Mary Beth.

India had told Cate Rossi that DI Paramo's death was not a murder. And that was the official version of course. But neither is she convinced that he committed suicide, despite his personal problems. And now Cate Rossi's stepmother dies in a tragic accident at home. Too much of a coincidence? Was it anything to do with this man Cate Rossi saw? She doesn't see how it could be as he wouldn't have any idea that he had been spotted. Not unless someone told him of course. And he somehow got hold of the file. Did DI Paramo have another copy of the file he took home? The file she is looking at is a photocopy. She's not sure what to do at this point, but decides she will remain quiet and keep her eyes and ears open. Wait and see who the new DI will be.

# 15

The man is disturbed by a nosey neighbour as he peers into the empty flat. He's too late. They have moved. He's been here several times already and the flat has always been in darkness. Now it appears to be empty. 'Are you looking for Cate and Marco?' the woman asks.

'Yes, I'm just visiting Sydney from Brisbane. Thought I'd take the opportunity to catch up with them. It's some time since I've seen them. Do you know where they've moved to?'

'Somewhere up in the Blue Mountains I believe. But they both work at that Architect's practice over in Church St, in Parramatta. You might catch Marco over there. Not Cate though, she'll be at the hospital with the baby.'

'Yes, how is the baby?'

'He's doing well apparently. They're taking him home soon.'

The man knows the name of the company she is referring to. He'd phoned the number he'd taken from the Brant's house and discovered it was an architect's practice and that both Mr. & Mrs. Rossi work there. He'd checked it out, but decided it was too public and he doesn't know what Rossi looks like. With hopes dashed at their home, he'll now have to visit Rossi's office sometime.

Marco and Cate had been hoping to take Milo home to the new house that morning, but there had been another scare with him in the early hours and Milo is now back on assisted breathing. While Cate and Marco wait to speak to the doctor, Cate finally mentions her sighting of her mother's murderer and that she re-visited the detective. Marco is furious with her.

'That's what brought on your premature labour isn't it?' he says accusingly. 'And you put our son's life in danger because of it, all because you *thought* you saw someone who looked like the man you used to sketch all the time.'

'We don't know if that brought on the early labour. The doctors haven't been able to give us a definitive answer on it. And it's not as if I went looking for him Marco. You're being unreasonable. How could I have known the man would be there, of all places, right on our back door? And it was the murderer by the way. Or his twin brother. I'd know him anywhere. And if he goes to see that priest regularly I could have bumped into him at any time as I was walking around the area.'

'You're right, I'm sorry,' he finally says. 'It's just that it has all been such a worry. Milo's life in danger. And Janet dying. As well as the move and getting the house ready. It's all been too much to deal with all at once.'

'Then there's the mysterious death of the detective as well,' Cate adds. This was something she hadn't told him as yet.

'What do you mean, the detective's death?'

'The one I was in communication with. The detective who handled my enquiry. I told you I went to see him.'

'Yes and …?

'Well he's dead now as well. They wouldn't tell me anything other than it wasn't in the line of duty and he wasn't sick.'

'He probably died in an accident or something. Like

Janet.'

'Maybe. A little too convenient for my liking. There is a woman detective who worked with DI Paramo who offered to see me, but I said I was too preoccupied with Milo.'

'And that's how you need to leave it Cate. You *are* too preoccupied with Milo. He has to come first. You are *not* to go anywhere near the police.'

Cate has never seen this side of Marco. Angry and aggressive. She doesn't like it at all. But maybe it's just his concern for her and Milo.

'I won't,' she promises him.

The doctor tells them that Milo will need to remain on assisted breathing for the time being. 'His lungs are just too weak to breathe on his own. He seemed to be doing very well the past few days, but clearly we were a little too optimistic.'

'When do you think he will be strong enough to try to take him off it again?' Cate asks, concerned.

'We'll test him again in another few days.'

Marco is scowling at Cate after the doctor leaves them. She is sure he is blaming her for Milo's condition.

'Look I'm going to have to return to work tomorrow Cate. I just can't bear being in here for another minute anyway. And work is piling up. I'll take some more time off when Milo is ready to be discharged. I'm going home tonight. I need a decent night's sleep.'

Cate finds Marco's attitude quite hostile and feels herself starting to react to him. She would like to ask him to stay a little longer so they talk things through further, but he leans over, kisses her on the cheek, says he'll call in after work tomorrow and abruptly leaves. After he's gone she feels relieved. Perhaps it is better that he didn't stay or they both might have said things they'd later regret.

# 16

**Manchester, UK, March 2000**

At twenty-five years old, Adhita Acharya is the youngest ever woman to be appointed a professor of Mathematics at a UK University. In fact she is the youngest appointed professor of either gender in any faculty. Lecturing throughout her PHD which she accomplished at 21, Adhita spent several years as a senior lecturer and research 'reader' for universities in London, before being appointed to her recent position at the Victoria University of Manchester.

Adhita has a small apartment situated on her campus so that she can work late into the night when the urge takes her with an easy return home in safety. She also regularly works at home. Her bijou home provides a convenient excuse to prevent the family visiting too frequently. She is however looking forward to Cate's visit, even though she will have to give up her lovely bed to Cate for the duration of her visit. Adhita's couch is an old friend though, she has spent many a comfortable night's sleep on it.

Cate was her only close friend growing up and she has greatly missed her since her return to Australia. Adhita has a few male friends, one in particular, but it's not the same as having a giggle with a female friend. She had planned to travel to Australia after completing her PHD, but she didn't want to leave Naniji and by then Cate was involved with the man she eventually married and Adhita thought she would only be in the way if she went out to Australia. Now sadly, it would seem, a family tragedy is bringing Cate back to England.

Adhita had received an urgent request a few weeks back from Cate to come to Manchester to see her saying that she needed to leave Sydney without fully explaining the details. Her email said "I've just gone through every parent's nightmare – but I can't face writing or talking about any of it just now."

After Adhita had emailed Cate in November with news of her new appointment that was due to start in January and asked Cate if she'd given birth yet, she'd eventually received a friendly email back congratulating her about the job and telling her that they had only just brought their son Milo home as he had been so ill after being born prematurely. Cate also told her the news of Janet's death, the move to their new house and how she was feeling so zonked out from lack of sleep. Apart from a Christmas card Adhita had heard nothing further, despite having sent Cate three further emails - until her recent request and then a follow up email with details of her flight. With Cate travelling alone (as she had said 'I' not 'we') and from what she'd said in her email about coming to Manchester, the odds are that the baby died, and Cate and Marco had split up, but she can't bear thinking about that and has made a decision not to push Cate for information. It will be up to Cate if she wants to discuss the matter. She just wants to make sure Cate's visit is as stress free as possible.

Cate's flight was due to land at 3.30pm, and it's now 4.20pm. Adhita'd had to re-arrange her afternoon tutorials with her PHD students in order to meet her. With no vehicle of her own she has borrowed a colleague's car to collect Cate. When Adhita finally arrives at the airport she is unable to drive right up to the arrivals exit so she is forced to park the car and walk across to the terminal. Will she recognise Cate after so long? Outside the entrance doors she spots a hunched over person who looks vaguely familiar, taking desperate drags on a cigarette. *Smoking? No surely that can't be right?* Adhita approaches the woman cautiously, convinced it can't be Cate. The woman looks up, recognition dawning and a smile that doesn't quite reach her eyes spreads across her face.

'Adhita!' she calls and quickly stubs her cigarette out in the ashtray the smokers are huddled around. The woman grabs her suitcase and hand luggage and drags herself across the pavement, dropping her bags again to give Adhita a hug. She can smell the remnants of the cigarette on Cate.

'Since when have you been a smoker?' Adhita demands.

'Oh, it's a temporary thing,' Cate replies waving her arms dismissively. 'I just started a few weeks ago, to the horror of my family. You're not going to start lecturing me about it as well are you? I just needed one after that horrendous journey.'

'Well, I might if you keep it up, but let's get your things to the car. I had to borrow one as I don't own one myself and I promised I'd have it returned by 6pm.'

Adhita notices Cate limping and that she is clearly in pain.

'Have you had some kind of accident? I can't help noticing that you are limping.'

'I had a bad fall. Almost lost my leg. But it's a lot better now.'

'Oh, how did that happen?'

'If you don't mind Adhita, I'd rather not talk about it at the moment. I can't face talking about anything that happened back home right now.'

'Sure. Of course. So it was a difficult journey then? You look exhausted.' Adhita asks, to change the subject.

'Well I couldn't afford business class so I was squashed into economy. There's never enough room and although I took a tablet, I only slept briefly. I had a rather large man beside me all the way from Singapore who hogged part of my seat as well as his own. I asked whether I could be moved, but the flight was full. It was bloody uncomfortable.'

'I can imagine. How long are you over in the UK for? Are you just intending it to be a short visit or staying here for some time? If you are staying where are you planning to settle?'

'I've obtained British Citizenship through my mother, and travelled on a British passport so I can stay as long as I want. Although I still have my Australian passport as well. I don't know how long I'll be here. I just intend to take one day at a time. I will probably go up to Yorkshire for a while, where my mother was born. We visited it briefly before we went back to Australia if you remember, but I'd like to spend more time there.'

'You'll need a car for that.'

'I plan to buy one. A second hand one anyway. I'll have to buy an automatic unfortunately - with my leg. I don't like automatics, but I can't manage manual gears at the moment. Do you know anyone that might be able to help me with that?'

'Oh I'm sure some of the men in the department would be only too willing to lend a hand. You can pick up a pretty decent banger for about £500 upwards. I've been thinking about buying one myself.'

'£500! Jees that's so cheap. It would cost thousands in

Australia to buy a second hand car that is anywhere near decent.'

'It's only cars like BMWs that hold their value here in the second hand market. Most others vehicles depreciate quickly. About 25% a year on average apparently.'

'You seem to know a lot about it?'

'Not really, I've just heard people discussing it at different times. Men usually and you know me, I always retain figures in my head and can quote them at random.'

They both laugh at that. Some things never change.

'So what's Manchester like?' Cate asks on their journey back into the city.

'I don't really see much of it. I'm so engrossed in my work. But from what I have seen, it's a thriving city, full of young people. It seems to be the 'in' place to live at the moment. Manchester of course used to be the heartland of the textile manufacturing industry, throughout the Industrial Revolution, so there are old warehouses, mills and factories everywhere. Some of them, that have stood empty for decades after the decline in the manufacturing industry, have been converted into trendy loft style apartments. Others have been demolished to make way for new apartment buildings. There's new buildings going up everywhere. Huge towering blocks. You'd probably pick up plenty of work in Manchester if you wanted it with all the building going on. The next Commonwealth games are being held here in 2002 and there's plenty of building development focused around that as well.'

'The Olympics are being held in Sydney this year. Thank goodness I've escaped the madness and chaos that it's going to bring to the city. I don't want to be tied down to a particular job at the moment anyway. I'd like to do something different for a while and then, when I'm a bit more sorted, I might look at a more long term position.'

Adhita glances at Cate and suspects by 'sorted' she means when she is able to face life without her husband and child. She wonders where Marco is now. And presumably complications arose from baby Milo's premature birth and he must have died or Cate surely wouldn't be travelling alone. Having never had children or a husband, Adhita can't imagine what Cate must be going through. She can see Cate's body slumped sombrely into her seat. She needs to distract her. 'Did you know that Manchester had the first passenger steam railway that ran between Manchester and Liverpool?' she says chirpily.

'If it ran between Manchester and Liverpool, then both cities had it first,' Cate replies. 'Not just Manchester. And if I remember correctly from my history lessons, the first train set out from Liverpool and on its journey claimed the first rail accident victim. So you could say Liverpool had it first.'

'Yes, you're right. Liverpool was the port all the textiles were sent to for export. They were manufactured here in Manchester.'

'Did *you* know that we call sheets, towels and other household items 'Manchester' in Australia? People usually say the 'Manchester' department or shop, rather than linen department. It must have been called that after this city.'

'But you Australians are all a little bit mad. What strange terminology to apply to sheets or towels. Naming them after a city rather than saying linen.'

'Well if you are going to get pedantic, linen is actually a cloth woven from the stalks of the flax plant. The linen cloth used to be used for making sheets, as well as clothes, but nowadays as you know sheets are mainly made of cotton. Likewise towels. So calling sheets and towels 'linen' is also strange really. It's just a blanket terminology that someone in the trade probably applied to the goods and it became common use, long after they stopped using the linen cloth. Companies shipped textile products to Australia from Manchester and originally the workers at the docks probably said, "The Manchester textiles have arrived" – or "the goods from Manchester have arrived". Knowing how we humans become lazy with words, especially when you work in the same environment for years, I imagine over time it was probably reduced to "the Manchester's docked" and the term stuck. I've never called sheets or towels Manchester because my mother never did, but Janet, my stepmother, always called it that. I think it's a generational thing as well – or it depends where you come from. But more modern houses in Australia are built with a 'linen' cupboard in hallways, they are never referred to as a 'Manchester' cupboard. Weird.'

Adhita smiles. The distraction has worked. Glancing at Cate she can see she is now sitting straighter and is more alert. 'Language is weird,' she says. 'It's also fascinating – but not as fascinating as numbers.'

'Not to you anyway.'

'No, and here we are,' Adhita announces as they pull into a carpark sandwiched between a range of large buildings. 'This is home.'

'What floor do you live on?'

'I'm on the second floor. I'm afraid there is no lift. We'll have to lug your bags up the stairs. Will you be okay with that? How's your leg? Can you manage stairs?'

'Yes, I just need to take it slowly. The doctors in Australia say I will always probably limp a little. It's considerably better than it was. I'm lucky to still have it, they did consider amputating below the knee.'

Adhita shudders at the thought of Cate of losing part of her leg. She can't imagine how that would have affected Cate on top of everything else she must have gone through. She wonders if Cate's 'fall' was a failed suicide attempt. Not that she can imagine Cate doing anything like that, but losing a child might make a person suicidal. 'Okay, let's get your bags over to the entrance for starters. You can wait for me there. I just have to drop the car keys back to my colleague.'

They unload Cate's bags and wheel them over to the entrance. There is a fine mist of rain and it's very cold, but once they enter through the doors Cate can feel the warmth radiating off the heating system in the entrance of the building. Within minutes she needs to remove her coat, but as she is shrugging it off she decides she needs to keep it on as otherwise it will just be another thing to haul up the flights of stairs.

Adhita returns quickly and takes Cate's large suitcase. 'You take the small one,' she insists when Cate attempts to take it off her.

'Okay, but I am not a complete invalid – just so you know.'

'I didn't think you were. I just thought as you are very tired and I'm not, it would be easier for me to carry the large case.'

'Fair enough. Thanks.'

Cate looks around as they enter the flat. There is one largish room that serves as a living room and dining room. The dining table is covered with books and stacks of paper and there is a laptop computer surrounded by more papers. She can see a very small kitchenette off the dining area.

'You don't cook here much I gather, with such a small kitchen?' Cate has also noticed the absence of the lingering smell of food.

'No, I can have all my meals in the halls if I want. Most days I have one meal there and maybe just prepare an evening snack and some breakfast for myself here. When I become fed up with Western food, I cook a meal here.'

'Where should I put my bags?'

'In the bedroom, it's through here,' Adhita says walking towards a door. Cate follows her and sees that there is a small bathroom and one bedroom with a double bed.

'You're sleeping here. I'm on the couch,' Adhita informs her.

'No, no, it should be the other way around. You are working. I'll take the couch.'

'No, I'm quite comfortable on the couch thank you. I always sleep there on the rare occasions my family turn up to stay. That way I can work at my table if I want without disturbing anyone – or them disturbing me. I just have to ensure I have enough clothing items I need for the next day and I'll be fine.'

'Are you sure? It doesn't seem right that you are giving up your bed.'

'I'm absolutely sure. This way works better for me. Just one thing – no smoking allowed in the bedroom.'

'I wouldn't anyway. I won't smoke anywhere in the flat.'

'Oh, you can smoke in the lounge if you want. Some of my colleagues smoke and I let them have the odd one here if they pop in. I don't particularly like it, but I always open the windows if they do and leave them open overnight. By the next day you can't smell it anyway.'

'But you will be sleeping in there. If I want a cigarette I

will go outside.'

'Okay. Would you like a shower or bath? I have either option here, although it's only a shower over the bath. And I thought we could go out for dinner this evening – that is if you are not too exhausted. What do you think and what do you fancy?'

'I'd love a shower to freshen up. I feel filthy after that flight. And I'm quite hungry. I ate very little on the plane. You know I wouldn't mind an Indian meal tonight. I haven't had a decent one for a long time. There isn't a huge selection available in Sydney. Where we lived in the mountains there were none. If I wanted some Indian food I had to cook it myself.'

'So you still cook some of Naniji's recipes?'

'Yes of course. Even Marco liked the food I cooked and he'd never eaten Indian food before I made it for him. Although I had make him meat dishes as well. Did I tell you he came from an Italian family?'

'Yes, you did.' Adhita notices Cate talks about Marco without any bitterness. Perhaps they parted on friendly terms. 'But with regard to Indian restaurants,' she continues. 'There's not any real Indian restaurants here in Manchester. Not that I've discovered anyway, as I don't go out that much. There's plenty of what are *called* Indian restaurants, but if you remember most of them are actually Pakistani restaurants. The Tandoori houses. There's a good one about a ten minute walk from here. I've eaten there with colleagues and the food's quite tasty. They have plenty of vegetarian food there as well.'

'I forgot you're a vegetarian. Presumably if you eat on campus most days they must cater for vegetarians. What are the meals like? If it's anything like my university in Sydney, the vegetarian meals were rubbish – the majority of Australians being great meat consumers.'

'They're nothing to write home about, but passable. There's quite a few vegetarians on the staff and plenty amongst the students. There'd be loud complaints if the standard was really poor. I'd generally give them six out of ten for their efforts.

'How would you rate the Tandoori House?'

'Probably an eight out of ten.'

'Good enough for me.'


Feeling refreshed after her shower Cate is looking forward to the meal. To say she ate very little on the journey was a bit of an understatement. All she'd had was a mouthful of a greasy pasta and a small square of cheese that came with two tiny crackers after their departure from Sydney. The rest of the meal was inedible. She'd had a croissant for breakfast. And several cups of tea. Apparently during her brief sleep she had missed the evening meal after Singapore. Cate had woken just as the stewardess was removing a food tray that was in front of her. She could see that the food had been eaten and she certainly hadn't had the pleasure (or displeasure as she didn't know what the meal had been) of doing so. When she looked at the man beside her, he also had a tray of empty containers in front of him and she was convinced he'd helped himself to her food. She was tempted to complain, but in the end couldn't be bothered. The man was overweight, and clearly needed the additional food as the servings were so meagre.

'We can catch a taxi back to save your leg,' Adhita says breaking the silence of their walk to the restaurant.

'Might be best, I'm not used to walking any great distance on it. The physio and doctor said I need to exercise my leg regularly, building up gradually, not attempting to do too much at once. So far, I have only walked around the corridors of the rehab unit or around my father's house, and of course airport terminals.' What Cate doesn't mention was that she had not been allowed to walk around the grounds of the rehab unit, although she did sneak outside briefly a few times with one of the men on duty there – which is when she had started having the odd cigarette. Limited to exercising through the corridors was in itself challenging. Both at the hospital and the rehab unit she became 'That Woman'; whispers of 'that's the woman who …' following her around each time she emerged from her room. Cate would feel the eyes of other patients and staff boring into her as she moved around. She was seldom greeted with friendliness by the strangers she was amongst, and they kept their distance from her as though they were afraid she might be contagious. Occasionally she'd hear 'poor thing, did you know …..'. And if Cate turned to look at them they would cast their eyes downwards or turn away.

'Do you still experience pain with your leg?' Adhita asks her.

'Yes, every day. They had me on a cocktail of drugs. I still have a heap of them with me. I avoid taking them as much as possible, but sometimes I need to take something or I can't sleep.'

'Did you manage getting in and out of the shower alright? I never thought of that – you having to climb into the bath.'

'I managed. I had to do little manoeuvres, sitting on the bath first, balancing using my hands while swinging my legs over, then taking the weight mainly on my right foot before standing up. It was the same when I got out.'

'It would be much easier for you to manage if you had

a walk-in shower. Especially with that bath, it must be 600 millimetres off the floor. I've never seen a bath that high before.'

'Yes, it was easier in Australia. Most places there have walk-in showers. Let's just hope wherever I end up I'll be lucky enough to have one.'

'Here we are,' Adhita announces stopping outside a small restaurant entrance.

When they have ordered and are nibbling on a poppadum, Cate asks Adhita how she is settling into her new job as a Professor.

'I love it, although there are the usual wearisome prejudicial issues to deal with. Most of the men in my department resent me. I believe they think I am too young, added to the fact that I am a woman. And an ethnic minority woman – that is how they view me. There's never been a woman Chair of Mathematics at the university. Apart from a young PHD female student who is an associate lecturer in the department, the remainder are men. A small fraction of them, say 15% are welcoming, the other 85% are resentful much of the time. But you know, I just ignore that, cut through all the divisions and get on with things. Because I don't react to them, they forget their resentments and actually will work harmoniously with me for an hour or two, before it rears its ugly head again in some way.'

Cate smiles at Adhita's regular use of mathematical language. She seems to unknowingly insert it into many of her conversations.

'There is talk though of amalgamating with the other University here, the University of Manchester Institute of Science and Technology,' she continues. 'I just hope that doesn't happen any time soon. The men in my department would just love that in some ways, because I'd be certain to lose my job if that happened. I'd like at least a few years to complete some research. I am working closely with the professor and some of his staff from UMIST – that's the shortened name we give the other university.'

'So no time for any love in your life then?'

'I don't know about love, but I'm certainly involved in an intimate relationship.'

'Oh, that's great. Who is he then?'

'The professor at UMIST. It just happened one night after a long evening of working together at my place and has become a regular thing.'

'By the way you say 'thing' so dismissively, I'm assuming it's not serious then?'

'Neither of us have the time. Our work is more important, but we all need some relief or diversion from work as well, don't we?'

'How old is he?'

'He's in his early 40s. Quite young to be a Professor as well.'

'Do your family know?'

'Not at all. My parents would have a fit! For years they have been organising gatherings with other Anglo-Indian Hindu families who just happen to have an eligible single man of marriageable age for me to meet. But I'm just not interested.'

Cate refrains from asking Adhita if she ever aims to have children. Her wounds are too raw to bring up that subject. They are prevented from further discussions on this topic with the timely interruption of the waiter bringing their meals.

'Oh this smells delicious,' Cate says, her mouth salivating. Apart from one small starter of Chicken Tikka that Cate ordered to come with the rest of the dishes, they have chosen a range of vegetarian options. The waiter plods back and forth to the kitchen bringing their numerous dishes until every surface of the table is covered with them.

'What we can't manage can go into a doggy bag to take home,' Adhita whispers.

Back at Adhita's flat later they sip tea, reclining on the sofa, fully sated. 'I enjoyed that so much, thanks for taking me there Adhita. I do like my spicy food. I've missed it so much - having to endure plain hospital food for months on end.' Adhita smiles and remains silent. 'Thanks for not asking as well,' Cate adds.

'I know you'll talk about it when you're ready.'

'To be quite honest Adhita, it's a relief not to have people plying me with questions like "How are you today?" or "How are you *feeling*?" It made me want to scream. I'm just glad to be away from it all. I'm not ready to talk about anything at the moment.'

'I can see that.'

'Have you mentioned anything about me to anyone here at the University?'

'Gosh no. It's none of their business. I did mention what little I knew to my family though, in case you met up with any of them or spoke to them on the phone and they put their foot in it by asking awkward questions.'

'That's okay. Look, do you mind if I head off to bed now. I'm absolutely shattered.'

'No, not at all. Let me just collect a few things and the bedroom's all yours.'

Cate opens the heavy curtains covering the windows just enough so that she can see daylight when she wakes. She also opens the window a little as is her habit when sleeping. It is so nice to be able to sleep in a room without the sealed windows and air-conditioning that she experienced at the hospital and rehab unit.

When she first wakes, needing the bathroom urgently, it is still dark. There is a bedside clock, but she doesn't bother to glance at it. The pain in her leg wakes her again and it's still dark. She takes two tablets and a sip of water from the glass she has brought to bed with her. This time she glances at the illuminated electric alarm clock. It is 3.19am. The tablets knock her out and she has vague recollections of stumbling to the bathroom again a couple of times. When she wakes again it is *still* dark and, glancing at the clock which reads 4.05am, she is confused. Surely she had been asleep longer than that? She's sure she's been to the bathroom a few times since going to bed. This is like that film 'Ground Hog Day' she thinks, except that every time she wakes it is still dark with barely any time seeming to pass. Perhaps her journeys to the bathroom were just dreams. Shrugging with indifference, she settles down and soon drifts off again. When she next wakes she can finally see daylight through the gap in the curtains. Glancing at the clock she can see it is 7.08am. She stretches her stiff limbs. The bed is very comfortable. She feels completely refreshed and fully recovered from her lack of sleep on the plane.

Not sure if Adhita will be awake, she limps out quietly to the bathroom for a wash.

'So you've finally emerged then?' Adhita says startling her. 'Thought you were never going to wake up.'

'It's not even 7.15 yet. I'm not that late am I? What time do you normally get up?' Cate asks following Adhita into the living room.

'You went to bed on Thursday night. It's now Saturday

morning.'

'What? You've got to be kidding me!'

'No, I kid you not. You have been in bed for 32 hours and 39 minutes. That's some sleep you had.'

'No wonder it was constantly dark each time I woke up. I had to get up for the bathroom a few times – I think. Definitely once and I vaguely recall another few times. I took some tablets at one point. They must have really knocked me out.'

'I checked on you a couple of times, just to make sure you were okay, but you seemed to be sleeping blissfully, so I didn't disturb you.'

'I'm really sorry. I had no idea.'

'No need to be sorry. You clearly needed the sleep.'

'You say it's Saturday. Are you working today?'

'No I've organised to have the weekend off. I usually meet up with colleagues from UMIST at the weekends, but I've pulled out of that with you here. We could go and look at some cars if you like. I've provisionally lined up one of the guys in my department. One of the nicer lecturers. He said he'd be willing to help you today. I've to phone him if we want to do that.'

'You surely don't want to be spending your day off traipsing around looking at cars? I could go with the guy on my own, if you'd rather do something else. It'll be fine. It's just if I want to buy anything I'll have to get hold of some money. I don't have enough cash and would banks be open on a Saturday? I have traveller's cheques with me.'

'I can get you some cash. I have a daily limit of £300, plus I have some on me. There are exchange places in the city that would cash your traveller's cheques as long as you have your passport with you. Also the building Societies are open on Saturday mornings. One of them might cash your cheques. Tim said he'd mark out some automatics in the lower price range for you. I'll give him a ring once we've had breakfast. He might still be in bed now, being a Saturday.'

'Do you mind if I have a wash and dress quickly before we eat breakfast?'

'No, I'll prepare everything while you do that.'

When Cate returns to the living room Adhita has steaming cups of coffee and a plate of warmed croissants waiting for her. 'I've phoned Tim. He's coming around about 10. That'll give us time to catch a cab into town, grab some money and be back to meet him.'

'Okay great. Thanks.'

'If you feel comfortable with him I might stay behind while you look at cars if you don't mind. There are a pile of assignments I could mark. If you buy a car today, you will need my visitor's sticker to put in the window when you come back with it. Otherwise they will clamp you. We mustn't forget that.'

'Right. I'll have to follow Tim back if I buy a car or I'll get completely lost.'

'I'm sure he'll suggest that. Don't worry. It'll be fine.

Adhita insists that she is welcome to stay on with her indefinitely, but Cate know she will just be disrupting Adhita's work routines and love life. Cate thinks the ten days she's spent with Adhita is more than enough, but promises to return to Manchester later in the year.

Cate hopes by then she will have stopped seeing Marco everywhere in the streets of Manchester (or anywhere else). Each time she ventured out to explore the city, she'd caught glimpses of Marco walking either ahead of her, or behind her in the crowded streets. Her rational mind knew it couldn't be him, but she found herself hobbling hurriedly after him, or turning back towards him only for him to suddenly vanish. When she caught up with 'Marco' a few times, she realised the solid tangible man she'd approached actually looked very little like Marco. It was only the height, build and hair colouring that bore any resemblance. She'd had constant internal dialogues in her head after such sightings. Arguing with herself about whether she had actually seen Marco – or not.

Cate's mind veered from *'No. I'm not really seeing him'*, to *'but I am seeing him!'* The only rational explanation she could come with is that in a heavily populated city there are bound to be many people who look alike. The possibility that she might be losing her mind is quite frightening and so she pushes these thoughts from her head and decides it's time to move on - and that she most definitely won't share her sightings of Marco with anyone (just in case she is losing it).

# 17

**Parramatta, November 1999**

The new Detective Inspector had transferred from the Blacktown Station in a sideways move. DC India Hargreaves thinks he is a surly sod. A man of few words, he speaks in an abrupt and uncultured manner, and seems to be displaying all the hallmarks of a chauvinistic attitude towards females. She does not feel inclined to approach him with her thoughts about DI Paramo. DI Paramo, despite his latter self-abuse with alcohol, had been an excellent detective and a pleasure to work for. He always had an agreeable manner, even when he was issuing firm instructions to those below his rank. You could never take offence with his approach as, even when he was being serious he afforded respect to all colleagues. DC Hargreaves has witnessed her colleagues reacting with anger towards this new DI – not that he seems to notice. She herself has bristled several times at his poor communication skills. How good he will be remains to be seen.

Carrying the cup of coffee he has demanded she make for him, she knocks and enters the DI's office. He is busy scribbling notes and acknowledges receiving the coffee with a grunt. It's as she is looking down at him she realises what it was that seemed wrong about the death scene at DI Paramos's flat. She turns abruptly and heads towards DCI Pritchard's office. She knocks and, not waiting for an answer, enters his office. He is talking on the phone and indicates that she should take a seat. When he ends the call he looks up at her saying, 'What can I do for you DC Hargreaves? You seem to be all excited about something. What is it?'

'When we found DI Paramo I sensed something was wrong with the scene sir. As you might imagine I was a little distressed to find the DI like that, a man I have served under for the past two years, and I couldn't pinpoint what the problem was at the time. I've just taken a coffee into the new DI and was watching him writing with his right hand. I realised then what it was that had bothered me. I was used to seeing DI Paramo writing with his *left* hand at the same desk. DI Paramo's head wound was on the right side of his head, meaning he would have, supposedly, used his right hand to shoot himself - if that's what happened. DI Paramo was left handed sir.'

'No, he was ambidextrous. He could use both his right and left hand. We cleared that up at the post-mortem.'

'I know he was ambidextrous sir, but not for everything he did. He mainly wrote with his left hand and, whenever he used his service gun, I only ever saw him use his left hand for aiming and firing. I went with him to the practise range several times and I have seen him draw his weapon on cases we've been involved in. He never used his right hand - he only ever used his right hand to support his left hand. I don't think he shot himself sir. He wouldn't have used his right hand if he was going to shoot himself. I think the scene was staged.'

DCI Pritchard is silent for a moment before answering, 'Powder residue was found on Paramo's right hand. And only his fingerprints. The man clearly took his own life.

He was a very troubled person over the past few months.' And was facing possible disciplinary charges Pritchard thinks. But he wasn't going to tell young DC Hargreaves that. His guilt at the final words he had uttered to Paramo have been keeping him awake at night since the discovery of his body.

'But sir, don't you think we …..'

'That's enough DC Hargreaves. Now if you don't mind, I have several reports to write.'

'Yes sir.'

After Hargreaves leaves his office DCI Pritchard sits thinking for a few moments. Might there be something in what she has said? Should he be looking into it again? Surely it was an open and shut case of suicide? Certainly DI Paramo must have made quite a large number of enemies over the years with his successful convictions. That could make a long list of potential suspects to look into which would take weeks of further investigation. And use up a substantial portion of his budget only to reach the same conclusion. No, he decides finally. The man took his own life. And that's an end to it.

DC Hargreaves is very disappointed with DCI Pritchard's attitude and believes he could at least look more closely at the evidence. He had worked with Joe Paramo for many years. Didn't he owe it to him to complete a more thorough investigation? It was fairly easy to stage a suicide, but there was always something that could be detected or queried if it was not a suicide and if one looked closely enough. Like the unlikelihood of him using his right hand to shoot himself. That surely is enough to instigate a fuller investigation? The DCI has made it clear that he is not going to do this though. Probably worried about his precious budget he's always going on about, India thinks. She had been tempted to mention the case Joe Paramo had been working on, but she suspects the DCI knows all about it. That must have been the reason Joe said he wouldn't involve her because, for some reason, the DCI had wanted to quash it. Why on earth would that be? Surely not just because the man whose identity Joe wanted to discover had contact with the bishop?

Maybe it's time to move on and request a transfer. She's not sure how long she can bear working under this new DI. In the three days he has been here he hasn't given her one task appropriate to her rank. Just things like photocopying reports and then acting as a delivery service around the building. When she pointed out that the admin staff did these tasks he just gave her one of his looks, remained silent, and held the files out for her to take. He has also asked her to make the odd telephone call that, once again, the admin people could deal with and today she's on coffee duty. Coffee duty! It's a joke. She never minded making a coffee for Joe Paramo. She would just routinely make one for him when she made one for herself. He would reciprocate the favour for her as well. She can't imagine this one ever making her a coffee.

India's considering starting her own little investigation. Following up on Joe Paramo's case. That would keep her mind busy. She'd have to do it unofficially though, as she is not prepared to share any of the information with the new DI or talk to the DCI. Not until she knows more.

She's also reviewing her options. She's no longer sure whether she chose the right career after University. She knows that a number of the men she works with resent her. Most of them began as probationers at eighteen and worked their way up through the ranks. She had also served time as a probationary constable, but with her degree, added to the fact that she is a woman, and the force was dramatically short of women in detective ranks, she'd moved rapidly into her present position. The only female detective in the station. There are a few female constables in uniform and the usual female administrative staff, but no other female detectives. If she leaves the force some of her male colleagues would only brag that they were right, that being a detective isn't suitable for women. Her family would be pleased if she left but would undoubtedly add 'told you so' type comments. They had not wanted her to join the police force, earmarking more salubrious careers with greater financial benefits while she was still completing her HSC. Perhaps she should be seeking promotion instead.

India places a call to the Diocese's office asking for Bishop Byrne. She's told that he has gone home for lunch but will be returning shortly after 2pm. She thanks the woman on the other end of the phone and decides she will take a late lunch today as long as no urgent business is thrown at her. Not that this is likely to happen. The new DI still has her on light duties. She asked him why she was relegated to these yesterday and he had the cheek to say he believed he was giving her duties commensurate with her rank. A likely story, seeing that DC Khan is the same rank as her and had been tasked with duties they normally would share. When she had pointed this out to the DI he'd acted surprised. Bloody male chauvinist! She's even noticed that the men in the squad look surprised when she is left behind on call outs. And they don't look happy about it. Perhaps they are starting to respect her more.

She has put in a request for her Sergeant's exam and

just hopes that she can transfer out of here as soon as she passes it. There is no point in whingeing to the DCI. That isn't the way things are done. She will just have to find an opportunity to deal with it appropriately herself.

At five minutes before 2pm she is parked down the road from the bishop's residence. A few minutes later she watches him leave and after waiting a further five minutes until he is out of sight, she emerges from her vehicle and heads towards the doors with her notepad.

A woman she believes is the nun, Mary Beth, answers the door to her knock. 'Hello, I wonder if Bishop Byrne is in please? I called the Diocese office and they said he'd returned home for lunch.'

'I'm afraid you've just missed him. Is there anything I can help you with?'

'Perhaps. You wouldn't be Sister Mary Beth would you?'

'Yes, I am. How did you know?'

'My name is DC Ruth Kelly,' she says using the name of one of their uniformed staff at the station and flashing her badge quickly at the nun. 'I'm just following up on a matter that my DI accidentally became involved with a few weeks ago. I'm afraid he died suddenly the day after a member of the public approached him and the paperwork has been sitting on his desk since then. I found your name in the notes he had written. Apparently he called around here on the same morning that he died and was given your name by the cleaner, to contact later.'

'Oh how terrible. He died you say?'

'Yes, rather unexpectedly. The matter he was following up,' she began hurriedly moving on to the main point, 'was that a member of the public was passing here the day before – it would have been late in the afternoon of October 13th and saw a visitor of the bishop's leaving. As he was getting into his car he dropped a rather expensive small silver case, like an antique cigarette case, only it didn't have any cigarettes in it. It was empty. Anyway the woman who saw this was too far away from the man for him to hear her calling out to him and by the time she had reached the place where his car had been, the man had driven off and the bishop had closed the door. She found the case lying in the gutter and picked it up.'

'Why didn't she knock on the bishop's door and give it to him?'

'Well apparently she was in the late stages of pregnancy and her waters had just broken. As it was her first child all she could think about was getting to the hospital quickly. It was her husband who bumped into DI Paramo later at the police station, just as DI Paramo was leaving for the day. The husband explained the situation about his wife finding the case, and her going into labour and he passed the item on to the DI. DI Paramo returned to the office, mentioned it to me and was going to pass it on to me to deal with, but decided he would deal with it himself, which is why he came around here the next morning.'

'Goodness me. So much going on. I don't know how you keep track of it all. How can I help you then?'

'We need to know the name of the bishop's visitor, and ideally, a contact number so that we can let him know we have the item. He might have bought it as a gift for someone and is wondering where it is. I wonder if you would have the name of this man. Do you know who it was or does the bishop keep a diary where his name might be entered?'

'I don't know who the man is, but if you would like to

come in for a moment I can check Bishop Byrne's diary.'

DC Hargreaves follows the sister into a smart office situated a few rooms down the hall. So far, everything was going to plan. 'It would have been October 13th,' she reminds the nun as she watches her leaf back through the pages of the diary.

'Oh I remember him. I didn't actually see him – well not properly anyway. I prepared some tea for them and took it into the lounge, but the man was looking out of the window with his back to me, so I didn't see him properly and didn't speak to him. Very smartly dressed he was. The bishop had answered the door himself that afternoon. But I remember the bishop's little joke about him later. Bishop Byrne had written the initials JB here in his diary. After the man had gone the bishop made a reference to his visitor being a Jim Beam man – that is an alcoholic beverage I understand, while he, the bishop, was a J & B man, referring to the whisky brand he likes a glass of in the evening. Now whether the man's nickname is Jim Beam or that's his real name I don't know. Of course the bishop's initials are JB standing for Jonathon Byrne. He joked about being a J & B man which match his initials. So it stands to reason that this other man has the same initials as the bishop has written them in the diary.'

'So you think his name is possibly Jim Beam?'

'I couldn't really say. I only know what I've just told you. Oh and one other thing. The bishop said he hadn't seen JB – that's how he referred to him, for about 15 years, before meeting him that day, but that he'd known him since they were young.'

DC Hargreaves realises no further information will be forthcoming. It is clear that the nun doesn't know his real name. She will have to speak to the bishop herself –

something she doesn't want to do - or she could use Sister Mary Beth as an intermediary. 'Well thank you very much for your help. I wonder if you could ask the bishop for the man's full name and contact details. And explain the situation to him. I could contact you tomorrow to follow it up. It's just a silly little thing that I would like to resolve as soon as possible. But it is a rather valuable item. I'm sure the owner would want it returned to him.'

'Well I'll do my best. Bishop Byrne is a very busy man. I don't always see him if he has functions to attend. He has tomorrow crossed out in his diary so that usually means he won't be here.'

'Okay, well I will call in a few days then. Could I take your number here please?' Sister Mary Beth writes the number down and passes it to her. 'Thanks again for your help.'

DC Hargreaves believes Joe Paramo would applaud her Oscar winning performance this afternoon. She thought her idea of the empty silver antique cigarette case was rather brilliant. Something small and valuable that someone might want returned. If they weren't a smoker, it might be a gift for someone else as she'd mentioned. It was the idea she had come up with for him and, had he lived, would have probably made use of it himself. Well at least she has some initials and his name is possibly Jim. It's a start.

When India manages to reach Sister Mary Beth a few days later, she is unable to proceed any further when she hears what she has to say.

'I'm afraid the bishop's reply was rather cryptic,' the Sister starts. 'First of all he said that he didn't think Jim Beam- and he did refer to him as Jim Beam, would buy a cigarette case for *anyone as he gave up smoking in his teens and doesn't approve of it. Then he said, and this is the strange bit – he said "you'll find him in the same place."'*

'What is that supposed to mean?'

*'I really couldn't tell you. He just laughed and walked out the door. I don't think I am going to glean anything more sensible from him about this Jim Beam. I'm really sorry.'*

'Okay, well it was worth a try. Perhaps the man will come forward to report the loss himself, although after all this time I doubt it. Thanks for your help anyway.'

*You'll find him in the same place.* What on earth could he have meant?

## 18

Cate and Marco are finally able to take Milo home to the new house in the mountains towards the end of November with strict instructions that they have to keep him indoors for the first couple of weeks and restrict the number of visitors. They agree that work on the house has to stop for the time being. Cate is happy that the new kitchen and bathroom have been installed and all the rooms have been decorated. Marco had wanted to replace all the windows and sand the floors before they brought Milo home, but this has been put on hold. The bare wooden floors have just been vacuumed and washed repeatedly. They cannot take the risk of exposing Milo to the dust that sanding them would create.

On a visit with her father on their second day at the house, Rosie asks Cate if she can come and stay with them to help out with Milo.

'It will be a welcome distraction Cate. I can't face working over the holidays from uni after mum …..,' she trails off, unable to finish.

'Of course Rosie. I'd love you to come. To be honest I was dreading being alone. Marco'll be out at work all day.'

'I don't mind sharing Milo's room. You have the single bed in there as well as his cot.'

'We'll probably be having Milo in with us, in the bassinet for the first few weeks at least, so you would have the room to yourself.'

'That depends on how well Milo sleeps through the night,' Marco interjects. 'If he constantly cries through the night, I was planning to de-camp into the single bed in his room. I won't be able to function at work if I don't have any sleep.'

First I've heard of this, Cate thinks. But he expects me to function as a *mother* without sleep.

'Oh of course. Well, I can sleep on the couch,' Rosie says. 'That's not a problem.'

With Rosie around at least four days a week, Cate manages to snatch a few hours' sleep here and there. Milo is not a baby who sleeps for long, waking after short naps with a cry that would wake the dead. If Rosie hadn't been there some days, Cate is sure she would have collapsed with exhaustion. In the hospital, nurses shouldered much of the responsibility for looking after Milo but the reality of looking after a tiny baby has left her completely drained of energy and thoroughly exhausted. She thinks she must be doing something wrong with Milo crying so much and wishes she had Janet on hand to seek her advice. Cate really misses Janet's presence in her life.

Cate had promised Marco that Milo would be her priority, and of course he is, but with Rosie helping her out, surely she could take some time to do some up to date sketches of the murderer. She worries that she will forget what he looks like now if she doesn't do some soon. Cate is unsure though. If Marco finds out she's done them it might trigger his anger again. Things have been slightly strained between them since their argument at the hospital. With her exhaustion from little sleep, and Marco often sleeping in Milo's room there's been little intimacy between them.

Cate made the decision to do some new drawings. She's managed to complete two in the short time she's had available while Rosie took Milo for a walk. But they are tucked away, hidden in her home desk.

When they were first married, Cate had shown some of her earlier sketches to Marco, but she's not about to show him these latest ones. She knows he would be angry if he did see these. Cate understands that he might be concerned for her and Milo, but surely she should do something about the man she saw? What if the man is living in Sydney now? It would be an opportunity to finally bring him to justice.

If she's honest with herself though, Cate hasn't enough energy to be contacting the police or dealing with this. What she desperately needs above all else is sleep.

The man watches two men leave the architectural office. He is sure one of them is Rossi. He's walked past the entrance a few times and seen there are pictures on the wall of people he assumes are staff, but he's been cautious about actually going into the premises for a closer look. He enters the reception asking for Marco Rossi. He's told that he is not in the office at present, but should be back later if he'd like to leave his name. He declines but asks what time Mr. Rossi might be finishing work for the day, telling the woman that he'd like to catch him before he leaves. He searches the labelled photographs of the firm's male architects on the wall so he now knows which one is Rossi. He is in such a hurry to leave he forgets that Cate Rossi also works there and doesn't look for her photograph. Too late now. He will no doubt see her soon enough.

Shortly before 5pm he's back waiting outside the office once again. He watches as Rossi pulls out of the small car park. He pulls out and follows him.

'Marco,' the receptionist calls out to him as he enters the office the next morning, 'did that man come back to see you in the afternoon?'

'No, he didn't Anna. What did he look like again?'

'I could show you on yesterday's security tapes if you want.'

'Okay, if you line it up, I'll just dump my bag and make a coffee. I'll be back.'

When Marco returns to the reception he finds the receptionist fast forwarding through the video tapes. 'God this system is antiquated. About time we updated it,' Marco says.

'You need to talk to Graham. It's nothing to do with me.' She stops the tape at the time she had been looking for and moves it slowly forward until she reaches 1.17pm. 'This is him,' she says pointing at the man who can be seen entering the practice doors. 'Do you recognise him?'

'He is familiar,' Marco says leaning in for a closer look. 'But I can't say that I can place him. He's probably someone I have had dealings with in the past. I wouldn't know how to contact him though because I can't recall where I know him from. Thanks anyway Anna.'

'No worries,' Anna replies.

It's not until later the same day that Marco remembers seeing a man who looked very similar in the petrol station at Penrith the previous evening. While he was filling up with petrol, he'd noticed a man who had pulled into the pump behind him. He was wearing sun glasses, but he's sure that it was the same man. What colour was the car? White or silver he thinks. He can't really recall. Funny, he thinks - if the man knew him, and had come looking for him at the practice, why didn't he approach me? He surely would have recognised me? Was he following me? No that would be ridiculous. Surely if someone was following him they wouldn't be brazen enough to be filling up with petrol at the pump behind him? But actually he hadn't seen the man filling up. Just standing at the pump as though he was intending to fill up. He doesn't recall seeing him in the petrol station shop or in the forecourt when he left. But then he wasn't actually looking for him anyway. Just going about his business. It can't have been the same man he decides. He had the general looks of prosperous middle aged businessmen who he sees regularly at the practice. Probably just a coincidence.

Cate is walking back from the shops with a few groceries a few days later, trudging along exhausted. She had thought the fresh air would shake her out of her lethargy, but it hasn't helped. Checking that the road is clear, she takes a few steps onto the crossing when she hears the squeal of tyres. She looks up startled as she sees a car driving at speed towards her and realises that there is little possibility of avoiding the imminent impact.

# 19

**Yorkshire, April 2000**

Cate arrives in the small town of Hawes at 11.15am. It has taken her just over three hours to drive from Manchester in her new second-hand car. Thankfully the car she bought, finally paying out a little over a £1000, has performed well and there have been no problems.

As Cate steps out of the car her first thoughts are that she hopes she is not going to start seeing Marco here in this small country town. If she does she'll know she really is going completely bonkers or ...... . *Stop!* She tells herself. *Get a grip.*

Cate hasn't booked accommodation anywhere in Hawes deciding to take a chance and look around. The tourist season is in its infancy as the Easter break does not start until 23rd April this year, much later than usual, so Cate doesn't think the B & B's will be full until then. It's only 3rd April now. She finds a parking spot and walks around the town looking for a decent place to have lunch. They'd breakfasted early this morning and Cate is ready for a meal, although it's only 11.20am. She spots an interesting looking café and just as she is about to enter she spots a sign taped to the window:

# Waitress wanted for the season
# Room available if required

The only other couple in the café leave as Cate enters. She orders a vegetable soup and French bread. She notices the woman serving seems to be on her own and wonders if she dares to apply for the position. The woman is friendly and polite and the soup is very tasty which helps her make the decision. She orders a wedge of Victoria sponge with tea to follow the soup and, when she steps up to the counter to pay, introduces herself and enquires about the position.

'Not being funny or anything, but how do you think you would manage with that?' the woman says nodding towards her leg. 'And would you be willing to stay on for the season or are you just travelling around wanting something temporary? I notice you have an Australian or New Zealand accent. I can't tell the difference between them.'

'I'm Australian and I'm looking for some temporary work, but I'd be willing to stay on for the full season and I'm sure I'd be fine with my leg. It's getting better all the time. It was broken in a car crash,' Cate says to pre-empt any further questions. 'I no longer need a walking stick.'

'You'd have to muck in and do bits of everything. Including washing up.'

'I'd be happy to do that. I'd also be interested in the room if it's still available.'

'It is, but I can't show you it now. You'll have to wait until the lunch rush is over. Not that it's that busy at the moment with tourists, but many of the locals come into town on Mondays and come in for lunch.'

'I could help you out now if you want, if you think you are going to be busy.'

'Have you done this kind of work before?'

'Yes, I waitressed part time while studying in Sydney.'

'The wages aren't great, but I'd pay you £4.00 an hour with the room and meals during the day thrown in. And of course you will earn some tips as well. We share those, placing them in a bowl under the counter back here, and then divide them up each day. It's mainly the tourists who give tips, not the locals.'

'So the £4 an hour includes the use of the room? I wouldn't have to pay rent or other bills on top of that?'

'No, it's all included.'

'Sounds fine to me. Would you like me to help you today?' Adhita had told her that the minimum wage was £3.70 an hour and Cate had been worried if she took casual work how she would pay her living expenses. With some meals and accommodation included, plus tips she would actually be earning a reasonable wage.

'Tell you what, you can have a trial today. The girl who was going to help me has let me down. I'll pay you for it instead. If it works out then the job is yours. You can leave your bag and coat just off the kitchen in the store area. I'm Bernice Walker by the way.'

'Thank you Mrs. Walker.' Cate offers her the money to pay for her lunch, but the woman waves away the money saying she doesn't want it, it can be part of the deal today and insists Cate calls her Bernice.

From 12.15 on the café becomes crowded with customers. Cate and Bernice have to work flat out to cater to their needs. Finally at 3.30 they have finished washing the last of the pans and stacking the dishwasher again with further china, glasses and cutlery. Bernice announces that she is happy with Cate's energy and skills and asks if she still wants the job. When Cate nods in the affirmative Bernice says, 'It's busier than it was today in the tourist season. You'd start at 9.30am – we don't do breakfasts. Just morning tea, lunch and afternoon teas. Although we offer sandwiches or rolls throughout opening hours. We close at 5pm and we're usually cleared up by 6pm. You'd have half an hour for lunch, either before or after the rush, depending how busy we are and then another tea break in the afternoon. Are you still interested?'

'Yes, and I'm happy to be flexible with break times,' Cate replies.

Bernice puts a 'back in 5 minutes' sign up on the door and opens a door just along from the café entrance. It leads up a flight of stairs to another floor.

'My daughter Steph lives here. She works at one of the local banks.' Bernice says with obvious pride. 'The front rooms are hers – she has a living room and a bedroom. You would have to share the kitchen and bathroom with her. This would be your room,' she says opening the door to a generously proportioned white room at the rear of the property.

The room has a double bed, a small built in wardrobe, a chest of drawers with a television on it, a bedside cabinet, a small desk and chair, plus a single lounge chair. There is a duvet with no cover on it lying on the bed. There is a mattress cover but no sheets. Bernice tells her that she will find linen for the bed in the cupboard at the top of the stairs. The beige carpet looks almost new and the room is clean. There are light blue curtains hanging at the window – just as Cate prefers in a bedroom. She can't stand dark heavy drapes in the room where she sleeps. Cate says she's happy with it.

'I'll leave you to look around the bathroom and kitchen then. When you've finished pop back down. I'd better get back.'

Cate explores the rest of the flat, disappointed to find the bathroom only has a shower over a bath again. At least this one has grip handles that will make getting in and out of it easier. She notes there is a small table with two seats in the little galley kitchen, which means she will be able to eat in there rather than her room. There is also a washing machine and small dishwasher. With the water shortages they sometimes experienced in Sydney, Janet had always refused to have a dishwasher installed and there had been no room for one in their mountain home. At least there are no water shortages here Cate thinks looking at the drizzle that has started outside the kitchen window.

Cate goes back down to the café, where there are only two customers indulging in afternoon tea, to sorts matters out with Bernice. She produces her National Insurance card, which she had checked was still active while in Manchester and had it altered to her married name. Bernice insists she won't need her any longer today and suggests she settles herself into her room. There is parking to the side of the Café, and Bernice agrees that she can park there, but she will have to share the space with her and Steph who has a vehicle parked there and that it might involve moving cars around some days if one of them gets blocked in. After Bernice gives her a set of keys Cate leaves to collect her car, parks and takes her bags, one at a time, upstairs to her new room. She struggles and curses with her large case, wishing she'd chosen a smaller one to bring – but she'd packed for all contingencies – one duvet cover with two pillowcases and two sheets, one towel, plus winter and summer clothes. After making her bed up with the linen she has brought with her, Cate examines what's on offer in the linen cupboard. Most of the duvet covers are bright or dramatic patterned affairs and the sheets dark. Whilst she is not obsessively fussy, Cate prefers her sheets to be white or cream and with plain or subtle patterned duvet covers. She is however fussy about washing whites separately from darks, so she usually buys light coloured duvet covers so that the sheets and covers can be washed together. She will have to look around and buy some more linen. At least one more cover, pillowcases, and another towel she thinks.

She unpacks her clothes and toiletries and shoves her smaller suitcase under the wooden framed bed. The other she just manages to squeeze into the built-in cupboard. The room looks a little bare with no pictures or rugs. She can do without them for now. Perhaps when she has saved a bit of money she could look in some of the shops for something to brighten the room up. She's not sure what time she will have available for shopping. She forgot to ask Bernice if they closed any day of the week. There is a sign on the door of the café with opening hours so decides she will check that on her way out for a walk. Not that she needs a walk. Her leg is aching after a gruelling few hours work, but she needs some fresh air.

Noting that the café is open seven days a week, Cate pops in to ask Bernice if she expects her to work the seven days.

'Goodness me, no lass. I wouldn't expect that of anyone. My widowed sister works here at the weekend, giving me a break, and occasionally other days. But sometimes we swap that around, depending on our personal calendars. Steph works here Saturdays some weeks during the busy season. My other daughter comes in some days during school hours – she has little ones to take and collect from school. I also have a young man who helps out. You can either be flexible with days off or choose a particular day and I will make arrangements to cover once the season starts.'

'I wouldn't mind having one weekday off so I could look around shops when they are open in the different towns around here,' Cate tells her. 'But I wouldn't have to have the same day off every week. Is there any particular day that is quieter than others?'

'Not really…. not once the season starts. Why don't you have Tuesdays and Wednesdays off from next week and then we'll see how we go when the season starts. If you don't mind doing extra hours that'd be great. Weekends and Mondays tend to be our busiest times. We get a lot of day trippers at the weekends and Monday is market day.'

'Okay, that will suit me. I'm off for a walk now. I'll see you at 9.30 tomorrow then.'

Cate realises as she is leaving that she will be working eight days straight before her next day off. She'll need early nights to rest her leg. She had exercised daily around Manchester while Adhita was busy at work and could feel her leg strengthening daily, but being on her feet for over eight hours a day will be a dramatic increase. She just hopes her leg will be able to cope with it.

# 20

**Blue Mountains, Sydney, December 1999**

'Are you alright dearie? Do we need to go and ask someone to call an ambulance?'

Cate looks up and sees two silver-haired seniors gazing down at her as she lies on the road. She turns and glances across at where she had been walking a few minutes earlier, notices her crushed shopping and shudders. That could have been me, she thinks. In a desperate attempt to avoid being hit, Cate had twisted slightly and hurtled her body backwards, dropping the shopping as she dived towards the kerb. The car had missed her by a few centimetres. Didn't the driver see her? Surely he or she would have stopped if they had?

'No, I ….I'm okay. I think I've just got a few cuts and grazes,' Cate says examining the gravel imbedded in her bleeding hands.

'Stupid bugger obviously wasn't looking where he was going. And he could have at least stopped to see that you were alright. Typical male.'

'So it was a man driving the car?' Cate asks the woman.

'I didn't really see, did you hon,' she turns and asks the man beside her who shakes his head negatively. 'I just assumed it was a man. A woman wouldn't do that.'

Cate had only caught the briefest glance at the car. It had seemed a dark colour to her. 'Did you notice the colour of the car or where it came from?' she asks the couple.

'It was black,' the man says. 'Definitely black. A large black car. We didn't see where it came from. We were busy chatting to a friend and had just started walking off again when we saw what happened. I didn't have time to see the number plate either. Do you want to report it to the police?'

'Yes I will when I get home. But could I have your names and either a phone number or address. Would you be willing to be witnesses?'

'Of course dearie. We'd be happy to.'

Cate rummages in her bag for a pen and writes down their details. Her shopping is ruined and the couple help her clear the mess off the road, as best they can. She places the ruined shopping in a nearby rubbish bin and decides she can't go back to the shops in the state she's in. She needs to return home to clean up her hands and the other minor scrapes to her arms and legs. She thanks the couple and limps off towards home, rubbing her shoulder which she realises she has also hurt quite badly from her abrupt landing on the tarmac. She carefully checks the roads around her, making sure there are no other rogue drivers about. Cate is sure that there were no cars coming along that road before she crossed. Just some cars parked at the kerb. She hadn't taken any notice of them as she walked past. Had one of them pulled out suddenly or is it that she is just so tired she is not paying enough attention to her surroundings? Was it deliberate or just an impatient driver who hadn't noticed her?

Back at the house Rosie cleans Cate's wounds with concern. 'God Cate, you could have been killed.'

'I know. I don't know where the car came from. I

checked the road before I started to cross.'

'Did you manage to get the rego plates?'

'No and neither did the old couple who witnessed it. They only saw the last part of the incident when the car almost hit me.'

'Are you going to report it?'

'Yes I am. There's not a lot I can tell them though.'

Cate rings the police and reports what happened. She passes on the couple's details and asks if they intend to follow it up. She is told that they will log the incident and gather information but unless they have the registration there is not much they can do as there are no cameras in the vicinity of the crossing.

When Cate tells Marco later that evening he asks her what colour the car was. He relaxes when she tells him the witnesses told her it was a black car. He needs to stop being so paranoid.

The man waits until he sees the two sisters leave the house with the baby. The husband had driven off to work much earlier. He enters the house and quickly installs his listening devices. One in each of the three phones he's found in the house. The main one in the entrance hall and then the study and the master bedroom. He also installs further recording devices in the living room, kitchen and the main bedroom and then slips out of the house without being noticed.

Weeks pass and now the weather is better, Cate, often accompanied by Rosie, ventures out each day with baby Milo to enjoy the summer sun. With Marco off visiting his sister they have walked to the park again this morning and are sitting in the cool shade of the trees.

'Have you noticed how much cooler it is up here than at home in Beecroft?' Rosie remarks

'Yes, it's great now. I'm just worried about what it will be like in the winter months though. I wish we had central heating like we had in London.'

'Yes that was great wasn't it? I've seen antiquated radiators in some of the big old hotels in Sydney. Like the Metropole. So they must have had central heating installed a long time ago. I wonder why it's not more common.'

'I spoke to Marco about it. We could have some sort of gas conducted heating in the house, but it would seem that the combination boilers which operate radiators and hot water like we had in England, don't seem to be available here. It gets cold enough in winter, so I don't understand why. We've only got our wood burning stove in the living room and no heaters in the bedrooms. Marco said when he was growing up in the mountains they only ever had a heater in the living room. Never the bedrooms – and he claimed it was fine. I'm not convinced though. I would want Milo's room to be heated for him during the really cold months. Apparently it can get down to minus one regularly up here.'

'We've only ever had heating in the living room in Beecroft, but I don't think the temperatures are ever that low. I always find it cold in the winter though. Do you remember the hot water bottles we had when we were kids?' Rosie asks.

'Yes, I was always terrified I'd roll onto it and break it with water spilling out all over my bed.'

'Yes,' Rosie laughs. 'I was the same. Then Mum bought us those electric blankets. I hated them as well.'

'Me too.' They sit in silence for a few minutes. Cate

glances at Milo. He's sound asleep for now. The fresh air seems to work wonders at assisting him to nod off.

'How are you feeling about Mum now Rosie? You seem better.'

'It's been cathartic for me being up here with you and Milo. Especially with little Milo. I've been totally absorbed in your lives and being with him. No reminders around the house of Mum except for the photograph you have of us all in the study, but I avoid going in there. I've been avoiding going home much since your accident, using that as an excuse. I was very worried about you of course, but really it's about not wanting to face up to the memories in the house. I spoke to Dad about maybe selling the house and moving, but he said he couldn't bear to at the moment. He wants to hang on to the memories the house holds for him. I want to escape them. It's going to be awful at Christmas. Our first without her.'

'I know. Why don't you both come up here then? I know Marco and I are going to his parents at some point. But we could do that either before or after Christmas and you and Dad could come here for Christmas Day. We spent last Christmas with Marco's family, only seeing you all after Boxing Day. It's my family's turn this year.'

'I'll mention it to Dad and see what he thinks. You'd better sort it out with Marco first though. I don't want to tell dad we're invited here until you're sure.'

Cate is sure that Rosie has noticed the tense atmosphere between her and Marco some nights. Rosie usually returns home to Beecroft at the weekends to catch up with her friends and Dad, she claims, but Cate is sure it is also to avoid being around her and Marco.

'Okay I'll sort it with him later. He'll be back from his sister's soon. Shall we go to the shops before his highness wakes up?'

'Yes, and then I'll head home. Dad will be expecting me because it's Saturday. I just didn't feel like racing off this morning.'

They walk slowly towards the shops unaware that they are being observed.

# 21

**Hawes, Yorkshire, April 2000**

With the clocks having gone forward on her first weekend in the UK, Cate estimates she has about an hour of daylight left by the time she leaves the cafe. She decides to stick with a walk around the town today and to look for a medical practice to register with. She finds a medical centre on the outskirts of town and makes enquiries about registration. She is told their books are full, but that there is another practice on the other side of town where there are definitely vacancies, the woman at reception tells her, with a smirk. Receiving directions Cate walks back to the other side of town, finds the medical centre and enters. It looks as though they are just about to close as there is no one sitting in the waiting room. She notices that the doctor's names, apart from one, are Asian. Was that what that woman's smirk was about, she wonders and why there are vacancies? Cate completes the registration form and asks if there is a female doctor when she hands it in. She is told that Doctor Patel is a woman, so she asks for an appointment. She is told that she must see the practice nurse first for a general check so is given two appointments. Cate asks for the appointments to be at the beginning of the day due to work schedules, and receives slots for 8.30am on two consecutive days on Wednesday and Thursday.

Cate's first appointment with the nurse deals with further information gathering, taking of blood pressure and blood tests. When Cate asks what the blood tests are for she is told that they test a range of things including cholesterol, diabetes, thyroid, liver, just to ensure that there are no undiagnosed conditions. Cate refrains from providing details of her recent injuries and waits until she sees Doctor Patel the following morning. She hands Doctor Patel the letter she was given by the hospital in Australia once she had booked her overseas travel. She is supposed to have her leg regularly monitored. Doctor Patel asks her to remove her jeans and socks so she can examine the wound and take a pulse in her foot.

'There is a strong pulse. Are you exercising regularly?' the Doctor asks.

'Sort of. I am on my feet most of the day with my new job and I am quite exhausted at the end of my shift, so I have only been taking short walks around the town.'

'Perhaps you should find a job where you are not on your feet so much.'

'I will once the summer season is over, but I would rather persevere with this job for the next few months. When I have my days off I plan to take walks on the dales. Normal walking might help, don't you think?'

'Yes, it would, but you need to do the strengthening exercises as well. Are you doing those?'

'Yes I do them most mornings.'

'Fine, well make another appointment to see me in another month. If anything changes, come to see me sooner. Now what about all this medication you are taking?'

Cate produces the packets of tablets she has left – painkillers and sleeping tablets. 'I will need some more soon, could you write me a prescription for them?'

'How often are you taking the different painkillers?'

'I take two of the milder ones each morning. Then I sometimes take two of the stronger ones at night. It's only if I have a particularly bad night that I might take the sleeping tablets. I only take those a couple of times a week.'

'Well that's good. You mustn't become dependent on them.'

'I can assure you I don't want to. I don't like taking the painkillers either, but the pain is still too severe for me to stop taking those yet.'

'I can see that it would be. What about your other wound in the shoulder? How has that healed?'

'It's okay, although it gives me some pain as well some days. Particularly if I move my right arm around too much or if the weather turns cold.'

'Well again simple exercises can help with that. I assume you've been given some to do each day?'

Cate nods. The doctor types some notes on the computer and prints out new prescriptions. Cate thanks her and stops to make a new appointment for the following month before leaving the surgery. On her way back to the flat, she also pops into a hardware shop just as it opens its doors and buys herself a tall narrow clothes airer.

The week passes in a blur for Cate. The fine weather at the weekend brings crowds of visitors to the town and no sooner has a table become vacant than it's occupied with new customers. Bernice's sister Ros works with her throughout the weekend and they have a young man helping in the kitchen. Cate collapses exhausted each night after her shower, just having a piece of toast and tea before crawling into bed. One benefit of her exhaustion means that she sleeps soundly most nights and has not dwelt for long on thoughts of Marco and Milo. Instead she seems to be functioning on automatic pilot, maintaining a polite cheery front with customers that she can finally switch off when she finishes each day. It's only when some evenings the pain in her leg strikes with a rapidity that takes her breath away and keeps her awake, does she begin the torturous thoughts of her last days and moments with Marco and Milo. Thankfully though, she has had no further visual sightings of Marco.

Cate has only bumped into her housemate Steph on a few occasions. She seems to have a busy social life and is rarely home before Cate retires.

On her first Tuesday off Cate heads to a second hand shop she spotted on her first day in the town, but which was closed by the time she discovered it. She had seen through the windows that they had a collection of framed prints. She searches through the art and finds a Paul Klee print that she likes which she buys for £10. Also on her shopping list is bedding and towels. She looks at a shop selling linen at quite extortionate prices, but it seems good quality cotton, so she chooses a new towel, a new duvet cover and two pillowcases, giving her two complete bedding and bath sets now. Cate would normally change her linen once a week, but with her exhausting work schedule she's not managed to change them for ten days. She'd stripped the bed this morning and so she either had to buy new linen or make use of some available in the cupboard in the flat.

She'd discovered that Steph hung her washing over an airer in her living room, so Cate'd had to set the airer she'd bought up in her bedroom. She didn't relish the idea of sleeping in her room with wet washing hanging about, so with the one clothes wash she'd done so far she did it first thing in the morning so it was almost dry by the time she'd returned from work. The central heating is still coming on each morning for a short period and then again from 5pm each evening. It doesn't take long for her washing to dry in these conditions.

With her freshly laundered linen still slightly damp Cate decides to use the new duvet cover and pillow cases without washing them first. They feel all silky and smooth as she slips into bed that night.

# 22

**Sydney, December 1999**

As Christmas Day is falling on a Saturday this year, and Marco has happily agreed to have Cate's father and sister staying with them, Marco's parents have insisted Marco, Milo and Cate come up to them on Boxing Day, staying with them for a few days. Cate would have preferred to postpone the trip to Singleton until the Monday as Rosie and her father would be staying the night on both Christmas Eve and Christmas Day. She thinks it will be a bit of a rush and seem rude to usher them out of the house early in the morning on Boxing Day. When Cate airs these thoughts to Marco he assures her it will be fine, they just have to tell her father that they will be leaving early and, if he and Rosie want to stay on in the house and leave in their own time they are welcome to do so. Rosie has keys to lock up, he reminds Cate.

Christmas Eve finally arrives. They had discussed the possibility of eating out that night. Experiencing what it would be like to take Milo with them for his first public engagement, but Cate had decided it would be too awkward. She tells Marco they will have plenty of time to do that in the future and that she'd prefer to cook a meal at home. They decide to have a family gathering instead.

Marco's sister, her husband and three children have been invited as well her father and Rosie, so Cate prepares a cold buffet style meal which they can all help themselves to, sitting either at the table or out on the deck. Marco also barbeques some Tandoori chicken, and sausages for the young ones. Cate notices that her father is very quiet and when she finally grabs an opportunity to eat, approaches him with her plate of food and plonks herself beside him on the couch.

'You okay Dad? Have you had enough to eat?'

'Yes thanks Cate. I was just thinking about your mother.' Cate wonders if he means her real mother Julie or Janet. She assumes he means Janet and doubts he has thought about his first wife for many years.

'It's such a shame she lost her life so young and missed you growing up. She would have been so proud of you.' *So he is talking about her real mother!*

'Thanks Dad, I'd like to think she would. I often wonder what I would be doing now if she hadn't died. Would we still be living in Melbourne? Would I have gone to uni? You know, those sorts of things.'

'I'm sure you would have gone to university in Melbourne. And I'm sure that's where you would still be. I doubt your mother would ever have budged from there. But she might have persuaded you to follow in her footsteps and go into the teaching profession.'

'No, I doubt I would have done that. It was never something I aspired to. Why don't you think she would have ever left Melbourne?'

'She said she needed to be there - where she grew up and lived with her family. That's what caused our final parting of the ways. We were already separated when I was offered the job in Sydney. I attempted a reconciliation with her and asked her to come up to Sydney with me, but she wouldn't.'

'I know, she told me. I didn't fully understand it at the time.'

'If she'd have come to Sydney, then she might still be alive today.'

'I've thought of that too. But there's no point in dwelling on maybes, ifs and buts. What happens, happens Dad. Some things we think we could have changed with hindsight, but other things are always out of our control. If mum had called the police as soon as we arrived home on the day that she was killed, they might have come around to interview her and then she might not have been murdered. But she could just have as easily been murdered the next night. Or the night after. The man who killed her clearly had her earmarked.' Cate hesitates for a minute before adding, 'I saw him in Sydney recently by the way.'

'What? You saw *who* in Sydney?'

'The man who murdered mum. I saw him in Parramatta one day back in October. The same afternoon on the day I went into labour with Milo. He was dressed like a businessman. A bit like you do going to work. I immediately went to see the policeman I'd spoken to before about him, but we didn't have the opportunity to take it any further as I was rushed into hospital for Milo's birth. And the policeman mysteriously died a few days later as well.'

'My god Cate, you've never mentioned any of this. How did the policeman die?'

'Well we've all been a little preoccupied haven't we? With Milo and then Mum's accident. It just wasn't appropriate to bring it up. And I don't know how the policeman died. They wouldn't tell me.'

'Right. I don't suppose they are allowed to give out that kind of information to the public. Unless it was already in the news. Do you think the man you saw lives in Sydney now?'

'No idea. He might have been up from Melbourne on a business trip or he could live in Sydney. He might have always lived in Sydney. I've no idea. I saw him with a priest at one of those Catholic buildings in Parramatta. So the priest could tell the police who he is. There is another police detective I spoke to who wanted to meet with me to follow it through further, but Milo was still in hospital then and I just didn't have the time.'

'What about now? Are you going to do anything about it?'

'I might. I've completed a few new sketches to pass on to the police so I might contact them in the New Year. I just haven't had the energy to do anything. It's been 19 years now so a few more weeks is not going to hurt.'

The conversation Cate had with her father is a little distorted with the background noise of other people in the room. But later that night the listener has heard enough of what Cate has said in the recordings to realise he has to do something about it.

Christmas Day is very quiet. Janet had always traditionally cooked a roast chicken serving it with stuffing and baked ham, but whilst Cate decides she will stick with a traditional roast, she does roast beef and Yorkshire puddings, reminiscent of her mother Julie's favourite. She thinks this might deflect the gloom of Janet's absence a little as she knows that Dad and Rosie will be thinking of her. It's their first Christmas without her. The food is demolished with compliments but Cate can see their hearts aren't really in it.

Marco is doing some last minute wrapping of presents for his parents in Singleton that evening when his spool of sticky tape runs out. He's in the study, and looks around on the desk and the drawing board for another reel. There is none to be seen. He rummages around in the first few drawers of the desk hoping there might be some there, but is out of luck. In the final drawer he moves a pile of papers and one of Cate's drawing pads out of the way, thinking he might find some buried underneath. Still nothing. He is about to replace the papers and pad when curiosity makes him open Cate's sketch pad to look at her latest sketches. She said she had been sketching Milo. This clearly isn't the drawing pad she'd been using for Milo though, as, staring back at him is a sketch of the man he saw on the video tapes at work. A chill runs up his spine. He knows now who this is. Why he was familiar. He is older and heavier than in the drawings Cate had shown him several years before. Cate has captured him in a head and shoulders depiction and also in a full length sketch. He reaches for the phone and dials his office number. He knows no one will be there, but he needs to leave a message.

He waits for the answer phone to kick in and begins his message, 'Hello Anna, this is Marco. Look can you make sure you keep that video of the man who was asking for me a few weeks back. You know, the one you showed me. I know who he is now and I am going to need it. I'm changing my plans and I'm going to drive back from my parents in Singleton on the 27th. I will come into the office the following morning. I know some of you plan to be in then to sort out the computer back up for the millennium scaremongering. I just want to make sure you don't delete it. Okay. Thanks. Hope you had a good Christmas break. See you on the 28th.'

Marco hangs up and stares at the drawings for a further few minutes. He is sure now that this is the man who was at the garage that day. Cate hadn't said anything to him about these drawings. But then again, she hadn't said a great deal to him since they'd brought Milo home. Until a few nights ago. Cate had finally challenged him about his attitude when he returned home on Wednesday night. Rosie had returned to Beecroft earlier that day to meet up with friends and do some Christmas shopping. He'd gone straight into the study after giving Cate and a sleeping Milo a perfunctory kiss telling her he had to work on plans he'd promised to complete for the following day. His last day at work before the Christmas break. Cate had stormed into the study some minutes later and confronted him.

'I can't stand this coldness a moment longer Marco. We have to talk.'

'I have to finish these plans Cate. I'm not ignoring you …'

'Bugger the plans,' she'd shouted at him. '*We* are more important. We can't have family here over Christmas without sorting *this* family out. I'm sorry, but I just can't do it.'

So they had talked – for as long as Milo let them before waking again. Marco had admitted that he had been giving Cate a hard time. Blaming her for Milo's vulnerable condition at birth and subsequent health scares. Being resentful of all the time and attention she had given Milo and Rosie since they'd brought Milo home. He confessed to feeling neglected and had not known how to break the tension that had built between them.

Cate had admitted that she had been angry with him for not supporting her after Janet's death and for blaming her for Milo's near death episodes. She'd found it all so traumatic and had really needed him, but when he didn't seem to need her, she in turn had resented him. She also didn't know how to break the cycle of tension as she was so exhausted from lack of sleep.

When he thinks back to all those wasted weeks. At least they had made up now, apologising to each other and promising to do their best to communicate better in the future. Over the last few days they'd managed to recapture the loving intimacy and comfortable ease of their relationship prior to Milo's birth.

Marco thinks he should go straight to the police once he picks up the tape. Probably with Cate. He just hopes the tape hasn't been re-used. The question on his mind now is whether he mentions anything to Cate. About seeing the drawings. About the man possibly following him. He doesn't want to worry her or her father and Rosie who are in the living room watching some comedy film. He can hear their laughter. No, he decides he won't say anything and will wait until they return from his parents. After all, he reasons, everyone is with their families over Christmas aren't they? Nothing is going to happen.

Marco is unaware though that his phone call has triggered an alert to someone who has been monitoring their phone calls. There is an urgency to the situation now.

Early on Boxing morning Cate tiptoes into Milo's room to collect his bags of clothes and paraphernalia she had packed the previous night. Rosie stirs in the single bed and wishes them a good journey. She says she will see them all later in the week as she and her father are returning to Beecroft that day. Cate leans over and kisses her goodbye. Her father, dead to the world on the couch, does not stir, but Cate gives him a departing kiss as well.

There are few cars on the Putty Road as they wind their way across the ancient mountain road that will take them to Marco's family in Singleton.

The man waits until he is sure the father and daughter are no longer at the house in Glenbrook. All seems completely quiet. He enters the Rossi house and removes all the listening devices that he'd previously planted. He searches through the house and finds the drawing pad with the images of a man he'd heard the Rossi woman mention to her father. He can't help but admire her skill, she has the likeness spot on. He rips the pages out to take them with him. He finds a set of keys on the desk top which foolishly have a 'work keys' tag on them. Some people never learn. He takes these keys with him as well as the car keys for Cate Rossi's Toyota which are conveniently sitting in a bowl on the kitchen worktop.

Marco and Cate are greeted with the usual effusive welcome when they arrive in Singleton at his parent's house and Cate is relieved to relinquish responsibility of Milo to his grandparents and have a break. Other family members have driven up from Wollongong on the south coast, although they are booked into a local motel for the night. It is a noisy and boisterous gathering and Cate is thoroughly exhausted by the time they finally retire for the night. Cate has been expressing milk for Milo since his birth and so she is still unable to drink any alcohol. She has found it hard to sit around relaxing while others become more progressively drunk. Marco mentions in passing he wants to leave the next day. There is no opportunity for them discuss why he has decided this as she is sound asleep by the time Marco staggers to bed.

The next day is much of the same. Several times from mid-afternoon Cate suggests that they leave in order to cross the Putty Road in daylight, as she assumes she will be driving. She is nervous on that road at the best of times, and certainly doesn't want to tackle it at night. Cate is relieved that she isn't wearing her watch otherwise she knows she would be looking at it every few minutes which would seem extremely rude. She can't help sneaking looks at the mantle clock though and worries about how late it is getting. Marco however, enjoying being surrounded by his family, lingers until the sun has well and truly set. When Cate suggests they stay another night and leave in the morning he insists he is fine to drive, knowing Cate's apprehension of the Putty Road. He reminds her that he hasn't had a drink since lunch time, some eight hours ago and has eaten plenty of food to absorb the alcohol he'd consumed earlier anyway.

They finally make their farewells and prepare to set off. Marco's mother is very tearful at their departure. She pleads with Marco to spend another night, but Marco insists they have to return home as he has to go into the office on urgent business the following day. Cate is surprised at his mother's tearful parting who, although an emotional woman, is not normally as demonstrative as this. She is further surprised at Marco's statement about work. She understood that he wasn't returning to work until the New Year. She remains silent though as Marco's mother makes him promise that they will come over again in another few weeks bringing little Milo with them.

The heat off the tarmac, following a downpour, has shrouded the Putty Road in a drifting mist. The air is hot and humid so Marco has the air-conditioning turned on full with all windows firmly shut. With the noise the air-con makes Cate can barely hear him when he speaks. The road is rising steeply and she is just grateful that she is not driving. She is sitting in the middle of the back seat, next to Milo. Cate is tempted to ask Marco if he really is going into work tomorrow or if it was just an excuse he gave his mother, but decides to wait until they are home, fearful of waking Milo.

As they are heading along a rare straight stretch of road a car looms up behind them suddenly and swings out to overtake. The overtaking car lurches in towards them and Cate hears the impact of metal on metal. Marco swears and can't avoid the car swerving into the barricade. Their car swipes along the metal barricade and swings back onto the road. Marco slows down and yells, 'Jees, did you see that stupid bastard, he nearly ran us off the road! We're going to have a lovely scrape down the left side of the car and probably dents on the other. Just what we need! And it was a red Toyota, just like your car.'

'He's probably been drinking,' Cate replies concerned that Milo has woken, crying. She strokes Milo's head gently and it seems to calm him and Cate can just about see that he seems to have nodded off to sleep again. She checks that her seat belt is fastened tightly. She often releases it when she is in the back with Milo as it's easier to administer to his needs, but tonight she wants to remain firmly fixed under its reassuring safety.

'You might have to pull over Marco if Milo wakes up again – at the first opportunity I mean, not around here,' Cate says.

'Okay, let's just hope there are no other drunks out on the road tonight. I forgot to fill the car up with petrol on Christmas Eve anyway, so hopefully there might be a garage open as we hit Windsor. We can stop there and fill up.'

'We've got enough petrol to get there though haven't we?' Cate asks worried. 'The last place we want to break down is on this road.'

'Yeah, yeah, no worries,' Marco reassures her, checking the gauge which is displaying a quarter of a tank.

Marco thinks the petrol they have left in the tank will be fine. They've probably just about enough to make it home if there are no garages open. Or at least reach Penrith, where there's bound to be a petrol station open.

They drive on slowly, Marco nervous about putting his foot down. Much as he wants to get off this road as soon as possible he has been left shaken by the incident with the overtaking car.

As they pass a signpost warning of upcoming bend, Marco approaches it with caution but, despite this, before they reach the bend, the high beam lights of an oncoming car blinds him. The car seems to be heading straight towards him! He can't see the road and doesn't know which way to turn the wheel.

'I can't see a bloody thing Cate!' he shouts.

The car is still right in front of him. Should he swerve to the right of it? To the left he knows will be the barricade and beyond that a steep drop into a ravine. Just as he makes his split second decision to swerve right the car coming at him suddenly swerves in the direction he was planning to take and instead he carries on ahead. Too late he realises that he has missed the bend and they are heading straight through a gap in the barricade. He brakes frantically, but the car has already begun it's descent into the ravine.

A car turns onto a safety exit ramp down the hill, a short distance beyond the place where the Rossi's car went over, and stops. It reverses onto the road and drives back up the hill. As the car approaches the bend the driver slows and looks over into the darkness. Through the open window there is silence. Satisfied, the driver pulls out and heads back towards Windsor and then to Penrith where he will dump the car. He believes everything is taken care of now and once he retrieves his own car he can finally enjoy some well-earned holiday rest.

# 23

The car is buffeted repeatedly by the branches of trees. The glass in the windows on the driver and rear passenger side break and showers them with fragments. They slide sideways and crash into a tree base again on the driver's side as the car gathers speed and are jolted violently back to the left. Something smashes into Cate's cheek and her head is jerked sideways. She hears a snap as something sharp penetrates her shoulder painfully. Before can she look to see what has happened the car turns over and she grips the baby seat firmly to prevent it from moving. Marco is shouting, Milo is wailing loudly and she thinks she can hear herself screaming. Cate throws her arms over the baby seat in an attempt to protect Milo as the car slides down into the last part of its descent.

The car comes to an abrupt stop with a great deal of crunching and grinding. She hears Marco scream in pain then he is silent. The sounds of running water filters through into the car and Cate is terrified that they have landed in a river and will sink. There is no water coming into the car though and they seem to be stable.

Hanging upside down she is aware of a sharp pain in her shoulder. Turning her head is painful and she can't see a thing. Using her left hand she runs it across her right shoulder. There is something sticking out of it and she can feel blood oozing out of the wound it's caused.

Milo is silent but she can hear Marco breathing raggedly

from the front seat.

'Marco?' she calls. 'Marco are you okay? Can you move?'

'No. I've got a dirty great branch across my chest,' he gasps. 'What about you?'

'I'm not sure. Marco, Milo has gone quiet. I can't see if he's alright. I can't see anything!' she cries in panic. Milo has not cried since the car came to a standstill.

'Torch. There's a torch in the glove compartment if you can get to it,' Marco croaks.

'I'll undo my seat belt and see if I can crawl through.' Cate fumbles with her seat belt, pressing the catch over and over, but she can't release the mechanism. 'It won't undo Marco. I can't free it!'

'Slow down. Just take it slowly. Press down hard and hold it. Try again. You have to Cate. I can't help you. Be careful when you do release it, you don't want to drop awkwardly and damage your head or neck.'

Cate takes some deep breaths to calm her nerves and has another attempt. This time the catch releases and she falls onto the ceiling of the car with her head tucked and her arms protecting the back of her head. There are glass fragments everywhere. She sweeps them aside carefully, turns herself over and attempts to pull herself over the front seat. There isn't enough room for her to make it through. The head rest is too high. She can't crawl between the middle of the seats as she can feel there is a thick branch suspended across Marco. She's afraid if she touches the branch it will cause Marco further injuries.

'I can't fit through Marco. How do you remove the headrest?'

'Button on the side.'

Cate feels around the headrest until she finds what

seems to be a button and presses. The headrest comes away from the seat and she throws it behind her. Now she might be able to squeeze through. As she begins to shift her weight to the front of the car, it rocks precariously so she pulls back quickly.

'Oh God, Marco, I think we're on a ledge. If I come into the front it might tip us over. I think there's a creek or river out there. Maybe below us. We don't want the car to go into it.'

'See if you can …. can open your window and get out first …. then open the front door if it's safe.'

Cate can hear Marco's breathing is becoming more ragged, she has to do something quickly or they might all die. Luckily the Toyota Corolla model has manual windows, not these modern electric ones and she begins winding it down, or up in this instance, with the car upside down. Just as she thinks this is going to work the glass crashes back down in place. Something must have damaged the mechanism, she thinks. She tries the handle of the door and the catch releases triggering the interior light which still seems to be working, unlike the headlights which have both gone out, most probably broken, Cate thinks. Most of the damage to the car seems to be on the driver's side. She kicks the door wide open and the car rocks again. She waits for it to steady before placing her hand outside where she can faintly see and feel solid ground – rocks and ferns. She crawls out and frees herself from the car. It is pitch black outside and she can barely make anything out. She has to close the rear door again to move to the front of the car. Edging forward close to the car she finds the front passenger door handle and pulls on it. It won't budge, she has to move further forward. As she steps forward the ground gives way and she slips, screaming loudly as she falls down a rocky embankment to land in shallow water with her left leg twisted awkwardly under her. The jagged rocks of the embankment have ripped her clothes and gashed her skin. The bit of branch sticking out her right shoulder has been snapped off and its stump pushed in further.

Cate can hear Marco calling her name and she looks up. The car is white and she can just about make it out in the blackness around her. The front seems to be dangling over a rocky ledge hanging above the stream but angled down slightly at the rear. She doesn't know how far up it is, maybe only fifteen feet, if she can just make it up there. The coolness of the water is refreshing in the stifling heat of the night and she has an urge to just close her eyes and sleep, but she must get back up to the car. She takes some sips of water and throws some over her face to keep her awake. Pushing herself up painfully onto her knees and then to standing, she is aware that something is very wrong with her left leg from the knee down. She thinks it must be broken but she can't think about that now. Using her right leg and arms she gradually makes her way back up the embankment, dragging her painful left leg behind, calling out all the time and sobbing to Marco that she's coming. There is still no sound from Milo and Cate hopes it's something simple like that he has been knocked unconscious – nothing more serious - although she worries that could prove fatal for such a small fragile baby.

Cate grunts and groans her way back up to the car after what seems like an eternity and manages to open the front passenger door, this time, carefully kneeling on a narrow strip of solid ground. The angle of the car, is sitting higher on this side and the door swings shut again. She needs something to wedge it open. She crawls to the rear of the car and feels around the ground, picking up and discarding pieces of wood that aren't suitable until eventually she finds a solid large 'y' shaped branch. The enveloping darkness of the trees makes her sightless. Looking up she can barely see the night sky. If there is much of a moon tonight, its light is certainly not shining down here, she thinks. The ground she is kneeling on is wet. Her trousers are soaked through and she can smell petrol. She believes the petrol tank is punctured and is leaking down across the rear of the car on the driver's side. Thank god, the petrol tank is almost empty she thinks. It still concerns Cate that something might spark a fire, like you see in the movies.

Shoving the branch along in front of her she makes it back to the front passenger door and this time manages to wedge it open just enough to reach across to the upside down glove compartment. The interior light has come on again. The car rocks forward a little, but Cate thinks it will hold. Marco is silent and she thinks he must have passed out with the pain, but just as she opens the glove compartment she hears him mutter, 'Good work Cate. See how Milo is. Try the mobile as well. There might be a signal.' She looks up and can see that Marco is wedged tightly by a large thick branch between him and the steering wheel. He cannot move his arms but he turns his head and looks at her. She can see he is struggling with pain, but doing his best to put a brave front on it.

A jumble of items tumble out of the glove compartment along with the car manual. Cate can just about see with the interior light but she cannot see a torch. She moves everything around again until she finds what she believes may be the torch and is disappointed to realise it's very slim and small. The batteries won't last long, she thinks, with this titchy thing! The torch won't switch on when she presses the button so she shakes it, loosens and tightens the mechanism and it finally comes on. She spots Marco's work mobile phone lying on the ceiling next to him. She reaches across for it and eases back out of the car towards the rear passenger door. The torch shows a series of scrapes along the passenger side. From where we hit the barricade, she thinks.

'How do I turn the phone on Marco?' she asks him, realising she's never used a mobile before. They had been talking about buying one for her for months, but there always seemed to be other priorities to spend their money on.

'There's an arc that's supposed to represent a phone with a circle under it on the right hand side of the phone. Press it down and hold it for a few seconds.'

She follows his instructions and sees it light up. 'It's come on,' she tells him excitedly, 'I can call for help. How do I make a call?'

'See if there's a signal first. If there is it will be showing little bars in the top left of the screen.'

'There's nothing there.'

'Okay. Thought not. No signal. We're too far away from the phone tower. And too deep down this ravine.'

'Does that mean I can't use it?'

'You can't if there's no signal.'

'What use is the bloody thing then if you can't make a call?' Cate says in frustration.

She opens the rear door and crawls across to Milo shining the torch onto him. She has to swivel her head to see him properly. She can see his little chest rising and falling and small glass cuts on his arms, legs and face. 'Milo's alive Marco. I think he's alright apart from a few cuts. But he's hanging upside down. Should I release his car seat and place it so he is level?' she asks panicking. More than anything she wants to unclip him and hold him in her arms.

'No! You shouldn't move him. We don't know what his injuries are. Something smashed through Milo's window didn't it?'

'Yes, something hit me hard in the jaw and I have a piece of branch embedded in my shoulder. I don't know if it hit him though. Surely it can't be good for him to be upside down though. All the blood would be rushing to his head wouldn't it – like it does when you do a head stand.'

'You're not supposed to touch people who have received injuries Cate, you should know that.'

'But Marco ….'

'Look Cate, I know you've been hurt as well, but as you are the only one of us who is mobile, do you think you can climb back up to the road? You're the only one who can do it. We need help. And soon. I'm sorry I can't help you. And I'm sorry I got us into this mess.'

'It's not your fault Marco. It was that ….'

'No. I should've done what you wanted and left while it was still light.'

'There's no point in thinking like that Marco. You didn't cause this.'

There's no possibility of Cate freeing Marco and she would not even attempt to for fear of causing further damage, as he said. She doesn't know what to do about Milo. Should she listen to Marco and leave him as he is? Her instincts tell her otherwise. But perhaps Marco's right.

'I'll give it a go at climbing up to the road Marco, but I think my left leg is badly broken below the knee so I don't know if I can manage it. I'll have to try and make some sort of splint for it.'

'Right. Do…that… first.' She can hear through Marco's breathy efforts to speak that he must have serious chest injuries. And he sounds distressed. The sooner she brings help the sooner he can be released.

Cate pulls Milo's bag towards her and unzips it. She takes out some of his disposable nappies thinking they might make a good first padding for her injured leg. She has to rip the bottom of her trousers to get to her leg, which she can see is beginning to swell badly and is a funny shape. Undoing some nappies she wraps several of them around her leg. Each touch is agonisingly painful which makes the whole process very slow. Next she needs some timber. Crawling back out of the car she pulls herself up and hops around the rear of the car scanning the torch across the ground looking for solid strips of wood. She picks up and discards several pieces. There is nothing that seems suitable. Eventually she decides she will have to use several thin bits of branches and tie them together around the nappies. What to tie them with though? She remembers she saw some brown parcel tape amongst the items from the glove compartment. Probably left over from their move. She crawls back to the front passenger door that is still wedged open and grabs the tape.

'How's …it going Cate?' Marco asks.

'I've found some thick twigs which I'm going to try and hold around my leg with this parcel tape. I don't know if they will hold. Be back in a minute.'

She eases back out and sets about fixing the twigs. Some she has difficulty breaking to the right size, but eventually she has sufficient. She winds the tape carefully over the first stick, then adds the second until they are all in place, finally winding the tape around them all again several times. She has to unwind even more tape to break it with her teeth and then wraps this surplus around her leg. She's hoping, with the padding of the nappies and the splint it will ease the pain for her climb to the top. She's ready to go, but first must see if she can do anything to make Marco and Milo more comfortable. She rolls over and eases herself up using the rear of the car for support and hops along to the back seats. She reaches in and places Milo's travel bag underneath his head for support in case his baby seat moves. She tips some water from a bottle she had in the back for the journey on to her hands and rubs it gently around his mouth. She runs her hand across Milo's head and savours the warmth of his little body. She then touches his arm and eases back out to move to the front again. She finds Marco's water bottle and offers him some. It is awkward to reach him and difficult for him to drink dangling upside down and most of it dribbles down his face to his head.

'Sokay darling. I'll be alright. You need to get going and just get us help as quick as you can. And take the mobile, you might get a signal up on the road. Listen if I don't make it you must go to my office and ask Anna for the tape I left a message about.'

'What tape are you talking about?'

'No time. Cate …..just promise me you'll do it.'

'Yes, of course but you'll be fine, don't worry. Just stay positive. I'll be back with help as soon as I can.' Cate says doing her best to sound convincing. She's not at all sure he will be fine, but there's always hope. Cate can't kiss him without disturbing the branch so she reaches out and touches his cheek with the kiss of two fingers. She doesn't want to leave either of them, but knows she must. Before crawling out of the car, Cate grabs Marco's lightweight jacket and the remains of his bottle of water. Despite the heat she puts the jacket on and shoves the water bottle in the large side pocket and the mobile in the other pocket. She knows she is going to need water. Already feeling dehydrated in the heat, she is tempted to swig the whole lot down, but knows she must use it sparingly.

Unable to place weight on her left leg she hops around to the driver's side of the car and shines the torch down its length from the rear. The twisted metal marks the journey of their descent and she can see the large branch that has Marco imprisoned protruding through his window. Tears slide down her cheeks. He must be in so much pain, she thinks.

Shining the torch up the gully Cate can see they dropped have a hell of a long way down. She just hopes she can make it up there or no one will ever find them. She is thankful she changed from her shorts into trousers for the journey home, knowing it's going to be hell for her knees as she will need to crawl much of the way with her damaged leg.

With the torch held between her teeth she hops over to an area that looks promising for an easier climb, drops to her knees and begins to crawl, singing a slow mantra in her head *I, can, do, this, I, can, do, this, I, can, do, this,* over and over. The pain and exertion begin to take their toll. Even her jaw hurts from holding the torch with her teeth and from whatever hit her earlier. To distract herself she loudly groans out the mantra *Icandothis, Icandothis,* the words becoming jumbled and distorted with the torch blocking her mouth. It makes her forget about the pain and, at one point, she even has to stop for a moment and remove the torch for fear of dropping it when she begins to laugh at how ridiculous she must sound and look. If there was anyone to see her! She had been hearing her weird sounds echoing around her. In a way it is comforting and makes her feel less alone. *Right get yourself together Rossi, Marco and Milo need you to do this. I need you to do this,* she thinks and moves on. There are times when she has to stand and pull herself up over rocks as there is no way to crawl around them. After what seems like hours she stops to rest, takes a sip of water and turns off the torch to save the battery. The torch's light is becoming increasingly dim and she will need it for the rest of the climb. She closes her eyes for just a minute, but must have dozed off because when she next opens her eyes she can see the first stages of daylight peeping through the top of the trees.

Panicking that she has been asleep too long she turns to start the weary climb again and drops the torch. She hears it clatter down into the gulley and knows she has to carry on without it. At least she can see a little bit more now. By the time Cate makes it to the road at the top the sun has come up. After climbing over the barrier she collapses by the verge, takes her final sip of water and lays down crying. She's made it, she just hopes there will be traffic along the road soon. She remembers the mobile, sits up and takes it out of her pocket. The screen has gone black again. She holds the button Marco told her about and it lights up then switches itself off again. *What?* She presses it hard again and the light comes back on. There are still no signal bars. 'Bloody useless thing,' she tells it before pocketing it again.

It feels like almost every part of her body has been bruised and injured; she doesn't think she can move any further. She's feeling feverish, but is shaking as though she is cold.

Cate can hear the rumble of what sounds like a large

vehicle chugging up the hill. She attempts to pull herself up ready to wave it down but can't get to her feet and collapses again. She cries in frustration, this might be her only chance for another few hours!

She needn't have worried as the driver has seen her. He pulls over, jumps out and runs over to her.

'What's happened Missus?' he asks in concern.

'Our car was forced off the road last night. We went down into the ravine. My husband and baby are down there, trapped in the car. My husband is badly injured, I'm not sure about my son. He's been unconscious since the accident, although I could see that he's still alive. Could you take me somewhere to get some help please? We'll need ambulances, fire brigade or rescue services as my husband is trapped, and of course the police.'

'You don't look too good yourself Missus. I'll call it in on my CB. That'll bring help.' He returns to his cab, makes his calls then brings some food and drink out of his cab to Cate.

'I've got a sarnie here if you'd like one. Also some lemonade.'

'I'd love a drink of lemonade thank you, but I don't think I could eat anything.' He hands Cate his bottle of lemonade and she glugs from it greedily. Just the sugar hit she needs, she thinks. 'Do you know what the time is? I forgot to put my watch on when we left home, so I've no idea what time it is, except that it's early morning?'

'It's 6.10am. What time did the accident happen?'

'I don't know. About 11ish. Oh God so Marco and Milo have been lying there without help for more than seven hours,' Cate sobs. 'It was ages before I began the climb. I also stopped to rest for a moment at one point and dozed off. I must have been asleep longer than I thought or it just took hours.'

'So you say you were run off the road? What happened?'

'It was probably two different cars, I'm not sure. First of all, someone sideswiped us into the barrier when they were overtaking on our way to Windsor. Then a few miles further up the road a car came around a bend from the opposite direction heading straight at us – on our side of the road - lights on full beam. The light blinded Marco, my husband, who was driving. At the last minute the car swerved out of our way and then we were suddenly …….' Cate pauses sobbing. 'We crashed down into the ravine. It was back down there a bit I think.' Cate points down the hill towards a bend.

'I noticed there was a gap in the railings on the bend. I can't remember it bein' like that the last time I drove through here, a few days ago. Stone the crows, Missus, that's a long bloody drop down there.'

'I know. We're not completely at the bottom. The car's wedged on a large rock overhanging a stream.' I don't know if the stream is at the bottom either. I couldn't see in the dark.'

'Judgin' by the holes in your knees it looks like you crawled all the way back up here - in your state? I would say it would have taken several hours to do that.'

'My husband couldn't do it, he is too injured. He's wedged in by a large thick branch. I was the only one that could do it.'

'How old's the littlie?'

'He's ten weeks and five days old.'

'Jeesus Missus. I hope everthin's alright with him.'

'Me too. Me too,' Cate starts to cry again and wipes her brow with the sleeve of the jacket. She is feeling feverish again. Embarrassed, the driver turns away and says, 'I'll just go and call me mates and have a smoko. See what's happening. Would you like a ciggie?'

Unable to speak, Cate just shakes her head negatively.

Within 30 minutes several ambulances, police cars and rescue services arrive. One long stretch of the road on the ravine side is blocked off with temporary traffic lights. The semi-trailer driver gives his details to the police and Cate can see him pointing down the hill at the spot she thought they had gone over. He is then asked to move his vehicle. The driver waves farewell to Cate before he climbs into his cab and drives off.

Cate briefly explains what happened to the police and rescue services, plus she tells them about the state of the car with the leaking petrol, how her husband is trapped and how Milo has been since the accident. She asks if she can remain until they bring them both up, but with one look at her swollen face, her temperature and other injuries, the paramedics insist she needs to go to hospital immediately.

# 24

**Yorkshire Dales, April 2000**

On her Tuesday afternoon off from the café, Cate drives out through the Dales. She finds a picturesque remote spot, parks the car and sets off on her first walk following public footpaths. Alone, with no other matters clouding her thoughts, her mind becomes absorbed with memories of her loved ones. She alternatively laughs and then cries at anecdotal incidents involving Marco and/or Milo. Like the first time Marco volunteered to change Milo's nappy. The moment Marco removed the nappy, Milo let forth a stream of urine that arced beautifully to hit Marco fully in the face. She'd laughed her head off at this at the time, but realised she should have warned him of the possibility. She always covered Milo with a piece of towelling as she was changing him, just in case.

Pain builds in her chest and stomach becoming overwhelming and she stops under a tree near an outcrop of rocks, doubles over and drops to the ground and begins to wail with heart-wrenching sobs. Her wails turn to anger. 'Why?' she cries out. She stands and shouts this to the tree, the sky and the rocks as though they might provide some answers for her. She screams in rage shouting 'NO!' over and over again. Her voice echoes across the valley and flies back to her. The anger she has released seems to have created a healing energy that soars through her. It flows down to her feet and she walks over to sit on a rock and looks calmly about her. The place is beautiful and she imagines Marco and Milo with her at this moment. She doesn't feel alone. This is the first time she has been able to really let go and allow her grief to be freely expressed. At the hospital and rehab unit there were always people around her, staff, family, friends, or the police. She just shut down there, swallowed her sorrow but it was constantly bubbling away below the surface waiting to be released.

An hour passes peacefully and Cate decides to head back. It hasn't been a long walk, but enough. She notices her leg is not so bad this afternoon. Perhaps her wailing has released some of that pain too, she thinks, hopefully.

Alan Mathers, a retired psychologist, witnesses the private grief of the young woman. Living nearby, he regularly walks the dales for his daily constitutional. He notices the young woman stop under the tree and appear to collapse. He initially thought she was hurt and was about to rush over to her when he realises that she is sobbing. He then hears her cries questioning 'why?' and realises this is a young woman in grief. It is not something he wishes to intrude on. He turns to retrace his steps when he hears her scream. He pauses again and looks down at the young woman. No she seems fine. It was not his place to interfere so he heads home. He wishes he still had Bessie, his beloved Dalmatian trotting along beside him, but she had passed away just a few months ago. Maybe it's a good thing Bessie wasn't with him, as she would have certainly barked, disturbing the privacy of the moment.

Two weeks later he spots the same young woman heading down to the tree where he had previously seen her. She walks with an awkward gait, limping, and wonders what happened to her. He turns and takes a different route for his walk, unsure of her intentions today. As he proceeds the sky turns menacingly dark, the wind suddenly picks up and it looks as if it is going to rain any second. He turns back. Sure enough within minutes the heavens open up and thunder roars across the sky followed by lightning streaks. Head down, he dashes back towards his house, but then remembers the young woman. Surely she has gone home? He decides he must check before seeking the safety of his home. When he reaches the rise, where he saw the young woman heading down towards the tree and outcrop of rocks, he stops and looks. Visibility is poor with the heavy rain, but he is certain he can see a figure on the ground. She must be injured he thinks and makes his way down the hill to find the woman lying prostrate, her arms stretched out by her sides. Her face is towards the ground and he can see now she is conscious and seems to be sobbing. His attempts to speak to her are drowned out by a deafening clap of thunder followed by another streak of lightning that seems unnervingly close. He can't leave her here and he bends down, gathers her in his arms, and turns back towards his house. She is light as a feather and her clothes are soaking wet, not unlike his, but at least he has a warm protecting jacket, whereas she is clad in just a jumper.

'You can't stay out here in this storm, it's dangerous,' he shouts in her ear. He meets neither resistance from her body or verbal response and wonders if she can hear him or is in some kind of trance. He won't be able to carry her all the way back to his place. At some point he is going to have to put her down. About a hundred yards further on he has to stop. He lowers her to her feet and shouts in her ear, 'You will have to walk the rest of the way. It's not far to my house. We need to find shelter fast. Are you going to manage?'

The woman looks at him, her face covered in tear-streaked mud and remains silent. Keeping his arm around her shoulder he half drags, half walks her back to his house. When they reach the safety of his hallway he turns to her and says, 'What the hell were you thinking, staying out in that storm. Do you not realise how dangerous it is out on the dales when there is lightning?'

She just looks at him in mute silence. 'Look you need to get these wet clothes off and have a hot shower. You can put some of my wife's clothes on afterwards. They will be a little too large for you but at least they will be dry. Can you take your shoes off and follow me upstairs?' She nods. Finally, some response.

He shows her the bathroom and collects a clean towel and some clothes that might be suitable for her to wear. 'Come back downstairs when you have finished. I'll be in the living room and then I'll make us both a hot drink. Okay? I'm Alan by the way. What is your name?'

'Cate,' she whispers. He nods and walks away to his bedroom, takes off his wet clothes and takes a hot shower in his own bathroom.

Twenty minutes later the woman finds her way to the living room.

'I'm sorry if I've caused you any concern,' she says. 'I hadn't realised how bad the storm was. How did you know I was there?'

'I saw you heading down towards the tree when I was on my walk. When I noticed the storm brewing and hurried back home I thought I ought to check that you had

had the sense to leave.'

'But I hadn't. Thank you.'

'Now, would you like a nice hot drink?' he says standing. 'Tea, coffee, hot chocolate? Come and sit by the wood-burner.'

'I'd love a cup of tea thank you,' Cate replies moving across the room to a chair opposite where he has been sitting.

Alan returns a few minutes later laden with a tray of hot drinks, a bowl of sugar, a little jug of milk and a plate of various biscuits. He finds the woman standing at the French doors looking onto the garden.

'What a lovely spot you have here. It's beautiful.'

'Yes, my wife and I fell in love with the place as soon as we laid eyes on it. We just had to have it. It is almost twenty five years since we moved up here.'

'Where did you move from?'

'Lancaster. My wife found it difficult to remain there after the death of our son. She wanted to move somewhere with wide open spaces and peace and quiet.'

'You say the death of your son, he must have been young if you moved here 25 years ago.'

'He was young. Just turned 20. He foolishly joined the army, running away from his responsibilities when he was 19. He was posted to Northern Ireland and was killed just as his tour of duty was coming to an end. He'd left behind a pregnant girlfriend. Our only grandchild. Well she's not a child anymore, she's a young woman of 25 - and she is married and expecting her first child now, so I will be a great grandfather soon.'

'So you didn't have any other children?'

Alan turns and looks into the fire. No, he wasn't their only child. Should he say anything?

'I'm sorry I'm being too intrusive.'

'No,' he says. 'It was a long time ago now. We had a little girl as well. Rosie. She died when she was seven of leukaemia. She was two years younger than our son Brian.'

'So you know a lot about loss then, with the devastation of losing both your children.'

'Yes. And my wife 15 months ago. And my dog Bessie just a few months back.'

He can see her turning pale. She looks down at the clothes she is wearing and he wonders if she is thinking 'dead woman's clothes.'

'Oh my God. So much loss. How have you coped?'

No, she wants to know how I coped because she is struggling, he thinks. She hasn't asked about what happened to Sylvia. Not that I've mentioned Sylvia's name, he realises.

'With difficulty at times,' he says cautiously, not knowing who it is she has been grieving for. 'And what about you?'

'What do you mean?'

'Who are you grieving for?'

'How do you know that I am?'

'Well the state of you today out in that storm has given me a bit of a clue, and I saw you up there in distress a few weeks ago. That was a Tuesday as well.'

'Yes, one of the days that I have off from work.'

He remains silent. And notices that she hasn't answered his question. After a few minutes she finally begins talking.

# 25

## Windsor, New South Wales, December 1999

DC India Hargreaves walks into the lounge of her parents' house at Windsor. She'd arrived last night to dine with her family for the first time since her hectic Christmas duties. It's the morning of New Year's Eve and she is having a rare day relaxing when she notices the headlines from yesterday's weekly edition of the local paper sitting on the coffee table. The front page is dedicated to an accident that happened on the Putty Road last Monday. She had seen it on the news but at that point no names had been released. Out of curiosity she picks up the paper and reads the article, shocked at its contents. She grabs her bag, car keys and tells her parents she needs to go out urgently.

At the Windsor Police Station she asks to see whoever is in charge of the Putty Road accident. A DI Rob Ellis comes out to meet her. She shows him her ID badge and asks if she can have a quiet word. He takes her through to his office, offering her a coffee which she declines. When he asks her what she wants to discuss with him, she says, 'It's about Cate Rossi, one of the victims of the Putty Road incident last Monday. I believe I have some information that is relevant, if what has been printed in the local paper is true.'

'Well, we all know what the papers are like and how they like to sensationalise things don't we?'

'Have you spoken to Cate Rossi?' she asks.

'I spoke to her for a short time at the scene, but she hasn't been in much of a state to talk to since she was admitted to hospital. I was called out to the scene as the message that came in said it wasn't a straightforward RTA. Her injuries were quite serious, although she didn't seem to be aware of it at the scene. Wanted to wait until her husband and son were rescued. Good thing that didn't happen or she might not have made it.'

'Right. What were the extent of her injuries? The paper didn't say. Just that she received 'serious' injuries.'

'She required two operations – one for a serious leg injury and one to remove the remains of a branch embedded in her shoulder. She had a minor mandible break, but they haven't operated on that. Just bandaged her up. She also had many cuts from glass breaking in the car windows and she accumulated other gashes and bruises from crawling over stones. They managed to save her leg though.'

'So just minor things then,' India says drily. 'God, how on earth did she crawl back up to the road with all those injuries?'

'She urgently wanted to get help for her son and husband. Her husband was trapped and the baby unconscious.'

'Yes, I can see how she would have been desperate. Look there's a number of things you need to know that might help your investigation. And I think Cate Rossi needs protection.'

India Hargreaves can tell from his raised eyebrows that this surprises DI Ellis. She launches into detail, explaining everything about DI Joe Paramo and his investigation linked to Cate Rossi, including her own findings following Joe Paramo's sudden death. She explains why she doesn't believe Joe Paramo's death was a suicide. She informs him that Cate Rossi's stepmother also had a fatal fall at the

Brant home and died just five days after Joe Paramo and how she now believes it was no accident. 'Now this,' she says, 'and god knows what else has been going on. I think the murderer somehow knows everything. Maybe there were things Joe Paramo discovered but never wrote down. I believe that is why he was killed and why the Rossi car was run off the road.'

DI Rob Ellis whistles. 'Wow that is really taking conspiracy theories to the limit.'

'You don't believe me?' DI Hargreaves challenges him.

'No I believe you. Well I believe that *you* believe every word of it anyway. The body count is certainly mounting, if what you say is true. Two murders in Melbourne and possibly more in the Sydney area, all by the same man with a nineteen year gap.'

'It *is* true, for god's sake. For all we know there might have been many more deaths in the intervening years that we don't know about as well. But the man clearly thought he had got away with the Melbourne murders and then Cate Rossi and Joe Paramo become a thorn in his side almost nineteen years later. Somehow he finds out about it and starts killing again. Are you telling me you are not going to take it seriously?'

'That's the key question though. How did he find out about DI Paramo's investigation?'

'I don't know. Joe Paramo left work fairly early on the day he died. He didn't go to the bar that he normally goes to after work. Perhaps he went investigating further and had an encounter with this man, who later killed him.'

'If you think this man was behind the Putty Road accident, tell me how he could have set that up? How would he know they were going to be on that road?'

'I don't know. Followed them? Bugged their home?

Weren't they run off the road?'

'It would appear so from what Mrs. Rossi told us at the scene and what the semi driver told us that she had told him. But there were two vehicles involved in two separate incidents. It could have simply been a case of drunk drivers.'

'It could have been that, but I don't think so. The papers said the second car drove at them with high beam lights on. They wouldn't have been able to see what type of car it was. Or see if it was red like the first car that hit them.'

'Mmm. That's true. So why didn't he kill Cate Rossi straight away? She would be his main problem.'

'She was at the hospital with her baby for several weeks. She moved house. Perhaps he didn't know where she moved to, and then later found out. He might have made an attempt on her life before this – perhaps without her realising. You need to ask her.'

'As I told you she is not in any condition to talk to anyone right now.'

'So, what have you discovered with your enquiry so far?'

'I'm not really sure it's appropriate for me to be discussing that with you.'

'Why not? It's not as if I am a member of the public. I'm police as well.'

'Alright, I will tell you that a section of the metal barrier fence was mysteriously removed some time in the few days prior to the accident. Exactly where the accident occurred. No one knows how that happened. Our enquiries have revealed that it wasn't done officially. You can see it has been cut rather roughshod with some sort of electric tool. We have appealed for witnesses to come forward but so far there has been no response. The semi driver told us that there was no gap in the barrier when he last drove up there – just over a week ago, and he is sure the gap was not there when he drove home to Singleton on Christmas Eve.'

'I read your appeal in the local paper. Although it was quite discreetly worded so as to not panic the public I noticed. What you've told me is another tick towards my conspiracy theory.'

'Yes. Look, this is not the first I've heard about everything you've told me. Although you have put a new slant on it. Mrs. Rossi's father has been in here making similar claims and asking for protection for his daughter. He doesn't suspect his wife's death is linked though. Unlike you.'

'So why did you act all surprised and then let me take you through everything I said without mentioning that?'

'I was surprised at your opening statement to me. Then I wanted to hear what your perspective on it was.'

'So you are taking it seriously then?'

'I wouldn't go that far.'

'So what are you going to do?'

'I will look into everything you have said. As I told Mr. Brant. I have contacted Melbourne regarding the murder of Cate Rossi's mother in 1980. I'm still waiting for their reply. It is a difficult time of the year to be gathering information. I will contact your DCI and find out what he has to say about your old DI.'

'I don't want my DCI knowing that I have all the information on Joe Paramo's investigation. He went to the DCI and look what happened to Joe.'

'Are you suggesting that he is involved in this somehow?'

'No I'm not. Not directly anyway. The DCI is no murderer. But he could have innocently passed on information that filtered through to someone who was. He is a practising Catholic and there is a bishop who seems to know the potential killer. Not that I'm suggesting the bishop knows he is a killer. He probably has no idea about the man he calls Jim Beam or JB either. The DCI is also neurotic about his budget. He seems to be convinced that DI Paramo committed suicide and won't spend the money to look into it further. Sure Joe was cut up about his wife leaving with the kids. Sure he'd become a heavy drinker in his last six months. But he was not depressed about it all, more pissed off that she received the bulk of the money from their house sale and that she had custody of the kids and moved them a long distance away, when she was the one having the affair. I think he was just lonely really. He never drank on duty. He was a bloody good detective. He doesn't deserve to have his death recorded as a suicide.'

'Were you involved with him?'

'You mean romantically? Sexually? Absolutely not. He was my DI for two years. I greatly admired and respected him. That's all.'

'Fair enough.'

'Do you want a copy of the file I have that DI Paramo created? It's not at work. I have it at home, but not with me today. My parents live up here and I was visiting them today when I spotted the article in the local paper.'

'Yes, I would like a copy of the file. Thank you. So you're from around here then?'

'Yeah, born and bred. Look can I have your assurance that you won't tell my DCI about my involvement in it? I've put in for a transfer and if he knew he might cancel it and discipline me.'

'If that's what you want. I wouldn't like to see your pretty life come to an end,' he says grinning.

'It's no joking matter! You need to be careful as well.'

'Oh I intend to be. Was there anything else?'

'I thought I might go and visit Cate Rossi – that's if you don't mind. I have had contact with her before and she said she might come and see me.'

'Righto that's fine. Let me know if anything comes of it. I suspect she won't be in a mood for talking though. I couldn't get anything out of her when I saw her yesterday and I suspect it will be even tougher to get her talking today.'

'Okay, I'll get back to you if I learn anything. Thanks for your time DI Ellis.'

'Call me Rob.'

'Okay thanks Rob. I'd say call me India, but most of the males I work with seem to have a problem with my name.'

'I don't. I think your name suits you and it's kind of ironic isn't it?

'What is?'

'That when you think of women from India you tend to associate them with brown skin, dark hair and big dark eyes. You're the antithesis having fair skin, blonde hair and small blue eyes.'

'Small blue eyes?'

'Sorry, I didn't explain that very well. Your actual eyes aren't small. But they seem to be slotted perfectly into your face with no 'lids' showing, unless of course you shut your eyes. Most Indian women I've met have large lids showing.' He pauses for a minute and then adds 'Ah. I can see by your face that I ought to shut up now.'

'Might be best. I do know what you mean though. I hardly ever put eye shadow on because you can't see it with my lids. Unless I close them of course.'

'Glad we got that sorted out. Do you fancy going out for a drink sometime?'

# 26

**Yorkshire Dales, April 2000**

'My husband and baby son died in a car crash we were involved in last December. I was the only survivor. I spent a few months first in hospital and then in a rehabilitation unit following the crash. My stepmother died just a short time before that as well.'

'How old was your son?'

'Ten weeks and five days old. He'd barely lived any kind of life before he was snatched away.'

'So you're suffering from survivor's guilt as well as grieving. Oh I know all about that.'

'I'm sure you do.'

'How did the accident happen?'

'It wasn't an accident. It was murder.' And she pours out her whole story. From the murder of her mother in 1980 to the sighting of the 'murderer' last year followed by the recent spate of deaths. And all of those deaths possibly linked to her mother's murderer. It's a story that shocks him and he can see why she carries the weight of guilt, sorrow and anger. He can hear it all in her voice. When she has finished he makes a few appropriate comments and then decides he needs to steer her thoughts away from events in Australia for the moment.

'So ...why did you come to our little corner of Yorkshire, all the way from Sydney?'

'My mother was born in Hawes. Her family emigrated to Australia when she was a young girl. We visited Hawes briefly when I was sixteen - our family lived in London from 1987-1991. I thought it was beautiful and always wanted to return one day. I had hoped to find some of my mother's family here one day, but I haven't looked as yet. I've been a little preoccupied with work and well… you know. I had to leave Australia because I didn't want to put any other members of my family at risk. Also my life was in danger.'

'Yes, it probably was, given all that you've told me. I can understand why you would want to leave. But you bring all the memories and emotions with you. My wife realised that when we moved here. She said she at least had some breathing space here though and she found the Dales provided a healing environment.'

'Yes, I'm finding that as well. I'm finally able to grieve. I was just numb after the crash, I didn't really want to live. I didn't care much about anything.'

'And now?'

'Now what?'

'How do you feel about living now?'

'I find I do want to live now. We had so many plans. Marco and I. I can't do any of those things with him now, but I can do other things. I don't know that I will ever *get over* Milo's death. I don't know that I want to. My friends in Sydney kept telling me that "I had to move forward," or "move on with my life," after Marco and Milo's death – "to get over it". As though they were both obstacles I had to remove in order to do so. I can't do that, it would be like denying their existence. But I can continue living and take pleasure in things. Not just existing. And remember them with love.'

'I don't think we ever 'get over' the death of one of our

children. We learn to continue living without them. Or not. Some people are unable to.'

'Did your wife manage to? What was her name by the way?'

'Sylvia. Yes, Sylvia did manage to eventually. She was dealing with the living on a daily basis so was forced to in a sense. She was a qualified GP and began working in a practice in town which she took over some years later when the senior GP died.'

'Not the one on the North side?'

'Yes that's the one.'

'I've just registered there.'

'It's an excellent practice, although my wife was not popular when she brought in a couple of Asian doctors some years back. Mind you one of them was born in Bradford and has a broad Yorkshire accent. The dust has settled now and everyone who attends the practice seems fine about being treated by doctors from other cultures.'

'I think the initial reaction to them was probably just through ignorance. People from small rural towns wouldn't have much experience of living in a multi-cultural society like those who live in big cities such as London or Manchester. Unless they had lived in a city themselves at some point. So I imagine it might be fear of the unknown. And it's possibly a hangover from the Empire nonsense when Britain ruled over countries like India, Australia and others on the African continent. Back in those days, which is still in the living memory of many people in Britain, Britain ruled the waves. They were the superior beings. Therefore all the people from the other countries were inferior. Load of bloody nonsense. I experienced a bit of that type of snobbery against Australians when we lived in London before. Especially at the private school

I first attended for a short time. Some of the kids were so ignorant. They even thought there were kangaroos hopping down the street everywhere.'

'Oh and here was me thinking the same.'

Cate looks at him with uncertainty, not sure if he is serious. He holds his face completely straight for a moment before breaking into a smile.

'Just kidding. Yes, you're right, it is ignorance. A fear of the unknown as you say. And sheer snobbery. We British can be quite good at that.'

'Many Australians are pretty good at snobbery as well, believe me. My stepmother was particularly skilled at it.'

'You haven't mentioned any brothers or sisters. Did your stepmother not have any children?'

'Oh didn't I say? Yes I have a sister – also called Rosie. She's four years younger than me – well three years and seven months to be more precise. Her mother brought me up after my mother's death. Janet her name was, the one who died in suspicious circumstances less than a week after Milo's birth.'

'So you've lost two mothers in your life.'

'Yes.'

They both sit and stare into the comfort of the fire, alone with their thoughts. Finally a rumble in his stomach reminds Alan that he didn't eat much for lunch.

'I'm about to make myself a meal. Would you like to join me?'

'I really should be getting back. I don't want to put you to any trouble.'

'It's no trouble at all. When I cook a meal I cook enough to last for four meals usually. I might eat the same thing for two nights in a row and then freeze two other portions so that I don't have to cook every night. It would make a change to have company.'

'What's on your menu tonight?'

'I was going to cook beef chilli con carne. I like it with sour cream and cheese over a jacket potato. With a little side salad. How does that sound? If you don't like the sound of that I could always do something different.'

'That's just how I like chilli! Marco thought I was strange having it like that. He always wanted it served over rice and wouldn't have the sour cream or cheese with it either. So usually when I cooked it I had to do rice for him and a jacket potato for me.'

'That's settles it then. You're staying. You said it was your day off and so I would also assume you'd be returning home to eat alone. Come into the kitchen while I'm cooking and you can tell me all about your new job.'

It was while Alan was cooking that Cate asks him quietly what happened to Sylvia, assuring him if he doesn't want to talk about it she understands.

'It's okay. I can talk about it now without falling apart. She died in a car accident. In her case it *was* an accident though. She was on her way home from the surgery one night during a very cold spell. The roads out here aren't gritted very often and can be treacherous in the winter months. Her car skidded on some black ice and went over an embankment. The impact killed her instantly I was told - which was one small mercy – if it was true. However, she lay out there for several hours, undiscovered, so I thought how can they can positively know that she was killed outright? I tortured myself, just as I imagine you have done, with thoughts of her lying there dying alone, in the freezing cold and no one to comfort her. I was working in Richmond that day and arrived home later that night to find the road blocked by the police. That's how I found out.'

Cate nods her head in empathy and he can see she is fighting back tears.

'It's alright. I've stopped torturing myself now,' he says. 'The thing is I don't *know* whether she was alive for any time after the crash, so I decided I was torturing myself with unknown facts – something that I will never absolutely know. Eventually I accepted the medical examiner's statement that she was killed outright and that probably was true. It's pointless causing yourself additional pain about something you can never know.'

'Yes, I think I understand what you are saying. And you're right. I have been torturing myself with things I don't know the answer to as well. How long did Marco and Milo live after I left them to get help? Did Milo feel me touching him? Was he aware of anything? The doctors say he wouldn't have been. If I had known how serious his injuries were I would have stayed with him, released him from his baby chair and held him. Marco insisted that I should leave him where he was in case I made his injuries worse. He wanted me to get help and, of course, there was always the possibility that with help both of them would have survived. But they didn't and I didn't get to hold my baby ever again. Or see either of them again. By the time I regained consciousness after my operations and was able to communicate sensibly or absorb any information, it was several days later and both of them had been buried. Marco's parents decided they couldn't wait for me to be able to attend their funeral as the doctors told my family that my physical condition would prevent me from getting out of bed for many weeks. Their bodies were released for burial and so the funeral was organised quickly.'

'God I would have been livid if someone did that to

me.'

'I was initially. And I still feel angry when I think about it. But I understand why Marco's mother did it.'

He nods and begins busying himself with the food preparation while she sits on a stool at the breakfast counter. From what he can make out from the tragic story of her mother's murder up to her husband and son's death, she must be in her mid-20s. About the same age as his granddaughter. For someone so young she has experienced a great deal of tragedy. No wonder she is in such a state. He would like to help her if she will allow it.

'Would you like a glass of wine? I'm opening a bottle. Can't have chilli con carne without a glass of red. Or perhaps you don't drink red?'

'No I do. Just not that frequently. I could have half a glass as I will be driving. Thank you.'

'I don't think you should be driving in this weather. In case you hadn't noticed, the storm hasn't abated at all. If anything it has become worse. Why don't you stay the night? We have several spare rooms upstairs. You'd be doing me a favour, providing me with some company.'

Cate looks at him, clearly weighing up whether it is safe to spend the night in a stranger's house. Should he give her re-assurances? No, let her judge him on her own instincts. She climbs down from the stool, limps over to the French doors past the dining table and looks out at the storm for a minute.

'It does look very wild out there. And a little frightening. If you're sure, I'd be happy to stay.'

'Very sure. Now that's settled, you can have a *large* glass of red wine.'

# 27

### Windsor, New South Wales, December 1999

At the hospital DC India Hargreaves discovers that Cate Rossi has been placed in a small private room. There is a male police officer stationed outside her door. *So he has taken it seriously!* She holds up her badge to the uniformed officer. Without speaking he stands, nods and waves her in through the door he has opened for her. She finds Cate Rossi lying immobile, her jaw bandaged up, one leg raised on a small platform and she can see she has dressings on her right shoulder plus visible stitched cuts on various parts of her body. She quietly approaches the bed and introduces herself.

'Hello Mrs. Rossi. I'm DC India Hargreaves. We spoke on the phone a few months ago when you rang to speak to DI Paramo. Do you remember speaking to me?' Silence.

'I'm so very sorry to hear about the deaths of your son Milo and husband Marco,' DC Hargreaves says speaking quietly. *God this is so hard!*

Cate Rossi turns her head to look out the window. She doesn't acknowledge DC Hargreaves.

'I am currently up in Windsor visiting my parents, and I read about the crash you had earlier in the week in the local newspaper. I thought it was important to come and see you, given what's happened.' Still no acknowledgement.

'I've been to the local police and met the DI who

is investigating your accident and passed on what information I have. I carried on looking into DI Paramo's case as much as I could, concerning the man you saw in Parramatta on October 13th.'

That finally arouses her attention and Cate Rossi turns to look at DC Hargreaves. 'I had to do it unofficially,' she continues, 'I believe DI Paramo had been told to drop matters. I learned that the man's initials might be JB or his name Jim Beam. Does that ring any bells with you?' Cate Rossi turns her head from side to side indicating no.

'Are you able to speak with your jaw bandaged up like that?'

'Yes, but I have to speak like a bloody ventriloquist, barely moving my lips,' Cate Rossi finally mumbles. 'It's not easy.'

'No, I can imagine. Look I wondered if anything else has happened to you in the past few months. Any unexpected accidents?'

DC Hargreaves can see Cate Rossi eyes widen with surprise. She is quiet for a moment then says, 'Someone nearly ran me over several weeks back. I thought it was maybe my fault for not looking properly before crossing the road, as I was so tired.'

'The car that almost hit you didn't stop?'

'No. You think it was *him*?'

'Possibly. Did you report the incident to the police?'

'Yes, and gave them contact details of witnesses, but there was nothing they could do. I couldn't give them the registration details or the make of car.'

'Right. Any other strange things happen?'

'Marco refused to stay at his parents for another night saying he had to go into work the next day – but he wasn't due back until the New Year. Just before I left Marco to crawl back up the ravine, he made me promise to go to his office to collect a tape that he left a message with the receptionist, Anna, about.'

'What kind of tape was he talking about?'

'I don't know. There was no time to explain. I know we have video tapes at the reception for security. Perhaps it was something to do with that.'

'Would you mind if I went to see this Anna as you are unable to at the moment? Your husband worked in an architect's practice in Parramatta didn't he?'

'Yes he did. We both did. You can go to see Anna if you like. I don't know what it's about. But if it was something special that Marco was organising for me, I want it.'

'Yes of course. I will bring it up to you. How long do you think you will be here in hospital?'

'I don't know. They might send me to a rehab unit in another few weeks.'

'Did you ever complete that new drawing you were going to do for DI Paramo? He'd made a note about it in his files.'

'Yes, I did a couple of sketches recently. One a head sketch and another full length one showing how his body looks now. They are in a sketch pad at home, in my bottom desk drawer.'

'Would you mind if I collected them from your house? Only I'd like to pass it on to the DI who is investigating your accident up here.'

DC Hargreaves realises she has made a mistake mentioning the word 'accident' to Cate Rossi, seeing tears well up in her eyes as she turns her head away once more. She is not sure how to retrieve the situation. Just as she had Cate talking to her.

'Mrs. Rossi?' she says placing her hand on Cate Rossi's

arm. 'I'm very sorry if I've upset you. I can't begin to imagine how you must be feeling. But I'd really like to move things forward on this matter if I could. To prevent any more deaths. Four deaths in the past few months is just too many. This man has to be stopped.' Once again, DI Hargreaves realises she has put her foot in it. Thinking out loud, she hadn't meant to say anything about 'deaths.'

'Four? In the past few months?' Cate Rossi asks her with startled eyes. 'Who are you talking about?'

'I'm sorry, I shouldn't have said anything. Nothing can be proven. It's just my personal belief.'

'Who?'

'DI Paramo. Your stepmother. Your husband and son.'

'My stepmother? And the detective? How did he die? You wouldn't tell me when we spoke.'

'I shouldn't really be telling you now either.'

'How?' Cate Rossi insists.

'A shot to his head that was staged as suicide. At least I believe it was staged. But I'm just a lowly DC. Our DCI wrote a report that ensured it was ruled a suicide. It was not adequately investigated to my thinking'

'And you think my stepmother was killed as well, staged to look like an accident?'

'Yes. That is my belief. But I need to stress, it is only my belief.'

'No I understand. I did question it myself.'

'And two attempts on your life now as well. So would you mind me collecting the new drawings from your house? Do you have any others there as well?'

'I have a load of them in a box in the attic. Old ones, from the past. I only kept the better ones. No it's okay,' she sighs. 'I don't want to go back there anyway. I can't face it. Take the whole damn lot away. The keys for the house are in my bag in my bedside locker here. They brought me my bag after the car was cleared out. And you know it was no accident. It was murder.'

DC Hargreaves nods and walks around to the other side of the bed and removes Cate Rossi's bag. She rummages around until she finds a set of keys. 'These them?' she asks holding up a set of keys on a koala key ring.

'Yes.

'Do you have a security alarm system at your house?'

'No. Marco and I discussed the possibility of putting one in. Neither of us have ever lived in a house with one, so we decided against it.'

'Okay. I'll return them as soon as I can. Look, just to let you know your father has spoken to DI Ellis about your mother's murderer. The murder in Melbourne. Your father seems convinced that the same person is responsible for running you off the road. Why he thinks that I am not sure. And he raised a query on Detective Paramo's death. But he hasn't connected it to your stepmother's death.'

'Right.'

'And one more thing. What day did you drive up to Singleton?'

'We went early on Boxing morning. We had Christmas Day at home with my father and sister. Why?'

'Just gathering all the facts. Is there anything I can do for you before I leave you in peace?'

'No, thank you.'

Cate is relieved to see DC Hargreaves leave. Despite what everyone thinks is best for her, she prefers to be alone with her misery. When she had first woken from her surgery in the intensive care ward her brain had been quite muddled. She couldn't think clearly. When she finally remembered everything that had happened, she asked about Marco and Milo and was met with stony silence. Angered by this she began to pull the lines out that were attached to her, despite her woozy state. If they weren't going to tell her then she was damned well going to find out herself. Her actions had caused chaos and she was rapidly sedated with an injection that knocked her out once again.

The next time she woke her father and Rosie had been there. And some detective called Ellis. It was Ellis who gave her the devastating news that neither Marco nor Milo had made it. They were both found dead at the scene. She hadn't wanted to believe it – it was just some horrific nightmare she was caught up in. Ellis had said he would return in a few days to speak to her again. When he popped in yesterday she couldn't speak to him.

Her father and Rosie had seemed prostrate with grief for her and the loss of more loved ones in the family, but she couldn't speak to them either. She couldn't speak to anyone. She'd just felt hollow inside. Empty. Apart from a crushing pain in her chest, despite the strong drugs they had her on. She'd believed it was her fault. If she hadn't taken so long to climb the ravine, they would have been rescued sooner and would both be recovering now.

One of the doctors at the hospital had come to see her the next day and explained the seriousness of Marco and Milo's injuries. He claimed that even if the two of them had been treated immediately after the accident the outcome would have been the same. They might have lived for another hour or so, but no longer. Marco had died from severe internal injuries, and two injuries had contributed to Milo's death. His brain had been badly shaken in the descent and something large and heavy had knocked him on the side of the head. Probably the same thing that had broken her jaw and pierced her shoulder she thought afterwards. The information eased her guilt a little, but didn't stop the pain. The same doctor informed her that the operation had saved her leg, but she might never walk properly again. It seemed like a very small sacrifice to pay compared with the loss of Marco and Milo.

Marco's parents and his sister, who also lived in the mountains, had been in to see her this morning, before detective Hargreaves's visit. Questioning her about what happened. With hostility. Marco's mother wailing that she knew he shouldn't have left that fateful night. Cate recalls how she had pleaded with him to stay another night. Mother's instinct Cate believes. She couldn't talk to them either – especially after discovering they had buried her husband and child without her knowledge or agreement early that morning. She was seething with resentment. They explained defensively that the doctors had told them that she wouldn't be able to leave her bed for weeks and they just couldn't leave 'the boys' lying around in refrigerators over the New Year. With the publicity the accident had attracted, they had managed to speedily arrange a funeral. Their old local priest from the Blue Mountains had been willing to hold a service and a funeral company had provided the other necessary arrangements. Apparently they had planned for it to be a quiet affair, with just the family attending, and 'the boys' had been buried together in one of the family plots Marco's father had purchased many years ago and where his mother, who'd died earlier in the year, is buried.

So many of Marco and Cate's friends and acquaintances didn't even know about Marco and Milo's death or have the opportunity to attend the funeral. Who was going to tell them? Cate's sure many of their colleagues at the practice will be upset to know that they have been excluded from the funeral.

The police knew how they had died and so didn't need to hang on to the bodies Mr. Rossi senior had explained to her. Bodies. Cate had shuddered imagining Marco and her baby lying in refrigerators. Imagining them lying buried deep in the ground is even worse. Marco and she had never discussed what should happen if one of them died. It just never seemed conceivable that one of them would die so suddenly. She doesn't know if he would have preferred burial or cremation.

Now with DC Hargreaves' visit her guilt has returned. The detective thinks it was because her mother's murderer was after her that her husband and baby have died. So it is her fault after all. She'd thought it was a drunk driver at first, but the more she'd thought about it, the more it seemed like a deliberate act. Both incidents. A drunk driver wouldn't behave like that. But how could *he* possibly know they were on the Putty Road? How could he have set the accident up like that? It makes no sense. And her stepmother? Janet murdered as well as DI Paramo? Finding the house in Beecroft she can understand – her father is listed in the phone book. There are not many Brant's in the Sydney area. It wouldn't take much sleuthing to find the right house. If he did kill Detective Paramo then he might have picked up the Beecroft address from him as well. But why kill Janet? Perhaps he had been after her, not aware that she was married and no longer living there. How can she live with the guilt of that? Face her father and Rosie knowing she is responsible for Janet's death? And their lives might be in danger as well. She will have to warn them.

DC India Hargreaves finds the drawing pad in the desk

drawer just as Cate Rossi described. However there are no sketches in it. The pad is blank. She looks closely at it and can see that some pages have been ripped out. *The bastard has already been here!*

She can see the loft hatch has a hook ring and searches around looking for something appropriate to open it. In the hall cupboard she finds the hook pole and pulls on the catch revealing a fold down-ladder. She unfolds the ladder and climbs up. There is a light to her right and she switches it on. She can see the roof area has been boarded for storage and it is safe to climb into. There are a number of boxes up here though, and she will just have to look in all of them. None of them are labelled. She rips the sealing tape off the first four and sees that they hold only books. The fifth one seems more promising as she can tell it is Cate's box with a few girly books and a number of large sketch pads. She takes them all out and starts looking through them. Some of them contain a range of drawings of different scenes and images. She's good, Hargreaves thinks. But they're not what she is looking for.

The final two she opens have still life sketches on the first pages and then the remainder of the pads are full of images of the same man. This is them. A similar face to the copy she has in the file. Only not so patchy and grainy. These are originals. There is something familiar about the face staring back at her, but she can't place it. No doubt he resembles someone she's seen on TV or something, she thinks. She laughs at a couple of them that are more caricatures, depicting him in shackles and behind bars in comic strip prison stripes. If only …. She carefully returns all the other sketch pads to the box, tucks the sketch pads she wants under her arm, turns the light off and climbs down, folds the ladder back up and closes the hatch.

So you didn't go into the loft. At least we have these. Checking her watch she sees it is 2.49. If she hurries she might make it down to Mr. Rossi's office. It is considered a normal working day but she knows many businesses shut altogether between Christmas and New Year, or close early so that staff can prepare for the evening's celebrations. She is not sure of the name of the company or if they are working today but she knows where they are located.

In Parramatta she finds a skeleton staff group still working at the architect's practice. The doors are locked, but a knock on the door holding up her police badge gains her entrance. She explains why she is there and asks if they have heard about Marco and Milo's death. They haven't. No one has thought to let them know yet. Like her, they had all seen the news about the accident, not connecting it to the Rossi family, but hadn't seen any updated news, naming the victims. The staff are all shocked when she fills them in, and they stand in stunned silence. The few women present begin to sob. At some point she is going to have to tell them that the funeral has already taken place as well. Rob Ellis had caught up with her just as she was leaving his police station earlier and warned her about Mr. Rossi's parents arranging a hasty burial and suggesting she shouldn't mention it to Cate Rossi at the hospital.

'Is there someone here called Anna?' she asks needing to move on to her reason for being here.

'Yes, that's me,' one of the sobbing women answers.

'Marco told his wife Cate that if he didn't survive his injuries from the accident he wanted her to collect a tape that he'd left you a message about.'

'Yes, I picked up Marco's message on Tuesday when we came in, but unfortunately we'd been burgled over

Christmas. All the security tapes were taken and the recording equipment damaged. I've been ringing Marco, but not received any reply. Now I know why,' she says bursting into tears again.

'Anything else damaged or stolen?'

'Things had been moved on some of the desks,' one of the men says, 'but nothing we could see that was taken. And the alarm system was damaged. It was quite strange.'

'What was on the tape that he left you a message about?' she asks Anna.

'If it is the one I think he was talking about, then it showed a middle aged businessman who came in asking for Marco, said he'd be back, but didn't return. I showed Marco the security tape footage and he said the man was familiar but didn't know who he was. That's all I know. I'm not even sure the tape hadn't been recorded over, but now we don't have it anyway with the burglary.'

'You don't think we were burgled just for the tapes do you?' the same man asks.

'I'm not sure. Can you hang on a moment? There is something I want to get from my car.' DC Hargreaves runs out to her car and collects one of Cate Rossi's old sketch pads. She returns to the office and opens the pad at a sketch of the man. 'Would it have been this man by any chance who was recorded on the security tape?' she asks, showing the sketch to the woman called Anna.

'It could be. Only he was a lot older. I'd say that drawing looks more like it would be the man's son.'

'Okay thank you very much.' she says closing the pad. 'Do you know what day Mr. Rossi left the message for you?'

'Yes the message log said it was left on 25th December. Christmas Day.'

'Did Mr. Rossi mention in the message what day he'd be returning to Glenbrook?'

'Yes, he said he was travelling back on 27th and would be in work the next day.'

'Okay that's great. Thank you. Have you reported the burglary? Did the alarm system go off? And when did this happen?'

'Yes and yes,' the same man says, 'the alarm was activated momentarily in the evening on Boxing Day. I received a call about it from our security firm. They did a pass by and everything seemed in order. Only the alarm was no longer working. There was no sign of forced entry. All of us were away at the time so we weren't able to follow it up immediately. As everything seemed okay according to the security report, we left it until I could come in on Tuesday. The entry door wasn't forced so, maybe, whoever did the damage, had keys. Or it was someone who knew how to open a locked door. We've had a constable around who took details. We had to report it for our insurance claim.'

'Did Marco have his own set of keys to enter the premises?'

'Yes he did. You don't think he did it do you?'

'No, no, of course not. He was in Singleton with his family on Boxing Day.'

'Right, yes, he said they were going up there. Where's Cate now? Is she still in hospital?'

'Yes, she's at the Hawkesbury and probably will be for some time, although she mentioned that they might be sending her to a rehab unit in another few weeks. She sustained a serious leg injury.'

'Right. We'll organise some flowers and arrange a visit. Thanks. Bloody awful news. Marco's been with us for the past six years. And Cate for three years,' he says with his voice wavering. 'Marco was a beaut bloke. One of the best. And a great architect. We'll miss him very much. We'll need to find out when the funeral's being held. You don't know anything do you?'

'Yes,' she says uncomfortably. 'Look I need to let you know that Mr. Rossi's family buried their son and grandson early this morning. Cate didn't even know about it or attend of course.' She can see their mouths forming an 'O' and knows they are about to protest, but she hasn't the time to become entangled in their thoughts on this. It is nothing to do with her. She decides to ignore their reaction and ploughs on, 'So if you see her you mustn't mention it, unless she does. She would have been very upset about it all. Apparently his family wanted a 'family only' affair. I'm sorry I have to get back to Windsor now. Thanks for your help.' DC Hargraves turns and hurries out of the building, knowing she has left a group of angry people grieving behind her. They are likely to be greatly upset about not being informed of Marco's death and the funeral arrangements. And she can't blame them. Mr. Rossi had worked with them all for some years. She hates the part of her job where you have to give distressing news to people.

Before returning to Windsor, DC India Hargreaves calls into her flat at Pendle Hill to collect DI Paramo's file she had hidden there. Although she plans to hand it over to Rob Ellis, she wants to make an additional copy for herself. As she is driving back to Windsor, she thinks that the file she has is probably a photocopy of a photocopy, which is why the quality of the images have deteriorated so much. She now has original drawings from Cate Rossi's sketch pads, similar to the one in the file. If one of the original sketches had computer enhanced aging applied, they might have an idea of what the man looks like now. She doesn't think Cate Rossi will be willing to complete another sketch of the man she saw in October. She will have to tell Cate that the pages have been removed; and with that, the knowledge that the man had no doubt entered the Rossi home. He is clearly a professional as there were no signs of forced entry. She wonders if Rob Ellis will consider it important enough to get the techies in looking for any trace evidence he might have left behind.

DI Rob Ellis is still in his office when DC Hargreaves arrives back at the Windsor station. Clearly he has informed staff that she can enter the building freely as she is waved straight through on arrival. She knocks and enters his office and is pleased to see his face light up when he sees it's her.

'I've been very busy since I last saw you,' she tells him. 'But I've discovered that our man has been as well'

'Oh, do tell.'

She fills him in on her conversation with Cate Rossi, and her visit to the Rossi house to retrieve the new drawings only to discover the pages have been removed from the pad. She places the collection of the old original drawings from the loft storage on the desk in front of him, explaining that whoever had been in the Rossi house had not been aware of these. She then goes on to tell him about her visit to the architect's practice where the security tapes that had captured the man had been stolen in a burglary and, finally, telling him that she'd collected DI Paramo's file from her flat.

'Yes, I can see you have been a busy bee. So you think the suspect broke into the Rossi house, removed the new drawings and then broke into Marco Rossi's office to remove the security tape?'

'Yes I do.'

'And how would he know about the drawings and the tape?'

'Like I said to you this morning, perhaps he had their place bugged. His actions seem to confirm my theory on that. I forgot to mention that Mr. Rossi also mentioned the date he would be travelling back to Glenbrook in the message he left at his office. So again it suggests that someone was listening to the Rossi's telephone conversations. There was no sign of forced entry at the house, so the suspect is clearly a professional. Or he hired a professional to do his dirty work for him. We know there was definitely an illegal entry at the office as all the recording equipment was damaged and tapes stolen, but again no sign of forced entry. Perhaps if he entered the Rossi home first to take the drawings, he might have found Marco Rossi's keys to the office. He is likely to have left them at home while he was away.'

'Hmm. Possibly.'

'Will you organise for a team of techies to go to the Rossi's house?'

'I'd have to have Cate Rossi's agreement to it first, as we have no evidence of a crime being committed there. If it was a professional job as you suggest, I doubt there would be much to find anyway, unless we find bugs anywhere in the house. I will need to check with the father first to make sure he didn't remove the new drawings. He knew about them because he mentioned them to me.'

'Yes, that would be sensible to follow up first. But no matter how clever these professionals think they are, they usually leave some trace of their crime. By the way, I'd like a copy of DI Paramo's file before I hand it over to you. These old sketch pads containing Cate Rossi's earlier drawings are similar to the ones she passed on to DI Paramo. Only the ones in his file have been copied several times and are not very clear. I'd like a copy or two of the originals as well for my file. I had an idea on the way back about them, by the way.' She mentions about computer-enhanced aging and Rob Ellis agrees to put his computer expert on to it when she returns in the New Year.

DI Rob Ellis makes the call to Howard Brant while DC Hargreaves completes her photocopying. When she returns he is still on the phone.

'That was my super,' he says when he finally hangs up. 'He's given the go ahead for the techies to do a once over of the Rossi house as long as Cate Rossi agrees. And we'll do door to door enquiries to see if the neighbours saw anyone near the Rossi house. I've spoken to Howard Brant as well. He hadn't removed the drawings. He didn't know where they were and knows nothing about them apart from his daughter mentioning them to him over Christmas. He doesn't think his daughter mentioned them to many people. She was generally quite secretive about these particular drawings. He said his other daughter Rosie knew, but neither of them have mentioned them to anyone else, so you may be right about the place being bugged.'

'Do you want to go and see her tomorrow?' DC Hargreaves asks, 'or shall I?'

'I'd like you to, as she seems to have developed a rapport with you. On one condition though,' he says smiling.

'Okay, what's the catch?' she says suspicious of his motives.

'That you come out for a drink with me tonight to

welcome in the new Millennium.'

'Oh. I had planned to go to a party back in Parramatta, but I was worried about how I would get home from there. Taxis will be a nightmare. Were you thinking of something local? My parents would welcome me staying over. I saw very little of them over Christmas as I was on duty, which is why I have the New Year off. I wish you'd mentioned it earlier as I could have picked up something to wear when I called into my place. Now I'll have to drive home and back again.'

'I wasn't sure that I would definitely be able to go. But I've had enough of work and after all it's not just any old New Year, it's a new millennium. I have local friends putting on a do. I know the food will be good. And there will be some live music. It's a bit out of town on a large property, but not too far to walk if we can't get a lift - I'm sure someone would oblige us though. There will be plenty of people abstaining tonight, being a designated driver. I expect there will be fireworks as well.'

'It's a deal,' she says grinning back. She hadn't expected this. Although he is a bit of a joker, she finds Rob Ellis quite irresistible. And she wonders if his reference to fireworks is just simply those used for display or if he is referring to the other type one might experience between couples. A girl can always hope can't she?

# 28

When DC Hargreaves visits Cate in the morning on New Year's Day, the first day of the new millennium, and informs her that her drawings have been removed from her sketch pad at the house, Cate is positive her mother's murderer is behind it. She also tells Cate that a man apparently resembling her older drawings, although somewhat aged, had called into Marco's office some weeks ago and been captured on their security tapes, but that there had been a break-in at the architect's practice over Christmas and all the security tapes removed. Detective Hargreaves relays Marco's telephone message to Anna asking that she put the tape aside and explains that when the man had come into the office he had asked for Marco personally. Cate and Detective Hargreaves concur that Marco had somehow worked out who his visitor had been.

'He must have seen my drawings on Christmas Day. You say the message was left then?' Cate asks. DC Hargreaves nods. 'Well Marco was in the study that night, wrapping presents. He must have looked at my drawing pad. I noticed he was very quiet when he re-joined us. Could that be why he claimed he had to go into the office and wouldn't stay another night at his parent's place? Why didn't he say anything? Had he planned to collect the tape and go to the police without telling me?'

DC Hargreaves shrugs helplessly. Of course she doesn't have the answers to Cate's questions, but she suggests that

Marco's actions had simply been to protect Cate from any further worry or distress about the suspect.

Now Detective Hargreaves has gone, Cate's brain is whirling with thoughts about everything. It had to be the murderer who was responsible for taking both the drawings and tapes. Either personally or through someone he hired. So that means it was definitely him she had seen in Parramatta that day, not that she had doubted herself, and he somehow found out about her recognising him. Probably through actions that DI Paramo took, costing him his life as well. When Cate queried how the suspect (as DC Hargreaves called him – Cate always referred to him as her mother's murderer – now she would be adding that he was her son and husband's murderer as well) could have known about the new drawings and the security tape, the DC suggested their house and telephones might have been bugged. The mere thought of this man listening in to all their phone calls, conversations in the house, the arguments and the intimacy she shared with Marco sends shivers up her spine. If it was true, that would account for his knowledge of them being at Singleton and possibly following them. It also meant that he had heard conversations with her father and Rosie. She decides she has no alternative but to speak with them about the potential risk to them. When would it all end? She thinks the only way to put a stop to all this is if she disappears. She cannot face returning to the house she shared with Marco and Milo. Nor can she place her father and Rosie in danger and ever go to back to the house in Beecroft.

Cate has given her agreement for the crime scene technicians to check over her house, but she doubts they will find anything. This man seems to be way ahead of the police.

'So where did you two spend last night?' she asks her father and Rosie when they settle into her visitor's chairs that afternoon. She knows they went to the funeral early yesterday morning. She had been very angry when they first confessed their attendance after Marco's parents had visited her. But as her father had pointed out, Mrs. Rossi senior is a formidable woman and was insistent that the funeral took place when the opportunity presented itself and before the press could gain any knowledge of it. Of course they would go, what else did she expect? She was just angry that she wasn't there. It was her husband, and her child. She should have been consulted or at least told about it. But as her father reminded her she wasn't really in a communicative state, either physically from the effects of all the drugs, or emotionally, after discovering about their deaths.

'Oh, we just popped around to Tom and Sue's for a few hours', her father says casually. 'You remember the Wallace's don't you?' Cate nods. 'We didn't really feel like celebrating as you can imagine.'

'No. I had a pretty quiet one here too. I had the nurses turn all the lights off in here and lock the door. I could hear them jollying about out in the corridor, but I didn't want to know. Look I've something to tell you.'

Cate fills them in on all her conversations with DC Hargreaves about the drawings and security tape thefts, the planned visit of the crime technicians to the house in Glenbrook, the previous attempt on her life that was probably linked and the possibility that the house and phones had been bugged.

'I don't want to return to Glenbrook and I can't return

to the house in Beecroft when I leave here or rehab Dad, it would be putting you all in danger. I think it would be a good idea if you moved as well and had an unlisted telephone number.'

'You think he knows where we live?' Rosie asks startled.

'I'm sure he does. The Beecroft address would have been in DI Paramo's file. I didn't give him any other address. He'd had that in the file from 1992. It's likely that the murderer got his hands on that as a starting point when he killed the detective. DI Paramo's death was recorded as a suicide. That's what his DCI believed anyway, but others doubt it. So do I.'

'You don't think ….,' Rosie starts but can't bring herself to finish saying it.

'Your mother's accident?' Howard Brant finishes for her. He always referred to Janet as Cate's mother. 'Do you believe your mother's death *wasn't* an accident?'

Cate knows he is referring to Janet. 'I don't know Dad. But it may not have been,' she tells him. 'I'm really sorry.'

Howard Brant stands and paces about the room. 'It never occurred to me. Although it should have by now, given what's happened since. The bastard! And you're sure this Detective Paramo was murdered?'

'I can't be positive about it Dad, but I think it is likely from what I have heard.'

'What's the name of this DCI at Parramatta?'

'I don't know Dad, but there's no point in having any contact with him. The Windsor police are dealing with everything. As I said, I've given permission for them to comb through the Glenbrook house in the hope of finding some evidence. The murderer has clearly been in there and removed the drawings. I don't think the police are going to get anywhere with this though, so I've decided the best thing is for me to go away.'

'Go away? Go away where?'

'I thought I might go back to England for a while. I can't face the house in Glenbrook or returning to work. There would just be reminders of Marco and Milo everywhere. And it's not safe for me at Glenbrook or at Beecroft.'

'You don't have to do that Cate. We can sell Beecroft and move. You need to be with family and friends right now.'

'I can't see any of my friends Dad. They all have husbands and babies or young children. I just couldn't be around them. I know it sounds unreasonable, but I would just be jealous or angry seeing them with their happy families. And it's not safe to be around either of you. I don't want to put anyone else at risk.'

'If we move, that'll sort the problem. I can't bear the idea of you being alone in England.'

'I need to be alone Dad. For a while at least. Anyway, I can go and spend some time with Adhita. We're still in touch with each other. Also, I thought I could go back to Yorkshire for a while and see if I can trace any of my mother's family. Julie's family I mean.'

'What about this murdering bastard? Are you just going to let him get away with this?'

'There's not a lot I can do Dad. Look what happened when I did attempt to do something about it. I just can't put anyone else at risk. And I'm not strong enough to deal with it right now.'

'Alright Cate, you have to do what you think is best. What about the Glenbrook house? What shall we do about that?'

'The mortgage will be paid off once I put in a claim for Marco's death. I haven't been in a position to do anything about it yet. Could you and Rosie go and dig out the relevant paperwork for me? I would also like my personal documents, Mum's document box and the photo albums. All the documents are in files or small boxes in the cupboard in the study. My passport is in the top drawer of the built-ins in our bedroom. I'll have to apply for a visa to travel.'

'We'll find everything, don't worry,' Rosie assures her.

'Do you want to sell the house in Glenbrook? I wouldn't advise doing it straight away. Perhaps you could rent it out while you are away. We'd have to sort those floorboards out though. I could get someone in to strip and polish them for you. What about the furniture?'

'I don't want any of it Dad. Do what you like with it, you can ask Marco's parents if they want any of his things – but don't mention anything about the police's suspicions. Then they'd blame me even more,' Cate says exhausted by all this thinking, 'but I do want to keep all the plans Marco drew. Can you at least pack those up for me to store?'

Howard Brant checks with DI Ellis about when they might be completing their investigations at the house in Glenbrook. He doesn't want to start moving things around until they have finished. Ellis informs him that the techies will be finished by the end of the day which surprises him - that they would be willing to go to the house on New Year's Day. He imagined the DI saying it would be later in the week before they were finished. He and his daughter Rosie travel to the house on the Sunday and the first thing Rosie notices is that Cate's car is not in the driveway. Howard phones DI Ellis to query whether they had removed it as part of their investigation. Detective Ellis is not on duty today so he leaves a message for him. They spend the Sunday and Monday, a public holiday for the New Year, sorting, packing and clearing the house, although they return home to Beecroft overnight. In the attic they find numerous empty boxes from the move only a few months before and pack up Cate's and Marco's belongings. Howard phones Marco's parents updating them on Cate's condition (without mentioning anything else) and asks if they would like to have some of Marco's things. All the kitchenware they pack into separate boxes to store.

A quick call to DI Ellis again on the Monday afternoon confirms that the police hadn't removed Cate's car, nor had it been at the property when the forensic technicians had visited.

'It was definitely here when we left on Boxing Day, so we need to report it stolen,' Howard Brant tells him. 'Probably some opportunist who guessed they were away over the holiday, but we haven't spotted the key anywhere in the house – only the spare key, which Rosie found in one of the kitchen drawers. Rosie was sure the key would have been in the kitchen, in a bowl on the worktop, where Cate always leaves it, but I'll check with Cate in case she has the main key with her at the hospital,' he adds.

DI Ellis agrees to make an official note of the car theft after the registration details are passed on to him.

'We can't finish all this today Dad,' Rosie says an hour later. 'Why don't I come back during the week and do some more packing.'

'I'm not having you alone in this house Rosie. It is too much of a risk. No, I'll organise a few days off work. I haven't been in touch with anyone yet, but once they hear what's happened they will be fine. There is so much to do. I'll have to find suitable tradesmen to deal with the floors here. And we'll have to move all the furniture out before the floor can be done. I want to see some agents about our house as well. I think we'll be spending the next few months packing, Rosie.'

Another matter Howard Brant wants to deal with is the DCI at Parramatta. Howard thinks that man has a lot to answer for. Leaving Rosie with some friends, as he doesn't want her in the Beecroft house alone either, he travels to Parramatta during the week and enquires at the Police Station about the name of the DCI who managed DI Paramo. He is told his name is DCI John Pritchard and requests a meeting with him.

'I'm afraid DCI Pritchard does not meet with members of the public who walk in off the street,' he's told by a young constable at the front reception. 'I can get someone else for you if you would like.'

'I'm not just any member of the public. It's concerning the deaths of four people. Three of them members of my family. I want to see DCI Pritchard. He'd better see me, or I shall be taking this matter further.'

The young constable takes his name and asks Mr. Brant to take a seat while he seeks advice from his sergeant who is just returning from his break. The Sergeant places a call through to the DCI, who he knows is in as he saw him arrive just an hour before.

The DCI knows who Mr. Brant is, as he had received a call from a DI Rob Ellis from Windsor earlier regarding the man's daughter. Why he wants to see him when the Windsor police are dealing with his daughter's accident he is not sure. DI Ellis had also asked him about DI Paramo's death. What on earth that has to do with them he doesn't know, but decides he needs to see this man who is making threats. He makes his way down to reception and introduces himself.

'What can I do for you sir?'

'I'd like a word with you about the deaths of several members of my family.'

'If you are referring to the accident that occurred on the Putty Road last week, that case is being dealt with by the Windsor Police. I'm afraid I can't help you there.'

'It's about a lot more than that. Look, we can discuss this here in front of everyone or you can take me to a more private room. It's up to you.'

'All right. You'd better come through then.' DCI Pritchard answers, resignedly. He finds it wearisome dealing with people like Howard Brant these days. But he can tell he is not a man to be trifled with. He takes Mr. Brant through to an interview room, not offering refreshments as he doesn't wish to prolong the man's visit.

'How can I help you then?' he asks once they are seated at a table.

'My daughter came to this station last October to see a Detective Inspector Paramo. She had spoken to Paramo some years prior about witnessing the murder of her mother in Melbourne and presented him with sketches. When she came to see Paramo in October she had just seen the murderer here in Parramatta that day.'

'Yes, I am aware of that. The man she *believed* murdered her mother I would add though.'

'Well, the following day apparently, the same detective commits suicide and then my wife dies a few days later in a supposed accident falling down the stairs at our home, breaking her neck.'

'I'm sorry to hear that, but I don't understand what it is you are trying to say?' DCI Pritchard says becoming

230

frustrated.

'I'm saying that their deaths were unlikely to be suicide or an accident. DI Paramo had my home address registered in his file. The one where my wife died. He did not have my daughter's new name or current address. Somehow - and we believe it is the same man my daughter saw that day - somehow that man got hold of my daughter and her husband's details, probably accessed through information at my house. He then went to my son-in-law's work place, where he was captured on security cameras. It is likely that he followed my son-in-law home and so learned their new address. He then attempted to kill my daughter by running her down with a car. That attempt was unsuccessful. We believe he then went to their Glenbrook house where he bugged the house and phones so knew exactly where they were going to be during Christmas. He followed them on their return journey on 27th December causing their so called 'accident'. It was no accident. It was murder. My son-in-law and my grandson died as a result of it. My daughter has survived through a sheer bloody miracle. Recent sketches of the man, which my daughter completed intending to hand them over to this station, have been stolen from her house in Glenbrook. The architect's practice, where my son-in-law worked, was broken into over Christmas and the security tapes that would have shown this man were stolen. Nothing else. Just the tapes'

'I wasn't aware of all this,' DCI Pritchard mumbles beginning to feel uncomfortable. 'But you don't know that this is all connected to the man your daughter saw. Everything you have told me is just supposition.'

'I think it is more than that. And it is all connected. All the evidence that could identify the man has been removed. Who else could it be? And why did all this happen? Because *you* didn't do your job properly and look into DI Paramo's death. That's why.'

'Now wait a minute. We did look into his death. The man was a heavy drinker. He was depressed after his wife walked out on him. His death was a suicide. I wasn't the only one who thought so. My Chief Superintendent signed off on it.'

'How much time did you spend looking into his death? I would imagine no more than a day or two. Worried about your budget were you? I know all about budgets. My background is accountancy. Perhaps I should be talking to your Chief Superintendent as well.'

'No, that won't be necessary. What is it you want Mr. Brant?'

'I want you to go home tonight and remember that three other people, besides DI Paramo are dead, due to your incompetence. I want you think about that every night before you go to sleep. And I want you to do your job properly. To avoid any further deaths. I think you should be re-examining DI Paramo's death for starters.'

'I'd have to have sufficient evidence to warrant that.'

'You have sufficient evidence. Everything I have just told you. Speak to that bloody priest as well. He is the one person who can identify this man and tell you who he is. The one my daughter saw him with on that day in October.'

'I'm afraid that won't be possible. Unfortunately Bishop Byrne died of a heart attack over Christmas.'

'He's the bishop who died recently? He's the so called priest my daughter saw with this man?'

'Yes, I'm afraid so.'

'Well you need to be looking into his death as well.'

'He died of natural causes in the presence of others.

There are no suspicious circumstances.'

'Just like my wife.'

'I can't make any judgements regarding your wife's death. And I'm sorry for your losses. I will discuss re-opening DI Paramo's death with my superiors. I can't do any more than that.'

'Right. Well I'll ring you next week and see what's happening. My daughter cannot return to her home because of the danger this man represents and I now have to move home as well because I cannot take the chance of putting my other daughter's life in danger. That's how serious this matter is. The information DI Paramo had, has somehow leaked out to the killer.'

Howard Brant stands and refuses to shake the hand DCI Pritchard is holding out to him. Instead he turns and leaves the room without another word, slamming the door behind him.

DCI Pritchard is confused and worried as he looks at the closed door. He's also starting to feel angry. Who the hell does this Brant man thinks he is, coming in here making demands. It's not his place to tell the police how to go about their business! Surely this is all a mistake? They are just disparate incidences. A drunk driver running a car off the road. An accident in the home. A suicide. Death by natural causes. But what about the attempted hit and run, the missing drawings and the stolen security tapes? How do they fit in? He should have stayed at home today, instead of coming in to clear up some tedious paper work that he'd left over Christmas. He's still supposed to be on holiday. He decides that he will go fishing this afternoon as planned. He had thought of cancelling it after Jim said he couldn't make it, but perhaps that was a good thing after all. I need the solitude of fishing to give me time to decide how to proceed, he thinks.

# 29

DC India Hargreaves bursts into DI Rob Ellis's office on Friday afternoon on the verge of hysteria. 'Have you heard the news? I just can't believe it! It can't be just another coincidence. It just can't!'

'Whoa, slow down India. What news?'

'My DCI has been found floating in the water at Bobbin Head. He's dead. Apparently he was still on holidays and went fishing alone yesterday afternoon.'

'What's the word on how it supposedly happened?'

'From what I've heard, he was near the shore where it's rocky. They reckon he went into the water and probably hit his head on a rock knocking him unconscious. Then, of course, he drowned, as there was non-one around who saw it happen to pull him out. I'm not sure I believe any of it though.'

'Why not?'

'How did he fall into the water for starters? He was an experienced fisherman. I can't see him putting himself in a dangerous position where he might fall.'

'Carried away in the heat of the moment with a large fish hooked onto the end of his line?'

'Maybe. Just a bit too much of a coincidence though. Apparently Howard Brant went to see him yesterday morning. The Sarge on desk duty said the DCI left in a bit of a hurry afterwards.'

'Perhaps I need to have a word with Mr. Brant. Why

would he be going to see the DCI?'

'I don't know. But thank god no one in my station knows I've been involved in this case. I tell you, it's a bit creepy. Our only witness who could identify the suspect supposedly dies of a heart attack over Christmas, so now that is a dead end. The DCI knew about Paramo's case. Now he's dead. Oh and have you heard, our Deputy Commissioner died over the holidays as well. Not connected though. He had apparently been suffering from cancer for some time. I tell you they're all falling down like flies around me.'

'Are you here unofficially, or are you still on duty?'

'I'm off duty. I had an early start this morning. I finished at 3pm today and came haring up here. Didn't want to take the risk of using the phone.'

'Look I have a few things to do, but do you want to hang around and go out for a meal later?'

'I didn't bring any other clothes with me. Mind you, I do have a few things at my parents. Saves bringing too much back and forwards each time I visit and stay over.'

'How about I pick you up later? I might have some more news for you by then.'

'Okay. I get the message. You don't want me around.'

'It's not that. I have things to do. You'd just be twiddling your thumbs here, when you could be relaxing at your parents.'

'Okay, see you later.'

DI Ellis managed to make contact with Howard Brant on his mobile. He explained that he had been to see the DCI requesting that he re-open the investigation into DI Paramo's death (where Brant was hoping evidence of murder might be found leading to a possible suspect). He'd told the DCI that he thought he hadn't done his job properly regarding DI Paramo's death and that several other people had died as a consequence.

'I have to tell you that DCI Pritchard died in a drowning accident yesterday.'

*'Well that can't be a co-incidence. Surely. This is really getting out of hand. Is his death being investigated?'*

'Yes, but not by me. Could you tell me where you were yesterday afternoon Mr. Brant? Your name will probably crop up in any investigation as you were one of the last people to see him. It would be good to verify your whereabouts so I can pass it on to the relevant team if necessary.'

*'I was meeting with some tradesmen at my daughter's house in Glenbrook. I also had to wait in for the Salvos to collect some of the furniture, as Cate will not be returning to the house.'*

DI Ellis is sure that Mr. Brant is telling the truth, however he asks for contact details of both the tradies and the Salvo branch he contacted in order to eliminate him from any potential questions that might arise from the DCI's death. He also tells Brant that his daughter's car has been located and it is a write-off. Another insurance claim Brant will have to make on behalf of his daughter, Ellis thinks, as he begins to punch a new number into his phone.

'Did you manage to speak to Howard Brant?' DC Hargreaves asks first thing as she climbs into Rob Ellis's car that evening.

'No greeting again. This is becoming a habit Ms. Hargreaves.'

'Sorry. I'm just really worried about everything. I went to see Cate Rossi again just to make sure she is okay and that nothing suspicious had occurred at the hospital.'

'I would have heard if anything had happened.'

'Yes I'm sure, but it just put my mind at rest to see her again. Did you know she's going into a rehab unit later next week?'

'Yes I had been told. Not sure if we are going to be able to continue with the security measures for long once she moves though.'

'You have to. We can't leave her so vulnerable to attack. The papers and news all announced that she survived the car crash. The suspect will know. It would be easy enough to find her. It's all about bloody budgets isn't it?'

''Fraid so. The Chief Super has been on my back about it.'

'Have you mentioned the DCI's death to him?'

'Yes. I pointed out the connections, so he's willing to cover it for another fortnight. No more.'

'Hmph! All they care about are budgets. People's lives aren't important.'

'You know it's not as simple as that. We can't just keep providing 24 hour protection for weeks on end.'

'I don't see why you can't provide the security. It's not as if the uniforms covering it would be desperately needed elsewhere.'

'There are plenty of other jobs they could be doing. Especially over this holiday period. Anyway, to answer your first question, yes, I spoke to Howard Brant. He was at his daughter's house in Glenbrook all yesterday afternoon. And I have verified that with the tradies he had at the house and the local Salvos who collected some furniture. I've informed Howard Brant that the Chief says we have to withdraw the security and he said he might look at funding it himself. I also told him that we've located his daughter's car. It was dumped at Penrith in a bit of a sorry state. There's large dents and scrapes down the passenger side. Different coloured paint markings indicate it'd had some sort of collision with another vehicle. Whoever stole it probably didn't stop after the accident, but there's been no reports made to the police that link to her car. It might have hit an empty stationary vehicle, but for insurance purposes any owner whose vehicle was hit would need to report it and none have come in. The key was still in the car. Howard Brant spoke to his daughter and she said she *had* left the key in a bowl on the kitchen worktop. She might have left it in the car though, providing the perfect opportunity for someone to drive it away.'

'Weren't the Rossi's sideswiped in the first incident on the Putty Road?

'Yes, they were. What, you think the person who hit them might have used Cate Rossi's car?'

'Wouldn't be surprised if he did. We know the person of interest had been in the house. He could have just helped himself to the car keys. Her car is the same colour, model and make as the one that sideswiped them. Cate Rossi mentioned it to me.'

'Traffic are looking at it, but I'll get them to see if any of the paint scrapings match the Rossi's car that went off the road. And if they picked up fingerprints or anything else from it. The number plates had been removed and were found in the boot, so presumably whoever took the car used fake plates when they drove it.'

They drive in silence for a minute before India says, 'You didn't think Howard Brant had anything to do with the DCI's death did you?'

'No but, as Brant saw the DCI yesterday morning and was apparently in a rather agitated angry state, I needed to clarify his whereabouts.'

'Did you ask him why he went to see the DCI?'

'Yes, he wanted him to re-open the investigation into DI Paramo's death, and by all accounts told him what an incompetent bastard he was. Not that he used those words, but it amounted to the same thing.'

'Good for him. About time someone stood up to the DCI. I made an effort challenging his theories about Joe Paramo's death but, as I told you, he wouldn't listen to me. The thing that worries me is what did the DCI do after meeting with Mr. Brant? Did he make any calls to anyone? Meet anyone else? Someone he unwittingly put himself in harm's way with?'

'I doubt we shall ever find out seeing that there were no eyewitnesses to his fall.'

'His land line and mobile could be checked.'

'I'm sure they will have already done that, but I'll make a quick call tomorrow and find out who is dealing with his so called accident and ask them to check out his phones, if it hasn't already been done. As it was not considered a suspicious death, they might not have looked into his phones.'

'You should also suggest they take a closer look at the circumstances of his death.'

'It's not my place to do that India, but I will think about how to discuss the matter discreetly.'

'Why pussyfoot around it? Why not just mention everything that's happened?'

'You are assuming that those looking at his death are incompetent India. I can assure you they will do a very thorough job, especially as he was a senior police officer.'

'Okay. Point taken. So what happens next with the investigation?'

'We've hit dead ends with everything. Unless Cate Rossi's car yields anything. No witnesses to the removal of the metal barricade on Putty Road, no witnesses to the crash. Our appeal has brought in no concrete results. Just the usual crank calls. With the drawings and security tape gone we have no visual clues on him. Bishop Byrne was our last hope but with his death we have no one who can identify the suspect.'

'You do. You have Cate Rossi.'

'Who could do a drawing, but won't. I've already asked her. Anyway that will only give us visual clues. Not a name. Kirstie is working on the old drawings compiling a computer-aged composite.'

'I don't blame Cate Rossi. Look at it from her point of view. The first time she approached the police with her drawings seven years ago nothing whatsoever came of it. The second time she approached the police just a few months ago, her son is born prematurely and she has to go through the heartache of whether he will survive; the detective dealing with it suddenly dies, followed by her stepmother, and now her husband and son's death. It has all been too much for her. She is grieving deeply at the moment and can't cope with anything else.'

'I can understand that, but we're unlikely to catch the bastard without her help.'

'We say we understand it. But do we really? Yes we're all really gutted when someone on the force is killed. But it's not the same as losing close family is it? I've never experienced a loss like hers. Have you?'

'Yes. When my mother died. But she died of cancer. Not quite the same. I felt angry enough about that. If someone else had been responsible for her death I'd be wanting to do everything I could to help catch the person responsible.'

'Yes but Cate Rossi was also badly injured in the crash. She spent hours, in what must have been agonising pain from everything I've heard, climbing up that ravine, desperate to get help for her husband and child, only to find it was too late. Nothing could save them. She told me today if she had known that she would have stayed with them and waited to die herself.'

'A good thing she didn't know then. It could have been weeks or even months before the wreck was discovered.'

'Is the computer composite all we have? Nothing else? What about the search of the Rossi's house. Did that yield anything? And the door to door enquiries?'

'We have silvery white hair strands. Found in the study. Two of them actually. I've asked Howard Brant whether they had any visitors in the house with hair like that and he said no, but that the Rossi's had had some workmen in the house on and off before they moved in and that it was possible that the hairs eluded house cleaning. They're not hopeful of getting any DNA off them. I am still waiting to hear – that might bring a result. I'll be checking in Victoria as well. We have lots of fingerprints, but apparently they had a gathering on Christmas Eve with lots of people in the house. Plus all the workmen they've had at the property. It would take forever to eliminate all the known fingerprints. The father hasn't any idea who all the workmen were that came to the house, so I doubt we'll have much luck there. Marco Rossi organised many of them while his wife and baby were still in hospital, so Cate Rossi probably won't know who they were either. You didn't leave your fingerprints at the scene did you when you went to collect the drawings?'

'No, of course not. I was wearing gloves. I automatically glove up when I enter new premises. Especially ones that might have any connection with a crime. '

'Okay, I thought you would have. There were some

positive results on the door to door, but nothing that takes us closer to finding the suspect though.'

'What did you find out?'

'Neighbours spotted a workman in overalls and a cap, carrying a tool box, entering the grounds of the property a couple of times over the past few weeks, whereas Howard Brant told me all work stopped on the house when they brought their son Milo home from the hospital. He checked with his daughter who was also staying at the house with the Rossi's, and she confirmed they'd had no one in. Until this week there has been no authorised tradies going in or out of the house since the middle of November. So we have to assume that it was our man, or someone he hired. Neighbours saw nothing suspicious in his actions and didn't make a note of any vehicle he was driving. No one saw anything on Boxing Day or the day after. So that's all a dead end.'

'So …..what happens next?'

'If the Chief Super agrees, we'll run the computer composite in the press. Another appeal. It might bring forward some results. Otherwise there is nothing else we can do unless Cate Rossi's car yields something. The Chief already wants me to shelve the case.'

'Just like what happened with the original murders in Melbourne in 1980. I wonder how many others this man has killed over the intervening years.'

'Don't know. But I do know he's a clever bastard.'

'I'm convinced that it's something that Joe Paramo discovered or did that triggered this recent spate of deaths.'

'I agree. It all starts with him. He must have identified the killer and taken some action. But what did he do?'

'I'm pretty sure he went to see Pritchard.'

'So we're back to that. Was it something that Pritchard

did or something Paramo did? Or both?'

'It could be that Joe told the killer he'd talked about him to Pritchard and after Paramo's death when he saw Pritchard take no action decided to leave it, but then changed his mind.'

'Hmm. Well we could speculate about it endlessly. Now are we going to sit outside this restaurant all night, or are we going to eat because I'm pretty hungry.'

DC Hargreaves looks around surprised. She hadn't even noticed that they were no longer driving. 'Let's go. I could eat a horse.'

'I hope not, that might take all night. I had envisioned a nice romantic evening together and nothing would destroy that faster than talking about suspects and death. So no more work talk. Agreed?'

'Sure, but I just want to say what if …..'

*'India!'*

'Okay. Okay. Agreed.'

# 30

**Hawes, Yorkshire, June 2000**

Meeting Alan Mathers proved to be a life changing experience for Cate. There was an ease of communication between them from the outset and Cate saw him as the grandfather she never had.

Cate's first sleepover at Alan's had been her first night of relaxed drug free sleep (well almost drug free – she had consumed a glass of wine earlier in the evening – but that was many hours before she went to bed) she had experienced since she'd been hospitalised. Sleep at the hospital came easy with drug inducement, but after her first night at Adhita's in Manchester, Cate had avoided taking tablets to help her sleep. Her second night at Adhita's had been a nightmare (no doubt due to sleeping so long on her 'first' night). Unable to sleep she had started thinking about everything that had happened. As the night wore on she'd become increasingly angry with Marco. For dying and leaving her alone. For leaving his parent's house so late. Just as he had admitted in the car in those last minutes together. It was his fault. Each time she had these thoughts it coincided with a stab of pain in her leg. As though she was being prodded for her irrational and unfair thinking. She'd repeated arguments in her head designating blame - swinging from it being the killer's fault entirely, to her fault, and finally Marco's fault. She understood that her actions of going to the police and doing the sketches, triggered a reaction in the killer that led to the events. But hadn't her actions been the result of the killer's actions all those years ago in the first place? Exhausted by the blame circuit looping in her head, she had finally fallen asleep. It was the next day that she'd first spotted Marco in Manchester. She has since wondered whether Marco started haunting her because she had been so angry with him that night. Cate no longer feels angry with Marco, but wonders if he is watching over her and led her to Alan.

Cate learns from Alan that he is 67 and worked as a psychologist until retiring the previous year. He had originally qualified as a doctor, then went into mental health.

'What made you go into mental health?' Cate had asked him.

'I'd always been fascinated by the way the brain works. I initially went into psychiatric practice in a hospital, but became disillusioned with the way patients suffering with mental health were treated and just pumped full of drugs, so I did some re-training and moved into psychology instead, where I've never written another prescription.'

'Good for you. Did that mean you had to move into private practice?'

'No, for some years I was attached, part time, to Doctor's surgeries, but with National Health cutbacks, my work there came to an end. I continued part-time work in NHS hospitals but also started a private practice in the Yorkshire town of Richmond.'

'I've not been to Richmond yet.'

'I'll take you there next week if you like,' he'd said.

Alan had driven Cate to Richmond on her next day off where they'd had lunch and after browsing around the shops she'd picked up a new book and a colourful rag rug to add to her room.

Cate has stayed over at Alan's numerous nights since that first occasion. He has taken to suggesting she stay in 'her room' as though it was solely hers now. She always enjoys a relaxing sleep in her 'room', unlike the exhausted sleep she experiences in her room above the café. It is comforting for her to have something that resembles a 'home' in the UK. She has not been able to view her room at the shared flat above the café as home, although it is very convenient. When she first phoned home and mentioned her developing friendship with Alan, her father had questioned her closely, concerned whether Alan was suitable or appropriate for his daughter to be socialising with. Cate had laughed at his old fashioned attitude, but thought it was understandable given all that had happened over the past year.

Alan has visited the café where Cate works for afternoon tea a few times and she visits him not only her days off, but also some other evenings after work. She hasn't invested in a computer or lap top since being in the UK and Alan allows her to make use of his dial-up internet facility so that she can keep in touch with friends by email.

Cate is well aware that Alan has been using his psychology approaches with her some days and when she challenged him about it, he said he couldn't help but challenge *her* with some of the statements she makes about the deaths of Marco and Milo. She'd come to realise, from answering his questions, that the only true aspect of their deaths was how she felt. Thanks to him she is now conscious of the distinction between her feelings and thoughts or beliefs. Most of what she had believed or thought was based on either lies she had told herself or unknown factors. She still believes it is true that Marco and Milo died due to their close association with her, but she no longer feels responsible. She did not cause the car to be driven off the road. Someone else was responsible for that. Although not a 100% sure, Cate believes the guilty party is the same person who murdered her mother.

Alan had carried out an exercise with her one afternoon asking her to imagine the murderer was sitting in an empty chair next to her and asked what she would like to say to him. What she'd really wanted to ask the murderer was 'why?' but, as there was no possibility of receiving an answer from an empty chair, she'd told Alan it would be a pointless exercise and instead said she would actually like to physically and verbally attack him. Alan had thrown a cushion onto the chair and told her to 'go for it'. Feeling slightly foolish, at first she had feebly approached the cushion muttering some mild obscenities at it but, as Alan began asking her more questions, the rage erupted from her and violence was unleashed on the cushion which was subjected to language she had never previously used and a physical strength that she didn't know she possessed. When the cushion had flown across the room from her final punch Cate had burst into laughter, sat down, looked at Alan and said, 'I feel fantastic now!' and burst into laughter again.

The exercise had released the built up tension and suppressed rage, leaving her with a feeling of elation. Alan had nodded as though it was what he had expected.

It was since that exercise that Cate felt free to sketch images of the man again. She shows them to Alan the next time she is at his house and he asks her whether she plans to send them to the Australian police.

'No, I think I would want to take them with me. I'm not sure I would trust them to arrive safely into the right hands otherwise. I don't know how the murderer gained knowledge of my drawings in the first place. Detective Hargreaves wondered whether her Detective Chief Inspector said something to the wrong person – someone possibly connected to the bishop who the murderer had visited. I thought it was something Detective Paramo, my contact at the police, had discovered or done. But we'll never know as all three, DI Paramo, the bishop and the DCI are all dead now.'

'And you think the murderer is definitely connected to their deaths?'

'Definitely in the case of DI Paramo. His was the fake suicide. Not sure how you could induce a heart attack which is how the bishop died, but the DCI died in a so called 'fishing' accident where he fell from his rowing boat, supposedly knocking himself unconscious and then drowning. That death could well have been murder.'

'Do you know if the bishop had any diagnosed or undiagnosed heart conditions?'

'No, I wasn't given any information about his death. Just that he was the only witness who knew the identity of the killer and that he had died of a heart attack.'

'He may have had a pre-existing condition that led to his death, which might have been caused from shock or stress linked to the suspect – or something else entirely. But there are other ways to induce a heart attack.'

'Hmm. It's a troubling coincidence that the only person who could identify him died. Anyway, the police compiled a computer-composite of the man which was published in the paper, but it brought no results. I didn't see it, but Rosie told me it wasn't a great likeness to the drawings she had seen me complete last December. Rosie was encouraging me to do new drawings. But I didn't feel like doing any at the time. To me the drawings represented death. I believed, as you know, that because I had done the drawings, several people had died. I was afraid if I did any new drawings, more people would die and I didn't want that responsibility.'

'And now what do you think?'

'I don't think it was my drawings alone, although their existence was a contributing factor to the murderer possibly becoming desperate. It *is* likely that our house and phone were bugged, although when the police searched the place they found no evidence of that. The murderer most likely removed them when he took my drawings. There is no other realistic explanation for how the murderer knew about the security tape and drawings. He must have listened to conversations in the house or on the phone. But how he knew exactly which day we would return I don't know. We hadn't definitely decided what day we'd travel back. Although Marco did tell his mother he had to return for work and I know he left a message at work about the tapes.'

'It does seems likely that the killer bugged your house and phone. You told me that Marco had left a message with his office about the tape, perhaps he mentioned the date you would be returning on that.'

'Hmm. Quite possibly. I wasn't told if he did. Marco might have made a decision about our return date, wanting to return as quickly as possible to collect the tapes. I know he left the message on Christmas Day, and that it was about the tape.'

'It would therefore seem reasonable to assume that the

murderer either paid a professional to carry out this work, or he works in that field himself – or has knowledge of someone who does.'

'Yes I thought that and discussed it with detective Hargreaves, on one of her visits to me in hospital. I wondered if his contact was the DCI who died, but detective Hargreaves doesn't believe the DCI was the kind of person who would be involved in any kind of crime. She thinks he was too incompetent for starters, believing he only gained promotion through the old boy network and money background. But also that he was a religious man who wouldn't be capable of doing anything that would lead to the death of others. It's funny though that he died on the same day following my father's visit to him. My father went to see him in the morning and gave him a dressing down for his incompetence. He died that afternoon. I wondered if the DCI then had any contact with the murderer who decided he had to be silenced.'

'Hmm. His death *might* have just been an accident. Cate, I noticed when you were punching the cushion last week you made reference to *your* car being used to hit Marco's car the night of your crash. I was a little confused about that. What did you mean?'

'Didn't I tell you?'

'No. You've told me nothing about *your* car. Only Marco's.'

'Oh, well my car was taken from our house at some point after my father and Rosie left the house on Boxing Day. It was found abandoned and quite badly damaged in a suburb some miles away, several days later. When the police examined it they ascertained that it was my car that had been used to hit us on the Putty Road. The one that side-swiped us. They matched the paints. Marco even commented that the car which was disappearing into the distance, was the same colour and model as mine at the time. The number plates had been removed, so he obviously put fake plates on, otherwise Marco would have recognised my plates. We don't know for sure that it was the same car that drove at us shortly after and caused the crash, but we think it was. We think when the killer gained access to our house, he just helped himself to my car keys and probably Marco's office keys. The police believe whoever stole the tapes at the architect's practice used keys to gain entry. Certainly my car keys and Marco's office keys had been removed from the house, although the detective in charge of the crash asked me a few times whether I had definitely left the keys in the house and suggested that I might have left the keys in my car sitting in the driveway. As if I'd do that!'

'Hmm. Well it was a reasonable question to ask you. They have to look at all possibilities.'

'I suppose so.'

'You obviously didn't have an alarm system at your house if the killer was able to enter and walk about freely.'

'No. You don't have one here either do you?'

'No, never seen the need. Although a lot of people have them today and insurance companies are keen on them. Particularly in houses like this - in isolated places.'

'We didn't see the need for it. We supposedly lived in a safe area.'

'So ….. if you are not going to send your drawings to the police in Australia and you want to hand them in personally to particular detectives, when would you consider doing that?

'I might go back at the end of the summer. But I don't really want to yet. My grief is still too raw.'

'And what was his wife's name?'

'Catherine.'

'My grandfather was called Harold Scrope and his wife's name was Catherine. My mother's name was Julie.'

'Little Julie. Yes that was her name. My niece. Harry's eldest daughter. Now lass, you're not pulling my leg are you? Has someone put you up to this?'

'No, no. Really. I have my mother's birth certificate upstairs. And photographs of my grandparents and other people I don't know.'

'So your mother was Julie? What was the name of her daughter?' the woman says turning to her friend as though she might provide the answer. 'She was named after her grandmother, but it was a different name.'

'My name is Cate, spelt with a 'C'. My full name is Catelin.'

'That's it. Catelin. Well what a coincidence! Is that why you came here – looking for family?'

'Sort of. I first came here in 1991 with my family hoping to find someone then, but we only had a few days and I didn't have the time to look into Parish records. I came back in April this year and was planning to do some searches, only I have been very busy and haven't got around to it yet.'

'So how's your mother Julie? Why did she stop sending me cards?'

'She died I'm afraid. Back in 1980.'

'That'd be about the last time I heard from her. That Christmas. That's dreadful. You say she died, how did she die?'

'Look, I've got to get on with work now, but I'd love to catch up with you later or another day if you are busy. I could show you the photos and documents I have.'

'Of course I'd like to meet up with you again. You're my great niece. I was very fond of little Julie. She was only four when I last saw her. I was twelve years older than her. Sixteen when my brother left here.'

'Do you live in the town? I could pop around after work one day if that's convenient.'

'Yes, I do live in town. If you'd like to give me a piece of paper I can write down my address. Come and join us for tea today.'

Cate knows northerner's understanding of tea is different to hers. In Australia if someone says come for tea – they mean either morning or afternoon tea, or simply a cuppa. Here the reference to tea means a meal – that is usually eaten at what Cate considers late afternoon or early evening.

'I'll be working until 6pm and then would need to go home and shower. I could come after your tea if that's okay.'

'But you'd need to eat something lass, after working all day. No we can wait to have tea until you come. My husband Ray wouldn't mind. I can give him a snack to tide him over. There's only the two of us now. The children have all left home.'

'No really, don't wait for me. You have your tea at the normal time. I always have a meal here during the day and just some soup, toast or a sandwich later. I couldn't be there until about 7pm.'

'Well that is a bit late for us. Alright, but I'll save some afters for you.'

Relieved that she won't have to sit down to a meal with strangers, Cate fetches some paper for the woman to write her name and address on. She realises her great aunt hasn't mentioned her name.

'I'll see you at 7pm,' her aunt calls out to her as she is leaving. 'I've left the details on the table.'

'Great. Thanks. See you at 7pm.'

Before pocketing the bit of paper she glances at it and discovers her great aunt's name is Edie Frost with an address in Turfy Hill. She will need to check with Bernice where this Turfy Hill is.

Turfy Hill, Cate discovers, is just a continuation of the Market Place, the same road that the cafe is on but heading out of town. She finds the house, a double fronted stone cottage with a navy blue painted wooden door and matching navy blue windows. She had noticed the house on her walks around the town as it seems to be the only one that doesn't have either white plastic windows or white painted wooden windows. She knocks and is greeted warmly by her great aunt. Cate follows her down the hall to a low beamed large kitchen with wooden cupboards. The walls are painted a light green with white painted beams and ceiling, and white wooden doors lead on to a courtyard. Through the doors she can see they have a fabulous view over the surrounding dales. There is a large scrubbed wooden kitchen table in the centre of the room where a man of similar age to her aunt stands to greet her. Aunt Edie tells her this is her Uncle Ray.

'Ow do, nice t'meet you lass,' he says with a strong Yorkshire accent. Cate sometimes struggles with customer's Yorkshire accents in the café, having to listen carefully to what people are saying to understand what they are ordering. She has learnt what several words, previously alien to her, mean, but occasionally Bernice has had to translate things for her. She's hoping she will be able to understand Uncle Ray.

'Would you like a cup of tea lass?' Aunt Edie asks her.

'Yes, that would be lovely thank you. I love your house, I've noticed it before,' she tells them. 'With its dark blue windows. I thought there must be some rule in the town that houses had to have white windows or something until I saw yours. It's the only one I've noticed that isn't white. And one of the few that aren't plastic.'

'Well Ray is a joiner so he isn't about to have plastic windows fitted on his own house,' Edie comments while pouring water into the tea pot. 'And we have always had dark painted windows. They were red before, but the last time we painted them we decided to have the blue instead. They aren't the original ones though. Ray replaced those with wooden double glazed some years back.'

'I think it looks great. Being trained in architecture and design, I am all in favour of wooden windows. Plastic windows and doors wouldn't work in most areas of Australia due to the heat. It would cause them to expand. Nowadays, houses mainly have coloured metal ones, but sometimes clients want natural wood. I've always lived in houses with wooden ones.' She looks at Ray and continues, 'My grandfather was a carpenter/joiner apparently as well. Did you know him?'

'Aye. It was my father who trained 'im, t'en me.'

'That's how we met,' Edie interrupts pointing back and forth between herself and Ray, while placing side plates on the table in front of them all, plus a plate of small cakes and the teapot. 'I used to go down to the joiner's yard to see Harry sometimes when I was just a young lass, taking him lunch in the school holidays if he hadn't prepared something before he left home. Then of course Harry married, but I still used to go and visit him there sometimes. Harry was still working there when he left for

Australia. I was 16 by then and we, Ray and I, had just started courting. I'd seen Ray at school, but he was a few years older than me, so we'd never spoken there.'

Cate nods and smiles at them. She hasn't heard anyone use the term 'courting' for many years. And then that was mainly in old films.

'Did you just say you'd trained in architecture?' Edie asks pouring the tea and pushing the plate of cakes towards her, 'And help yourself. These are home made by the way,' she adds.

'Yes, I did a degree in Architecture and Design in Sydney, but didn't complete the additional training to become a fully qualified architect. I worked in an architect's practice though, doing drawings and visiting sites sometimes.'

'You won't find any of that kind of work around here. You'd have to go to one of the bigger towns or cities,' Edie says.

'I'm not looking for that kind of work at the moment, I wanted a change. The café suits me fine.'

'You sound just like Harry's young 'un did when she came over int' 70s,' Ray remarks.

'Do you mean with my Australian accent?' Cate asks.

'Aye,' Ray says, 'she were just a bairn when the family left here, so she would've grown up in Australia.'

Cate just nods and then asks them about their family. Edie explains that they have three children. One son and two daughters. One daughter Jane, the youngest, is a married secondary school teacher working and living in the nearby town of Kirkby Stephen and has no children as yet. Ray tells her Jane followed Edie into teaching, who then explains that she is primary school trained and still works part time at the local primary school. She tells Cate that she left Hawes to train as a teacher but returned to work in the local primary school when she qualified, not wanting to be away from Ray any longer. They married just over a year later.

'Of course I had to give up the teaching when I married. They wouldn't let you continue working once you married in those days. All that nonsense has stopped now and I returned to work part time in the local primary school when all the kids were in secondary school.'

The information is thrown at Cate with barely any interruptions apart from 'have another cake' – or 'do you want any more tea?' before continuing full pelt. Cate has to concentrate hard to keep up with it all. The other daughter runs a book shop with her husband in Richmond and has two children. When Cate tells Edie she went into a bookshop recently in Richmond, Edie tells her it must have been her daughter Susan's shop as it is the only one in town. The son, Richard is an engineer and is based in York with his wife and three children, but he apparently travels for his work. Many asides are thrown in about all the grandchildren – whose names Cate promptly forgets and she is still listening carefully when Edie suddenly throws in a question, asking Cate to tell her how her mother died. Cate has been dreading this, not sure how much to reveal, but in the end decides to be honest, about her mother at least. She tells them about her mother's murder and how she was taken to Sydney to live with her father, stepmother and half-sister Rosie.

'Why didn't your father let me know what happened to your mother?' Edie asks.

'I asked Dad when we were living over here in the late 80s if he knew whether Mum had any family left in Yorkshire and he said he was sure there were relatives, but he couldn't find mum's address book when he came to collect me from Melbourne and assumed the police had taken it for their enquiries and not returned it. So he was unable to contact anyone at the time. He said he'd later asked the police about it and they said there was no such thing in the evidence box. He asked Aunt Betty, mum's best friend, and she admitted that she had taken it to let mum's friends know, but it had been ruined by a leak in her house from the bathroom upstairs that damaged all her books on a shelf in the room below. That's apparently where the address book was. She hadn't thought about contacting relatives in England. She threw it away.'

'Well that solves that mystery then,' Aunt Edie says a grimace, 'but I'm sorry you had to witness that lass. It must have been terrible for you.' She places her hand on Cate's arm in empathy.

'Did they ever catch 'im?' Ray asks.

Cate swallows back the tears that are welling up and looking up at him says, 'No, and he's still murdering people.'

Cate explains how she spent years sketching the man and approached the police when she eighteen, but nothing came of it. Then how, just last year, she identified the man leaving a bishop's property near where she worked and most of what had followed since, until leaving to travel to England. She had left out the bit about her husband and son being in the car with her. She just didn't feel strong enough to speak of it yet and it seemed just too much to inflict on these people who were virtual strangers to her, despite being relatives.

'He sounds a right bad 'un.' Ray says shifting uncomfortably in his seat. 'Is there nowt police could do t'find 'im?'

Cate explains how her more recent sketches were

stolen from her house, which she hadn't included in her narrative, and how the computerised-composite failed to bring any results adding that she hadn't been willing to complete any further sketches for them at the time.

'I'm not surprised,' Aunt Edie sniffs. 'You had enough to deal with, recovering from your injuries from the crash. I noticed you had a limp – presumably that's a result of your leg injury?'

'Yes, but it's improving all the time. I walk on the dales some days. I have become acquainted with someone who lives out there and we often go walking together.'

'Not the doctor's husband? The psychologist?'

'Yes, how did you know?'

'I saw you talking to him in the café one day, when he was in there having lunch. Such a tragedy, the doctor dying like that. She was our doctor. He's all alone in that big house out there. I thought he might sell up and move into town.'

'I think he's quite attached to the house. He and his wife lived there for over 25 years and his granddaughter comes up to stay there with him - with her husband now as she is married and about to have a child herself. He says we're about the same age.'

'You never met anyone you wanted to marry yourself?' Edie asks.

Cate ignores the question and picks up her bag. 'Now I wonder if you might be able to tell me who all these people are in the photographs,' she says pulling out a few albums and placing them on the table. 'I know who some of them are. There's quite a few look like they might have been taken here in Yorkshire, so you would probably know them – you might even be in some of them,' she adds to Edie.

Ray excuses himself as soon as Cate presents the albums and leaves the women alone. For the next hour Edie is delightfully absorbed in explaining, picture by picture, who everyone is. Cate pulls each photograph out of the album and makes a note of their names on the back of each picture if she is not aware of who they are. It is gratifying to discover what their names are after all these years. Once they have finished with Cate's albums Edie collects her own albums and takes Cate through all the photographs of her family, which include further pictures of her great grandparents and grandfather as well as Edie and Ray's children throughout their childhood and the grandchildren.

'Our Susan takes after her grandmother, just as your mother did. You will see the resemblance when you meet Susan.'

'Yes I could see my mother looked a lot like one of the women in the older pictures. I thought she might be my great grandmother. Is she still alive?'

'No lass, she died last year. She was only 82. A shame you didn't get to meet her last time you came to Hawes. She would have loved to have met you. You would have been her only great grandchild at the time. Neither my son or Susie had any children back then, although both had one on the way.'

'Yes I would have liked to have met her too. I wanted to try to trace some relatives back in the early 90s but we had so little time here.'

'I also have some pictures of you and your mother,' Edie says placing another small album on the table. 'She sent me a new one of you both with each Christmas card. Can you bear to look at them?'

Cate nods and she spends time looking at the

photographs, some which she has already and recognises, but discovers other new ones as well. When she mentions this, Edie offers her the photographs which she gratefully accepts. Looking at her watch Cate is shocked to discover it is 10pm when Edie finally closes the last album. She is exhausted, makes her excuses and says she needs to walk back while there is still some light. Despite having experienced the long summer nights of England when she lived in London, it never ceases to amaze Cate how late the light finally disappears up here in Yorkshire. Just a few nights ago she and Alan had been sitting on his patio at 11pm and she could still see faint pink and blue sky in the distance. In Sydney it is always dark by 8pm even in the summer months.

'You must come for Sunday dinner one day,' Edie says as Cate is packing up her albums to leave. 'I can invite my daughters over. They don't have so far to travel and often come for a Sunday roast. They were your mother's first cousins, so they'd be your first cousins once removed. Although, as I was the baby of the family, my children are closer in age to you than they would have been to your mother.'

'I work every Sunday as a rule,' Cate tells her. 'I don't know whether I would be able to organise the time off.'

'I'm sure Bernice would be happy to oblige seeing as it would be for a family gathering - I mentioned to her today, before I left the café, that you were my great niece. I could ask her if you like.'

'No, no. I can do that.' Bernice didn't mention anything to me, Cate thinks. No doubt too busy. 'Just let me know when you might want to arrange something and I can ask her.'

'I'll talk to the girls and pop in one day to let you know.

As it's almost the end of June now there's just over three weeks left until the school's break up for the summer holidays. I know Jane is very busy at this time of year in her school, as are we in my school, and I'm not sure of the dates any of them are going away on their holidays.'

'Right. Well thanks for the tea and cakes. And for the company. And listen, I would rather you didn't say anything to anyone in the town about what happened to my mother or anything else I've told you tonight. I don't really want to become the subject of gossip.'

'I understand lass. Sadly all my brothers who lived locally are deceased now and my sister, as I told you, moved to Florida when she retired. My brothers all died too soon, but I still have nieces in and around the town and two sisters-in-law. Some of them are dreadful gossips. If I mentioned anything to one of them you can be sure the whole town would know very quickly. You can be assured I won't.'

'I'd rather they didn't know anything about my mother's death or any of the other things I've told you. I just told Bernice I had been in a car crash. Nothing else. I came to Hawes for some peace and quiet.'

'I promise I won't say anything. I will mention you are here to my girls though, of course, as I want them to come and meet you, but not about why. I'll just say you are working and travelling around England and we happened to discover each other in the café. I'll tell Ray not to say anything – not that he would, he is not the type to disclose any private business to anyone.'

'Thank you. I'd like to say goodbye to Ray – is he still up?'

'No lass, he'll be long in bed by now. Don't worry I'll pass on your goodbyes in the morning for you.'

Cate walks back to the Café deep in thought. She has enjoyed her evening with Edie, and meeting Ray, but is not sure whether the meal with other members of the family would be wise. They would be bound to ask questions she has no intention of answering. It could be awkward.

# 32

Over the next few weeks Cate has to fend off several of the cousins and the two widowed sisters-in-laws who claim to be her great aunts-by-marriage. Edie popped in to warn her that word had spread of her existence through Edie's daughter Susan telling one of her cousins in a telephone conversation. Cate repeatedly apologised and said she was unable to stop and chat to them due to work and so they didn't hang around for too long. Bernice told Cate that Edie was fine, but warned her to avoid engaging in conversation with the 'poisoned tongued cousins' and the sisters-in-law. Soon other local customers of a similar age to Edie, or older, would say things like, 'So you're Edie's great niece from Australia. I knew your grandparents and your mother when she was little.' It seemed to Cate as though most of the town knew her grandparents or mother. Or at least claimed to. Bernice was one of the few who made no such claim. When Cate asked her if she had known her grandparents as well she said, 'No we're blow-ins - we've only been here for the past 20 years, moving up from York. You'd think we'd come from another country from the locals attitude to us at first.'

Bernice assures her that the other locals who claim acquaintance with her grandparents are just being friendly, that there is no malice intended, and that she should take it as a sign of acceptance in the community. Cate can see that, as they mention it with genuine friendliness.

Edie finally comes to see Cate with some dates for the special Sunday meal where she will meet Edie's daughters, her first cousins once-removed. Cate had discovered the strange term of 'once-removed' meant that there was a generation difference – meaning her mother was by birth the first cousin and Cate the next generation down. Susan's children were Cate's second cousins because they were the same generation as her, although they were still young children. Her first cousins once removed were in their early thirties.

The date is set for the second Sunday in August, when everyone will be back from their holidays in Europe. Bernice readily agrees to her having the day off as she had covered an extra shift recently on a Wednesday so Cate really doesn't have an excuse not to go.

At her weekly Tuesday dinner date and sleepover at Alan's, Cate voices her concerns about the meal set for the following Sunday while they are sitting outside, Cate, having one of her rare cigarettes and biting her nails. Alan is smoking his pipe. Cate only smokes occasionally now, when she is extremely nervous.

'So what are your concerns?' Alan asks.

'I'm dreading it. I'm afraid they will ask a load of questions about my mother.'

'Where is that fear coming from?'

Cate thinks for a minute then realises what he is asking. 'Okay, it's from my thoughts. Which then makes me feel nervous and sick. But what if they do ask? What should I say?'

'What would you like to say to them?'

'You know you have an annoying habit of answering my questions with a question?'

'Well it's not appropriate for me to tell you what to say to them if they ask about your mother. What would you want to tell them?'

'I don't *want* to tell them anything. I suppose I could just say she died suddenly when I was only six and hope that they don't pursue it further.'

'And if they ask how she died? What will you say?'

'Nothing. I wouldn't trust them not to pass it on to one of the cousins like last time and then it would be all over town.'

'There you are then. You have answered your own question. You are going to say she died suddenly when you were very young.'

'What if they then think she either committed suicide or was a drug addict and took an overdose? I wouldn't want them to think badly of my mother.'

'Cate you can't know what they might think, remember. Whatever they think it's not in your control. You just need to decide what you are willing or not willing to discuss.'

'Yes, you're right. I'll just play it by ear then.'


Edie has extended her dining table in the front dining room, a room Cate has not seen before. There is to be nine of them for the meal. The couples arrive about an hour before dinner and after meeting them all and exchanging pleasantries, Susan's eight year old daughter, Phoebe, asks Cate why she limps. Cate just shrugs it off saying she had been in a car accident some months before leaving Australia, makes her excuses and disappears into the kitchen to help Edie.

'You shouldn't be here helping me lass,' Edie says. 'You're the guest of honour.'

'No it's fine. I'd like to help you.'

'Did you notice how our Susan looks quite a bit like your mother?'

'Yes she does. It felt strange looking at her.'

'Must bring back sad memories for you?'

'Do you have a dish I can put these potatoes in?' Cate asks choosing to ignore Edie's statement about sad memories.

'Yes that one on the range there with the lid. I think we're all set to go now. Shall we take everything in?'

Once everything is placed on the table, the family start helping themselves talking nineteen to the dozen. It's the first roast dinner Cate has experienced since coming to England and she savours every mouthful eating in silence, watching and listening to the exchanges taking place around the table. She can see that they are a close family. Cate loves Edie's Yorkshire puddings, which are served as small individual helpings and is disappointed to only manage to acquire one, whereas young Phoebe, the eight year old, piles three on to her plate without challenge. Edie starts clearing the empty plates away when everyone has finished and Ray disappears to collect more beers for the men. Cate is about to follow Edie with further dishes when Susan asks her about her mother – where she lives now and what she is doing? Edie has clearly kept her promise and mentioned no word of her death. Everyone stops talking to wait for her reply. 'My mother died when I was very young and so I moved to Sydney to live with my father and stepmother,' Cate eventually says.

'What did she die of? Was it cancer or something else?' Susan persists.

Cate pretends not to hear the question as she hastily exits the room with empty serving dishes. She finds Edie rinsing things in preparation for washing up and tells her what has just happened.

'What can I say Edie, if she pushes me for an answer about how Mum died? I just can't face telling her that mum was murdered.'

'Your mother was *murdered*?' shouts a loud voice from behind them.

Turning they see Phoebe with her arms full of more plates. Edie rushes over to rescue them from her precarious grip and says, 'I've told you before you shouldn't be listening into adult's conversations lassie.'

Pouting, Phoebe turns and rushes back to the dining room shouting, '*Muuum* cousin Cate's mother was *murdered!*'

Edie covers her face with her hands. 'Oh God, I'm sorry Cate. I was worried something like this might happen.'

Susie and her sister Jane rush into the kitchen, followed by young Phoebe and her brother Will. 'Is it true?' both women ask in turn. 'What happened?'

'Out you two,' Edie says to the kids. 'Back to the table or there'll be no desert.'

'Aw gran, I want to hear as well,' Phoebe moans.

'Out Phoebe. And Will. I won't tell you again.'

Cate looks at Edie and shrugs hopelessly. 'I don't really want to talk about this. Except to say that yes she was murdered because she was an eyewitness to the man who murdered another woman. So he came after her as well. That's all I am prepared to say. Now if you will excuse me Edie, I think I had better be going. Thank you very much for the meal. It was delicious and I've enjoyed meeting you all.'

Cate collects her bag and leaves the house.

The girls stand in stunned silence in their mother's kitchen after Cate's hasty departure. 'Was that really necessary?' Edie demands. 'The lass is upset enough about everything that's happened without Phoebe and you two stirring things up.'

'What do you mean everything that's happened? Is there more?' Susan asks.

'That's enough!' Ray says in anger, walking into the kitchen. 'Tis nowt to do with you. And don't you be going speaking to those mealy mouthed cousins of yours 'bout this.'

'No dad,' they chorus. They know their father is not quick to anger but when he becomes angry it is always best to remain quiet.

It is not Edie's daughters who spread the news, but young Phoebe, Cate later finds out. She told her friend at school in Richmond, who told her mother, who happened to be close friends with one of the cousins in Hawes. Word spread quickly around the town and Cate notices a number of the regulars coming in for snacks or meals, looking at her and whispering. It was the hospital and rehab unit all over again as she heard 'that's the lass … murder …'

Bernice found a teary Cate in the pantry after a particularly unpleasant afternoon later the following week. 'What's the matter lass? What's going on? What were they all whispering about?'

'You mean they didn't tell you?' Cate sobs.

'No *they* didn't – tell me what exactly?'

'Nothing. Would you mind if I remained in the kitchen washing up for the rest of the day? I can't face going out there again.'

'Yes, alright, but I want to you to tell me later what this is all about.'

Edie came rushing in just before closing. 'I've just heard what's been happening. I found out it was our Phoebe started it all by telling her friend at school in Richmond, who told her mother …. I'm so sorry Cate.'

'What is this malicious gossip that is being spread about Cate?' Bernice demands to know. She walks over to the door, turns the sign 'closed' sign and declares that they all need to sit down with a nice cuppa and sort it out.

Edie is reluctant to say anything so Cate explains about her mother's murder, which has been the subject of the gossip. 'It's not just about that, it's just brought up everything else that's happened as well.'

Cate looks at Edie. 'Tell her the rest lass, it's best she knows now.'

At length Cate explains the rest of the story. When she reaches the part that involved the car crash she turns to Edie. 'I didn't tell you everything Edie. You see my husband and 10 week old baby were in the car with me as well - only they died.'

Bernice and Edie look at her in shocked horror. 'I knew there was something troubling you deeply,' Bernice says. 'But I didn't like to pry as it was none of my business. You did your job well and that's all I asked of you. I can't believe what you've been through. It's just horrific.'

'Oh Cate, and you've been carrying all this alone,' Edie sobs. 'How sad.'

'Not entirely alone. I've told Alan Mathers everything and he has helped me a lot, taking me through some processes to help cope with it all.'

'He's a good man,' Bernice says.

'Yes he is. I'm sorry Bernice, I'm not sure if I can carry on working here. I'm sorry to let you down, but I had a belly full of the constant whispering when I was in the rehab unit learning to walk again. It was in all the papers you see. About our car being run off the road. And then later about my mother's murder and my stepmother's death. Some reporter did some digging and linked me with the different events. I really don't want to listen to whispers day in and day out again. What worries me is that someone might mention my mother's murder to someone who has links to the press over here. If the British press got hold of it they might do some digging and discover the more recent events like Marco and Milo's death. You know how the press like to sensationalise a story. If that happens then …..'

'I understand Cate, don't worry. I'll be sorry to see you go. You've been one of the best seasonal workers we've had. And your chocolate cake will be missed,' she winks. Cate has been making her famous chocolate cake each morning for the past two months, fed up with the so called chocolate cake that Bernice had delivered from a local woman. 'It just tastes of sugar,' she'd complained to Bernice one day. 'A chocolate cake is supposed to taste of chocolate.' And so she'd offered to make her version of a chocolate cake which they now sell out of each day.

'I'll give you the recipe and you can make it,' Cate laughs.

'Would you like to come and stay with Ray and me?' Edie asks.

'Thank you for the offer, but no. I think that would be disastrous for you and Ray. I'll ask Alan if he'll put me up for a few days and then I'll head off.'

'Where will you go?' Edie asks with a worried frown on her face.

'I don't know,' Cate replies, not keen to say she will head back to Manchester. 'Maybe London,' she adds.

'You're welcome to stay in your room upstairs until you're ready to leave. There's no rush.'

'You'll be wanting to find someone else to replace me and might need the room. Thanks anyway. I'll stay tonight if that's alright with you - and then phone Alan in the morning.'

'Phone him from here before you go up if you like. No need to go up to the call box. You need to get yourself one of those mobile phones.'

'My husband Marco had one, but it proved to be totally useless when we were run off the road as there was no signal in the area. I've had no desire to buy one since.'

'The signal's not so good up here in Hawes either.'

'What's the point of them then?' Cate asks.

'The providers claim they are going to improve reception in the area. '

'I wouldn't have one of those things if you paid me,' Edie says. 'Our Susan has one and she's always fiddling with it when she comes over or when we go to her house - sending texts she calls it - to her friends. Ray just put his foot down one day and said she had to put it away when we were talking and eating. She even brought it to the table with her one day! Can you imagine, sitting at the table playing with a phone. The silly thing beeps what seems like every few minutes. It's so rude!'

'Yes we've had much of the same experience with Steph as well. She's banned from using hers at the dinner table as well. I suspect these mobiles will become an integral part of our future though. All the young people seem to have one.'

Alan had welcomed Cate coming to stay without question when she had phoned him from the café. When she arrives at his place the following day he suggests she stay with him indefinitely, but Cate insists it won't work.

'It won't work Alan, not due to any sort of incompatibility between us, but because of the few gossips in Hawes,' she tells him. 'They are bound to discover I am here with you and make life uncomfortable for you.'

'I don't go into Hawes that often these days anyway. Not since Sylvia died. The only reason I tend to go there is if I need to see a doctor. Or more recently to see you at the café. I do my shopping elsewhere.'

'Besides, I don't have a job now and I need to earn money,' Cate continues. 'There will be greater opportunities for me in Manchester, with all the building work going on there. I might pick up work in my old field.'

'That I can understand. I will be sad to see you go though.'

'I will be sad to leave as well. Apart from the recent gossiping, I've enjoyed my time here. Working at the café - walking the Dales - meeting you. You have been very kind, helping me through my grief.'

'No you helped yourself through the grief.'

'With you facilitating me though. I would have still been stuck back where I was when you discovered me that night if you hadn't asked me all those questions I had to find the answers to.'

'You didn't *have* to find the answers, you chose to. You were willing to find the answers for yourself.'

'Okay, let's leave it at that shall we? Now what are we going to do today?'

# 33

**Manchester, August 2000**

Cate uses the bulk of her savings from working in the Café to pay for a hotel room for several nights and for the deposit, together with a month's rent on a small furnished one bedroomed flat not far from Adhita's place. She also has to pay a deposit to have the gas and electricity connected in her name. Apparently, this is the usual practice if you don't have a track record with any companies. It had not been easy to find a furnished flat.

'Apart from shared student housing, we don't let furnished properties,' was the stock answer she received from most agents.

The flat would not have been her first choice (or second or third choice for that matter), but with little to choose from Cate had grabbed it when the opportunity arose. Now she has to find work.

'You're looking 100% better,' Adhita remarks when they meet at Cate's flat before setting off for a meal several weeks later. 'The Yorkshire Dales must have agreed with you, you even have the remnants of a sun tan I can see, which is surprising for Yorkshire. Must be all that wind they have up there. Mind you, I seem to remember that you only need to be in the sun for five minutes before you start tanning with that skin tone you have.'

'There were hot sunny days as well,' Cate replies indignantly. 'And if you're talking about windy places, Manchester must top the charts. The tall buildings create wind tunnels that can knock you off your feet when you turn a corner! I nearly took off the other day. The wind caught my jacket, it billowed out and I lifted several inches off the ground. One of the girls at work told me Manchester is called 'The Windy City'. Not without reason.'

'I know. How do you think I acquired my sun tan,' Adhita says straight-faced.

'You daft thing!' Cate laughs.

'God help us – she is beginning to talk like someone from Yorkshire!' Adhita exclaims as she heads off for an inspection of the flat, which takes less than a minute, and returning comments, 'I thought my flat was small, but this is miniscule by comparison. Your living room and bedroom must be a quarter of the size of mine.'

'Yes, but the rent is manageable. It's all I need. At least there is a small table and chairs in the kitchen, so I can eat in there.'

'If you say so. Personally I'd feel a little claustrophobic.'

'I'm not here that often, as I'm working seven days a week at the moment, five days at my new job at the architectural practice and earning extra money over the weekends portrait sketching.'

Once her new telephone had been connected, Cate had called London to update Adhita about her return to Manchester, her new flat and the work she'd found. Adhita had been thrilled to hear Cate was back in Manchester, but said she wouldn't be back for another few weeks, as she was looking after Naniji while her parents were away.

'What about during the winter months? You won't be working at weekends then.'

'No, but at least it will be cosy and warm. And cost little to heat. I might buy a television then, and more books to read.'

'I wouldn't know about bills. I don't have to pay any for my place. The rent they charge me includes everything.'

'Exactly. If you did you'd have to consider those aspects when it came to choosing where you lived.'

'Why don't you buy a place? There's still places going for silly prices at the moment. As the dates for the Commonwealth Games approaches, prices will rocket. Compared to London, Manchester is very cheap. I'm considering buying somewhere as an investment to rent out.'

'I hadn't thought about buying. I'm not sure how long I will be staying in the UK.'

'Well even if you only stay for a few years, it would still be an investment. Values in Manchester are predicted to rise by at least 12% in the next couple of years. You would save on rent and have a better place to live.'

'But then I'd have to buy what you call the white goods and furniture. I don't really want to spend money on things like that.'

'It's worth it to have a decent bed and couch. Most of the furniture in my place is my own. The University only provided the cooker and curtains. The previous occupant conveniently left a bookcase and the table and chairs. Everything else is mine.'

'I didn't realise that. I must admit the bed here isn't all that comfortable.'

'I like my comforts. I don't sleep for long most nights, but when I do I want to know I am going to be comfortable. You could always sell things anyway if you went back to Australia.'

'I suppose. We had to do that when we left London in '91.'

'I'd give it some thought if I were you. Worth considering. Right, let's head off to eat and you can tell me all about your family in Yorkshire and the exercises that your psychologist friend took you through that you claim helped you so much.'

Cate spent the time at the restaurant talking about the new family members and Yorkshire and what happened with them, but she told Adhita she wanted to wait until they were back at her flat to talk about other matters.

When they were finally sipping tea a few hours later Adhita says, 'First of all you need to tell me what happened so that I can understand how this Alan helped you. I've suspected that Milo didn't make it and that you and Marco split up or something. Did you leave him or did he leave you?'

'In a way he left me, but not in the way you think. He died Adhita. With Milo in a horrific crash. That's how I hurt my leg.'

'Fucking hell Cate!' Adhita exclaims loudly. 'Why didn't you tell me? I've spent months thinking Marco might have been a right bastard towards you.'

'Adhita!'

'What? Oh for god's sake Cate, you're not going all prudish on me are you about swearing? Everyone swears. Even you, you hypocrite – although the worst I've ever heard you say is 'shit!' and that was years ago when you were frustrated about your drawings.'

'I've said much worse since. It's just that I've never heard you swear. Ever. And I didn't challenge you just about the swearing Adhita.'

'No. I'm really sorry. I wasn't intending to be disrespectful. It was just the shock. Tell me then.'

With several tearful stops Cate gradually fills Adhita in on the crash and how she felt afterwards. And how Alan helped her through the grieving process.

'So what you're saying is that all the thoughts you had swirling around in your head when you were in hospital were based on either lies or things you couldn't possibly know?'

'Yes. At the end of it all, the only aspect of it that was true were my feelings. Some things I was thinking might have been true, but I will never know.'

'Like what?'

'That Milo was suffering and I should have remained holding him until his death. The doctor said he was unconscious and wouldn't have known anything. But none of us were there and so how do we know he didn't wake up and cry out in pain, needing his parents. Marco wouldn't have been able to reach him.'

'Okay. I understand. You don't know if he woke in pain and you will never know, so there is no point in tormenting yourself with those thoughts. It is likely that what the doctor said is correct. That he remained unconscious throughout.'

'Yes. So I've stopped torturing myself with such thoughts.'

'That's good. You look so much better. Lighter. And your gait has improved.'

'That's all that walking on the Dales. Not exactly even ground for walking practise, but it somehow did the trick. Plus the waiting on tables for many hours each day.'

'Are you still experiencing any pain with your leg?'

Cate sighs. 'Yes, I still have pain every day, although I

seldom take painkillers for it now, only if I have a really bad night. The blood flow seems fine now. I've had several check-ups.'

'On a scale of one to ten, ten being the worst, how would you rate the pain now?'

'A three to four most days.'

'And what was it when you first came back to the UK?'

'A seven at least. Eight some days.'

'Well that's great news and I'm pleased you've come back to Manchester. It's better for you to be here than in a small town where you were exposed to gossip and pointing. That's the beauty of a city. There's so many places you can live and the population is so large, that if you don't like one place you can just move on to another. You can't do that in a small town.'

'No. But I did enjoy my time there though, apart from those aspects. It's a beautiful place to live. Although I love Alan's place I don't know if I could live way out in the country like he does. Mind you it's not like Australia. In Australia, way out in the bush, you could be hundreds of miles from your nearest neighbour or town. Alan is less than a quarter of a mile from his nearest neighbour and only four miles from civilization.'

'Not my cup of tea either. So ….. are you ready to talk about everything else that happened in Australia? All you've told me is about Milo's premature birth and the crash. What about everything else? Janet's death? I've gained the impression that there is a lot more that happened.'

'Yes, there was and I will, but not tonight if you don't mind. It would take most of the night and I have work tomorrow. Tell me how Naniji is. And all the news on the rest of your family,' Cate says changing the subject. She has been avoiding thinking too much about *him*.

The conversation about other events in Australia is forgotten with Adhita and Cate distracted with properties and their work. Adhita had decided, rather than invest in a flat or house, she wanted to purchase a whole semi-derelict warehouse next to one of the canals near Deansgate with her brothers and convert them into 16 apartments. Adhita asks Cate to draw up the plans for the conversion to submit for planning permission and works on persuading Cate to come in with them, so she can have one of the flats. The whole area is improving and Adhita believes it will be a sound investment. She sits down with Cate to go over the costings.

'Cate if you invest one sixteenth of the purchasing and building costs, complete all the plans, and help with project management, it would be a fraction of the cost of purchasing her own place independently. Look I've drawn up comparable costs here.'

'Yes I can see that, but I don't have enough money to cover those costs. I have some in Australia, from insurance pay-outs, and the rent of our home - but not enough.'

'Try the banks here, Cate, it's too good an opportunity to miss.'

After approaching the bank Cate discovers that they will not lend her any money on the venture. Once the conversion is complete, however, they will look at lending her money to purchase a habitable flat. Adhita and her brothers are planning on selling twelve of the flats and keeping one each apiece for rental. They had hoped that the sixteenth one would be for Cate. They have raised most of the necessary capital for the purchase and conversion through savings and re-mortgaging one of the brother's houses in London.

Finally Cate telephones her father asking whether he could lend her the money she needs until she can raise a mortgage. She knows he has the funds available as the new unit (apartment) he purchased with cash, although nearer to the sea where prices are normally higher than other areas, was a much lower purchase cost than the money released from the sale of the Beecroft house. The Beecroft house, where Cate had grown up, was in a desirable suburb. The house had also been huge and sat in large grounds. The back yard/garden was enormous and so the value of the Beecroft house far exceeded the cost of the new smaller unit. Her father readily lends her the cash and she nervously invests the money with the Acharya family.

Cate gains permission to use the facilities at her job out of working hours and draws up the plans, which she asks her boss to check. Once satisfied, she passes them on to the family and then they are submitted for approval. The planning process takes three months and while that is happening Adhita and Cate search for a suitable builder for the project and source fixtures and fittings. With recommendations from her employers, they choose one building contractor whose costings prove slightly higher than the original budget. Rather than raising further capital, they decide to proceed with the completion on all but the last remaining four flats (Cate's and the three rentals) and sell a few of the properties to raise the funds for the final conversions. The structure, layout and first fixes of plumbing and electrics of each apartment will be covered by their current budget, it is simply final fix wiring, heating, plastering, flooring and fixtures and fittings in the bathroom and kitchen that won't be completed on their apartments.

Eight months later the first apartments are ready and there is a waiting list of buyers. The apartments are all sold at full asking price and Adhita, her brothers and Cate are eventually able to proceed with the final work on the remaining apartments. A further three months later Cate is able to move into her two bedroomed apartment – one of the lucky ones to have a spacious outdoor terrace, rather than a tiny balcony. She manages to obtain a mortgage and re-pays the loan from her father.

'Just look at this space,' Adhita marvels walking around Cate's new living room. 'Even with all your furniture in here it still looks enormous.'

'That's because I don't have that much. And I don't plan on filling it up with much more either,' Cate replies. She had been economical with furniture, buying the bare minimum for her requirements. Apart from the beds, a couch and white goods, all her other purchases were second hand. There are a few more things she might buy, but she'd wanted to keep it low key so that when she returns to Australia there won't be too much to sell or dispose of.

The spare room is awash with boxes still to be unpacked and the only piece of furniture in there is a bed. Alan is due to come down next weekend so Cate decides he can have her bedroom with the en suite and she can sleep amongst the boxes.

# 34

**Manchester, August 2002**

The development of the City of Manchester in preparation
for the Commonwealth Games has enhanced its status to
being a leading International European City, providing the
largest Commonwealth sporting event in the history of
the Games. The city has been thriving on the international
crowds who have flocked to see the events; businesses
city-wide have prospered throughout the duration of the
Games and there have been large numbers of visitors to
various cultural events taking place around the region.
A partying atmosphere has prevailed amongst the locals,
proud to see their city so alive and buzzing. Flags of
the Commonwealth countries can be seen displayed in
windows of homes around the city and suburbs, revealing
the multi-cultural population of the city.

Cate, and her colleagues from the architect's practice,
received complementary tickets for events through some of
the contracts they had completed linked to the games and
so Cate had enjoyed an evening of exciting athletic events
at the new City of Manchester Stadium. It is rumoured
that it will convert to a football stadium and become the
home ground for Manchester City Football Club. Not
being a particular fan of football (which Cate calls soccer
in Australia) she would prefer to see it retained for regular
athletic events, but understands that it is football where

the money is and it will at least have more regular use. The papers say that music events will also be held there outside the football season.

Adhita had suggested to Cate that while the Games were on, she could rent her whole flat out for mega money, to visiting families from Australia who have relatives competing in events, and then stay with her at the university. Cate was tempted at the idea of boosting her savings but the thought of moving all her personal belongings out to a storage facility just for the extra money she might gain was too much to bear thinking about. She has, however, rented out her bedroom while she is sleeping in the spare room which is now fully furnished to accommodate personal visitors. Letting her bedroom with its en suite meant she could offer a stranger some privacy and at an affordable rate, and she only had to move her clothes and some personal belongings into the built-ins in the spare room rather than removing them entirely from her home.

The sister of one of the competitors from Australia is staying with her for two weeks, bringing in some handy extra cash. Her lodger is only around in the evenings during the first week and Cate has enjoyed sharing meals with her and chatting about home. Having the company of a fellow Aussie, Cate realises how much she misses interacting with Australians. She regularly seeks out any Australian films that are released at the cinema, or any Australian documentaries or films screened on TV in an attempt to connect to her roots. Her book shelves are filled with novels by Australian authors Rosie regularly sends her, as well as books with scenes of Australia, few of which are available for purchase in the UK. She even had a short foray into watching an Australian soap, one that she recognised as being filmed at Palm Beach in Sydney, but this was stretching matters a little too far, providing no emotional connection whatsoever and it was really targeted at teenagers.

Throughout the late Spring and summer months Cate also returned to Saturday sketching, in the dockside venue where she worked when she first arrived back in Manchester, so her savings are building up to cover either the cost of further study or returning home. Cate has been considering part-time training for the Masters of Architecture (MArch) at the Manchester School of Architecture – but she discovered that this would take four years to complete. She is not sure that she wants to remain in the UK for that length of time. Basically she is feeling homesick and wants to see her father and Rosie again. They had recently discussed the possibility of her father and Rosie flying over to the UK to spend Christmas with her this year, but Cate thinks she might prefer to go home instead. She is undecided at present. She has a fabulous place to live that costs her far less than she used to pay in rent. She enjoys her work. The people in her community and work environment are great. She earns a decent wage. So what is the problem?

The problem, she realised when discussing it with Alan on one of their lengthy evening calls, is that she has unresolved business to deal with in Sydney that constantly niggles away in her brain; the man who murdered her mother, quite possibly her step-mother and Marco and Milo. Also a number of other people outside her family circle. However, there is her own and her family's safety to take into consideration. Would she be able to take any action without fear of being pursued by him again? She is unsure whether the murderer has any idea of where her father and Rosie live, but if he is in the field of employment that Adhita suggested, then no doubt he will have access to information which reveals their address.

She had finally had a lengthy session with Adhita many months back, going over every detail of events from the first day she saw 'the man' in 1999, visiting DI Paramo again, Milo's premature birth, DI Paramo's death, her near fatal hit and run 'accident', Janet's death, the crash on the mountain road and the devastating events which followed. Also her subsequent conversations with DC Hargreaves and what the detective had discovered, including the theft of her drawings from her home and the security tapes from architect's office.

After expressing shock at the full range of events, Adhita had sat in silent contemplation for a minute and then said, 'It's obvious isn't it?'

'What's obvious, you've lost me?'

'Well the cryptic message that this woman detective received from the nun via the priest or bishop whatever he was – "that you'll find him in the same place". That's obvious. He's a policeman isn't he? And he meant that Detective Hargreaves would find him in the same place that she is. Where *she* works of course.'

'How did you come up with that? When Detective Hargreaves last came to see me, we pondered over it for ages and just couldn't work it out. We thought of something connected to the Church – meaning the same place as the bishop. DC Hargreaves looked into people working in the Diocese Headquarters and there was no one fitting the description.'

'I don't think the bishop was referring to himself – he was referring to *her* – that *she* would find him where *she* worked. You just need to weigh up all the probabilities.'

'God, you may be right. You know we never thought of that.'

'Can you contact this woman detective?'

'Yes, she gave me her parent's phone number in case I wanted to contact her. She didn't want me making any contact with her at work. She also advised me not to talk to anyone else in the police force about it. It was too dangerous given that two policemen had died in suspicious circumstances. I don't know if she would still be working at the same place anyway as she had put in for a promotion and a transfer.'

'Well why don't you try to contact her and suggest that this might be the answer to the riddle?'

'Yes I can do that.'

Over the following few months Cate tried telephoning the number that India Hargreaves gave her but each time she called it went straight to the answer machine. She didn't dare leave a message. Now she thinks it is about time that she attempted to make contact again after several week's gap. Over the weekend she calls at various times, but again only receives the answer phone. Perhaps the family are away on some lengthy extended holiday or have moved. But surely the number would be disconnected if they'd moved?

When Cate couldn't get through to the Hargreaves's house after her first few attempts she'd decided to take a chance and call Detective Ellis instead. Detective Hargreaves spoke highly of him, but Cate'd only met him a couple of times. When she went to dig out his card it wasn't where she believed it to be and couldn't find it anywhere. Cate was reluctant to try and reach Detective Ellis through the main Windsor police station switchboard number. His card had his mobile number listed and she would rather call him on that to avoid anyone else discovering what she had to tell him. Then when she was clearing out her things in preparation for her lodger the other week she'd discovered his card in one of her drawers. She'll try the number for India Hargreaves parents a few more times as she'd rather talk to her. Then she'll call Ellis if she keeps getting the answer machine.

Cate books a week's leave of absence from midweek to midweek so that she can shower some attention on her lodger, Diane, in the final days of the games and show her parts of Greater Manchester. Cate takes her to some of the posher suburbs where the footballers' mansions are, and the two of them have cream teas at various village tea rooms or gardens dotted about the region. Her lodger, from Melbourne, is due to fly out Wednesday evening, Cate's last day off.

With the university closed for the holidays, Adhita has been away visiting her parents and to escape the madness of the Games. She is due back today and they are planning to get together that evening. Cate taped the closing ceremony of the Games last night and plans to watch it while waiting for Adhita to turn up. Her lodger attended the closing ceremony and told Cate how miserable it was with all the rain when they bumped into each other this morning. Diane's spending the next two nights with her sister now the Games are over, but is due to return on Wednesday morning and Cate has promised to drive her to the airport in the evening for her flight back to Melbourne.

On Monday evening after preparing the meal for tonight's dinner, a vegetarian chilli, Cate sits down and begins watching the ceremony. Adhita arrives before it ends and she pauses the tape to welcome her back and pour them both a glass of wine.

'I've nearly finished watching the closing event of the games from last night, do you think you could suffer the last five minutes or so, otherwise I'll watch it later?'

'No, it's fine, you go ahead. I can think about work while you do that.'

'Don't you ever stop? I bet you've been working at your parents as well.'

'Just a little. Not all the time.'

Cate re-starts the tape and watches as the camera pans across the visiting dignitaries sitting in the same area as the Queen. She recognises the Australian Prime Minister and the British Prime Minister before it moves on to where the Queen is seated. Frowning she pauses the tape again.

'Hang on a minute. There was someone near the Australian Prime Minister who looks familiar. I'm sorry Adhita, I just need to go back and have a look.' Adhita sighs with obvious boredom while Cate re-winds the tape and presses play again until finding the section she wants. She presses pause.

'Look Adhita! Look at that man in the fancy police uniform or whatever it is supposed to represent. It's *him*. I'm sure of it. You've seen my latest drawings. What do you think?'

Adhita peers at the screen saying, 'It's hard to make him out clearly with all the rain that is pouring down at the stadium, but yes, he looks like your sketches around the face. The cap he is wearing doesn't really show him clearly though. And he looks even fatter than the drawing you made of him.'

'Yes, he does look a lot fatter, but it's him, I'd swear to it. He's here. In *Manchester*. Bloody hell. I *have* to find out who he is. And you were right. It looks as though he is a policeman. Some bigwig though. Otherwise what is he doing here?..... and he is amongst the dignitaries near the Australian Prime Minister. I hope they're not pals. That could prove awkward.'

'How are you going to find out who he is? You'll have to be careful.'

'I know. I don't know what I'll do. I'll have to think about it …. I know … Lydia, my boss, has a friend I met at a barbeque at her place a few months ago who works at the BBC as a cameraman. He might have been involved in filming the games. I'll go and see her tomorrow. I also need a copy of this video image blown up somehow. I'll have to find a company that does that.'

'You still don't have internet here do you?'

'No, I just use it at work in my lunch break or after work if I need to. Why?'

'You could look up companies that do video production on the net.'

'I can just as easily look it up in my Yellow Pages.' Cate picks up the directory from the shelf of a side table beside the couch and looks through the listings. 'There's a few companies listed here. I'll phone them in the morning and see what they can do.'

Cate begins pacing up and down the room. She is agitated and nervous all at once. This might be her chance to finally identify the man.

'Cate, come on, there's nothing you can do tonight. Let's eat and try to relax for a while.'

'Okay, but I'm not sure if I can eat much. It's a good thing that I decided to watch the rest of the tape. I was on the verge of abandoning it and was going to re-wind the tape ready to record over it. Then I would have missed him.'

Unable to sleep that night with her brain working overtime, Cate finally swallows a sleeping tablet which she still keeps a small supply of for painful-leg-nights and finally surrenders to sleep at 4am. The alarm rudely awakens her at 7.45 and she showers to clear her head of drowsiness and consumes several cups of coffee to make her more alert. At 8.30am she places the first call to one of the production companies but it is still too early. A recorded message informs her that the office does not open until 9am. She phones another company and this time they do answer. She explains her needs and that it is a matter of urgency. They agree they can do the work she requires and she arranges to drive over immediately.

The company creates several blown up stills for her, some cut in closely to the individual and others panned out showing the Prime Minister and other people nearby. They also make several copies of a short segment of the video just at the point where the camera closes in on the dignitaries and then the Queen. Cate thanks them and leaves their premises with her purse many pounds lighter, but believing it was worth every penny. Next stop is her office. She knocks on her boss Lydia's door and enters.

'Oh hi Cate, can't stay away? I thought you were supposed to be on holiday until Thursday?'

'I am. I've come to ask you a favour.'

'Oh, what's that then?'

'You remember at your barbeque you introduced me to the cameraman who worked for the BBC – I think his name was Michael?'

'Yeees. What about him?'

'Do you have his phone number handy? Only I have some footage and stills from the closing ceremony of the

Commonwealth Games and I wanted to ask him if he would be able to find out the name of a particular person in the shots.'

'He works for BBC North West. He wouldn't have been involved in filming the Games, although he was probably there much of the time.'

'I really, really need to find out this information urgently. Could you give me his number so that I can phone him?'

'What's the urgency? What's this all about Cate? I can see it's something that is distressing you.'

'I'd really rather not go into it at the moment if you don't mind. But if you would just trust me and believe me when I say it is very, very important that I find out who this person is.'

'Okay, I'll try and reach him now and then pass you over to him.'

Lydia makes contact with Michael and then passes the phone over to Cate who explains her need to identify someone caught on camera at the closing ceremony. She tells him she has still shots and a segment of the tape she can give him. He agrees to meet her at the Manchester BBC Headquarters in 30 minutes. Cate thanks Lydia and rushes off.

Michael meets her in the large entrance lobby and she shows him some of the stills she has.

'This is the man I want to identify,' she says after they exchange polite greetings. 'The policeman. At least he looks like a policeman. Only you must do it very discreetly. Not let it be known too obviously what you are doing. Is it possible for you to find out who he is?'

'This is a bit cloak and dagger Cate. Why all the secrecy?'

'Let's just say he is a rather powerful and dangerous man. And you wouldn't want him to know you were making enquiries.'

'What's he done?'

'I can't talk about that I'm afraid. But it is very, very important as I said on the phone.'

'Okay, I'll see what I can do. I will need to find out who all the dignitaries are. His name will come up amongst them. If I have a list would you be able to identify him from that?'

'It would be helpful if that is all you can obtain. An exact identification of that particular man would be better. But anything'd be great. Thank you. How long do you think it might take?'

'I don't know. I might have something by the end of the day. I can't promise though. Give me your phone number and I will call you later.'

'I don't have a mobile, it's just my land line at home. I'm on holidays until Thursday, so I'll be home again tomorrow.' Cate recites her number for him and he logs it into his mobile. 'I'll be waiting for your call. Thank you very much.'

Michael calls Cate at 7pm with the news that he has the list of dignitaries but that no one was able to identify her man. He offers to call around to her flat with the list as he has finished work. Alan has driven down following her phone call to him with the news. He thinks she shouldn't be alone while waiting for the information and insisted he was coming. Cate is grateful to have his company. He always tends to keep her balanced with his psychological approaches and she is certainly feeling a little off kilter at present. Cate had been about to serve up their meal when Michael phoned and arranged to come over. Alan suggests they wait as it is a one pot casserole that can simmer on a low temperature in the oven until they are ready to eat.

Twenty minutes later there is a buzz at the door and Cate presses the entry door release for Michael to come up to her flat with instructions on how to find her. Cate introduces Michael to Alan and, after Cate pours him a glass of wine, they sit at the table while he explains that no one knew who all the individual foreign dignitaries were, but that the country each person on the list comes from is noted beside the full names. He passes her the list and she greedily scans down to the Australians.

'This must be him,' she says showing the list to Alan. 'See, the initials of his first name and surname match the J & B that the bishop mentioned. But look at the name! What a joke!'

'The bishop?' Michael queries. 'Now you have me intrigued. This is not one of those cases of historical abuse is it, like we've been hearing about Catholic priests for some years now?'

'No, nothing like that. Thank you so much Michael for doing this. You don't know what it means to me.'

'No I don't, if you don't tell me ….. and I can see that you are not going to,' he adds.

'I can't I'm afraid. Not at the moment anyway. Would you like to eat with us? I have a casserole in the oven all ready to go if you would care to join us?'

'Meat casserole I take it by the smell? Thanks all the same, but I'm a vegetarian.'

'I had a veggie meal last night, but I'm afraid I gave what was left of it to my friend who is also a vegetarian, so she could have it again tonight. Sorry.'

'Don't worry, I've got plenty of food at home. I'd better be off. Here's your stills and the video segment you gave me.'

'Thanks again Michael,' Cate says standing and giving him a hug before he leaves.

'Phew,' Cate says flopping back onto the chair after Michael has gone. 'Step one accomplished. After 22 years!'

'You've accomplished that Cate. There's always a reason why things happen. You were clearly meant to be in Manchester at this point in your life so this could happen.'

'With a little help from friends. It would have been difficult to acquire this list without Michael. Do you think that name is real? I'm surprised no one commented on it in the press or something – except I suppose listing his middle name, Arthur, might have made the name less notable. Surely he couldn't attend an important event like that under a false name could he?'

'I doubt it. Now are you ready to eat? I haven't had anything since I left home and this wine is going to my head a little.'

'Coming right up, and I think I need another glass myself. To celebrate. And decide what to do next.'

'See I told you yesterday, you can't stay away can you?' Lydia remarks with sarcasm when Cate visits her again the next morning. 'Was Michael able to be of any help?'

'Yes he was and I'm fairly confident I have identified the man. But I'm sorry Lydia, I'm afraid I am going to have to give you notice. Notice as short as you are willing to permit. Only what I am about to tell you I would rather you kept completely to yourself and Stuart.'

Cate explains briefly about the trail of deaths and tells her how she believes the man she has now identified is vital to the cases. She doesn't explain to Lydia how or why he might be of importance, deciding she shouldn't confide too many facts to her. Cate stresses that she needs to return to Sydney imminently.

'My God Cate, what a tale of horror. I'm so sorry to hear about your husband and child. I can see now why you desperately wanted to know who he was and why you need to return to Australia immediately to attempt to sort this out once and for all. Don't worry. I'll explain to Stuart. You need to leave as soon as possible.'

'I don't think it's going to be an easy task though. I suspect he is a very important person or he wouldn't have been over here. He might still be here for all I know. Thankfully he doesn't know that I live in Manchester now.'

## 35

The man watches as the young woman enters the apartment block. He had observed her leaving last week and head off to the athletic stadium. The stadium was not an appropriate venue for what he has in mind. He waits until he spots a young man approaching and rushes over quickly to enter the main door at the same time. He hasn't been inside the block as yet, but he has walked around its perimeter and seen the young woman on her terrace. He therefore knows which side of the building her apartment is and he knows the number of the apartment from his information gathering in Sydney.

When he discovered that the Brant family had moved from their Beecroft house, he laughed. These people had no idea. They thought moving would mean they were untraceable. But unless they were no longer planning to drive cars, they would always be traceable through their driving licence and vehicle registration. He had thought that the Rossi woman would return there when she recovered from her injuries and he was right. However, the few times he visited the place he noticed security guards staked outside the premises. On a subsequent evening visit, he had seen her leaving with her family and a large suitcase. He had followed their vehicle and the security car to the international terminal so guessed that she was taking a trip somewhere.

Confident that the security guards would no longer be

in place once she had departed he had paid a visit to Brant family's new home approximately a month later. Once the father and younger daughter had left that morning, he'd entered the premises. From his observations of the small block he had seen the father entering the right hand door. There only seemed to be two units in the building with garages below. Entering any premises was second nature to him. Locks were never an obstacle – he had learnt from a master in his youth. Once again the elder daughter's address was listed in a personal address book he found hidden in the younger daughter's bedroom. It would seem that Catelin Rossi was now living in England. In Yorkshire. There was no urgency for him to deal with her for the time being. He wasn't prepared to take a trip to England. Besides that would be rather difficult to organise and explain.

However, when he was fortuitously offered the chance to travel to Manchester in England for the Commonwealth Games, it was an opportunity that he couldn't afford to turn down. Because, co-incidentally, that was where Rossi was now living. In his occasional surveillance and visits to the Brant home he had discovered this fact and it would seem that this was where she had finally settled. He didn't think she posed any risk for him there, but while he was in the city, why not kill two birds with one stone?

When he reaches the Rossi apartment door he is not sure whether to knock or simply gain access under his own steam. He saw her enter the building alone, however, there may be another person in there with her. She might share the place, although the few times he has seen her she has always been alone. It is a gamble he will just have to take. He decides to knock and carry out a surprise attack when she answers, otherwise she may see him entering through the door and scream, alerting neighbours. He knocks and waits. She answers the door with a smile that he quickly wipes off her face as he charges in, gags her with one hand and grabs her wrists with the other, pushing her against a wall.

'Good to see you again Catelin. I like what you've done to your hair. The lighter colour suits you with those big blue eyes. But you can't fool me.'

She struggles, attempts to shake her head and is making a lot of indecipherable noises. He needs to move quickly and silence her. Twisting her around so she has her back to him he snaps her neck to make matters easier. She has conveniently opened the terrace doors for him. In several swift strides he moves her across the room, out onto the terrace and places each of her hands on the rails to show fingerprints. Checking no one is around down below, he lifts her to an almost standing position and throws her from the railings, facing outward as though the distressed young woman has jumped. He has a quick nose around and thinks she must have visitors staying judging by the several suitcases he sees and the bedding folded on the couch. It looks as though she was in the process of packing a case herself when he disturbed her. Perhaps even planning to travel back to Australia. Good thing he has put a stop to that. He decides he'd better not hang around in case one of her visitors returns unexpectedly. He needs to drop the hire car back to the hire base, then catch a cab to the airport, to join the few colleagues that have stayed on for a further couple of days like him. He told them he would make his own way to the airport and a quick look at his watch reminds him he needs to leave now if he is going to make it on time.

# 36

DS Dhiren Khatri closes down his computer and sighs. Another afternoon and evening on duty at the competitor's village. Whilst he has enjoyed seeing all the competing athletes in the flesh, and his time there has by no means been arduous, he has found it extremely boring. Tantamount to babysitting. Something that would be better left to the uniforms. He doesn't see why detectives should be wasting their time with such tedious tasks. It wouldn't be so bad if he had DC Jaya Seth with him. He would pass the time looking at her any day. But sadly she has not been rostered on duty with him any of the days he has been there.

He stands and pushes his chair under his desk and is just about to leave when the young constable he has been daydreaming about walks into the room.

'Sarge,' she calls out to him, 'there's been a change of plan for you today. We have a jumper. You and I have to report to the scene.'

DS Khatri is momentarily taken aback before his brain connects the context of what she is saying. He thought at first she was referring to knitwear – but of course she means a suicide. Never a pleasant experience.

'Where?' he asks.

'Down at Deansgate. A block by the canal. One of those old warehouse conversions. Took a dive off a third floor terrace. Uniforms are there now and she's been pronounced dead at the scene. The boss wants us two to take a look. Sounds straightforward, but he wants us to check it out.'

The DS is not sure if this news is welcoming. At least he would have the pleasure of Jaya's company. Careful what you wish for! Suicides rarely necessitate the attendance of more senior officers which is why he has been placed in charge of the matter.

'Do we have a name?' he asks on the drive there.

'Well they located the apartment she took a dive from. The apartment is in the name of a Catelin Rossi. But uniforms found a passport in another woman's name in the flat as well as one in Catelin Rossi's name. They can't tell which one she is, although they think it might be the same woman with two passports. The passports show images of two young women with similarities.'

'You mean white?'

'Well that as well. No, they both have blue eyes, fair hair and are of a similar height. One is a couple of years older than the other. Whether they are two different people or Catelin Rossi has two passports in different names they don't know.'

'Sounds like it might be a bit more interesting. Have they found a note or last letter? What do we know about this Catelin Rossi?'

'No, no note. We know very little about her at the moment. That's what we will need to look into.'

'Right.'

At the scene they can understand why identification has proven difficult. The features on the woman's face are indistinguishable due to her hitting a metal bollard by the canal, slitting her face open. DS Khatri has seen some gruesome corpses, but this one makes him feel quite queasy. They are shown photographs which had been taken of the woman as she lay dead, before the medical examiner moved her. He looks up at the terrace and shudders. A long way down. Why would you choose to end your life this way?

'Can you give me an approximate time of death?' he asks the ME.

'No more than three hours ago I'd say. We'll know more from the post-mortem. There's very little blood here which doesn't seem in keeping with a fall of this nature. I would expect to see more.'

'So are you thinking the fall didn't kill her?'

'I'm not saying that. I'm just stating a fact. We'll have to wait for the post-mortem,' he says with finality.

'Okay thanks. Come on Detective Seth we need to go and look at the flat. Are there any SOCOs up there at the moment?' Suspected suicides are normally checked out by the team – in case the death is not what it appears to be.

'Yes, some of my colleagues are up there taking a look at the terrace – it's apartment sixteen on the third floor,' one of the SOCOs says.

The Scene of Crime Officers (SOCOs) have finished their work and are beginning to pack up. DS Khatri and DC Seth get the go ahead to enter the flat. He notices that the flat, or apartment as they tend to be called these days, is clean and tidy, apart from some bedding folded on the couch and a small case standing next to it. There are suitcases visible in both bedrooms – one lying open on the bed that appears to be in the process of being packed. Visitors? If so where are they now, he wonders? Is this a straightforward suicide or is there more to it?

A young SOCO presents him with not two, but three passports. One Australian passport in the name Diane Quinn, the other two, one Australian and one British, in the name of Catelin Rossi. He can see the women are quite different, but have a similar look about them. Catelin Rossi is currently 27, the Quinn woman turned 25 last March.

DS Khatri is just about to place the passports in an evidence bag when a young woman and an older man enter the apartment.

'Excuse me, who are you? And what are you doing in my home?' the woman asks. She looks up and sees a suited SOCO technician on the terrace and turns pale. 'What's happened?' she whispers.

'Are you Catelin Rossi? The owner of this apartment?'

'Yes.'

'Oh we thought .......,' DC Seth begins and then clams up. DS Khatri thinks she was about to say *we thought you were dead.'* He was thinking the same thing.

'I'm afraid there has been an incident.'

'What type of incident? Has there been a break-in?'

'I'm afraid it is a little more serious than that? Might I have your name sir?' he asks the man now standing at Catelin Rossi's side.

'My name is Alan Mathers. I'm staying with Cate at the moment, visiting from Yorkshire.'

'When was the last time either of you saw Diane Quinn?' he asks, believing now she is the deceased.

'Monday morning,' the woman says. 'Her sister was competing in the Games and now the Games are over she went to stay with her sister in a hotel somewhere. I'm not sure where. Her sister is flying out with the team tomorrow and Diane is due to fly out this evening. Why, what's happened?'

'How well do you know Miss Quinn?' – They don't know she is dead yet so he refers to her in the present tense.

'Hardly at all. My godmother from Melbourne contacted

me via my father and asked if I would be willing to rent some cheap space to Diane for two weeks while the Games were on. I'd never met her prior to her arriving here in Manchester.'

'You say her sister was one of the competitors? For Australia I presume? And would you know the sister's name?'

'Yes. Her sister was competing for Australia and her name is Sandy Quinn. Please, I am feeling quite uncomfortable. Will you tell me what is going on?'

He scribbles the name down that she has given him and looks up at her. By rights he shouldn't say anything further until the family has been notified. But it is her flat after all.

'I'm afraid there has been an incident with Miss Quinn and she is dead. It would appear that she jumped off the terrace.'

He watches as Catelin Rossi's legs give way and is prevented from falling by Alan Mathers. He helps her across to the couch. 'No. No, no she wouldn't have done that. It's him, Alan. It's *got* to be him.' she says shaking her head.

Mathers looks as though he is about to say something to counter her statement, but has second thoughts and closes his mouth.

'Can I ask who you are referring to when you say – "it's got to be him?" Did Miss Quinn have an involvement with a man during her visit?'

'No, she didn't. She simply went to the stadium and returned here every evening – apart from the last couple of nights. Her sister wasn't able to socialise with her whilst the Games were in progress. As she was alone she wanted to stay somewhere where she had a bit of company,' she says with tears beginning to streak down her face. 'Oh poor Diane. She must have been terrified.'

The man, Mathers, places an arm around the Rossi woman to offer her comfort and whispers something gently in her ear. His words clearly have an impact on her and she begins to compose herself. DS Khatri waits a moment before proceeding with his questions. Clearly this Catelin Rossi believes she knows something and is saying that Diane Quin wouldn't have killed herself.

'Can you tell me who are you referring to then?'

'Someone who was probably after me. Poor Diane just got in the way – or maybe he even thought she was me. He's never really seen me close up, except the time he attempted to run me down with a car and that was nearly three years ago. I look quite different now. I had darker short hair then.'

'Sorry, you've lost me. You will need to explain what you are talking about.'

DS Khatri is shocked when Catelin Rossi pours her story out, but instead of showing shock, he frowns. If her story is true then she is talking about deaths stretching back to 1980. He was only a little kid then. Like she had been. He can't help but reveal his shock with her final statement about spotting the man she refers to as the 'murderer' at the Commonwealth Games closing ceremony sitting amongst the dignitaries. He looks at her, then at DC Seth. Is this for real? Everything she is saying about the supposed deaths can be verified so why would someone make up such a convoluted and tragic set of circumstances? It crosses his mind that she might have mental health problems and perhaps Mathers is staying with her to attend to her needs. She seems articulate and lucid enough, but you never can tell. He doesn't know if she can read the doubt in his face but she stands up, finds her bag and pulls out a set of still photographs holding one of them in front of him.

'This is the man you are looking for. I've written his name on the picture. You will need to hurry if you are going to catch him or he might leave the country. How long ago did this incident, as you call it, take place?'

'Several hours now. Can I ask where you two have been today?' He looks down at the picture she has handed him and does a double take. She's got to be kidding, he's sure of it.

'We went to my employer's office to tell them that I need to travel to Australia urgently. Now I have this new information I will need to return to Australia and see the detective who was handling matters back in early 2000. We then went to the university – the Victoria University Manchester that is, to meet up with a friend to update her. The three of us then went to lunch.'

'I will need the name of your friend at the university and details of where you went to lunch.'

'Fine, but you need to ring Manchester airport urgently to see if this man is booked on a flight today and try to prevent him from leaving the country if he is. And you can make a call to Australia to the Windsor Police Station in New South Wales and speak to a Detective Rob Ellis – he was the DI who was handling the case. I just found his card recently when I was clearing things out of my room. I thought I'd lost it. Hang on I'll dig it out.'

He waits for her to return with the card and excuses himself to make a call, leaving the apartment for confidentiality. He doesn't tell her that he cannot take much action without speaking to his DI. The DI isn't in at the moment, but he asks that enquiries are made with the airport and passes on the man's name. There would be a large number of flights departing today – if he is leaving the country he could be on any one of them – but is more than likely booked on a flight to Australia. It is going to take several calls to obtain this information. He reassures base that this is not a joke (at least he hopes not). He asks them to call passport control at the airport first to check if anyone of that name has passed through the system in the past few hours and to alert Headquarters if someone has or does. They can't possibly detain someone on this woman's say so, however he needs to initiate matters in case. He also provides the phone number of the detective in Windsor that Catelin Rossi has given him and asks them to call to confirm the enquiry he was dealing with that involved Mrs. Rossi. It will be very late at night there so he's not sure if they will be able to reach anyone, but there is a mobile number on the card. He tells them to wake the Australian detective if need be.

He receives a call back a short time later informing him that a man with the same name passed through passport control approximately two hours ago. So he is real. It might mean he is still there waiting for a flight, but it could also mean that he had already departed. If that is the case, it was going to complicate matters. His DI will not be pleased.

'The post-mortem revealed that Diane Quinn was dead before she hit the ground,' Detective Chief Inspector Steve Mills announces to his team at a midday briefing the following day. 'Probably only minutes before.'

'DS Khatri and DC Seth were able to locate the victim's sister and she has positively identified her sister through a prominent birth mark.'

'We've spoken to a DCI Ellis in Windsor, New South Wales, who's confirmed Cate Rossi's story about numerous deaths in Australia, including those of her husband and child. However, he has made it clear that although there was a person of interest they wished to trace, they have no evidence that this person is responsible for a fatal car crash that killed members of the Rossi family. They have little or no evidence linking him to the other deaths either. In fact they have no name for the suspect they wish to question.' There were sniggers around the briefing room when he finished.

'DS Khatri can you take over here and tell them what else has been discovered.'

'This man,' Khatri says pointing to a grainy photograph and a copy of a sketch Cate Rossi had given them that are tapped to the board, 'whose name was given to us by Cate Rossi, departed on a flight from Manchester International less than an hour after passing through customs, so even if we were in a position to detain him as a person of interest it would have been too late. Uniforms did door to door enquiries at the apartment block which revealed that a man, possibly fitting the description, followed a tenant into the building. But the tenant can't be absolutely sure as he only had a momentary glimpse of the man who was wearing a hat shadowing his face. The man had climbed the stairs whilst the tenant caught the lift to the second floor, so it was only briefly at the front door that the man had been seen and the tenant hadn't noticed whether the man had been driving a car. There is a security camera at the entrance to the block by the buzzers so that tenants can view their callers, but there are no other security cameras installed in or around the building. The area immediately surrounding the block has no CCTVs and, so we have no idea if he was driving, and if so, what type of vehicle we might be looking for.'

'I have decided that CCTV around the block is a useless

line of enquiry to follow,' DCI Mills interjects. 'But I want all hire car companies contacted, both in the city and the airport to see if he hired a vehicle. I want CCTV at the arrivals entrance searched to see how the person of interest arrived at the airport.' Mills nods for Khatri to continue.

'We've identified the hotel he stayed in during his visit to Manchester. SOCOs are currently doing a search of his room. He checked out yesterday morning so the room has already been cleaned, but as no-one else has been booked into the room we are taking a look anyway. We have some trace evidence on the victim's clothing so we're looking for a match.'

'DI Traynor,' DCI Mills says, 'can you follow up on the SOCOs and allocate tasks. We'll re-convene this evening at 5pm. Thank you everyone.'

What DCI Mills did not tell his team was his enquiries had revealed that their person of interest was the Commissioner for Police in New South Wales. He initially dismissed the possibility that this person could be involved, but after interviewing Cate Rossi he is more open-minded.

When the search results are shared amongst the team that evening no record had been found of the man in question hiring a car at the airport or from any other companies in the city. At least not under his given name. CCTV showed him arriving at the airport in a taxi and the taxi driver in question had been tracked down and he'd confirmed he'd collected the man from the hotel in the city.

The SOCO search provides a few clear fingerprints, fibres and several hairs. It will be some days before there are any DNA results and DCI Mills has promised to forward them to the DCI in New South Wales to see if they match any collected by his team.

Mills has not told DCI Ellis the name they have as yet, or the fact that their person of interest is the Police Commissioner for New South Wales. He wants to wait to see if any of their evidence matches the little Ellis has collected. He hasn't made Cate Rossi aware of the Commissioner's position either, although she kept saying he must be someone important. There is a lack of evidence both in Australia and the UK, with no trace of him at her apartment, although Mills is hopeful some of the fibres found at the hotel might match some found on the victim's clothing.

Mills has cleared Cate Rossi to leave the country and she is due to fly out in the next few days. She claims she intends to return to Australia to see that justice is done and prevent this man from killing anyone ever again. He wishes her luck with that – if she is right about her man it will not be an easy task. She will be pitching herself against one of the most powerful men in the state.

# 37

Cate telephones her father at his place of work, which she hopes is a secure line, to pass on the dreadful news of Diane's death and how she had spotted the man on TV at the Commonwealth Games, warning her father to tighten security at his house. She is afraid to call him at home in case the land line is being tapped. After thinking about it, she is convinced that the murderer must have gained entry to her father's home to discover her location in Manchester. How else would he have found it? The only other person who had her address was Aunt Betty in Melbourne who had passed it on to Diane. She is sure the leak didn't come from that quarter. She hasn't given her address to any old friends or colleagues, citing security reasons and only keeps in touch with them by email. She has not told her father the man's name, although he insists the Manchester Police should be able to discover it. She gives him assurances that they are working on it. She is afraid if she gives her father the man's name, he will take some rash action that could endanger his life. She'd been horrified when she'd learnt he'd been to see the Chief Inspector at Parramatta some years before and then found out that the Inspector died later that same day.

Diane's tragic death has given Cate the strength and courage to return to Australia to deal with this man once and for all. She is not sure how she will accomplish this and she doesn't know where she will stay. Clearly her father's home is out of the question. Likewise all her friends. She cannot endanger anyone else in her enterprise. The only person she trusts is DC Hargreaves, but she has still had no response from her telephone calls to the parent's house. She decides not to call DI Ellis, but she knows the Manchester police have been in touch with him.

Alan is still staying with Cate and will see her off at the airport. They'd packed all Cate's personal belongings which are being placed in storage until Cate decides whether she will return to the UK. The flat will then be rented out, furnished. Adhita is having use of her car. The removal men have just unloaded the last of the boxes into the storage unit and Cate shuts the door and fixes the padlock which she will be passing on to Adhita for safekeeping.

'Well that's everything,' Cate sighs sadly to Alan, who has barely left her side since they'd encountered the police in her flat. Cate had to have emergency repairs carried out on her apartment door after the Police forced entry. The door has since been replaced. Adhita and her brothers, as freeholders, are now planning to install security cameras in and around the building. It will increase service charges, but they can't afford to have a re-occurrence like Diane's death ever again. Owner-occupiers in the building agree.

On their return journey to her apartment Alan voices his concerns. 'I understand your need to return to Australia, especially in view of Diane's death Cate, but I am worried about you. How you are going to prove he was responsible for the deaths of Marco and Milo I don't know. And how are you going to have him arrested? If he's the top man there who can you go to? How are you going to achieve all that without putting yourself at risk?'

Cate has had this conversation with Alan and Adhita several times already. She knows they are only worried for her safety and are also trying to make her think matters through clearly, but she can't give them the answers they are seeking as yet. She doesn't know herself what she will do. Internet searches at Adhita's place revealed that the man is the Commissioner of Police and was stationed at Parramatta when she saw him in 1999, meaning he would have had access to vital information that enabled him to commit his crimes.

'I know Alan. I'm worried as well, but I promise I will do everything I can to ensure my safety. I can't say more than that at the moment. I don't know what I will do until I arrive and find DC Hargreaves …..if she is still in the force. It will also depend on any results the Manchester police find. DCI Mills has told me he will be forwarding the information to the detective in Windsor. If all else fails I will have to go and see Detective Ellis. I have the photographs from the Commonwealth Games and the video footage. Thank goodness I didn't leave them in the apartment that day or he might have taken it all.'

Cate has her last meal with Alan and Adhita that evening. She makes every effort to steer the conversation clear of her impending trip. Her flight leaves at 8.20am so it will be an early start for her and Alan, who plans to drive back to Yorkshire after he has dropped her at the airport.

'Safe journey Cate. For goodness sake, please don't take any unnecessary risks,' Adhita pleads with Cate as they have a tearful farewell outside the university grounds. 'Promise me.'

'I promise I will do my best to stay safe Adhita. Here's the keys to my car, storage unit and apartment.' She passes

Adhita the sets of keys. Although Cate has arranged letting of her apartment through an agency who will also manage everything, she wants Adhita to have the keys as a back-up measure. Adhita has also promised to strip the linen on the beds and remove them for laundering once she and Alan have left tomorrow. Cate is keeping one set of keys herself.

'Look after my car,' Cate shouts back at Adhita as she and Alan walk away, 'I'll be back as soon as I can.'

When they return to Cate's that evening, Cate announces she is shattered and needs to go to bed. She wants to ensure both she and Alan have a decent night's sleep before their respective journeys tomorrow.

'Take care my dear,' are Alan's parting words at the airport quick drop the next morning. Cate has insisted he merely drops her at the departure entrance with no need to come into the terminal. It would simply prolong his day unnecessarily. She looks back waving one more time before entering the terminal doors.

# 38

**Sydney, August 2002**

Cate has not told her family of her arrival in Australia. They would have insisted on coming to meet her at the airport and she can't take the chance that they might be under surveillance. She doesn't know if the Commissioner realises yet that he has killed the wrong person, but she's not taking any chances. She spends the first night in a hotel at the airport and then catches a train into the city, changing at Central for a train heading towards Windsor.

From Windsor Station she walks to the hotel she has booked into which she reserved through her Sydney Airport Hotel. She is not sure if it will suit her, but it is close to the centre of town, and is convenient for walking everywhere. She will need to hire a car at some point, but prefers to keep her costs down for the time being.

The hotel building is an old historic Colonial design with its name and the date of 1863 built into the frontage just below the parapet. Cate likes the look of it, with the large veranda running across the street front. She hopes the noise from the road, plus the bar and restaurant she can see downstairs, doesn't go on until late at night disturbing the accommodation rooms. A motel would be quieter, but she is concerned that a motel would leave her too vulnerable, so this will have to do for now. The room she is shown to is quite spacious with a double bed, a small table with two chairs, built-ins, a small couch and an en suite. There is also a wall-mounted air-conditioning unit and a television. The room faces the back of the building so she won't have access to that wonderful veranda, but it will no doubt be quieter she thinks. For an old hotel it is luxurious. Most older hotels don't have many en suite rooms. She'd noticed a public phone at the end of the landing on the way up to the room and, after dumping her bags, calls the Hargreaves house again. But there is still no answer. Cate wonders if they have moved. There is a phone book on the shelf and she looks up the name. There are several Hargreaves listed but she finds the one matching the number she has and notes down the address. She has been given a small map of Windsor and can see the street is a short walk away, so heads off.

The house, close to the town centre, is a brick built, detached, double fronted single storey of old colonial design. Cate notices that the front lawn is mown, and the garden looks freshly weeded so someone must be looking after it. There is no answer to her knocking and she can see the shutters on the windows are all closed. They must be away. Just as she is about to turn away she hears a woman's voice from behind her asking, 'Are you looking for the Hargreaves?'

Cate turns to see a middle-aged woman standing on the path. 'Yes, ....well no ... actually I was looking for their daughter India,' she tells her. 'I know she doesn't live with them anymore, but I wanted to make contact with her. I've been trying to get hold of the Hargreaves for some weeks by telephone, but there is never any answer.'

'That's because they're away dear. Mr. Hargreaves is currently working abroad. I live next door and I promised I would keep an eye on the place since their son recently moved out,' she says as though Cate needs an explanation as to why she is approaching her. 'You'll find India down at the local police station – that's if she is on duty or not out and about. You do know she is a police detective don't you?'

'Yes, I do. Thank you very much for your help. I'll go down there now.' Cate wants to leave but the woman is blocking her way on the path.

'Of course she might be off somewhere with that husband of hers,' the woman continues and remains standing on the path.

Not wanting to show her surprise at this snippet of information Cate says, 'I've been abroad myself for a few years, so I haven't been in touch with her for a while.'

'Been married for over six months now. India and that detective husband of hers.'

'So India is based up here now? She's moved from the Parramatta station?'

'You *are* out of touch my dear. She left Parramatta more than two years ago. Went to Penrith first. Now she's here. You do know she's now a Senior Sergeant don't you?'

'No, but I'm not surprised.' Cate doesn't really know police ranking, but does know enough to recognise that a sergeant is a higher rank than a constable, and so that a senior sergeant must be at least one step up from a sergeant. 'Okay, thanks again,' she says to the woman. 'I'd better get down there. Can you direct me to the police station?'

The woman finally moves, walks out to the pavement at the front of the house and begins directing Cate with verbal directions accompanied by many dramatic arm movements. Cate stifles the urge to laugh and has difficulty concentrating on what the woman is saying. She thanks her again and hurries off before her smile gives way to laughter.

At the police station Cate asks for Detective Senior Sergeant India Hargreaves before realising that this is no longer her name and she has no idea what her married name is. It makes no difference, the constable on the desk clearly knows who she is talking about. Cate doubts there would another detective based at the station by the name of India.

'I'm afraid she's not in at the moment, but we expect her back shortly if you'd like to wait,' the constable says.

'How long do you think she'll be?' Cate asks.

'Apparently she's on her way back.'

'Okay I'll wait,' Cate replies taking a seat beside a nervous looking young man who is called away a few minutes later. She wonders what he is here for. Cate had never been in a police station in her life until she went to the one in Parramatta when she was eighteen and met DI Paramo. She thinks about his death being recorded as a suicide. If that verdict could be altered it would make a huge difference to his family.

When her mother was murdered the police interviewed Cate briefly at their house and again at Aunt Betty's where she had been taken until her father came to collect her. They never took Cate to the police station at the time, although her father went there before they left for Sydney.

The entrance door swings open and Cate recognises India Hargreaves immediately although like Cate, she has let her hair grow which she has tied back in a ponytail.

'Detective Hargreaves?' Cate says standing. Detective Hargreaves swivels around showing surprise and recognition on seeing Cate. 'Can we have a private chat somewhere?'

'Cate Rossi isn't it? I thought you were living in the

UK?'

'I was. I have some news to update you with if we could speak somewhere privately.'

'Of course. Do you want to do it at the station here or go somewhere else?'

'I don't mind, as long as we can't be overheard,' Cate says lowering her voice to almost a whisper.

'Hmm. Why don't you come through to one of the interview rooms?'

Detective Hargreaves leads Cate through to a room that smells unpleasantly of sweat and she's not sure what else. There is one small high window with bars. Cate wonders if this is where they interview potential suspects. It doesn't look like the type of room she imagined they might use, as it doesn't have a mirror like she's seen on television shows.

'Would you like a tea or coffee? I am going to make one for myself. I just have to go and collect something and then I'll be back.'

'Okay I wouldn't mind a cup of tea thanks. Just a little milk …. but would it be possible to open that window to let some air in here before you leave?'

'Yes sure, it does pong a bit.' Detective Hargreaves pulls a chair over, climbs up to reach the window and yanks it open with some difficulty, grunting and groaning as she does so. 'Ugh. Don't think that's been opened in a while. Back in a tick.' Detective Hargreaves jumps down and disappears leaving Cate alone. The air is cool outside and the smell in the room immediately begins to improve.

About ten minutes later Detective Hargreaves returns laden with two mugs and a file under her arm. 'Just wanted to locate the file in case we need it,' she says by way of explanation for her absence. She passes one of the mugs to Cate, offers sachets of sugar which Cate refuses and taking a seat opposite her, looks up and says, 'So what is this updated news you have for me?'

'There's been another murder. In the UK this time. At my flat. I think the murderer thought he was killing me, but unfortunately for my lodger, he killed her instead. We were a similar age and height and both had long fairish hair. As you can see I have lightened my hair in recent years. Anyway, because he's never really seen me up close I imagine the murderer thought it was me, although the only facial feature we had in common were blue eyes. The police in Manchester have been investigating and I believe they contacted DI Ellis about me? Have you heard anything?'

'I have – but only that the police from Manchester called to verify the story you gave them and that they were investigating a suspicious death linked to you. They were unable to tell us if the death in the UK was connected to anything we had investigated here, but promised to send any evidence that came to light. We haven't had anything through as yet – not that I'm aware of. I've been out all morning and DCI Ellis is not in at the moment. Were you aware that we had both been promoted?'

'I learnt about your promotion and that you were now stationed here from a neighbour of your parents who I saw this morning when I went to your parent's house. I've been phoning there, trying to reach you or leave a message with your parents to call me, for the past few months. She tells me congratulations are in order as well – that you've married.'

'That'd be Mrs. Watson from next door. She likes to think she's in charge of the place while my parents are away. Yes I am married now. So you'd been phoning me for months? Even before this latest murder? My brother and his wife were staying there until last week. They never mentioned you calling.'

'No, I just kept getting the answer machine and didn't like to leave a message. The reason I was phoning you was that after talking to my friend in Manchester she thought the killer must be a policeman. She thought the remark of the bishop "that you'd find him in the same place" meant *you* would find him at your station at Parramatta. So I was wanting to discuss this possibility and see if you knew anyone with the initials JB based at Parramatta. Those *are* his initials, he *was* based at Parramatta and now I know for sure now who the killer is and his current position.'

'Oh ….how were you able to discover that when apparently there were no witnesses as such to this latest death? The UK police have not mentioned this. Have you told them?' India asks racking her brains to think of someone with those initials at her old station.

'Yes, I gave them his name, but they explained that they could not release the identity of the person until there was further proof. I have no such reservations, as this man has been in my head since I was six years old.' Cate produces the drawings that she re-did whilst in Yorkshire and the photo stills from the Commonwealth Games.

'These drawings are a replica of the ones that were removed from my house in Glenbrook. I re-drew them a few months after arriving in the UK. As you can see I've done quite a few of them. These photographs are stills taken from a video recording I made of the closing ceremony of the Commonwealth Games that have recently taken place in Manchester. It was quite by accident that I noticed him on the TV coverage in the group of dignitaries seated not far from the Queen. As you can see I have written the name of the man on the photographs. A friend of a friend, who knew the people filming there was able to provide me with a list of visiting Australian dignitaries and I spotted his name. As you can see his first name and surname make the initials JB. The initials you gathered through the bishop. I'm sure the Manchester police know his position in the Australian police, but they didn't tell me. I found out from an internet search.'

Detective Hargreaves looks at the picture and whistles. She had just made the connection before Cate Rossi produced her drawings. She opens the file in front of her and attempts to see some resemblance between Cate's original drawings from 1992, the copy of the ones she completed in late 1999 and the photographs. She can see there is a striking resemblance.

'I know he is the Commissioner for Police in New South Wales,' Cate tells her, 'and I know it will prove very difficult to move the investigation forward. How can we proceed? Who appoints the Commissioners?'

'The State Minister for the Ministry of Police appoints the Commissioner. Um...I'm ...I'm not sure how we can proceed Cate. Do you mind if I call you Cate?'

'No Cate's fine. Can't we go to this minister then?'

'We'd need more evidence than these drawings and still shots. We can't go to the Minister with just your story. If we'd had the footage from your former employers here it might have helped, but again it wouldn't be enough. We need forensic evidence. And we have none except some mitochondrial DNA picked up at your home in Glenbrook, which we are not even sure came from the suspect. I'll have to discuss it with my DCI. DCI Rob Ellis – and by the way, he is the man I married.'

'Oh.....well congratulations. Did you transfer here

before or after your marriage?'

'Before. I doubt I would have been able to transfer here if we were already married.'

'You know Marco and I used to work together. Well, in the same practice anyway. We didn't see each other all day, every day. He had his own office and was out quite a bit of the time.'

India nods. 'Yes, Rob and I don't see each other all the time either.'

'Does Detective Ellis know the Commissioner?' Cate asks suddenly, frowning. India thinks Cate might be concerned about possible conflicts.

'Not personally no. But we all know who he is of course. I knew his face was familiar when I saw your original drawings. Now I know why. He has changed considerably over the years, but you can still see his features clearly from the older drawings. You have captured him well.'

'I've become a bit of an expert at sketching people. In fact I was doing pencil sketches of people at an outdoor market in Manchester for extra cash occasionally. So..... what can we do? There must be something. This is definitely the man, Detective Hargreaves – sorry are you known as Ellis now?'

'No, I still use Hargreaves professionally.'

'Okay, as I was saying – he is definitely our man. We can't.... we just simply can't let him continue to get away with this!'

'I understand that you believe he is. And I'm sure you're right. Never took to the man the few times I saw him in person. He does bear a striking resemblance to your drawings. But as I said, it is simply not enough. We need evidence ....witnesses.'

'I am a witness. Anna where I used to work is a witness.'

'Yes, but you were six years old at the time of your mother's murder. If I remember correctly no one took you seriously then. They are not going to now twenty odd years later. The receptionist at your old employers did manage to see him once, very briefly. But that proves nothing except that he asked for your husband by name. He could claim that he was looking for an architect and that your husband had been recommended to him. It is still not sufficient evidence.'

'But there was the break-in at the office with the tape conveniently removed and the equipment broken.'

'Circumstantial. It could be argued that someone else was responsible for that. The police who investigated the break-in found no forensic evidence whatsoever to link anyone to the crime.'

'What about this mito…this DNA thing.'

'We'd have to match it to him. And at the moment we don't have grounds for attempting to do so. Even then I am not sure it would be considered enough. It has been used in cases in the USA for convictions. I'm not sure that it would be here. Most criminal cases in Australia involving DNA have been based on what is called nuclear DNA.'

'I don't really understand the difference. God, this is so frustrating!'

'Mitochondrial DNA is DNA that can be obtained from degraded samples when no Nuclear or let's say 'normal' DNA can be obtained. For example from skeletal remains or hair. I'm not sure I fully understand it myself – I haven't done that much reading on the science - but apparently it is a DNA that can be traced through the female line and provides so many matching markers. It apparently shows a match between siblings and so can be useful when looking at familial matching and they are also talking about the fact that it can be used to trace ancestry – but I'm afraid not much use to us for this case. Not without further evidence or cause to take samples from him.'

'So what are we going to do? Until this man is charged and imprisoned I can't have any contact with my family. I can't put them at risk. As yet he may not even realise that he killed the wrong woman in Manchester, but if he does find out then both my family and I will become targets. I can't live my life. He's destroyed enough of it already. We'll never be free until he's caught.'

'I know. I realised that back in 1999. And I'm really sorry Cate,' Hargreaves says reaching out to touch Cate's hand. After a moment she continues. 'So I assume you aren't staying with your family then?'

'No, they don't even know I am here. I am staying at a hotel in Windsor.'

'Can you let me have your details? I will speak to Rob – DCI Ellis that is, and he can chase up the Manchester Police – see if they have found anything. Then I will be in touch.'

'Okay. I'm keeping a very low profile here as you can imagine.'

DSS Hargreaves catches up with her husband DCI Rob Ellis and fills him in on her meeting with Cate Rossi and all that it revealed. He is astonished by the news, but also worried. How the bloody hell are they going to proceed? He promises to follow up contact with the Manchester Police, but reminds her that the UK is currently nine hours behind them so he's unlikely to have any successful contact until early evening. They agree to remain at the station until contact is made.

At 6pm India pops her head around his office door and

asks, 'Any joy?'

'Yes I've just been talking to Steve Mills – my counterpart in Manchester. I'm waiting for an email to come through now. They have some mitochondrial DNA, nuclear DNA and fingerprints. They had no luck matching fibres found in his hotel room to those found on the dead Australian girl. So there's no evidence to link him to that crime. Should be interesting though, to see if any of our evidence matches any of theirs.'

'If they are a match what are we going to do Rob?'

'I think we should make an appointment with the Minister as a starting point. I don't know if it's even possible to make an appointment with him. I haven't mentioned it to the Chief Super. I don't dare – it might spell the end of my career – and possibly yours. He knows the Commissioner and they're quite matey from what I can make out. Going to the Minister could be a gamble as well. He might be great mates with the Commissioner as well.'

'I know. We're in an impossible situation. But I think the present Commissioner only got the promotion because of a lack of other candidates. When he stepped into the deputy Commissioner's post after his predecessor's death back in late 99, it was because he was the popular choice at the time. But when the previous Commissioner retired earlier this year I heard that others turned the position down, so who was the minister left with? I think he obtained the position by default, so they might not be mates. I've been doing some digging by the way.' She pauses to watch his reaction. She never knows if he will be pleased or annoyed at her initiatives.

'Go on. Don't keep me in suspense then. I assume you mean digging into facts about our illustrious leader?'

'Yep. Turns out he started his career in Melbourne.

I always thought he was from the Gold Coast. That was how he was presented to us when he took up the position of Assistant Commissioner. But no, he moved there for promotion from Melbourne. He was a Detective Sergeant at the time of Cate Rossi's mother's death. The other woman who was murdered the day before, Mia Adjudovic, worked as a civilian at Melbourne Police Headquarters. Bishop Byrne also came from Melbourne and moved to Sydney sometime in the late 80s. I discovered that they attended the same secondary school in Melbourne. So it all fits. The Commissioner would have known the Adjudovic woman. Julie Brant, Cate Rossi's mother lived a few streets away from the Adjudovic crime scene. According to Cate, she and her mother witnessed him leaving what was probably Adjudovic's block the day of her murder – and saw him there again the next day. If he was a DS he would have very likely been part of the investigation team. He obviously knew the bishop as well. They presumably kept in touch – although if you remember that nun told me that Bishop Byrne said he hadn't seen JB for more than 15 years or something.'

'I agree it all fits – but it's circumstantial. We need hard evidence. Oh wait. The email from Manchester's just appeared in my box. I'll print it all out. Why don't you go and make us both a cup of coffee so we can look at this at leisure. Then we can go out for a meal to discuss our plan of action.'

'You know how I feel about making my superiors coffee. But seeing as it's you I'll make an exception.'

'What I want to know,' India starts as she returns with their coffee, 'Is why we didn't piece this all together back in '99? According to Cate Rossi, she mentioned everything to a friend in Manchester who immediately hit upon the fact that the suspect had to be a policeman and the bishop's clue meant to look at my place of work in Parramatta.'

'Well to be fair to us, we did discuss the possibility that he might be a cop, but dismissed it because Cate Rossi said the man looked like a smart businessman. The receptionist at the architect's practice said much the same thing. The majority of us cops don't resemble smart businessmen. Especially middle aged ones. They just look like worn out cops, sometimes wearing ruffled suits they've often caught a few hours' sleep in, in their offices, while on a big case. Or we just wear more casual clothes, not smart suits. The higher ranking officers don't wear suits. They wear uniforms, so we wouldn't have considered them. Then there was the link with the bishop and the Church.'

'I suppose. But *we* are the detectives. *I* should have made the connection. We should have considered other options – like how he might have knowledge of bugging devices for starters.'

'Yeah I agree. We thought he must have hired someone. And you don't like to think that someone in the force would be connected to murders do you?'

'I'm sure it's happened before. Especially back in 50s, 60s and 70s. There were lots of crooked cops around then. The Commissioner would have started his career on the tail end of that corruption era in Victoria. He would have the knowledge of how to keep a crime scene clear of all evidence – even before DNA.'

'Yeah – he's certainly not left much around at any crime scene. But this evidence was gathered from his hotel room where he thought he was safe. The British police managed to acquire some even after the room had been cleaned. Okay, here's what the emails tells us. Let's have a look. I'd like to get out of here some time tonight!'

The pair huddle together over the paperwork and compare findings. The mitochondrial DNA looks like a match to them. The fingerprints and other DNA doesn't match anything in their files.

'So it looks like the hairs we found in the Glenbrook house were from him,' India says.

'Yes, but I'll have to have one of our techies compare the mito DNA just to make sure. We're no experts on this. Okay let's call it a night. I've had enough for today.'

A match for the mitochondrial DNA was confirmed by the technicians. The Ellis's discuss the possibility of collecting DNA somehow from the Commissioner, but as Rob points out the Commissioner's DNA from the hotel room will obviously match any DNA they might manage to collect from him. The mito DNA could mean a link to someone related to him. It still doesn't prove absolutely that *he* is their suspect, although they are both convinced that he is. The evidence is slim and does not give them a great deal to take the case forward.

# 39

Cate Rossi sits fuming in her hotel room. She has thought long and hard about the Commissioner. Detective Hargreaves has been to see her with up to date information as promised and although there is some evidence from Manchester that matches the mitochondrial DNA collected from her Glenbrook home, it is the only evidence they have on him. The detectives claim it is still not enough proof to move forward with any further investigations in Australia. They discussed the possibility of obtaining an appointment with the Minister, but as India pointed out they really need more evidence. Cate has come to the conclusion that the only way that they are going to catch this monster is if she is used as bait. It is not what she really wants to do, but she can't see any other way around it. He needs to be *caught* in the act of committing a crime. There is always the possibility that she will lose her life in the process. She has no wish to die now, although she did several years ago, but is willing to risk losing her life if it means the man is caught. She rings the station and makes an appointment with DCI Ellis and DSS Hargreaves for that afternoon.

'So what do you think of the idea of using me as bait?' Cate asks them both.

'We don't normally use members of the public in those circumstances. It is usually a police officer who is made up to look like the person we are wanting to be the bait,' Rob

Ellis tells her.

'But I think it needs to be me,' Cate says.

'I think it poses too much of a risk to you,' India Hargreaves says.

'I know it's a risk, but I can't see how else we are going to catch him. There are several ways we could do it. We could do it quietly - say for example me making a challenging phone call to him and then go to my father's place and wait for him to take action. He obviously knows where they live and must have been there to obtain my Manchester address. Alternatively I could challenge him loudly in a very public place .... I don't know ... like at his office or the police Headquarters – with an audience - or at a press conference where there'd be even more people. Personally I prefer the second option as it places him publicly in a poor light where many questions will be asked. He'll be furious. And will react.'

'I think the first option – a quiet attack will be better. We need to keep this low profile. Otherwise there could be dramatic repercussions,' DCI Ellis states quietly.

'Such as?' Cate asks.

DCI Ellis pauses. He is not sure he should be spelling it out for this woman. A member of the public who has personally suffered so much due to one person who happens to be in the force. She is looking at him with those big blue eyes that hold so much sorrow - and innocence. He decides to take a gamble. He believes she will see the sense in what he has to say. 'Well for example, the Head of a CID team in one of our other state capitals was done for corruption a few years back and then virtually all the team lost their jobs, even though there was no concrete evidence against them. Also, all the convictions the dirty cop had been involved with were overturned and many guilty crims were released from jail – including a number of murderers.'

'Well maybe all his convictions need examining anyway. Who's to say he didn't commit some of the crimes himself?'

'No, that would be a nightmare. Seriously. His convictions will automatically be examined once we have evidence of his guilt - without the need for blaring publicity. To involve the press would just produce a relentless campaign against NSW, Queensland and Victoria Police – anywhere he has been stationed. It would damage the force irreparably for many years to come. It would make our job impossible. I'm sorry I cannot agree with an approach that involves the press. If, and when we catch him, those sort of decisions will be taken out of my hands. But I believe my superiors would also insist it is kept quiet.'

He can see she is weighing up the options. The need for revenge perhaps? To crush this man and to make it known who was responsible for all the suffering she and her family have endured. She opens her mouth as though she is going to speak or protest several times, but each time remains quiet, swallowing her words. Finally she speaks.

'Okay, you're right. I will agree to do this quietly on one condition. And that is that, if I can obtain evidence of Detective Paramo's murder, the enquiry is re-opened and a different ruling given on his death. He was working to help me find my mother's killer. I owe it to him and his children. It is just so wrong that his children will grow up thinking that their father didn't want to be with them anymore and chose to end his life, when we all know that was highly unlikely. Also, I would want all the crimes against my family noted on the files, even if they are kept 'top secret' or whatever you do when you don't want information released.'

'I don't know Cate,' India interjects with a worried frown. 'It's very admirable of you to make that condition about Joe Paramo particularly, and I understand you want the crimes committed against your family resolved. I have always wanted to see a different verdict on Joe Paramo's death as well. But even if we have your father's place under surveillance and others inside, he still might find a way to get to you before we can. He is such a devious bastard.'

'Hang on India – I mean Detective Hargreaves, if Mrs. Rossi is willing to do this, I think it is certainly worth a shot. We've discussed the impossibility of the situation. I think this might be just the ticket to nab him. Then we'll have irrefutable proof. You could wear a wire as well,' he says to Cate Rossi. 'And see if you can get him to confess to his other crimes.'

'We'll need to approach my father at his office first. He doesn't even know I am in the country,' Cate Rossi says. 'It's all dependent on his agreement and he might not give it. If not we'll have to set the scene up somewhere else.'

'Okay, use my phone to call your father now and arrange to meet with him,' Ellis says standing. 'If he says no, we'll have to rethink the situation. Detective Hargreaves, a word outside please.'

Cate and Detective Hargreaves visit Howard Brant's office that afternoon. The weather has turned cold and rainy so Cate bundles herself up in a coat and dons a hat and scarf to disguise herself further. Just in case his office building is being observed. She knows that is probably very paranoiac thinking, but the killer might have discovered that she is not dead – you never know with the internet these days. One day, when she was in England talking to Rosie on the phone, Rosie happened to mention some UK celebrity's death – Rosie knew about it before it had appeared on the news in the UK, through the internet. The killer might be keeping her father's office under surveillance, although she can't see how he could possibly do his job and carry out so much surveillance. However, he had managed to have time off work to stalk her family in the past. He could of course be paying someone else to assist him as well.

Her father greets her warmly, but he is not happy to hear of her plan to use herself as bait. Cate has told him that they have discovered the man's name and profession, but she tells him she can't discuss the details with him at the moment. 'I have to do it Dad, there's just no other way to stop this man.'

Her father eventually concedes, but insists on seeing Detective Hargreaves who Cate calls into his office. 'I'm not happy about you using Cate as bait in this situation,' he tells Detective Hargreaves. 'In fact I'm very surprised that your superiors are planning to use Cate at all.'

'I can assure you….,' India Hargreaves starts, but Cate cuts her off.

'Dad it's not Detective Hargreaves's fault. It was my idea. I have persuaded her boss to go along with it. So don't take it out on her. Detective Hargreaves isn't happy about it either.'

'Okay Cate, okay. If you think it is the only way we can put an end to all this, then I'll agree. On one condition only. Rosie is not involved in it all. It's bad enough one of my daughters putting herself at risk. I will not allow another one to do so. Rosie will have to move out of the unit for the duration. You will have to find someone to take Rosie's place.'

'That won't be a problem,' Detective Hargreaves assures

him. 'We can put Rosie in a safe house somewhere – with protection just in case.'

'Thank you. That would ease my mind considerably. Rosie and I have been talking about it – not while at home I might add, just in case we have been bugged - and we think he picked up your English address from the address book she had hidden in her room. I told her not to write it down or keep it anywhere at home, but you know what she can be like – she loves her pretty little address books. She hid it thinking it was safe. As if anything is safe from that mongrel! I thought of moving again when I heard what happened in Manchester - but there's no point until this is resolved. He always seems to find out where we live.'

Cate and India Hargreaves look at each other. They are aware of how he would have traced them, but can't say anything at present.

## 40

Cate spends the next couple of days writing her 'speech' while the Detectives organise everything. She doesn't want to forget anything, so the speech will be with her to use as a prompt. The days seem to drag as she remains largely ensconced in her hotel room, only venturing out if Detective Hargreaves accompanies her.

They have someone keeping any eye on the Commissioner's movements during the day at Headquarters. The Commissioner is to address the press at 3pm today with a presentation of crime statistics compiled in his report. No doubt completed by one of his minions, Cate thinks, as he has been busy stalking her family, breaking to their unit and repeating much of the same process in Manchester. As well as masquerading as an upright citizen of Australia. It's a shame the press and public will probably never find out that he is the greatest criminal of them all. Cate suspects that there is an intention to silence him permanently, if the opportunity arises, so there will be no trial. No blaring publicity. It will just be one big cover up. She would have preferred him to serve time thinking about his crimes. But that would involve her going to court as well. Not that she would mind giving evidence against him, it's just the publicity it would generate that is not appealing.

Cate wants to make her challenge to him before his conference, hoping it might put him off. At 1.00pm on 'D' day, as Cate has taken to calling it, Detective Hargreaves collects her, accompanied by two other officers. A further unmarked car follows them across to Dee Why where her father's unit is located. They have ascertained that the Commissioner is safely preoccupied at Headquarters. Cate is briefly reunited with Rosie who has taken some time off work and will be whisked away by officers to an unknown destination. A lookalike female officer, sporting a red wig, will be taking her place at the unit and pose as Rosie in a staged exit later that evening and again the next day if necessary. Several officers are to remain with Cate at her father's house, including Detective Hargreaves. DCI Ellis has named it 'Operation Goldfinger' to those involved – a touch of irony given the man's name.

As soon as Rosie departs Cate places her call through to the Commissioner. She is told he is unavailable at present, taking no calls as he is preparing to leave for a press conference. Cate assures the woman that he will take her call. 'Tell him it's Catelin Rossi.' Sure enough she hears an angry voice in her ear.

'Is this some kind of practical joke?' he barks.

'No Commissioner. My name is Catelin Rossi. I'm sure you know who I am. Yes I am still alive. That was my lodger you killed in Manchester. You are due to give a speech this afternoon about the clear up of crime statistics in New South Wales. I would like to ask you Commissioner when you are going to take responsibility for all the murders you have committed.' She can hear his audible intake of breath.

'Namely - Mia Adjudovic, in Melbourne Australia in December 1980. My mother Julie Brant also in Melbourne in December 1980, a murder that I witnessed. Detective Inspector Paramo in Parramatta on October 14th 1999. Janet Brant, my stepmother on October 19th 1999. My husband and baby, Marco and Milo Rossi on the Putty Road December 27th 1999. Detective Chief Inspector John Pritchard January 6th 2000 and more recently Diane Quinn, Manchester England August 7th 2002. Yes, Commissioner, as I said you killed the wrong woman in Manchester. I'm still very much alive and calling you to account.'

'Lies! All lies. Who is this?'

*Really? Is that the best you can do?* 'Oh, I can assure you I'm Catelin Rossi. Sorry, have I missed some Commissioner? I'm sure there are plenty more, only I don't know all their names. What about Bishop Jonathan Byrne – did you cause his death as well? Well I'm ringing to let you know that I have arranged to speak to someone here in Australia about this. The Manchester police know all about you as well. You'll not doubt be hearing from us shortly.' Cate slams the phone down. 'Bait set,' she confirms to Detective Hargreaves.

Howard Brant and his 'daughter' make a loud exit from the unit at 8pm that night. Cate stands visibly at the front window of the spare bedroom, waving at them. If the Commissioner is out there he will see that she is purportedly alone in the flat. If he's been listening then he would have heard their 'scripted' conversations (with the fake Rosie pretending to have a bad cold). The unit has been scanned for listening devices. None had been found, but they are not taking any chances.

Cate wanders into the sitting room and waits. Her father and 'Rosie' are scheduled to return at 11.30pm unless told otherwise. The hours drag by but the killer doesn't appear. Cate is worried that this could go on for days while she has to remain cooped up. When her father and 'Rosie' return, relieved that all is well, they decide to retire for the night.

The Brant unit at Dee Why is one of only two sited on a large block of land that once held a single home. It is not a new building, but an 80s development where the convenience of its layout was never considered Cate thinks. The sloped driveway leads down to two double garages. Behind the garages are laundries, workshops and store rooms that lead out to a shared garden. There is no entrance to either unit from the garages, but there is a gated side footpath leading to the laundries at the rear and to the garden. Entrance to each unit is gained through a set of stairs up the side of the garages where there are separate entrance doors. One leads to the Brant unit, the other to the unit upstairs. The Brant unit, which is three bedroomed, spans the length and breadth of the building, with an external terrace sitting over the laundry rooms downstairs. The terrace spans the width of the building and can be accessed either through the living room or from Howard Brant's bedroom. At present there is no access to the garden from the terrace. Howard Brant's plans to have one installed has been repeatedly delayed due to builders letting him down. Now it is preferable that there is no direct rear access to the unit. The upstairs unit is set over two floors and has recessed terraces on each level to take advantage of the ocean views. The height from the ground to the front bedrooms in the Brant apartment would make it difficult for anyone to enter the premises from there. It is believed the killer is more likely to enter through the front door, doors having proved no obstacle for him in the past. There is a possibility that he might gain access to the garden and climb onto the terrace, entering the unit that way and so all options are being covered.

Detective Hargreaves will be sleeping in the second single bed in the spare room near Cate. The fake Rosie will be taking it in turns with the two other officers to remain awake in the living room while one naps in Rosie's room. The police officers and Detective Hargreaves are to remain completely silent throughout the operation using only sign and gesture to communicate. Detective Hargreaves wants to have someone placed in Howard Brant's room as well, but he refuses the intrusion to his privacy. She is concerned that the Commissioner might enter the flat in the middle of the night with a different plan of action, making Howard Brant vulnerable. Hidden cameras are installed in the entrance hallway, the living room and Howard Brant's bedroom. There are further officers stationed around the neighbourhood, including DCI Ellis. If DCI Ellis had his Chief Superintendent's complete confidence, he would have been allowed more options and been able to watch the movements of the Commissioner at all times. As it was he was restricted to one ex-colleague at Headquarters keeping him abreast of any news. Apparently the Commissioner disappeared with the Minister and deputy Commissioner to an unknown destination following the conference. The Commissioner has not returned to Headquarters, nor has he returned home, where DCI Ellis has another surveillance car. He appeared at the conference dressed in his full uniform but is unlikely to approach the Brant household wearing that. He has to make a change of clothes somewhere. Does he have a second home – an apartment they know nothing about – or a storage unit somewhere?

Neither Cate nor Detective Hargreaves manage much sleep, both on alert for the slightest change in sound. Several times one or the other sits bolt upright in bed, alarmed by different noises they hear that prove to be nothing.

At 7.45am the following morning, Howard Brant and

'Rosie' once again exit the flat with Cate waving at them from the bedroom window. Cate is again fitted with the wire that they had placed on her the day before. The morning drags on without disturbance until 2.03pm when a voice in Detective Hargreaves's headset gives the warning from one of the plainclothes officers parked outside that an elderly disabled man in a small black vehicle has parked nearby and is walking towards the building. Hargreaves signals to her team to be on the alert. The officers tell her they are unable to determine the man's exact age, as he is wearing a cap, but say he doesn't appear to look anything like their suspect. A few minutes later they hear the entrance door to the upstairs unit slam and Hargreaves gives the signal for the team to stand down. Everyone relaxes and one of the officers makes them all fresh cups of coffee before they retreat to their respective rooms.

Sitting in the front bedroom Detective Hargreaves thinks about the neighbour that they heard entering the unit on the next floor. All her instincts scream at her that something is very wrong. She is sure she remembers Rob mentioning that the occupiers were away. That was something they checked out surely? She walks quietly out to Cate in the living room and beckons her to follow her into the bathroom where she runs water at the sink.

'Do you know the people who live in the upstairs unit?' she whispers to Cate.

'It was a young couple before I left for England,' Cate whispers back. 'I don't know who lives there now. Why?'

'I just have an uneasy feeling about it. I'm sure they are supposed to be away. We need to get hold of your father and check it out. You go and sit in the living room. I'll warn the others.' She walks silently to the other rooms indicating with gestures to expect some action. She pulls out her mobile and dials Howard Brant speaking to him in whispers from the bathroom. He confirms that a young couple live there, but he is sure they are still both away at present as he had told her DCI. They were travelling to the young woman's home country, the Netherlands, to visit family and were due to be away for eight weeks. Howard Brant tells her that they left around July 20th which would mean they were definitely still away. It could of course be someone coming to water their plants or just check on the place for the owners, but Hargreaves doesn't think this is the case. The description of the man entering the building is supposedly that of a disabled old man but Detective Hargreaves is sure it is the killer attempting to disguise himself.

He may know that the neighbours are away as well if he visited both units before heading to Manchester at the end of July. They should have checked all this out more thoroughly before the operation commenced. Poor preparation, Detective Hargreaves admonishes herself. They had wanted to involve as few people as possible. The more civilians that knew, the more potential leaks or mistakes could be made. However by not physically checking out the neighbour's unit, they've left themselves exposed and the family, particularly Cate, in greater danger.

Of course she may be completely wrong. But they have to prepare for the worst. The most likely place he may attack from is the terrace, she thinks. She knows the upstairs unit has its own terrace that is staggered back from the Brant one. If he were to lower himself off the upstairs terrace he would land on the Brant's terrace. To do that in front of the living room would be too obvious so he is likely to land outside Howard Brant's bedroom, believing him to be gone for the day. They have left the curtains drawn in his bedroom. He is likely to enter the unit from there. She tiptoes silently into Howard Brant's bedroom and pulls the two officers out of there, moving one into the spare room and one into Rosie's bedroom. She then returns to the bathroom, repeating the water trick, alerting her external colleagues to the possibility that it is the suspect who has entered the top unit, as the occupiers are abroad, and asks them to be ready at her signal. She receives no reply from the officers outside the unit and all her fears are realised when Rob shouts an urgent message down her headset that the suspect *is* on the premises. How could he know for sure? She doesn't have time to become involved in a discussion about it though.

Detective Hargreaves warns Cate with gestures that the suspect is upstairs and may enter through her father's room. Cate nods, turns her wire on and moves into the kitchen that leads off the living room and starts preparing some food. Detective Hargreaves thinks Cate being in the kitchen will at least offer her some protection, with handy knives if necessary. The only victim the suspect has shot was Detective Paramo and so she thinks he will attempt to use one of his usual methods, strangulation, breaking the neck or throwing her off the terrace when he attacks.

Cate is genuinely preparing a chicken curry for tonight's meal. She feels secure with a knife in her hand chopping up vegetables. She can feel adrenaline coursing through her body and there is a slight tremor in her hands. If it is him upstairs, it will be first time she has encountered him at close quarters face to face. When she was six years old and hiding in her mother's wardrobe, he was well under a metre's distance from her, but not aware of it.

She looks up and there he is, just standing inside the living room door, watching her, holding a gun with a silencer pointed directly at her. Cate gulps, swallowing her fear. She hadn't even noticed the living room door open. She thinks that if she drew him again today she would now be depicting a bloated ugly pitted face. Not that she ever thought him attractive or handsome. He was beyond that. But now she sees his evil deeds etched deeply into his soul. His eyes are like two black holes. She was never able to make them out clearly from the wardrobe all those years ago, but thought they were a cold grey. Her grip on the knife she is holding instinctively tightens. For a moment she fantasises about plunging the knife deeply into his body. Again and again. One thrust for each life he has taken of her family members. Could she really do that? Yes she believes she is capable of it – certainly in her head. And she will not hesitate to defend herself if he attempts to attack her before back up arrives.

'I thought you'd come,' she says brazenly to him.

'It's about time we met face to face Catelin, - the girl with nine lives,' he says sarcastically walking further into the room. 'Although you've only used up four of your lives, this is where it is going to end today. I suspected you might have been at your mother's house on that day all those years ago, but clearly I didn't do a thorough enough search. I decided you'd gone to a relatives for the night or something as your bed was made and the room clean and tidy. My kid's rooms were never that tidy. A shame I missed you in Glenbrook with your fast action leaping out of the way. I almost had you there. Then finally I thought I'd never see you again after Putty Road. The way I set that up was pretty ingenious I thought. How on earth did you survive that one? Must have been very painful for you to climb all the way up to the road. I hear you nearly lost your leg. And Manchester. Well I believed I definitely had you there, but it seems it was some other patsy took your hit.'

'You've accumulated quite a collection of victims haven't you?' Cate says. 'Detective Paramo and my stepmother included.'

'The wop detective thought he had me, but drinking was his downfall. I soon sorted him.'

'And my stepmother?'

'Wrong place, wrong time. Unfortunate for her.'

'Why my mother?'

'She saw me leaving the Adjudovic place the day before. Nearly ran me over. I followed her and saw where you lived. When I saw her stop the next day on the corner near the crime scene and that she'd spotted me, I knew she had to be silenced.'

'So why did you kill the Adjudovic woman in the first place?'

He sighs. 'Yes Mia. She was the start of all this. She was out with me at a club the night before. We were having an affair weren't we? The nosey cow copped me attacking the club's owner and decided she had to report it. I couldn't let her do that. It could have been the end of my career and marriage. I had a couple of kids. If only she had kept her nose out of my business, none of this would have happened.'

'Why involve my husband and child? They were innocent bystanders in all this.'

'No, your husband had clocked me. I heard a message he'd left with his work saying he *knew* who I was – whatever he meant by that, and he obviously planned to take some action as he said he was changing his plans and returning to work sooner to collect the tape with me on it. So he had to go as well. Your child was an unfortunate casualty of that.'

So Marco had definitely seen her new drawings and realised he was the same man who'd been captured on the camera at work Cate thinks. She wants to scream at him, abhorred by his callousness. But she needs to gather more evidence.

'What about John Pritchard? Was he on to you as well?'

'That incompetent fool? No. He'd questioned me when you came back in after spotting me in '99. Seems Paramo had told him your original drawings were of *me*. But Pritchard came up with a plausible argument about you mixing me up with what the killer looked like all those years ago because I was at the scene investigating Mia's death. Which I was of course. Pritchard really believed that trauma caused confusion in witnesses. Especially in such a young child. In fact it was *his* suggestion. But your father came in stirring things up. Pritchard rang me internally to tell me he was considering re-opening the investigation into Paramo's death. You could say Pritchard died *because* of me, but I didn't lay a hand on him.'

'What do you mean?'

'I knew where he'd be that afternoon. I needed to talk to him and I arrived just as he was bringing his boat back in. I called out to him. He turned, looked at me and suddenly twisted back around. I don't know what was going through his mind, or what he was planning on doing, but he tripped, falling and hitting his head on a rock nearby in the shallows. Landing face down in the water. There was no-one else around so I knew he'd drown. I just left him to it. He obligingly silenced himself.'

'And Bishop Byrne?'

'Johnny Boy? Nothing to do with me. I hadn't seen him for months. Although I did ring him to wish him a Merry Christmas and asked him kindly not to speak to anyone about my visit in October or reveal my identity if anyone came to see him. Seems he had his heart attack later that day. He was never a particularly strong character.'

'So ....how's this going to pan out? You can't shoot me surely. How would that be explained?'

'No, I won't shoot you, but the gun is to persuade you to move out onto the terrace where you will take a dive.'

'Again? Can't you be more creative than that? That was the one you tried in Manchester with Diane Quinn. But they know you killed her first.'

'I had to shut her up. She was making too much noise. Now be a good girl, put the knife down and move out here.'

'Sorry, can't oblige. You'll have to make me. Besides, it's only one level down to the garden. You can't be sure that a fall there would kill me.'

'It most likely would if I dropped you head first onto the concrete path. But I will shoot you if I have to.'

'But how would you explain that Mr. Bond? James Bond. I have to say you are nothing like your fictitious namesake - although he does have a habit of shooting people. But he is made out to be the good guy with his shootings. Unlike you.'

'I was born before that bloody fictitious character was created. Those books and films have been a bloody pain in the neck much of my adult life with people laughing about my name. That's why I go by the name of Jim. Not James.'

'So how many other people have you shot besides Detective Paramo?'

'Plenty in my time, in my line of work.'

'I imagine some of the ones you've shot might account for some of the unsolved murders in all the places you have served.'

'I've enjoyed our little chat Catelin, but it's time to stop. Stop procrastinating and move out here. I know what you think. You think someone is going to come charging in on their white horse and save you. Well you'd be wrong. The two plain clothes outside are out for the count. They won't be helping anyone. I could always make this look like a burglary gone wrong.'

'Plain clothes? What are you talking about?' Cate asks this with genuine shocked surprise. Is DCI Ellis outside somewhere lying dead? Not more deaths?

Bond looks at her and hesitates. Perhaps she didn't know about the protection. Doesn't matter anyway. They won't be helping anyone anytime soon. He begins to move towards the kitchen when the door behind him bursts open.

'Police. Drop your weapon now!' shouts a female voice. He looks around and sees one female and two male officers aiming guns at him. Shit, he thought she was alone. Listening on a device in his car before entering the upstairs unit, he hadn't heard anyone but Catelin Rossi. He had installed a bug some months earlier, but thought he no longer needed it. After receiving the phone call from the Rossi woman he had activated the device and heard nothing that alerted him to the presence of others today. Only her singing at times. He'd checked outside and only seen the one vehicle. What now? It's not in his nature to capitulate. His weapon is still aimed at the woman who has been the bane of his life for several years. He fires his weapon several times at her while at the same time he can hear the guns of those behind him firing. He doesn't feel a thing, but looks down and can see several shots have entered his body. *At least I took the bitch with me* are his last thoughts before collapsing on the floor.

'Cate?' Detective Hargreaves calls out in a panic before entering the kitchen area. She sees Cate Rossi lying prone on the floor. Oh Christ, he's killed her! She bends down and touches the lifeless figure of the woman she was supposed to protect and sobs. I've failed she thinks. I left it too long. Cate was doing such a brilliant job at gathering information from him that Rob kept saying, 'wait'…..'wait', until it was too late. With three guns aimed at him, the last thing they expected was for him to open fire. They should have realised he was not about to leave Cate alive. After all his failed attempts. She can see blood trickling down the side of Cate's head. She feels for a pulse. There is a steady beat. She's alive!

'Call an ambulance,' she yells to her colleagues.

# 41

India Hargreaves searches over the rest of Cate's body and cannot see any other wounds. Just the one on the side of her head. Looking more closely she can see it is just a shallow wound. Cate stirs and shakes her head. 'I think his shots missed me,' she mumbles, 'but I bashed my head hard on a cupboard handle as I went down. Did you get him and did you hear everything clearly?'

'Yes, we got him and you did brilliantly Cate. Everything he said has been recorded.'

'Is he alive?'

'I'm afraid not.'

'Shame. I would have been happy to know he was rotting in jail for the rest of his life. At least it's all over,' she says before promptly passing out again.

Cate is taken outside the unit when the paramedics arrive and her wound, which proves to be minor, requiring just a couple of stitches, is tended at the scene. The paramedics were told that she hit her head in a fall. Cate refuses to go to hospital, so she is to be carefully observed by family overnight in case she's sustained concussion. Detective Hargreaves arranges for Howard Brant to collect Cate and the overnight bags they had packed. She'd told them the day before that it would be necessary for the crime scene technicians to spend time at the unit if there was any action.

Crime technicians from the Windsor station had been

on alert waiting for instructions to attend the scene if required. DCI Ellis has called them and they are on their way to two locations.

'What happened with Dave and Phil?' India asks Rob when they finally meet up just inside the Brant unit after the crime technicians arrive.

'After notifying us of the man approaching the unit, we lost contact with them. I suspected something was wrong so we moved in to check it out. He'd shot them both and knocked them unconscious. Not to kill them I don't think, just to put them out of action. He'd used a silencer which is why no-one heard the shots.'

'Are they going to be okay? I saw no sign of their car when we came out.'

'No we moved the car several blocks away, while radioing in for help. I didn't want ambulances turning up here to collect them before we had any action. The sound of sirens might have scared Bond off. I had Johnno follow them to the hospital. He's just phoned me. They've had emergency surgery and they're both going to be okay.'

'Thank Christ for that. The last thing we want is more deaths. I've left Greg and Pete dealing with the neighbours. Quite a few of them heard the gunshots coming from the unit and then of course saw the ambulance. We've told them that a visiting family friend had a fatal heart attack and Cate just had a fall when she fainted after seeing the friend die. We played it all innocent about the gunshots, claiming it was probably a car backfiring. I'm sure they know they're just being fobbed off, but most of them have returned home. A few are still hanging around.'

'Okay, good work. We found a listening device in the car Bond was using. So there was one in the unit.'

'How did the techies miss that?'

'Guess we'll soon find out.'

'What about the car he used to travel here?'

'Dave gave me the rego plates when Bond pulled up. After checking it I discovered it was registered in a different name at an address near Parramatta. We didn't think it was his but I despatched someone to have a look anyway. Seems Bond had a small industrial unit at his disposal where this car was kept. We've split the techies up and one lot are there checking it out at the moment.'

'Have you spoken to the Chief Super?'

'Yes, I'm waiting to hear back from him as to whether we need to call in the local boys. He thinks not, that the big guns will probably want to keep it low key. But he said there might be issues that arise with the locals anyway, as word will filter through about our two wounded at the local emergency hospital. They might turn up there. Johnno will sort it anyway.'

'So does the Super know it's Bond now and that he's dead?'

'Yeah he knows. You know we gave him Bond's nickname of Jim Beam for the operation, but once we had Bond's confession recorded I phoned him again and told him who he really was and what had happened here. I thought he'd had a heart attack or something from the groans and then silence at the other end of the phone. He couldn't believe it. Said he wants full reports as soon as, so expect to be spending the next few days tied to a desk. You'll all have to hand your weapons in as well. He's contacting the deputy Commissioner and the Head of the Ministry of Police right away to decide what they are going to do. It's up to them now.'

James Arthur Bond was pronounced dead, photographed and removed from the scene later that night, long after the crowds on the street had dispersed. An announcement was made to the press that Commissioner Jim Bond (as he was known to the public, to avoid sniggering associations with his eponymous namesake) had died suddenly of a heart attack whilst visiting friends that day. His family, a son and daughter still residing in the Gold Coast, were informed. His ex-wife, also a resident of the Gold Coast, was told of his death by her children. They were told that a formal identification of the body had been carried out by colleagues, but that there would be a delay in receiving the body for a funeral as a post-mortem had to be carried out because it was a sudden death. Arrangements were being made for a death certificate to be issued for the family stating the cause of death as a heart attack.

Cate and her father were re-united with Rosie that evening in a city hotel where Mr. Brant had booked rooms for them all to stay.

'Tell me everything that happened Cate. I want all the gory details,' Rosie demands over their meal.

'Not here, Rosie. Not tonight,' Howard Brant hisses.

'Let's drink a toast to my two mothers,' Cate says changing the subject. She raises her glass. 'To Julie and Janet who now have some sort of justice.'

'To Julie and Janet,' her father and Rosie echo.

'What about Marco and Milo?' Rosie asks. 'Shouldn't we drink a toast to them as well?'

Cate hesitates. It doesn't seem right to her to be toasting them. Her emotions are still too raw. 'No, to justice,' she says thinking of all of Bond's victims.

'To justice,' they all chorus, clinking their glasses.

'Of sorts,' Cate adds.

DCI Rob Ellis makes contact with his counterpart DCI Steve Mills in Manchester by email officially informing him that the suspect in the Cate Rossi investigation is now deceased, and that they would not be continuing any further enquiries. He also states that they found no evidence linking the deceased suspect to the murder of the young woman in the Manchester flat. Of course this was all correct. There was no hard evidence. They had Bond's confession, but the last thing they needed was the UK police informing the young woman's family in Australia who the suspected perpetrator of the crime was.

'I saw your Commissioner of Police died recently,' Steve Mills remarks to Rob Ellis when Ellis phones him to confirm receipt of his 'official' email. 'Of a heart attack I read.'

'Yes, an unfortunate premature death, one might say.'

'Should I be looking for anyone else in connection with the Diane Quinn murder?'

'It's up to you, but I wouldn't waste my resources if I were you.'

'Understood.'

# 42

## Windsor, NSW, December 24th 2002

Cate has a meeting with Detectives Rob Ellis and India Hargreaves this morning for an update on what has happened since she last saw them. She steps off the train at Windsor enjoying the warmth of the summer heat. Alan had invited her to stay in England for Christmas, as she loves a hot Christmas dinner with cold blustery weather outside. There's nothing cosier than sitting around the fire after a feast, but her father and Rosie had really wanted her to return home. Alan had his granddaughter and her family coming to stay with him for Christmas this year anyway and with two young children the house wouldn't have had its normal peaceful calm. Cate is also not sure she is ready to be around young children just yet.

Following the death of Commissioner Bond, Cate had returned to England, remaining there for almost four months, tying things up with the intention of returning to Australia permanently. As the apartment was already let, Cate stayed with Adhita whilst in Manchester. Adhita decided she would like to buy Cate's tenanted apartment if Cate would throw in her car as part of the deal when she finally left the UK. They agreed a price for the apartment and set about completing the necessary legal work.

Cate had spent some time with Alan in Yorkshire and met up with her great Aunt Edie and her husband Ray.

Not in Hawes though. Apart from Alan and Adhita, who knew the truth, Cate had told everyone the suspect responsible for the murders of members of her family had died suddenly, and that the cases had been closed. She made no mention of his name – or his prominent position. Her father and Rosie knew now who he was, but they had agreed to keep the secret.

Alan and Cate had spent some time in London, exploring sites neither of them had ever seen. Whilst there Cate had visited Naniji at Adhita's childhood home. They also took a road trip up to the west coast of Scotland, visiting Glasgow and exploring a number of lochs. Cate has many wonderful photographs of her and Alan from the memorable trip.

India Hargreaves meets Cate at reception and takes her through to Rob's office. Steaming coffees are waiting for them on the desk, as well as a plate of biscuits. Special treatment, Cate thinks.

'So tell me what's been happening with the cases while I've been away?' she asks DCI Ellis.

'An internal investigation was launched into the Commissioner's death detailing events leading up the shooting. Your statement and the recordings played a vital role in that enquiry. His death was considered unavoidable in the circumstances and all officers involved cleared. As promised, Joe Paramo's death was immediately re-investigated and the verdict changed from suicide to murder – by persons unknown the family were informed. His family were duly compensated with his pension and a trust fund established for his sons. It was decided that the death of DCI John Pritchard would stand as previously recorded as his wife was already receiving his pension and it was, strictly speaking, an accident, even if his death could have been avoided.'

'Okay what about the first murders in Melbourne. My mother and that other woman?

'Bond has been cited as the person responsible for the murders of Mia Adjudovic and Julie Brant in Melbourne, Janet Brant in Sydney and causing the deaths of Marco and Milo Rossi in the Putty Road crash. When investigators recently looked into the unsolved Adjudovic crime file they discovered samples of hair had been discovered at the Adjudovic flat that had been found between the cushions on the couch. Bond, as one of the investigators, either overlooked this evidence, or considered it unimportant, believing it would never be linked to him. Testing on the hairs revealed a match for him. Thanks to you we have his confession on record and the hairs just confirm his presence in her life. The files on the two Melbourne murders have now been sealed, as have the files on your husband and son's death. Your stepmother's death was re-examined and a different verdict recorded. Again the file has been sealed.'

'Is that so they can't be made public?'

'Yes. As I said, we wish to avoid the police being targeted over these crimes. So Mrs. Rossi, I think that's all we really need to cover with you. Was there anything else you want to ask?' DCI Ellis does not think it is appropriate to mention that there is going to be a lengthy internal investigation, that is likely to take several years, to re-examine all James Bond's cases. Internal Affairs committees have been established in Victoria and Queensland to deal with this task. It was not thought necessary to do the same in New South Wales, as by the time of his promotion to the NSW force, Bond was no longer directly running cases.

'Yes. Did you ever discover whether Bond had a listening device at my father's unit?'

'Yes, he did have one embedded in the extractor fan over the stove and was only detectable when the device was activated.'

'Crafty. And clever. But surely if we'd been using the extractor while cooking, he wouldn't have heard anything?'

'No, he wouldn't have. But most people don't have extractors on for hours at a time. Well if you don't mind, I'm sorry, but I have a meeting to attend. Stay here and drink your coffee. Help yourself to biscuits. You can catch up with Detective Hargreaves,' Ellis says standing.

'Thank you for filling me in.'

'It's us that have *you* to thank for helping to resolve these cases. Thank you for all your input.'

'I'm sure you are aware that it has been my life's mission to bring my mother's killer to justice. It's because you two were willing to support me that I achieved it. Once I went to the police, there was no going back for me. It just took a long time to happen.'

'But you were drawing danger to yourself the whole time in doing that Cate,' India interjects.

'Hmm. Literally I suppose. In drawing the murderer, I attracted danger - not only to me though.' Cate says with a serious face.

'Well goodbye Cate Rossi,' DI Ellis says, reaching out to shake her hand.

'So you've severed ties with England now and are back in Australia for good?' India asks her once Rob has gone.

'Yes, although I have a few close friends there and some relatives I will be keeping in touch with.'

'Your family here must be pleased that you are back

home. What are your plans?'

'Oh eventually I'll go back to uni, to complete my qualifications as an architect. In the future I might set up my own small practice.'

'Good for you.'

They chat for another fifteen minutes and then Cate says she must go. At the reception Cate reaches out and hugs India. 'Merry Christmas, India Hargreaves Ellis.'

'Merry Christmas to you too Cate.' They release each other and smile before Cate turns and leaves.

# Epilogue

## Sydney, Saturday 6th December 2014

Cate looks around the room at the assembled crowd chatting over plates of food. Some standing, some sitting, some at the dining table on the covered terrace. It's her 40th birthday celebrations and all the people she loves are here today. Well not quite all. Not in any physical presence anyway. There are those who are no longer with them, like her mother, Janet, Marco and Milo. And Alan Mathers, who sadly passed away earlier this year. Alan had made the journey out to Australia to see her in early January the previous year, staying for a couple of months, to escape the harsh winter months in Yorkshire. She suspected when they waved farewell at the airport it might be the last time she'd see him.

The departed pass through her thoughts briefly every day. She sends silent wishes to them. She no longer feels that deep stab of pain that she used to when she thinks of Marco and Milo. It's not that she has 'moved on' – an expression her friends were fond of using. Wherever she moves to, 'they' accompany her, but instead of continuing to grieve for their loss, she celebrates their existence in her thoughts. Fifteen, Milo would have been on his last birthday. She'd tried to imagine what he'd look like now, supplanting Marco's face on teenage shoulders. But even a visual recall of Marco has become less tangible as the years pass. Possessing no photos of her own of her and Marco in her house, her memory of Marco has faded. Her father had boxed up all photographs of her life with them from the house in Glenbrook and they sit, no doubt mouldering away, in his storage room. Once, she'd looked through them after her final encounter with the Commissioner, but then packed them away never to re-visit.

She has a photograph of her and Milo though that she keeps in a drawer of her bedside cabinet. On Milo's birthday each year, she visits their grave in the Blue Mountains where they are buried together. The grave is always well tended. Marco's parents, now retired and living back in the mountains, visit it regularly. Cate exchanges Christmas cards with them each year, but has never seen them since the day they last visited her in the hospital and gave her the news of Marco and Milo's burial. She knows that deep down she has never truly forgiven them for that, despite understanding their reasons. She would have liked to see Marco and Milo one last time to say goodbye and they deprived her of that possibility. She is also aware that her resentment towards them has prevented her from having any direct contact and cost her emotional turmoil. She believes Marco's parents also harbour some resentment towards her. Resenting the fact that she'd survived. It came across quite plainly from Marco's mother, on that final visit. And blame. Blaming her somehow as though she may have contributed to the crash. They still believed it was a drunk driver who caused the crash but the questions the mother raised that day at the hospital indicated her thoughts also lay in some imaginary actions of Cate's in the car and her subsequent inability to seek help sooner "because Marco was such a good driver" she'd said "and wouldn't have crashed without some other *problem*" – like

Cate. "If only you'd got help ……" Mrs. Rossi had started saying before her husband had stopped her.

Cate's thoughts are interrupted at that moment by a gathering of children all vying for her attention. 'Auntie Cate, Julia won't let us play with her toys,' moans her nephew Cameron who is tugging at her skirt. His younger, four year old sister Katie is standing shyly behind Cate's daughter Julia, peeping around with hopeful eyes, her fiery red hair and green eyes the image of Rosie at the same age.

'I told him that you said we couldn't get any of them out until later, and that we had to eat first,' says an indignant Julia. 'Isn't that right mummy?'

'Yes you are quite right Julia, I did say that. Once you have all eaten you can go into the playroom. But you can't just grab food off the table – especially the cake. You need to ask your parents to put together a plate of food for you. And then you can eat at the table outside.'

Cameron storms off in a temper to find his mother, yanking his friend Leo with him, son of Cate's old school friend Emma. 'She's probably only got girly things to play with anyway.' Cate hears him say contemptuously as they depart.

'Julia, why don't you take Katie's hand and I'll take Seth here and we'll go and make you all a plate of food.'

Seth, Adhita's six year old son had been standing silently at her side waiting to hear the outcome of the dispute over the toys. He was a lovely natured, clever child, who observed everything going on around him. With only six months between them, Julia and Seth were best of friends. Katie, Rosie's youngest, adored Julia and trailed around after her everywhere when they visited.

When the two universities in Manchester had merged in 2004, Adhita had applied for, and secured a position at Sydney University, deciding it was about time she kept her word to Cate and moved to Australia. Naniji, the main reason she had remained in the UK, had passed away in 2003, so there was nothing holding her there anymore. It provided the perfect opportunity to escape her domineering family. Rather than a few hundred miles distant, they were now thousands of miles and several oceans apart. In 2006 Adhita had married Ewan Campbell, a Science Professor, who was Scottish by birth, and had immigrated to Australia with his family when he was 15. They now had two little boys, Seth who was six, and Jack who was 18months old. Motherhood and a marriage based on love suited Adhita. She had softened around the edges and although still a bit of a workaholic, family was her priority.

Cate's father, who turned 63 this year and wouldn't even consider retiring, was here with his new love Jacinta who was only eight years older than Cate. The jury was still out on her in Rosie and Cate's opinion. They understand their father's obsession with her though as she is a very attractive woman and her Spanish accent draws people like a magnet. It was strange how her father was always attracted to women whose names began with 'J'. He said it was a co-incidence. But his last fling had been with a woman called Joanna and the one before that was called Jackie. Then there was her mother Julie, and Janet, her stepmother. His mother's name had been Jean, which Cate and Rosie thought might have something to do with it. He had been delighted when Cate named her daughter Julia.

On her resettlement in Sydney, Cate eventually returned to university and completed her qualifications as an architect. It was during her final year that she met and subsequently married Sam Maynard, a successful author of history books and lecturer at the University. Since Marco's death she'd had no involvement with any men. The thought of doing so never even crossed her mind and she clearly emitted firm signals of unavailability to any men in her environment, as none ever approached her. One day in 2006 she found herself sitting next to Sam on a bench in the university grounds. They'd exchanged friendly banter and when their paths crossed again one day in the canteen, it seemed natural to share a table. Cate found herself responding with ease to Sam and a close friendship soon followed.

The large airy modern house they now live in was designed using a combination of the plans Marco had originally drawn up for replacing their Glenbrook house (long sold) and amendments Cate had made to suit their needs. Cate had had three pregnancies since she had married Sam. Julia, their first born, was now six. The same age she had been when her mother was murdered. Named after Cate's mother. Her second pregnancy two years later resulted in a miscarriage at four and a half months. Another little girl who would have been almost four now. It was several years before Cate fell pregnant again resulting in the birth of their son Lewis who is 13 months old and currently asleep. Cate and Sam have agreed they will have no more children.

Cate piles plates full of food for Julia, Seth and Katie and takes them out to the covered patio where the smaller dining table is set up for the children. No sooner does she have them settled when her father shouts out the door that Lewis has woken. She turns ready to enter the house when Sam appears at her shoulder.

'I'll see to him, you stay here and enjoy yourself,' he says and dashes off before she can protest. She feels very fortunate to have such a loving husband and such beautiful children. Cate looks up at the sky, a sunny cloudless day and steps out into its warmth. Yes all her loved ones are here she thinks.

# Author's Notes

When writing I like to embed my fictitious characters into real places. The history surrounding Australian name places, both pre and post European settlement is interesting. As a former history teacher I love to read historical information about the places authors set books. For those readers who like history and live outside Australia the following information may be of interest.

### Parramatta

Parramatta was 'founded' the same year as Sydney was settled by the English (1788). Chosen by Captain Arthur Phillip (leader of the First Fleet that established Sydney) as a suitable site for a farming settlement, it was originally called Rose Hill, but was re-named Parramatta in 1791. The name is believed to derive from 'Burramatta' – a name or word used by its first inhabitants. However fundamental misunderstandings occurred in communications between the Europeans and the original custodians of the land. The Europeans called all the 'aboriginal' inhabitants around the Sydney region the 'Eora people' or 'Eora tribes'. 'Eora' when translated means 'from this place'. There were in fact approximately 29 different 'clan' groups all with different names, different languages, land boundaries and cultures across the region. Whether 'Burramatta' meant the name of the area or was a word that had a completely different meaning has been lost in time.

Parramatta lies 14 miles (23km) west of Sydney and originally could only be reached by river from Sydney Cove. In 1790 the town of Parramatta was laid out and in 1793 the first road was built for overland travel between Parramatta and Sydney.

In 1799 Old Government House was built, which is the oldest public building still standing in Australia today.

In 1820 the infamous second Female Factory was opened in

Parramatta to house female convicts and their children who were used as slave labour. It was a factory, marriage bureau, hospital, asylum, prison and supposedly a place of 'refuge' where the women lived and worked. Named as a 'factory' due to the manufacture of linen and woollen products, the 'factory' was the first to export goods from Australia. It operated a three tier class system with those in first class allowed to earn money by taking on additional work, after they had completed their daily work load. It was generally guaranteed that those in first class would eventually be assigned a 'master' or gain a 'husband' and be able to leave the Women's Factory. For those unlucky enough to be in the second or third class tiers, with inadequate food rations and poor conditions, it was a place that most female convicts dreaded entering. Life expectancy was short in the lower tiers, particularly in third class where they were expected to carry out backbreaking work equivalent to their male counterparts (e.g. rock breaking). The Factory still stands today and is part of the Cumberland Hospital.

The first railway arrived close to Parramatta (called Parramatta Junction) in 1855 and was extended to the present Parramatta station in 1860.

In 1938 Parramatta was granted 'city' status which means it is a city as well as an area (or suburb) of greater Sydney.

It would necessitate a whole book to do justice to the history of the original land custodians of the Parramatta region, but I will summarise it in brief. The original inhabitants of the Parramatta region are now recognised as the 'Dharug' (or Darug) group whose land stretched into the Blue Mountains. For groups like the Dharug people, the land boundaries they lived within meant these were their hunting and feeding grounds and where they moved about taking care of the land. They didn't have fixed permanent settled communities with houses and crop growing (until the Europeans attempted to force this on them) but they would build shelters and there were various edible native plants that grew in their region that they would consume.

There were pockets of resistance against the Europeans as traditional hunting grounds were taken. In some raids or attacks, crops were burnt, livestock killed and some Europeans killed or injured.

Following a smallpox outbreak in 1789, the 'Eora' people population was decimated around Sydney and left groups struggling to survive. In the early 1800s some groups were provided with 'camp' areas and food and blanket rations. Governor Lachlan Macquarie gave grants of land to the 'Dharug' people to 'farm' and created a 'native school' in Parramatta. This stemmed from a misguided well-meant attempt to 'civilise' the people and bring Christianity into their life, without any understanding of their culture, a pattern that was repeated across much of the British Empire.

## The Blue Mountains

The Blue Mountains were originally named 'Carmarthen and Landsowne Hills' (in different sections). However they were re-named the Blue Mountains due to the distinctive blue haze that hovers over them. The mountains are covered in oil-bearing Eucalyptus trees. The dispersed droplets of oil from the trees together with dust particles and water vapour in the air form the blue haze.

The Blue Mountains, which are a small part of the Great Dividing Range that stretches down the eastern side of Australia, lie 31 miles (50km) west of Sydney to its foothills. Glenbrook is the first suburb of the mountains along the Great Western Road (or Highway).

Needing more farming and grazing land to support the Sydney colony, the mountains were first crossed by European settlers in 1813 to discover if there was suitable land that lay beyond it (and they discovered there was what seemed like an endless expanse of suitable land). The indigenous people of the region (the Dharug in the first parts of the mountains and the Ghundengarra in the further reaches of the mountains) had been travelling through the mountains for generations, but the European settlers wanted to find a suitable route to build a road which was completed by convict labour in 1814 and known as the Great West Road. When the Europeans began to settle land beyond the mountains the indigenous population retaliated and a war broke out.

Apart from some military outposts there was little European settlement in the actual mountains after the road was built. However following the discovery of gold in the 1850s (in locations beyond the mountains), more and more people crossed the mountains and

Europeans beginning to settle there. Further suburbs were established and when the first coal mine was opened in the late 1870s, the population of the mountains swelled.

The first railway opened in 1867 that took travellers part of the way across the mountains. The famous 'zig-zag' section of the railway was built to complete the crossing to Bathurst and opened in 1876.

The higher areas of the Blue Mountains can experience snowfalls for approximately five days each year in the winter months.

**Windsor (the town where the fictional DI Rob Ellis and later India Hargreaves are based)**
The town and district of Windsor was the third settled area in the new colony established in NSW. Settled in 1791, the area was of vital agricultural importance in feeding the inhabitants of Sydney. Originally called 'Green Hills', it was accessed by coastal inlets and up the Hawkesbury River. In 1794 the first road to Sydney was built, some 35 miles (76ks) distant. Governor Macquarie renamed it 'Windsor' after its namesake in England.

Once considered a country town, with Sydney sprawling ever outwards, Windsor is now classified as an outer 'suburb' of Sydney.

With the Hawkesbury River silting up preventing shipment of goods, the railway at Windsor was opened in 1864, however it was not until the 1990s that electrification came to Windsor and was linked to the Sydney 'suburban' rail network.

The original inhabitants of Windsor were again the Dharug people who objected to the loss of their traditional hunting and fishing grounds along the river. There were regular conflicts between the settlers and the Dharug people for many decades until the Government once again 're-settled' them.

**The Putty Road** (where Cate and Marco are run off the road) opened in 1823 and runs for 108 miles (174km) across country linking the towns of Windsor and Singleton (a mining town in the Upper Hunter Valley region). Large stretches of it, where Putty Road crosses the mountains, are narrow, steep and winding. The road can be treacherous in poor weather conditions. It is bounded on the east and west by national parks that are Unesco World Heritage Sites and listed as the Greater Blue Mountains.

It was the original route out of Sydney through the North West to areas settled in the Hunter Valley and a long circuitous route back to Newcastle on the coast until a more direct road from Sydney to Newcastle was built. There is a village called Putty (on the Putty Valley Road) which lies in a valley a few kilometres from the Putty Rd and 50k from Singleton.

There has been suggestions that the Putty Road might have acquired its name due to its original dirt surfacing that became 'like putty' in winter months. It has been called different names since it was built and had route variations, but when it was upgraded after the Second World War (during the war it was apparently called Military Rd and was of strategic military importance) it reverted to its original name and took its current form.

# Chocolate Cake Recipe

Note: This recipe can be adjusted according to the size of dish you wish to bake in. The main thing to remember it is a similar mix to a traditional 'sponge' type cake and that for every two ounces of flour, margarine (or butter) and sugar that you use, 1 egg is required (with further adjustments to note). It is not intended as a layer cake that has a cream (or buttercream) centre filling. I tend to bake it in a rectangle shaped dish – a stainless steel, or enamel baking dish (that of course has slightly rounded edges at each corner). Sometimes I use a square silicon baking dish. I created it in pounds and ounces, so metric measurements provided are approximate.

For a baking dish that measures approximately 7" x 9 " (or 17.8cm x 22.8cm) you will need the following (that is if you want a cake with depth however if you don't mind a shallower cake you can take it down to the 4oz and two eggs):

For the cake
6 oz (170g) of caster sugar
6 oz (170g) of margarine, spread or unsalted butter (when using a margarine or spread, make sure it is one that you can bake with)
7 oz (just under 200g) self-raising flour (preferably organic)
3 large eggs
1.5oz (42g) pure cocoa powder (not drinking chocolate). If you don't want the chocolate flavour to be too rich, reduce the measurement of cocoa to 1 oz or 30g. If you want it to be a stronger chocolate flavour increase the cocoa to 2oz. The cocoa used will give different results, so I would suggest using a good quality brand.

For the Icing

60g dark chocolate (it doesn't have to be cooking chocolate, but it needs to be one with at least 60% cocoa solids. In fact I often use Waitrose Continental dark chocolate for the icing as it's very tasty – it has 72% cocoa solids).

75g icing sugar

30g butter (and it preferably should be real butter – any butter e.g salted is fine)

2 tablespoons of milk

Almond flakes to spread on top of the icing (if you don't like nuts – or are allergic to them you can leave the icing plain. It is best to avoid adding any further sugary toppings like chocolate flakes or hundreds and thousands).

Step 1

Preheat your oven to: gas mark 4, 180c or 160c if you have a fan oven. Boil the kettle and mix the cocoa with a small amount of boiled water to make a paste that it easy to scoop into your mix. You don't want it too watery – or too thick or you won't get it out of your bowl. By mixing the cocoa with the water it makes the chocolate flavour stronger. Allow the cocoa to cool before using. There is slightly more flour required when you do this to balance out the liquids against the solids. If you add your cocoa dry then the flour quantity required would reduce to 6 oz.

Step 2

Mix the margarine or butter with the sugar to a creamy consistency.

Add the eggs and sift a little bit of your flour into the mix and beat.

Sift the remaining flour, add your liquid coco paste and beat (throwing it all in together after beating in your eggs and using an electric mixer is fine).

If you don't have a specific flour sifter, just use a mesh strainer for sifting.

Step 3

After greasing your tin, place the mix in it and bake. Test the cake after 35 minutes by sticking a knife into the highest point. If any soggy mix shows on the knife it will need to cook further (even if it is dry I usually give it another few minutes). Depending on the accuracy of your oven it might need 5 – 10 minutes more.

When cooked take out and allow to cool before attempting to remove the cake from the tin. In fact I often leave the cake in the tin until after I have iced it and then cut it up to place in a cake tin. I do this to avoid the disaster of the cake breaking as I remove it. If you line the tin with greaseproof paper then removing it is not an issue. The cake is also easy to remove from a silicon baking dish.

ICING

When the cake has cooled start you're icing mix by melting the butter gently over a very low heat. When melted add your icing sugar and whisk briskly (I usually sift the icing sugar to reduce potential lumps). Immediately after add the dark chocolate and milk and keep mixing to remove any lumps. Do not allow the mix to bubble or boil. When it is quite smooth spread on top of your cooled cake and sprinkle flaked almonds on top. The icing will set fairly quickly. When it is set it is ready to eat. Enjoy!

If you are making a larger cake than the 6 oz one, you will need to increase your icing quantities. If you have any icing over – don't let it go to waste!

You can leave your leftover icing in the pan until you want to use it later and then add a few more tablespoons of milk, heat it gently (again don't allow it to bubble) and pour it over some vanilla ice cream and add flaked almonds or chopped nuts. It makes a great hot chocolate fudge sauce to have over your ice cream!

# Acknowledgements

Huge thanks to Laura and Judy, who read this book when it was hot off the press and gave valuable feedback. Particular thanks to Judy also for her invaluable proofreading and editing skills with notes of 'needs sorting' or simply '?' indicating there was some confusion that needed clarification with clearer writing.

I'd also like to thank the professional manuscript assessor (who shall remain nameless) whose report provided some justified criticisms about the structure and aspects of my writing that needed revising. It prompted me to do necessary re-writes and consider changing the structure to how I had original planned it (but hadn't been brave enough to do as I'd been worried it might irritate readers). I would recommend any writer use a professional to evaluate their manuscript – it does make you think differently. He also complimented me on the original story line and thought it showed great promise. So it wasn't altogether negative and motivated me to take action.

I'd also like to thank Steve and Lyn Horton. Lyn for training me in technical matters where I was completely clueless (and still am rather hopeless) and Steve for his suggestions on promotional approaches.

It is surprising how many books go to press with errors (including those from professional publishing houses), despite the many hands they pass through. Any mistakes I've missed in this book are entirely my own. Hopefully there aren't too many!

## About the Author

L.E. Luttrell was born in Sydney, Australia and spent the first 21 years of her life there before moving to the UK (although she spends a few months in Australia each year). After working in publishing (in the UK) for a few years she went on to study and trained as a teacher. From the 90s she spent many years working in secondary education, although she's also had numerous other part time jobs. A frustrated architect/ builder, L.E. Luttrell has spent much of her adult life moving house and wielding various tools while renovating properties. Drawing Danger is the first of her books to be published. More will follow in 2018.

L.E. Luttrell lives in Liverpool, Merseyside.

Lightning Source UK Ltd.
Milton Keynes UK
UKHW012136050719
345653UK00001B/90/P